ALL THE SKILLS

— BOOK FOUR —

ALL THE SKILLS

— BOOK FOUR —

HONOUR RAE

Podium

Published in 2026 by Podium Publishing
www.podiumentertainment.com

Podium

To the citizens of Texas.
Who have the best barbecue and, hopefully, the best sense of humor.

ALL THE SKILLS

— BOOK FOUR —

CHAPTER 1

Arthur and Brixaby stood on a hill and looked out at the city ahead of them.

It was . . . hard to miss.

Entirely encircled by steep brick walls, the buildings inside were arranged by height. The ones at the city's edge, closest to the wall, were the shortest. Each row farther back was built slightly higher, allowing windows or balconies to peek just over the ones in front. This repeated, row after row, until the buildings reached over twenty stories high in the middle.

Every building seemed to be made of different materials, varying in color and texture. Some buildings were in several colors, giving them a patchwork look.

He wasn't sure if it was impressive or impressively ugly.

"I smell no dragons."

Arthur glanced at Brixaby, who had his head cocked to the sky. He barely seemed interested in the city at all.

"Not a surprise," Arthur said. "Most cities back in our kingdom only saw dragons when there was an eruption nearby. I didn't even see my first dragon until I was twelve years old."

Brixaby gave an exaggerated shudder. "Then you must be glad I am in your life!"

"It's made things interesting," Arthur said dryly. He gestured back to the city. "Have you figured out what we're here for?"

The dark dragon's gaze dropped to the city again. He shrugged. "The card only tells me where, not what. It probably assumes we already know what we're looking for. Now that we are close, the map has been updated to the middle of that city." Then his head turned to look at the stand of nearby trees, though not with any urgency, as if he'd just heard something. He looked like he was considering something.

Come to think of it . . . the trees were strange. They were of a type of oak Arthur hadn't seen before. But that wasn't what made them interesting—it was the fact they were here at all, so close to such a large city.

From their vantage point on top of the hill, he had a good view of the area before the walls. It was all scattered forestland with some straight dirt roads that led directly to arched openings in the city walls.

No farmland. No cultivated areas. And apparently, no one had ventured out of the city to cut firewood.

Very odd.

Arthur's train of thought was interrupted when Brixaby suddenly said, "I wish to hunt."

"Hunt?" Arthur echoed.

"Yes!" Brixaby's chest swelled with pride. "I think it would be delightful to hunt proper prey for once. Not just small animals like rabbits or cats."

Cats? Arthur almost asked before he decided he didn't want to know. "I thought you liked your food cooked," he said instead.

"I do. I will hunt it, and you will cook it. Several delightful-smelling creatures in this forest remind me of venison."

Now Arthur got it.

His dragon had gone from the size of a parrot to the size of a small donkey. He wanted to try out his teeth and claws—or maybe his new card powers. They'd both gained some over the last few days.

"If you're hunting, I'll scout out the city. We'll meet here this evening when the sun touches the horizon." In his mind, Arthur reactivated his Nullify card, which worked on his Return to Start. But that could be lifted by either of them at any time. "Key in your Return to Start here, just in case."

"Yes, it would be inconvenient if either one of us were sent to the Mesa Free Hive." Brixaby crouched as if ready to take off. Then he paused. "But if you encounter trouble, you will regroup here, yes? I am a dragon. But you . . . have no claws." He looked faintly pained.

"I'm a Legendary cardholder linked to a Legendary dragon," Arthur said, summoning his inner Brixaby. "Trouble will find itself in trouble with me."

This seemed to mollify the dragon. With a snort, he sprang into the air. Though he kept low, within the branches of the trees. No need to attract attention from this kingdom's hives . . . whoever they were.

Arthur waited until the sound of his droning wings faded. Then he turned to the city.

There was no way he would be able to hide who he was forever. As soon as someone realized he was linked to a dragon, the local hives would come calling.

And once it was known he was a Legendary cardholder, he'd likely find himself entangled in local politics.

Being a Legendary rider had its downsides, but it also gave him the strength to say no to whatever someone wanted from him.

Straightening his shoulders, Arthur started down the hill toward the city.

One of the weirdly straight dirt roads lay at the bottom of this hill. He walked along it toward his destination. The tall buildings made an excellent beacon.

Walking briskly, he soon came up behind a large cart hitched to some plodding oxen.

That was where he found his second oddity. The cart was . . . weird.

Arthur knew carts. He'd traveled with a trading caravan for some time when he was twelve. Those were basic open-air carts, with the contents usually covered with tarp or blankets to keep off weather or thieves away.

These were wide flatbed carts that contained two identically large wooden boxes that fit perfectly flush on the edges of the cart and stood so high they would have touched the low branches . . . if the branches had not been sharply cut to avoid them.

And on top of these boxes sat four people in blue uniforms. Each faced a different direction, likely keeping an eye out for brigands. The one in the back saw Arthur and called out to him.

Arthur couldn't understand a word the woman said.

Thinking that distance had muddled the sound, Arthur responded with a friendly wave. His hands were empty, of course. Anything that could be a weapon was stored in his Personal Space.

The cart was going very slow, so Arthur easily caught up to them. As he did, the guards stood.

Two of them were visibly armed with a spear and a sword. The other two were barehanded, but Arthur suspected they had cards to defend themselves.

Another guard called out. The words were . . . nonsense.

Another language?

Everyone Arthur had ever met spoke the same language, though there were accents.

One time, he found a Polyglot Tongue card, though. Too bad he'd never taken it. He'd thought it was pointless at the time.

Where in the world am I? Arthur wondered, but it didn't matter.

The guards were waiting for a response. Arthur could only shrug and say, "I don't understand you. Mind if I walk on past?" He pointed.

The guards exchanged glances, and one said something else in a string of syllables and vowels that made Arthur wonder how he'd even made those noises.

The tone, however, was universal: caution.

"I just want to get past." Arthur pointed again. He hadn't slowed. If push came to shove, he didn't need their permission. "Don't attack me."

There was little enough room on the sides of the road, but he began to edge past.

One man, who he suspected was the leader because the others kept looking at him, frowned down at Arthur. Then, after a moment, he signaled for him to pass . . . even though he already had.

"Thanks," he muttered.

When he got to the front, he nodded to the driver and did a double take at the oxen. They were dark brown and woolly with massive heads and tiny black horns. Arthur gave them a wide berth.

Then he looked down and saw that the wheels of the cart weren't following well-worn ruts in the road. They were fitted to a metal bar that had been sunk in—a rail of some sort that ran at a perfectly straight line on either side of the road.

He glanced again over his shoulder at the cart and noted the size of the four huge beasts and how slow they were moving despite the help of a rail. Whatever they were carrying was heavy.

As Arthur walked on, he kept a light thought on his Phase In, Phase Out card, just in case someone took a shot at him. But though he heard muttering from the guards he'd passed, no one did.

A quarter mile ahead, he saw another cart—this one had the same dimensions with the same large boxes. Only it was green with nonsensical gold writing looping on the back.

It was also rolling up to the city wall, and several guards had already come around to chat with the driver.

There were more guards along the top of the wall. A lot of them.

One guard turned from the green cart and saw Arthur. He called him over.

Unable to understand, Arthur showed his open palms in an exaggerated shrug. "I don't understand you."

"Oakee, oakee," the guard said, and led Arthur toward the wall to another guard who was seated at a small portable writing desk. From the more ornate uniform, he looked to be in charge.

The two gabbled, and then the seated one stood and approached Arthur.

"Do you know my language?" Arthur asked.

The man's eyebrows rose. "A Fabergé. It's been a while since I've seen one of you."

"A . . . what?" At least the man spoke his language, though Arthur wondered how well.

"It's what we call your kingdom. Like the fancy egg, yeah? All your weird buildings come to a point, like an onion." He tented his hands and chuckled.

"Since you have no name for yourselves, we had to come up with something. So? How did a Fabergé man find himself here?"

Arthur, always ready to level up his **Deception** skill, already had a story in mind. "I bought a trip from a portal card user, but he was only a Common, and he had the wild card of his set. Made for a random destination." Arthur shrugged. "I didn't care."

The man eyed him. "Criminal?"

"Some might say so," Arthur said. "My family was sentenced to the border for my father's crimes." This wasn't too much of a lie, to muddle things in case the man had a truth-detection card.

"We've heard of such practices," the man said. "It's barbaric to condemn an entire family for the crimes of another. But we still don't tolerate criminal behavior here. If you're caught stealing, you'll regret it."

"I'm not a thief. I'm looking for a fresh start."

"That's what all thieves say. But you'll be able to prove yourself. I'm Domingo the"—he said two words that sounded like she-raff—"on shift, and you're at the border of—" The next few words must have been in his language because they were incomprehensible . . . and long. "We're the last of our great state. Did the portal drop you close to the city?"

"Yes, the buildings are hard to miss."

"You're a lucky kid. Wandering that forest isn't wise."

"Why?" Arthur asked. "Does it belong to the local baron?"

"No such nonsense here." Domingo looked like he was going to say more, but at that moment there was a commotion behind them.

The plodding cart was coming in at a greater speed, the driver snapping the reins and cracking a whip over the back of the oxen to hurry them up.

Arthur would have felt sickened, except the guards at the top of the boxes were standing again. One threw out a lightning bolt at something behind them.

"Seems you'll see for yourself. Stand behind me," Domingo said.

The guards on top of the wall went on alert and called out to one another.

Then Arthur heard whistling from the trees. The sounds of scourglings.

The attack happened in a flash.

Several scourglings with massive bulbous heads and gray hides, like mockeries of a cart-beast, sprang out from between the trees. One of them split its head in half and clamped its oversized teeth on the neck of one of the oxen.

CHAPTER 2

There were four scourglings in total.

Arthur started forward with the intent to help, but a heavy hand landed on his shoulder.

Domingo pushed him back. "Don't bother," he said, sounding almost bored. "We have professionals to handle this."

Arthur looked around wildly. "But those are scourglings! There's an eruption—!"

His eyes scanned the treetops, certain that he would see or hear Brixaby at any moment. The dragon wouldn't ignore something like this.

He looked for signs of a rising eruption cone as well. But there was nothing in sight. Come to think of it, he hadn't felt the slightest bit of an earthquake, either. Was the eruption farther away? Why hadn't the local dragon hives contained the scourglings?

While Arthur reeled, the unlucky ox was pulled down by the scourgling. It bellowed and kicked but was hampered by the yoke it was tied to. Then the scourgling bit down with a crunch over its head and the ox went still.

To their credit, the guards had acted quickly. They immediately began firing on the attacking scourgling. One used his spear as a ranged weapon, pointing the tip end at the scourgling and launching bright yellow bolts at it.

The other two guards jumped down from the top of the cart and took on the scourglings with hand-to-hand fighting. One, the swordsman, must've had some kind of body-enhancement card. He moved so fast that Arthur only caught flashes of him.

The scourgling he was fighting fell, missing a front leg. Then, with another movement, the back leg came free as well.

The one scourgling that had managed to reach the ox suddenly emitted a screeching cry and backed up, the thickest part of its body glowing. But this wasn't the light of ready-to-harvest cards. As Arthur watched, equal parts fascinated and horrified, the thing self-immolated, fire suddenly erupting from its chest cavity and engulfing it.

Meanwhile, a few of the guards with ranged powers at the top of the wall started taking potshots at the remaining scourgling.

They seemed to have this well in hand. Some of the guards up top were even taking bets on shots.

Arthur blinked. He hadn't seen people stand up to scourglings like this before. Not in an organized fashion. Usually people ran, even if they had combat powers, because where there was one scourgling, there were likely others on the way. They overwhelmed people in waves and brought with them disease and death. Already some of the foliage was beginning to wilt.

Yet while these guards treated the threat seriously, they didn't seem surprised or even overly alarmed. This seemed like a common occurrence.

Just as he had that thought, three more oxen-sized scourglings lumbered out of the brush, whistling a challenge. And then, beyond them, a true monster emerged. It had the same body shape as the other scourglings, like one of those odd brown oxen, only with no fur and with outsized jaws. Only, it was easily twice as big. And where the hump of fat over the shoulders would normally be, additional limbs emerged. They were twisty, whiplike tentacles that lashed this way and that. It was a mega-scourgling. One of the more powerful, Rare beasts.

When the mega-scourgling entered the fray, everybody paused, as if sizing up the new threat.

Domingo said something in his language that had the flavor of a curse. And just like that, the fight turned earnest, where it had been almost casual earlier.

Orders rang up and down the high wall behind Arthur. Suddenly, everybody who could was shooting at the mega-scourgling. But its hide must have been thick enough to shrug off every hit. It treated them like an annoying bee sting at worst. The side benefit was that the ranged attacks happened to kill the other three normal-sized scourglings, but that was only a happy accident.

One of the mega-scourgling's wildly flailing tentacles shot out and snapped against the wood frame of the cart. It splintered as if it had been hit with an explosive card charm, and thick splinters struck two of the guards standing nearby.

"Do you have a knife or something metal?" Arthur yelled to Domingo.

"You want to go at that thing with a knife?" Domingo looked at him like he was crazy. "Get back, kid, and let the professionals handle it."

I am a professional, he wanted to say, and wished that Brixaby were here. His dragon's Stunning Shout would knock that thing for a loop. But . . . it might also hurt the guards standing near it.

The mega-scourgling turned to snap up at the remaining guards on top of the cart, who'd taken to harassing it to keep it away from the injured. The one with the self-immolation charm was sitting down, meditating. Arthur's guess was that the man's particular card had a strong cooldown on it or it had sucked his mana dry.

The fast swordsman tried his hand at the mega-scourgling but couldn't seem to get past the whiplike tentacles. Arthur saw him retreat, his shirt torn and blood coming off his shoulder.

No one could seem to penetrate the skin.

Well, I can, he thought, and with a twist, he moved past Domingo and ran straight at the mega-scourgling.

Domingo called out after him, but Arthur ignored him, grabbing a shovel out of his Personal Space.

One of the whiplike tentacles lashed out, passing through Arthur as he phased out. This gave him a few precious moments to run up to the thing. He quickly had to use Phase Out again as another tentacle lashed at him and the first came back for a return swipe.

This particular card could be mana hungry when his body was phasing through many objects at once. He'd only get one shot at this. Mentally holding on to his Phase In, Phase Out card, he ran through the side of the scourgling. His mana dropped like a stone. But when he came out the other side, he made sure the flat end of the shovel was stuck inside the scourgling.

Then he phased back into reality.

Its hide was impervious, but having a large shovel lodged in your chest would give anybody a bad day. The scourgling shrieked a sound like nails on a chalkboard, rising up as if ready to come down on Arthur and squish him. But as it did, it revealed a soft belly.

Finally, one of the guards on the rooftop nailed it with what looked like a wind bolt edged with razor blades. Intestines fell free, and Arthur wisely backed away, letting the guards wear it down now that he had proved it was not completely invincible.

The thrashing scourgling landed sickeningly on the handle of the shovel still sticking out at its side, driving it in further. This seemed to hit something vital. It collapsed, and a few moments later, it was dead.

A cheer went up from both the top of the wall and the wagon.

Domingo came up to Arthur, looked at the fallen oxen, and spat. "Shame 'bout the by-son." Then he looked at Arthur. "Seems like you do have some tricks up your sleeve, though."

Arthur wasn't amused. He looked around, suspicious of every bush and tree. "There have to be more where that came from."

"There are always more," Domingo said with a laugh. "As I was about to tell you, the damn forest is full of the things."

"Then why aren't you gathering to fight them off?" Arthur wanted to know.

"What, this wasn't enough excitement for the day?" With another laugh, Domingo slapped his shoulder and then walked off to inspect one of the fallen scourglings.

Flummoxed, Arthur stared after him. He had to be missing something . . . and he was a stranger here, so he shut his mouth and tried to observe instead.

The guards from the wagon were all smiles. They had lost two of the oxen, one from the initial scourgling attack and the other, unfortunately, from friendly fire. But this didn't seem to bother them overly much. A couple of the guards went to unhook the bodies and reestablish the line.

Meanwhile, more guards came to inspect the scourglings along with Domingo, commenting to each other in their language, laughing and joking. The most attention went to the mega-scourgling. People gathered around its head and traded comments, looking like how he remembered the men from his village used to when they hunted deer and scored a huge buck. One even went so far as to whip out a measuring tape from his pocket to size the head.

There were smiles all around. He didn't get it.

Then, naturally, they started harvesting. This was the part that Arthur dreaded. He'd seen people get vicious when there were cards or card shards up for grabs.

Indeed, several shards were pulled from every one of the minor scourglings. Domingo attended to the mega-scourgling himself. He pulled out a full Rare card and held it up to cheers.

Instead of fighting, the guards turned the shards over to Domingo, who made a show of tucking the card and the card shards away in a bag that was too small for its size. It must've been some kind of spatial enchantment bag.

Domingo returned to Arthur. "That was a Rare beast," he said. "Good, good. It won't be long now."

"Long? What do you mean?" Arthur asked.

"You're here to try for the . . ." Domingo uttered more incomprehensible words before adding, "Right? Looks like the whole area is almost ready to pop."

Pop? Arthur pensively looked around for a scourge-eruption. "I don't know what that is."

That earned a surprised laugh out of him. "Kid, you've come at the right time. If you don't know what that is, you've got the luck of the demi-scourgling. Here." He gestured for Arthur to follow him back to the desk, then wrote on a slip of paper, stamped it with ink that glimmered with a card-anchor charm, and handed it over. "Get into the city. This note will hook you up so you don't need a translator following you around. Then get signed up for the . . ." Again, he uttered that string of words. It sounded impossible to twist a tongue that way. "With Rare beasties emerging at any moment, you'll want to get in on that action." He winked.

A guard standing next to the oxen called out to Domingo, who turned and waved that he'd heard. Then he looked back at Arthur expectantly.

The man was busy, and while Arthur had many questions, he knew his answers would be found in the city.

"Would you sign up for the . . . uh . . ." He wasn't going to embarrass himself by trying to repeat the words. "If you were in my place?"

"Kid, I'm going in myself! Now, hurry along through that gate. Anyone hassles you, show them that note."

It was a dismissal. Instinct told Arthur to just obey. Domingo wasn't his friend; he was a guard, and Arthur did not want to stand out or be too suspicious.

Arthur took the piece of paper, nodded, and left.

He stopped in front of the archway that led to the city and glanced back the way he'd come.

Scourglings didn't just appear from the forest. There had to be an eruption site somewhere.

And as he turned and looked again at the city with new eyes, he realized that if one thought about it from the right angle, the buildings that started short and grew taller and taller farther back vaguely resembled an eruption cone.

CHAPTER 3

With only some lingering apprehension for Brixaby, Arthur headed into the city.

Just past the wall, he stepped into a busy, crowded twisting street filled with a multitude of shops, all in different, often clashing, colors. Most were strung with banners in eye-popping colors, as if every single one was trying to outshout the other for attention. In addition, some had buskers who would regularly yell at passersby. They in turn had to compete with other street performers who used both native skills and card powers to interest the crowd.

It was all overwhelming, like the thickest part of a festival at the busiest, most hectic part of the day. But as Arthur strode along, his ears ringing with the sounds of all of it and his eyes dazzled by the lights of a performer who had just set off some sort of silent fireworks charm, he had the feeling that this was a normal occurrence.

It was so different from the forest that lay just outside the walls.

And Arthur realized, with a feeling he couldn't quite put a finger on—Apprehension? Amusement? Pity?—that these people were celebrating and yelling and buying and eating less than fifty feet away from where a mega-scourgling had killed two oxen and threatened the lives of guards.

They had been separated only by a wall with, by the looks of it, some sort of sound enchantment. Arthur glanced up to see if he could spot any of the guards patrolling the wall from the other side, and found he couldn't.

Sound and sight enchantments, then.

The people here hadn't known there was any danger at all.

And if that mega-scourgling had broken through, they wouldn't have been prepared.

It reminded him uncomfortably of Mesa Free Hive. Only they'd been protected by living in desolate wastelands. These people were protected by . . . what? Ignorance?

He shook his head, then had to forcefully wave off a vendor who, for some reason, wanted to aggressively sell him wooden beaded jewelry. The woman followed him for a few steps, coming close enough to try to drop a necklace over his head. Arthur ducked and walked away. She yelled at him in another language he couldn't understand.

Increasing his pace, he felt the road slope upward, which likely aided in creating the height of the buildings.

Dragon hives had been built from the cones of ancient eruptions, back when the world was more dangerous and the cones grew so high that some of them touched the lowest clouds. Those cones were long dead, though, with not a sign of scourglings around them.

But if this was on top of an active eruption cone, shouldn't the scourglings be coming out of the top, and not from the forest?

Stranger and stranger.

The frantic atmosphere lessened a bit as he went up the hill. The crowd grew thinner, and it gave Arthur room to breathe. There were still plenty of vendors, but they weren't nearly as aggressive.

Now he took a few moments to actually take in what the shops were selling, and he found a little bit of everything. Some had clothing, some bits and bobs, others household goods. He even saw one or two cards for sale, securely locked behind enchanted glass, and runes that probably fed into security-card anchors.

He paused anyway to get a look at them. Both were Commons.

Perfect Apple Honey Butter Every Time
Common
Skill
The wielder of this card will be granted the supernatural ability to create apple honey butter. Using mana, the wielder will be able to create apple honey butter with unusual ingredients.

The Strength of One and a Half Men
Common
Body Enhancement
The wielder of this card will be granted a temporary, once-in-a-24-hour period, boon of strength. The wielder's strength attribute will be increased by 1.5x for the duration of 20 minutes without any bodily damage or exhaustion afterward.

They were both minor cards, but a little unusual in that they didn't have major drawbacks. That often was a problem with Common cards. They either had some double-edged sword drawback, giant mana consumption, or an extraordinarily long cooldown.

Arthur briefly wondered how much these cards were. When he glanced at the amount written beside the cards, he remembered he couldn't read this language.

So . . . how could he read the cards?

That stumped him. He remembered when he had first looked at his Master of Skills card as a boy. He'd been so illiterate that he could barely read the description and didn't know its function until he had placed it in his heart deck. From there, it had been stamped on his heart, his soul. He hadn't needed to read to know what the card could do.

Later, of course, he'd learned to read, and figuring out other cards hadn't been a problem.

He'd ask Brixaby for his thoughts later, but he suspected the answer was some version of: cards are magic. Placing his first card in his heart had activated his heart deck, and so he had magical sympathy with all other cards.

And since the first card in his heart had been Legendary, he might have more magical sympathy with other cards than the average person.

It was strange, but he couldn't linger. Arthur moved on.

The shops in this upper district had enough room to put up signs. Not that Arthur could tell what they said. It was all in that script that looked so overly pretty and loopy, he was surprised anybody could read it.

There were still a few vendors here and there. He stepped over to a couple who didn't seem busy and showed them the note that Domingo had stamped for him.

Most ignored him, but one or two glanced down at the paper, up at Arthur, then pointed him in a different direction down the street or off around the next corner.

Wherever Domingo had sent him, it was deep within the city. By the time he had taken about fifteen turns, he'd completely lost his sense of direction. Then, to make things worse, he felt the ground rumble under his feet.

Scourgling earthquake! Arthur thought, and then felt a little bit of relief because if that were the case, at least this place would make some sense.

Until he saw everyone quickly scrambling to the sides of the street.

Arthur did as well, and just in time, as the rumbling was revealed to be an entire herd of those woolly oxen running down the street.

The animals weren't pushed along by card powers—at least not that Arthur could tell. Instead, they were hurried along by men and women on horseback with wide-brimmed hats, yelling and whooping as they went.

The people who had been forced to the sides of the road didn't seem to mind. In fact, they laughed and cheered. A few daringly reached out to touch the big brown woolly oxen as they ran by.

Finally, that cleared out, people retook the road, and Arthur continued on his way.

Then, abruptly, he found himself directly in front of the shop he was looking for.

He could tell because the swooping characters matched the ones that were written on the note. He suspected the stamp was some version of Domingo's signature.

Underneath the local phrasing were other lines of characters, all stranger than the next. And some were arranged vertically.

Then, near the bottom of the list, was something that he could read: *Language translation card anchors.*

Though the actual script it had been written in was a little weird. It reminded him of those ancient enchanting books that he and Brixaby had stolen. He thought whoever had written this might've done so with outdated information.

Walking in, Arthur was greeted by a woman who sat behind a wooden desk. She spoke in words he didn't understand, of course. In answer, he showed her the slip of paper.

She glanced at it and then called to the back of the shop, which was partitioned off by a wall.

A man soon bustled out. He was in his thirties with dark hair, spiked up for some reason, and equally dark eyes that held a sly expression as he beheld Arthur.

"Welcome, welcome," he said, coming around the desk. "From the Fabergé kingdom, right? It's been a while since we've had a traveler from those parts."

He spoke smoothly without any hint of an accent at all.

"So I've heard," Arthur said. "Where I come from, everybody speaks the same language. I'm a little overwhelmed here."

"Well, you've come to the right place. For the right price, of course." The man took a stack of papers Arthur hadn't noticed sitting on the desk and handed it to him. He shuffled them around, and Arthur noticed that all the papers were written in different languages. Finding Arthur's, he handed it over.

It was a basic list of services, and finally, prices he could understand.

His stomach sank. All of them were priced not in coins, but in card shards.

The list started out with temporary card anchors that were usually painted on the skin using a staining oil. Those lasted a set amount of months before wearing thin and having to be reapplied.

Arthur ignored these. He planned to be away from the kingdom for a long time, which meant he needed to plan long term.

The next most expensive option was a permanent tattoo—assuming the tattoo itself wasn't damaged—and only translated the local language, which was called Texan.

No, if Arthur was going to do this, then he wanted a universal translation option.

Those, naturally, were the most expensive. There were several different versions of a card-anchor tattoo:

- Audio understanding translation for 20 languages – five Rare card shards
- Speaking translation for 20 languages – five Rare card shards
- Two-point anchor for audio understanding and speaking – nine Rare card shards (1 shard savings!)
- Reading translation for 20 languages – five Rare card shards
- Written translation for 20 languages – five Rare card shards
- Two-point anchor for reading and writing – nine Rare card shards (1 shard savings!)
- Four-point anchor, speaking, audio, reading, and writing for 20 languages – one Rare card*

*Financing available; speak to store management.

From the sly grin on the man's face, Arthur suspected that financing came with some strict terms. He'd heard of people selling their services for card shards before, signing contracts that were downright predatory.

He wasn't going down that road.

Unfortunately, Brixaby quickly gobbled down any card shard unless Arthur carefully hid it away. And even then, the dragon usually managed to weasel it away from him, given enough time.

Not that he had to try hard recently: Arthur had wanted him to be as strong as possible for whatever they faced in their new kingdom. Long story short, he didn't have a card shard to his name right now.

But he did have other options.

"Do you take trade of high-quality goods, or just cards?" Arthur asked, tapping the four-point anchor option.

The man made a show of sucking his teeth and thinking. "It depends on the good. And of course, I'll have to get it appraised, friend."

"Well, between you and me, you may want to keep what I have . . . between us." Arthur made a show of looking around. "I hate to part with it, but I have no means of selling it anywhere else without an understanding of the language."

The man's eyebrows raised. "You've piqued my interest. Come with me, but don't try anything funny. My safe room is enchanted with more security than you'd believe. If you try anything funny, you will be dead twenty ways before you even realize it."

"No tricks," Arthur said. "I deal in good faith." This was a complete lie, but he wasn't looking to scam anyone today.

Well, at least not this guy.

Though he did wonder what those security runes looked like.

The man, who Arthur noticed still had not introduced himself, led him to the back, then locked the door behind them before turning around to look at Arthur, one eyebrow raised. "I suppose you've got a card for me to look at? Something you stole?"

"Better than a card," Arthur said.

And from his Personal Space, he pulled out one of the enchanting books he and Brixaby had stolen from the Mesa Free Hive's council.

One of the primers.

He handed it over, and the man stared at the title for so long that Arthur would have wondered if he had trouble reading it, except for the fact that his expression was of pure disbelief. Then he started paging through quickly.

The book, consisting of enchanting secrets, were kept strictly that: secret. Anybody could tell this was an old book, but it was a primer, a way to get a student started. Perfect for beginners.

Arthur wasn't a complete fool. He and Brixaby had already read through this book. And, using Arthur's Eidetic Imagery and Mental Bookshelf, the information was there forever.

The man looked up. He'd schooled his expression rather quickly, but Arthur had still caught the gleam in his eyes. He knew it was worth a lot. And, more importantly, so did Arthur. "What do you want for this?"

"That is the equivalent of a Rare enchanting card," Arthur said, "or even better."

"It's old as dirt, kid. The techniques are outdated—who even knows if anyone practices like this anymore?" he said, proving he knew something about enchanting.

"Doesn't matter," Arthur replied. "It's enough to get started with, and it's not under lock and key with the enchanters' guild."

The man looked at him closely.

"It's in Fabergé Kingdom script. Not many people read that."

"You do, which makes you the only one who can translate it for others to buy," Arthur said. "But if you don't want it—" He reached out as if to take the book back.

The man drew away, book still in hand. "Don't be hasty now!" And Arthur knew that he had him.

They went back and forth. Arthur knew these goods were good, so he pressed for every advantage. And even though he knew he could use the Subtle Influence card that Valentina had given him . . . he held himself back. So far, his **Haggling** skill was up to the challenge.

The only real hiccup came when the man looked at him with an expression that Arthur wasn't sure he liked.

"Are you running from the Fabergé Kingdom because you stole this beauty?"

"My reasons for being here are my own."

"The Reshuffling, aye. I'm not judging, I'm only saying that there's work for people with sly hands."

"I'm not a thief," Arthur said, a bit harshly.

The man grinned. "I suppose you bought this fair and square, with receipts and all."

Arthur ignored that, and thankfully, the man moved on. He did say, reluctantly, that it was worth the equivalent of a Rare card.

"It's better than a Rare card," Arthur said.

The man sucked his teeth again. "You want shards on top of this?"

"No," Arthur said. "I don't even want an anchor."

That stopped the man cold. "Why not? My work is solid—I have testimonials."

It was a reverse of their previous positions. Now he was trying to sell Arthur, and the way he kept one hand flat on the top of the book said he did know its true value.

"I'd need two tattoos, and one wouldn't work."

"I assure you they would—"

"All I need is lessons," Arthur said quickly. "And a ten-second use of your card."

"My card?" He recoiled, one hand flicking up as if to cover his heart before he caught himself. "Why?"

"Have you ever tried to tattoo a dragon?" Arthur asked with a grin.

CHAPTER 4

Arthur had to push every one of his skills in his Stealth Class—especially Silent Movement and Evasion—to the limit to make it up to the top of the wall undetected. Then there was the matter of avoiding the guards who were patrolling there.

It hadn't been his first choice, and certainly not his best choice. But he'd been unaware that the exits out to the forest shut down at sunset.

He was stuck inside the city, unable to make it to the hill where he was to meet Brixaby.

As soon as the dragon figured out he wasn't going to arrive, he was going to come looking.

Arthur only hoped that he wouldn't make a big scene.

The top of the wall was a wide walkway, with plenty of shadows from outcroppings and large stationary ranged weapons to duck and hide behind.

Even better, Arthur found a helmet hanging on a peg at the top of the stairs. He put it on, and at a glance—from far away—he looked a lot like a normal guard, most of whom wore cloaks over their uniforms to keep off the chill.

He strained his ears, listening to the sounds around him. The moon was a thin slice in the sky, leaving little but starlight. The forest beyond looked peaceful. No one would ever guess that there were any scourglings there.

A familiar voice intruded into his head: *Arthur, you better have a good reason for not meeting me at the hill.* A pause. *But you had better not be dead, either.*

Arthur looked around but still didn't hear the droning sound of Brixaby's wings. Then it occurred to him. Of course. The dragon had the same Stealth capabilities.

Taking a chance, Arthur dropped his own Stealth, took off his helmet, and waved wildly in the air, hoping to catch the dragon's attention. If he heard him in his head, then he must be within shouting distance.

Unfortunately, because it was Brixaby, his shouting distance was . . . quite the distance.

Finally, he heard the droning buzz of wings from straight above. Turning, Arthur pointed to a building several rows back. This one was especially high, rising above its immediate neighbors, almost to the height of the buildings in the row behind it. Arthur had already scouted it out and saw that, despite the height—or maybe because of it—no one had set up a patio on top of the building. Perfect.

The buzz wavered, then grew fainter. Brixaby understood. Now Arthur just had to meet him.

He climbed down the wall, exchanging glances and nods with people who were coming up. Their eyes slid off him. He wasn't invisible, just so unremarkable as not to be noticed.

Reaching the bottom, he ditched the helmet and made his way to the building.

Now came the hard part. Arthur had leveled his **Climbing** skill, among others, at the Mesa Free Hive. That had been mostly for fun. Now it was about to come in handy. The building was not only tall, but its exterior, made of pale stone, had become unusually pitted by the elements, rough enough to allow for some handholds.

Some people still roamed the streets, so Arthur chose the shadowed side of the building.

Arthur concentrated on his **Climbing** skill, then activated his 20-Point Spree card for a boost of strength. His finger grip increased, and he smoothly hoisted himself up, setting the toes of his boots into the rough edges. Soon, he was past the first set of windows and still climbing.

He didn't dare look down, and had to trust that Brixaby wouldn't let him fall if he lost his grip.

It was a cold night, and despite his enhancements, his fingers became numb. More and more often, he had to stop, hold on with one hand, and shake the other out.

Windows were a problem, too. He had to move right and left to avoid windowsills, conscious of every moment for the sound of someone spotting him and shouting.

The rough stone, which was so helpful for handholds, was painful to hold on to. His minor healing card helped whenever his skin tore.

Thankfully, it was only about four stories up. He reached the top of the roof, out of breath and winded, despite his cards and skills.

Brixaby had already alighted on the roof, looking down his long pointy muzzle at him with an expression that was less than impressed.

Arthur noticed his claws were shiny with wet blood.

"You . . . found the scourglings?" Arthur guessed.

The dragon jerked in surprise. "Scourglings?!"

Arthur shushed him as he rolled back to his feet. "Yes. I guess you didn't. There are scourglings in the forest."

"What?" Brixaby beat his wings in an automatic response, lifting a few feet in the air, shocked and angry in equal measure. "I smelled no eruption. Where is the cone? The dragons? What are the hives doing?"

"There's no eruption . . . Brix, this place isn't like home," Arthur said with a light laugh. Though, deep inside, he felt a twinge. Who knew he would feel homesick? Ruthlessly, he pushed it aside.

"Let me explain," he said, "and I think I found out why your card brought us here."

A few hours ago

"My name is Dannill," the salesman told Arthur. "But everybody calls me Danny Boy."

Arthur refused to call him that, but he gave the man a polite nod. Now that they'd come to terms over the worth of the book, Dannill was in high spirits.

"So, you really are a dragon rider?" Dannill gave him a long look, then snorted. "Well, weirder things have happened. Can't say that I didn't dream about being a rider as a boy, but as a man, it always seemed so limiting, tying your heart to something else for the rest of your life. I suppose that link can be broken?"

"No," Arthur said, "not unless you want a very angry dragon on your hands."

That was not the whole truth, but he wasn't about to spill hive secrets. There were riders who would do anything to upgrade their cards another rank. Dragons, being natural magical beasts, could not upgrade their cards along with them.

It ended with sundering the link between dragon and rider, an ugly scenario Arthur didn't like to think about.

"Where's your dragon?" Dannill asked.

"In the forest," Arthur said.

Another hard look. "All right, I suppose I couldn't tell if you're lying or not anyway, so what's your deal?" Dannill asked. "Why in the world would you want my card, and why do you think I would ever agree?"

"It would only be for a moment. I have a Rare power copying card," Arthur said, once again playing with the truth. He did, in a way.

"Oh, really?" Dannill's eyebrows shot up. "You want to sell that?"

"It's a heart card," Arthur said.

"Well, you're here for the Reshuffling, aren't you?"

"The what? You mentioned that earlier."

Dannill rattled off a few more words, but Arthur didn't understand any of them. Finally, Dannill raised his hands in exasperation.

"It's the whole reason the city is so full. Word from the other city-states is that their Dark Hearts are almost bursting, ready to overflow, too. It's going to be a boom year, let me tell you."

"Start from the beginning," Arthur said, annoyed. "Explain it as if someone has just been dropped into your kingdom."

"Right, right, you're a dragon rider. Well, first, it's a city-state. We're not under any kingdom, and we don't have any hoity-toity nobles up in our business. And if you are one of them—"

"I'm not," Arthur lied.

"Well, if you *were*," Dannill said with emphasis, and Arthur wondered if he had some kind of lie detection card, "then you can just knock off thinking that it will do you any good around here, because it means less than a cow pie at noon. You get me?"

The man had been nothing but ingratiating before, but speaking of his annoyance at nobles, there was a gleam in his eyes that reminded Arthur of the Mesa Free Hive. A fierce, hard-won sort of independence. Arthur nodded.

"Now, all the city-states have a Dark Heart at its center. It's like the yolk in an egg. We're on top of a scourgling cone, if you haven't noticed. The ancient dragon riders killed it, but not completely. Just enough so it can seed out scourglings."

"Seed out scourglings?" Arthur repeated, staring at Dannill as if he was an idiot. "But the scourge-rot—"

"Now, now, everyone's carded. It's mandatory at twelve. Either your parents get one for you or the government loans you one—and I do mean *loan*. Most people have to pay off their card loans for years until adulthood, but it's better than getting the rot. And half these buildings are for farming. That way we don't have to worry about the rot poisoning the land. Heck, they're under so many enchantments to keep the crops clean inside, it'll make your head spin." Dannill flashed a grin. "Now that we've shaken hands on the deal for your book here, I don't mind saying that enchantments are big here." He patted the book.

Arthur stared at him, horrified. He remembered the havoc just one scourgling nest had caused in his hive. Joy had been hatched, already close to death because the scholars' guild had let several cards go to rot, spawning a handful of scourglings—including the Mind Singer.

Later, while dealing with Whitaker's records, he had learned that quite a few lower-ranked dragon eggs around that time had simply not hatched.

The scourglings were the antithesis of life.

"And the hives just . . . let you? They don't care?"

"No hives," Dannill said. "We're not one of those kingdoms."

"But what about your eruptions—"

The man grinned. He looked like he was enjoying himself. "No eruptions, either."

"What, why?" he spluttered. "How?" If they'd found a way to stop the eruptions that had plagued Arthur's own kingdom . . .

"No idea." Dannill shrugged. "But if you don't mind me saying, you're focusing on the wrong thing. You're aware that scourglings operate in cycles, aren't you?"

"Cycles of decades," Arthur said. "We're in an upswing right now in my kingdom." That was putting it mildly. Apparently, the rate of eruptions was currently way out of the norm, even for a peak.

"Well, here it's usually seven to twelve years. It looks like we're on the low end of seven years, but it's still peaking. This year is promising to be a bumper crop," he said with a smile.

"You're not *harvesting* scourglings, are you?" he asked, thinking with growing horror about what the Mind Singer had been doing to those baby dragons . . . what she still might be doing in some new, faraway place.

"No, no, no, the scourglings are only a side effect. It's the hive—the Dark Heart. Think of it like a beehive. You have the honeybees, yes? They sting, they're quite unpleasant, but you also have the honey inside."

Arthur started to shake his head, then stopped. "What's the honey? What makes all of this worth it?"

"Now we're getting to the good stuff." Dannill smiled at him and answered his question with another question. "Where do cards come from?"

"Dragons," he said immediately, "and card shards . . . and scourglings."

"And scourglings come from their own hives." He pointed downward. "Strange things happen down there. Our people figure there's such a tight mass of magic and power, it sorta warps reality. The dungeoneers have used the Dark Heart of hives as testing grounds, with the power to fuel it. So, we use the blighted scourglings as a yardstick to tell us when it's ready for harvest, for us to grab all that honey."

"What's down there?" Arthur asked, certain Dannill was drawing out the answer.

"Magical laws are bent down there, so close to a source of magic. They say . . ." Dannill paused for effect ". . . you get what you truly *need*."

That resonated with Arthur. It had been what he asked Brixaby to search for. His heart started to beat fast, but he kept it off his face as he asked, "You've been down there?"

Dannill straightened. "I have, and it's no secret. I had a Common card that helped me print out paper almost perfectly from the original. I was a simple scribe. My parents were able to buy me a Common card soon as I turned eleven and a half. I was lucky enough that they could afford one, and I didn't have to go into debt for them. It was meant for my brother, but he didn't survive the scourge-sickness."

Arthur suspected that was a common story. Being around even a dead scourgling hive was not healthy at all. He once ran across a report of a city that had been blighted with a scourge-eruption—not too different from the one he and his graduating class had attended, only on a larger scale. Many people stayed because the city had been only half destroyed by the scourglings. But disease had run rampant through the uncarded, especially among the children. Birth defects as well.

Now it was practice to abandon any place that had a hive eruption and treat the area with dragon soil to reclaim it. He shook his head.

Dannill continued, "I didn't want to be a scribe, knew I had better things ahead of me. So at fourteen, I went down to the Dark Heart. Delved three dungeons. I know you're new here, so let me assure you that's quite the accomplishment for a kid without a combat card. My reward was two Rares in languages that allowed me to start my shop here. Exactly what I needed.

"And I wasn't the only one who got lucky. Other people found the secret to a craft they had long been looking for. Others, key shards. Have you ever heard of key shards?"

Arthur shook his head.

"It fits into any slot of the same rank card. Sometimes you have shards, but you can never get that corner piece, or there's just one piece that doesn't fit quite right, no matter how hard you try. Well, a key shard will always fit into it as long as it's the same rank." He paused for another dramatic moment. "And they almost always provide special cards from a set. Some call them the Jack cards."

Arthur's eyebrows raised. He'd heard of special cards, but they were rarer than . . . well, Rare cards.

From Dannill's grin, he knew he had his attention.

"So what is it that *you* need?" Dannill asked.

That was what he had Brixaby ask his Call of the Heart card, a seeker card. "I need to find out the secrets of the scourglings, how to destroy them," Arthur said automatically.

The man snorted. "Honorable, but no. That's a want, a duty. What do you need?"

He wasn't wrong.

"I need . . . to complete my set." It was the first time he had ever verbalized it, but he also knew that completing his Master set meant killing his cousin, Penn. There wasn't any love lost between the two of them, but . . .

And yet, even as Arthur said it, that didn't feel right, either. It felt like something he *should* say, like his first answer. Something that Brixaby would say, even.

Arthur shook his head as if to wipe away his last answer. "I don't know what I need."

"Well," Dannill said, "if you don't know now, chances are you'll figure it out in the depths of the Dark Heart."

"Of course you want to complete your set. As do I!" Brixaby exclaimed as Arthur's retelling wound down. "I want to become the strongest Legendary in the world!"

Arthur looked at his dragon, amused. He wished that he could know himself as well as Brixaby knew himself.

"Well, the first step is learning the local language, and I have it all planned out. Dannill's waiting for us, but he'd only agree for a second book. I trust you have another one of the basics?"

Brixaby snorted. "I'll be glad to get it out of my Personal Space. What is the point of hoarding books if you have a Mental Bookshelf?"

That was pointedly aimed at Arthur, who ignored it. He liked books, and he wouldn't admit to a twinge of guilt about selling some . . . even if he had the contents completely memorized.

As soon as he was seated at the base of his dragon's neck, Brixaby took off, and they were buzzing over the top of the city. Arthur briefly worried about alarms—scourglings did fly, after all—but no bells or shouts rang out.

"We are not scourglings," Brixaby said dismissively when Arthur mentioned his worry. "Where is this building?"

"There. I had it lit up with card-anchor lights."

They found Dannill sitting out on the top of his roof, where he'd built a terrace.

And he wasn't alone. He had brought several rented armsmen, who stood off to the side, hands on visible weapons in case Arthur did anything silly.

They were dealing with cards after all.

Word of Brixaby is definitely going to get out soon, Arthur thought, but he'd had no real hope of keeping it secret.

Several guards looked in awe at Brixaby's arrival as he settled down.

Brixaby arched his neck and preened as people stepped closer to get a look at him.

"Welcome, welcome," Dannill said, though his eyes were on Brixaby. "You really are a dragon rider, aren't you? I'd half convinced myself you were insane. Is it true that dragons speak like men?"

"Of course I do," Brixaby boomed, "and I'm smarter than most men, too."

"That you are," Dannill said with a grin so wide it looked like his face was going to split. Arthur suspected that his wish to see a dragon was more than just a boyhood dream.

"I don't suppose you would be willing to wear a banner, advertising where you learned to speak other languages—"

"No," Arthur said, before Brixaby could more rudely decline.

"Ah, well, I had to ask." Dannill led them to a table which had been set up with torchlights all around to ensure proper visibility.

At Arthur's prompting, Brixaby removed a book on basic rune security and set it on the table.

Dannill flipped through it, verifying all the pages were in order. Then it was his turn.

Dannill removed a card from his heart.

The guards watched with bated breath as Arthur took the card.

This was the riskiest moment for him. If the card was spell or charm based, his Master of Skills wouldn't be able to properly take it in. But he'd had reason to suspect it wasn't. Dannill's advertisement for card anchors hadn't mentioned a need to use mana, and card anchors were only as strong as the card they'd been linked to.

His guess was right.

Foundational Language Class

Rare

Knowledge

The wielder of this card will gain the ability to understand foreign languages at the foundational level, as if they had learned to speak it as a child. This card does not include written, sign, or purely text-based languages. There is no limit to the number of languages that may be learned.

Arthur slipped it into his card anchor. He was about to have Dannill speak, but the guards were already muttering to themselves in their native tongue.

"Why's the boss allowing this? Giving up his card? I don't like it."

"That's why we're here, isn't it?"

"I thought dragons were supposed to be bigger . . ."

New skill gained: Texan (Foreign Language Class)

Due to your card's bonus traits and bonus Foundational Language Class card, you automatically start this skill at level 5.

Good enough. He handed it over to Brixaby, who put it in a secondary core, grimacing because it was full. Quickly, Brixaby removed it again and returned it to Dannill.

Dannill looked at him. "That's it?"

"That's all I need," Arthur said. "Now, for the lessons—" Arthur stopped, realizing that Dannill had asked his question in Texan. And Arthur had not only immediately understood as he had with the guards, but had answered in kind.

It felt weird on his tongue. The vowels were not where he was normally used to them being. He opened and closed his mouth a few times, exercising muscles that weren't used to moving in that way.

Dannill gestured at the table, then sat him down for a bit of writing.

"Copy the lines," Dannill instructed. "I'll verbalize these out as you write the words. That should get you started. I used to be a scribe, so I do understand teaching reading skills."

Once Arthur had those skills, he could teach Brixaby.

And just like that, after several hours, Arthur knew the basics of reading and writing in another language. Despite the strong start, he wouldn't call himself fluent. But as these were skills, he would level them—and learn—at an accelerated pace.

And best of all, this was not a card anchor or tattoo that could ever run out of power or become damaged.

This was close to true knowledge, and much more valuable to him than any crutch or aid.

CHAPTER 5

Once Arthur and Brixaby had finished with the card and returned it to Dannill, the tension noticeably lessened among the guards.

Dannill turned to Arthur, all smiles on his sly face as he asked in Texan, "If you don't mind me asking, where do you and your fine fellow here"—he glanced at Brixaby—"intend to room for the night?"

To Arthur's chagrin, he'd forgotten to set something up. Ever since he left the apartment he'd shared with Horatio, a roof over his head had always been provided to him in some way or another. Now he had nowhere to rent, much less a place that would fit a dragon.

"I guess we'll stay the night out in the forest," he said slowly, practicing with the new language that still felt very odd on his tongue.

"Without a bed?" Brixaby swelled up indignantly. "You know I require at least three pillows at night."

"The forest?" Dannill sounded horrified. "That would be suicide. There are scourglings out there!"

"I'm not afraid of any scourgling," Brixaby said. "They should be afraid of me."

"Now, that might be the case, but I take it you still won't want to sleep out in the dirt," he replied, which earned a grumble from Brixaby. The man smiled wider at this. "How about you and I talk about negotiating a sponsorship deal?"

Arthur's **Haggling** skill tingled. "What's that?"

"Oh, it's a simple thing, really. I can tell the two of you are going to be big stars for the upcoming Reshuffling. People will want to know about you. There will be jealousy and intrigue and a cartload of curiosity."

This was starting to sound like a sales pitch. "So what do you want from us?" Arthur asked bluntly.

"I want to sell your likenesses in toys and drawings. You know, keepsakes for people to say they've seen you. How is your signature, by the by? People like signatures from famous folk."

Why? Arthur almost asked, but Brixaby beat him to it with another question.

"Why do you call it the Reshuffling?"

Still smiling, Dannill crossed his arms and leaned against the wall that ringed the rooftop. "Because after all is said and done, the whole shebang reshuffles wealth throughout the city. People with humble Common cards can come out with Rares. Rumor has it, even a Legendary is up for grabs." Dannill leaned in then, as if to impart a secret. "As I told your rider, magic is bent down there in the Heart—some rules are even broken. It's said that a person's heart deck can gain strange new powers."

Arthur and Brixaby glanced at each other.

But Dannill wasn't done. "It seems every time there's a Reshuffling, something new is discovered. A new power comes out the other side. So you can see why people are excited. They want to know who are going to be the new movers and shakers in the city, and a dragon rider is a good one to bet on."

"We aren't going to be staying long term," Arthur said, wanting to be crystal clear.

"That hardly matters, does it? You're still exciting. Have you ever heard of a 'limited time promotion'? All I'm saying is, in exchange for room and board up here"—Dannill gestured with open arms to mean the roof of the tower—"you let me sell your likeness around the city."

"Room, board, and food for myself and for Brixaby," Arthur said.

"Of course, of course," Dannill replied quickly.

"And crafting supplies," Brixaby added. "Me and my rider will need to prepare for the Reshuffling. Not only will we take it seriously—we intend to win."

"I'm not certain it's something anyone can win, per se," Dannill said, "but I appreciate the enthusiasm."

Brixaby wasn't done. "We will also require basic construction supplies to build higher walls against the wind, and two beds to be brought up. Also, what do your people know of chainmail?"

Arthur stepped back to let his dragon manage the man, throwing in a few suggestions when Brixaby's demands became too . . . dragonish.

As they went back and forth, Dannill's smile became less bright as he slowly realized Arthur and Brixaby weren't going to sign away their advantage for free.

"You're asking for supplies enough for months," Dannill said a bit sourly.

Arthur shrugged. "When is the Reshuffling supposed to start?"

"Can't say," Dannill admitted. "But I've heard it's weeks out. We have experts study that sort of thing and judge when the Heart is ready to burst—you can't overplay these things and wait too long, because if it does ever burst . . ." He shuddered.

"You end up with a scourge-eruption?" Arthur guessed.

Dannill pointed his fingers at him with a clicking noise. "You got it. And no one wants that."

Privately, Arthur thought that the city was already close to playing with fire—or playing with scourglings, which was even worse. But this wasn't his kingdom. Besides, he didn't want the Reshuffling to happen right now. Cressida and Horatio were two weeks away at best.

If this event was as good as Dannill said, they could stand to benefit.

Plus, he had been in this city for a day and had already learned something new about scourglings no one else back at home did: Dark Hearts preempted a scourge-eruption.

If we can find a way to look for those, we could get people out of the way before an eruption occurs. We might be able to stop it altogether.

Brixaby returned to haggling, and Arthur pulled his thoughts away from that prospect to continue.

Finally, they came to an agreement where Arthur and Brixaby were able to use the rooftop terrace as a pseudo-apartment, with a few more additions for comfort.

Dannill had his men go down to his shop and return with canvas and wooden poles they could use to construct a roof against the wind. It was the dry season, which meant no storms were predicted, though apparently a Reshuffling tended to affect the local weather, so that wasn't guaranteed.

With promises that the crafting supplies would be delivered in the morning, Dannill and his guards took their leave through a trapdoor that opened on the corner of the roof.

As soon as it shut behind the last man, Arthur slipped a piece of thin wood under the catch, effectively bolting it into place.

Brixaby eyed him. "Why bother? If anyone sneaks up on us during the night, I will just throw them off the roof."

"I'll sleep better if the door's locked," Arthur replied. "But if someone does make it up here around the trapdoor, go ahead and give them a good flying lesson."

Then he set about setting up the wood and canvas into a serviceable roof for the two of them. Dannill had provided nails and a hammer, and there were already grooves on all four corners of the terrace to fit in the ends of the wooden poles.

To his mild amusement, both Arthur and Brixaby received starting levels in Construction.

"You know," Arthur said as he tied off the ends of the canvas to the final pole, "you could make a good life for yourself by ferrying supplies like this back and forth through the city. You'd just put the stuff in your Personal Space, fly to wherever they want it delivered, take it back out again, and get paid."

Brixaby jerked his head back in an exaggerated eye roll. "I am a dragon, not a courier service."

Arthur grinned. "Plenty of purples are couriers."

"I am a Leg—"

Arthur stopped him with a look, and for once Brixaby modulated his voice. "I am a *Rare*," he grumbled in case anyone was listening. This city-state may not look to any hives, but word might spread faster if it became openly known that he and Brixaby had Legendary cards.

Louder, Brixaby added, "I do hope Joy and Sams arrive on time."

"Me too," Arthur admitted, and glanced at the single cot bed brought up for him. Brixaby had been given a wider pallet to sleep on, and he'd already claimed the thickest quilt to stretch across it. "But we'll have to figure out a different place to stay once they're here. Sams won't be able to land on top of this roof without bringing the whole thing down."

In the back of his mind, he wondered if Cressida would mind sharing a bed with him. It wouldn't be the first time they'd shared sleeping quarters . . . though in Mesa Free Hive, nothing had happened. The dragons had been much too young, they were all squished together, and . . . Arthur had chickened out.

He regretted it even though he wasn't sure he could have done anything differently with Joy being injured and both dragons poking their nose into their riders' business like young children whenever they were awake.

"Arthur, do you think dragons can go down to the Dark Heart?" Brixaby asked suddenly. He seemed unusually anxious.

"I don't see why not for you and Joy, though I suspect Sams might have a problem with narrow tunnels."

Brixaby visibly relaxed. "Then we shall need to buy him a body-modification card. I want all in my retinue to accompany me."

This, Arthur knew, was Brixaby's way of showing that he cared. "It's smart to have everyone grow in power at the same time," he said with a nod. "There's no point in gaining power if you leave everyone else behind."

Something twinged in his heart, and he thought of Dannill asking him what it was he needed down in the Dark Heart.

But when Arthur tried to chase that thought down, he found he couldn't follow its path. Perhaps it had been nothing.

Arthur woke early the next morning just as the first rays of the rising sun hit him in the face.

I need to put up walls on the east side, he thought grumpily, sitting up. At least the view was spectacular—an unfamiliar city and a forest that lay beyond the far walls.

Glancing at Brixaby, Arthur noticed that the dragon, who had made a big show last night of making up his pallet bed on the other side of the terrace, had shifted it during the night so it lay right beside Arthur's bed. Wisely, Arthur decided not to mention it.

Instead, he looked at his waking dragon and said, "Let's go out and fly."

Brixaby went from groggy and barely awake to perked up in a moment. "Yes, since we are to be sponsored by Dannill, we should make ourselves known to the city. Only . . ." He looked at Arthur. "I thought you wanted me to be a *secret.*" He said this last part with mild distaste.

"Not much chance of that now," Arthur said. "Dannill's guards will probably talk, if they haven't already. Besides, if we're going to have our likeness spread around and . . . sign things, we may as well make a splash."

"Good. I am not meant to be a secret," Brixaby said. "Let's fly. What are you waiting for? Why are you still in bed?"

Things had been hectic since Brixaby had grown to his current size. Unlike most dragons who grew with meat and time, Brixaby grew on a diet of cards and card shards. Thanks to ingesting a Legendary card, he was finally big enough to bear Arthur's weight in flight.

Unfortunately, they'd only had time to fly while in battle. No time to actually enjoy being in the air together. Arthur didn't even have a proper dragon saddle. Luckily, he always had his **Dragon Riding** skill to lean on.

He settled himself on Brixaby's back right at the base of his neck. It was the only spot that was devoid of sharp backward-facing ridges.

The more Brixaby grew, the spikier he became.

The moment he was seated, Brixaby beat his four wings, and they flew straight up into the air. Then, once he gained a little height, they shot right toward the middle of the city, weaving his way up and around buildings.

They passed people who were having an early morning breakfast on their balconies. Arthur waved at them—one dazed-looking person waved back.

People pointed from the street as Brixaby dived down low, skimming over the tops of night-shuttered vendor booths. The wind wash from Brixaby's wings made the colorful flags and banners flap.

At Arthur's whoop of exhilaration, Brixaby climbed into the air again, turning this way and that to avoid low-slung clotheslines that were strung between buildings. Arthur shifted his weight along with him, moving with his dragon as an active participant.

He was rewarded with another **Dragon Riding** skill level, bringing him to level 18.

Arthur pointed. "Let's take a look at the tallest buildings. There's something weird about them."

They were coming up toward the very center of the city, where a grouping of high buildings seemed to stretch to the sky.

As Arthur and Brixaby drew closer, it became clear the buildings were stacked so close together that there wasn't any room between them. And in the rare places there were gaps, it was filled by a rock wall every bit as sturdy looking as the one that surrounded the city.

The drone of Brixaby's wings changed tone as he once again stopped moving forward and began to climb straight up. And up. And up.

They crested the top to discover that the buildings bracketed an entire city block on all four sides.

And in the middle sat . . . a pit.

Looking at it, Arthur had no doubt that this was the Dark Heart of the city. The pit was so deep that he couldn't see to the bottom. Yet as he stared, he got the impression of something . . . pulsing down there. His eyes wanted to slide away. He was looking at something that should not be.

The hair rose on the back of Arthur's neck. It was all too easy to tear his gaze away and back to the buildings. There were no windows facing the Dark Heart. Just blank walls, as if no one could stand to look into it.

He swallowed through a throat that had gone suddenly dry. "Brix, don't fly down there."

"Of course not," Brixaby replied. "You heard Dannill. It's not ready to be harvested yet."

Arthur exhaled a little breath of relief, glad he wouldn't have to talk him out of anything foolish. Dragons could be very insistent on killing scourglings.

"Let's see what's on the other side of the city."

Brixaby complied, and soon they were flying at breakneck speed out toward the opposite side from where they'd come in yesterday. It wasn't too different— more buildings in that staggered height.

Then they were over the wall and out over the forest again. Only then did Brixaby lower his speed, favoring a more sedate pace. The land was completely uncultivated, as if it hadn't been touched by human hands at all.

Arthur looked around in satisfaction. After all, this was a brand-new king- dom, a whole new part of the world to explore. He wanted to see what it looked like.

"Climb higher, Brix. As high as you can!"

Brixaby buzzed on—not to the height of the clouds, but so high up that the green tops of the trees were smaller than a pinhead.

Only then did Arthur catch a shadow out in the distance. He pointed. "What's that dark spot? The ocean?"

"If it is, I should like a swim."

"You can swim?"

"How hard could it be?" Brixaby asked.

But as they got closer, that smudge against the horizon expanded and also resolved itself. Arthur's stomach sank.

"That's not the ocean. That's scourge-deadlands."

"It's not all dead," Brixaby said. "I see something ahead."

Arthur didn't, but with a neck-jerking change of direction, Brixaby started flying directly to the south. They were still headed toward the deadlands, but as they drew closer, Arthur saw a strip of darker color running through the gray, dead dirt. Pounded soil that indicated a road.

And beyond that, Arthur spotted tiny moving objects along the road. It was an oxen caravan.

"How desperate must people be to cross the deadlands?" he wondered aloud. People who were uncarded would be at great risk of becoming sick.

Though, his own childhood village had been on the edge of the deadlands, and there were rumors that bandits camped out miles into the dead areas. But it was a place hostile to life in every way. Nothing could grow. The water itself was poison, and if scourge-dust got into lungs or an open cut, people would sicken and die.

"Brix," Arthur said as another thought occurred to him. "How far does this extend?"

"As far as I can see." Brixaby sounded mildly bored, as if nothing out here could interest him. "Past the horizon. Why?"

"Cressida and Horatio," Arthur said with a feeling of sick guilt. "They'll have to cross all of this to get here."

After that, much of the joy was drained out of the flight. Brixaby turned back to the city and their rooftop home.

But they weren't alone. The trapdoor had been broken open, and three stern officials dressed in uniform were waiting for them.

CHAPTER 6

Brixaby circled around the top of the tower a couple of times to give himself and Arthur a view of the people waiting for them. As he did, he fanned out his extra set of wings in what anybody who was used to working with dragons would know was a display of aggression. Judging by the unimpressed look of the authorities and some curt gestures to come on down and land, this seemed to shoot right over their heads.

Brixaby turned his head to glance at Arthur. "Should I give them a Stunning Shout? Perhaps just to that little one off to the side?" He gestured with one claw toward the only woman out of the three.

Arthur winced. "No, let's see what they want with us first." He hesitated. "But if they try anything, remember what we talked about last night?"

"Oh, yes, the flying lesson." Brixaby boomed this out loud enough for the authorities below to hear.

Brixaby came in for a landing in a way that only a dragon with his specific body type could. That was, straight down while managing to keep his body perfectly level. It was an elegant move, and one that happened to throw a wash of air straight downward, kicking up a satisfying amount of dust into the faces of the authorities.

Wisely, the woman and two men moved off to the side of the rooftop terrace to give the landing dragon some space.

Their uniforms were a slate-blue color—now fairly dusty—and accented with gold trimming. The smallest of the three, the woman who had her hair up in a severe bun, also had extra gold pieces added to her left shoulder and the side of her arm. By the way the other two unconsciously gave deference to her, Arthur suspected that she was the leader out of the three.

Sure enough, as soon as Brixaby had fully landed and snapped his wings shut, she was the first to step forward. The larger, more burly of the two men kept half a step behind her, just to the right, at her shoulder. He carried a notebook in his hand.

"I assume you are Arthur and Brixaby?" the woman asked, her voice dry. She stood in a parade stance, her arms folded behind herself, and she didn't look intimidated in the least. "I am told that you've been given an understanding of our language, so please don't play any silly games."

"We can *both* understand you," Arthur said pointedly as he dismounted from Brixaby. He didn't extend his hand for a shake, and neither did she. "Yes, I'm Arthur, and this is my dragon, Brixaby."

"I am Oversheriff Walker," she said, "and I speak on behalf of the mayor in these matters."

Arthur's eyebrows rose, and just before he could speak, Walker continued, "From which kingdom do you hail? And I assume you come from one of their hives, as well?"

Arthur, of course, already had a lie ready on the tip of his tongue. "I've heard you call it the Fabergé Kingdom. And we come from Strawberry Moon Hive."

This lie wouldn't hold up to scrutiny, especially if somebody had active communications with his old kingdom. He and Brixaby weren't exactly the type to blend in with a crowd. But if he could delay the secret inevitably coming out, he certainly would.

Walker nodded. "We checked the records, Rider Arthur, and we saw that you two have not been formally signed up for the Reshuffling."

This wasn't a question, but Arthur treated it like one anyway. "We just came in last night. I wasn't aware that we had to sign up at all."

Walker nodded to the man behind her, who started writing in his notebook. "Well, we'll get you signed up right now, and of course, you will have to pay your entry fees. You will be given one week from today," she said, and fell silent as the man—her assistant?—stepped forward to ask basic information, including the spelling of both their names and their ages.

Meanwhile, the third man stood slightly off to the side of the other two. From his practiced stance, Arthur suspected that he had some kind of combat card. He was backup in case this went south.

Arthur turned his attention back to the man with the notebook. He had a little bit of trouble with spelling his name, considering the letters between the two languages were different. But Walker broke in and stated that his name was common enough in their kingdom. Though the way that they said it grated on his nerves. An extra emphasis on the "er" at the end that made his name sound whiney to his ears.

Brixaby tried to convince the man his name was spelled with two X's, but Arthur saw he only put down one.

"Well, now that we've got that out of the way," Walker said briskly, "we're here to explain the rules around here. New Houston is a free society, mind you, and we don't want any kingdom business interfering with ours."

"I don't intend to bring any part of the kingdom with me," Arthur said. "Brixaby and I came here to get away from that sort of thing."

She hummed under her breath but didn't say anything else. "There is another matter. I spoke of entry fees before."

Arthur nodded, unconcerned. He figured that Dannill would take care of that. He was selling their likenesses, after all, so he wanted them to look good.

Walker continued, "There is a way that you could easily make enough to take care of those fees, and also make the complaints about your little adventure this morning go away."

Arthur stiffened. "Complaints?"

She glanced to the side at the man Arthur was starting to think of as her secretary. At her nod, he read off what looked like a prepared list. "Disturbing the peace; using a flying card, power, or skill without proper licenses; and of course, failing to register a dangerous animal."

"I am no more an animal than you are," Brixaby interjected, "though I certainly am dangerous."

The man continued, "In addition, you have been directly implicated in causing several different accidents throughout the city. There are reports of at least three different cart accidents that could be laid at your feet."

"What do you mean? We didn't touch any carts!" Arthur asked, annoyed.

Walker answered this one with a snort. "People were watching a dragon fly only a few feet above their heads. And that meant that they weren't watching where they were going. Plus, you startled several animals, and there is one report of a small herd of bison becoming fretful enough to stampede."

He didn't even remember seeing a bison pen. That was the name these people had for those woolly oxen.

Crossing his arms, Arthur gazed at her with a steady look. He wasn't going to allow himself to be intimidated, and he had a feeling that Walker was going somewhere with this. He just wanted her to get to the point.

Reading his expression, her lips twitched up in a very, very small smile. "As it happens, there is a way that you can pay your fees, make these complaints disappear, regain good favor among the citizens, and also earn extra money on the side."

Now they were coming to the meat of it, and Arthur suspected, the real reason why these three were up here. Everybody in the city seemed to have their own particular angle.

"And that is?"

"The Dark Heart is reaching its peak of power, so it's spawning more scourglings than usual. We've had reports from Undersheriff Domingo that you were of some help with a mega-scourgling, and that was without the assistance of your beast. What do you say about helping us out again?"

"Of course we will," Brixaby said before Arthur could get a word in. "I would have done it anyway. Scourglings should not be allowed to roam free." And just in case anybody got the idea that he was doing this out of the goodness of his heart, he added, "Also, most of those were Rare-type scourglings, yes?" His greed was obvious.

Walker shook her head. "Most will be Commons and Uncommons with some Rare. But you would be deputized on behalf of an undersheriff, and as such, you would not be allowed to keep any of the harvest. This is *law*," she said, "and if you're caught keeping cards or shards from a harvested scourgling, that is a crime punishable by jail time, dragon rider or not. All harvests go into the city vault, and the resulting cards are then given out to children who have come of age." She gave them a hard look. "You are dragon riders, so you know how important it is that everyone be carded as soon as they can."

Which was admirable and all, but Dannill had mentioned that children and their families had to pay back the cards with steep loans. And the cynical part of Arthur doubted that a Rare-ranked card would go to an orphan or somebody without any connections.

But the other part pointed out that even one Rare-ranked card was worth many Uncommon cards, and even more Common ranked. Those would certainly go to children in need. Even a Common card could stop scourge from taking root.

"I understand," Arthur said. "However, Brixaby and I are searching for new cards, too. We intend to prepare for the Reshuffling. So we demand first right— at a fair price—for any Rare card that we harvest."

Arthur, if we kill a scourgling, the harvest should be ours, Brixaby muttered in his head.

Arthur glanced at his dragon, nodding his head in what he hoped was an acknowledging look that said, *Trust me.*

Brixaby backed down.

"That is . . . reasonable," Walker allowed. "But we won't allow any shenanigans. You will be scanned for your existing cards and shards on your person before and after any battle. And yes, our particular scans do show cards in extraplanar spaces."

Well, there went Arthur's half-baked idea to shove anything interesting into his Personal Space. But he still had something else in mind. "You mentioned pay?" he asked.

"I think you'll find it more than reasonable. The standard pay is one Rare card shard for every mega-scourgling taken down. The same rate for lesser-ranked scourglings. Common for Common, and so on."

"Then it will be one card shard for myself, and one for Brixaby," Arthur said. "He is a person, even if he has scales and wings."

"I do like card shards," Brixaby added with a toothy smile.

Walker hemmed and hawed about this for a few moments, but Arthur sensed she would agree. Mostly, he had put up this front about the pay to keep up appearances. He didn't actually care. He had his own plans.

In the end, she agreed. "Fine. Let's get you scanned in."

The man who had been watching silently—the one that Arthur had thought of as the combat backup—came forward with an enchanted stick polished to a dark sheen. Runes glowed up and down its sides, unfamiliar ones. Arthur longed to take it and study it for himself, and he could see Brixaby's sharp attention.

"This is an enchanted scanning wand," the man said. "If you have any cards that are sensitive to magic or mana, you may feel a reaction, but I can assure you it's perfectly safe and won't negatively affect you in any way. Think of it as a seeking tool. It only counts the number of cards and shards in your possession."

Arthur hesitated. Discovering he was a Legendary-ranked rider now would lead to awkward questions. "What does it tell you about my cards? The type?" *The rank?*

The man shook his head. "No one would put up with that. It only reports the number of cards and shards in your possession. Nothing more."

That was interesting, and Arthur's Thief class immediately identified the easy-to-exploit loophole. If he changed out his cards for ones he'd just harvested, how would anybody know?

"Okay," Arthur said, "me first." He didn't think that this was a trap, but he would rather take the risk than have Brixaby do it.

The man waved the wand at him, which glowed a bright blue as it sensed Arthur's magical potential. He then rattled off a series of numbers to the man with the notebook—none of them made sense.

Judging by the complete nonreaction of Walker and her men, it seemed that the enchanted wand didn't recognize the rank or type of cards, just as he'd said.

Walker nodded and turned back to Arthur. "It seems that your secondary card anchor is quite full. It's not my place to say, but since you seem to have already found a sponsor here, you may want to consider upgrading it before the Reshuffling."

Brixaby's cards were recorded as well. It only took a few moments, and Brixaby did not twitch an eyelid.

Walker nodded again, satisfied. "Your current card numbers have now been recorded. At the end of every day, you will come to the sheriff's headquarters to submit yourself to a new scan. It will only take a few moments. Once we confirm you have the same as before with another scan, you will receive your pay."

"How will you know how many scourglings we've killed?" Arthur asked.

"You will collect the chips from the undersheriff that you assist. They will be the one who will verify your kill and perform the harvest." She fixed him with a firm stare. "It is *very* important that you do not harvest the corpse yourself without the presence of an undersheriff. That is a Class III misdemeanor, and it goes up to a felony if you're caught stealing the cards."

"Understood," Arthur said, though he had no idea what a misdemeanor or felony was. Some words, it seemed, didn't have direct language equivalents.

Satisfied, Walker and the two others returned back down the trapdoor, but not before leaving him a small egg-sized object that looked like polished quartz. "This is a card-anchor stone, given to most of our emergency services personnel. If you're called to assist, it will activate with a buzz, and there will be an arrow which leads you to the location. After you're done, the undersheriff will clear the stone, and you'll be open to take the next call."

Arthur took it, and he was a little impressed despite himself. "You guys seem prepared for this sort of thing. Have you had other dragon rider visitors?"

This actually earned a full smile from the woman. "No, but we do have other combat teams—adventure teams, as we call them here, who work with us in the same fashion. They're also sharpening their knives for the Reshuffling, so be aware of that. You may come across them, and my advice is to give way in case they want to kill the mega-scourglings first. Many of them have been here for years. They've earned their seniority. Do you understand?"

It seemed that wherever he went, he was at the bottom of the totem pole, but that was the risk of starting over in a new place. "I understand," Arthur said.

After that, the three officials returned back down the trapdoor.

The moment it closed, Brixaby plunged his hand within his own Personal Space and pulled it back with a woven bit of metal which he fastened over the top of the trapdoor. This would be much harder to break through. The piece of wood that Arthur had used earlier was now in splinters.

The oversheriff had acted pleasant enough, but this had been more or less a shakedown. And Arthur suspected that things would not have gone so well if he had said no to the request to help out the city. Luckily, that had fit into his agenda as well.

"You have a plan," Brixaby said.

"Of course I do," Arthur said. "Follow me."

At Brixaby's nod, Arthur touched him, and they both were transported into Arthur's Personal Space.

Normally, time stopped completely there, but Brixaby had natural nullification magic. It became a spot where the two could talk in peace.

Within an eyeblink, they returned to the real world with no one the wiser.

Brixaby flicked his wings in a self-satisfied manner. He was happy with the plan Arthur had outlined.

Then the dragon glanced at the card anchor. "You think that we will have to wait long?"

"No," Arthur said, "I don't."

He was proven right when, less than an hour later, the card-anchor stone started to buzz.

Arthur tapped the top to activate it, and a ghostly green arrow appeared over the top of the egg-like rock, indicating they were to head east.

CHAPTER 7

Following the ghostly green arrow that hovered over the card-anchor stone, Arthur and Brixaby headed to the east.

As they got closer to the wall, the arrow's direction shifted to the north. Their target was moving.

Frowning, Arthur bent as low as he could over Brixaby's neck without tipping over the side, scanning the ground for movement. The city officials had cut a road along the outside of the wall and trimmed the vegetation back all the way out to the forest nearly a quarter mile out. That made it easy to spot a line of four horsemen riding along it. The card anchor pointed right toward them.

Brixaby saw them as well and flew in their direction, but the horses the men rode began to get skittish. Unlike beasts near the hive, they hadn't been desensitized to the sight of dragons.

"Pull up, Brix," Arthur said. "Then come around and land a little farther down the road."

Brixaby grumbled, "Stupid animals. Have you ever tasted horse meat? Feh. Now, if those men were riding stags . . ."

His complaining didn't keep him from performing a tight turn midair and coming in for a perfect landing a hundred yards in front of the approaching group. The horses were still unhappy and refused their riders' attempts to make them approach, but at least none had bolted.

The riders didn't look happy, either. The undersheriff in charge wasn't Domingo. He was a portly man with one of those wide-brimmed hats that was so popular among the people here. An odd ball of light glimmered just above his right shoulder. Arthur was certain it was some kind of card power.

The man glanced at his fellows, one of whom gave a shrug, then he dismounted his snorting horse and approached Arthur and Brixaby on foot.

As a show of goodwill, Arthur dismounted as well.

The undersheriff had a slightly goggle-eyed look as he glanced from Arthur to Brixaby and back again. "Well, I suppose the rumors 'bout a dragon rider in the city are true."

"Don't tell me you called us over just to verify rumors," Arthur said.

That seemed to snap the man out of a little of his shock. "No, no, of course not."

"Good," Brixaby said. "Because I would have been most *displeased* if I could not fight scourglings today."

The man's eyes widened more when Brixaby spoke. But then, to his credit, he shook his head and focused on Arthur. "I'm Undersheriff Lopez. We've had reports of scourglings hitting caravan trains out in the deadlands, and I was told you could help."

Arthur frowned. "Scourglings don't erupt out of the deadlands."

The deadlands were so thoroughly desiccated by ancient scourgling attacks that nothing grew there. Not moss or lichen, or even more scourglings. It was one of the reasons why Arthur had not seen a scourge-eruption until he had gotten well away from his kingdom's borderlands.

That was the great paradox of scourglings—they killed all life down to the building blocks that plants needed in the soil. But they also needed that same life to spawn more of them.

Lopez nodded. "No, they spawn out of our side and then follow the smell of fresh meat back along the roads." His face twisted into a grimace. "Unfortunately, we don't get the reports of attacks until the event's well over. Word comes in from others who come across the remains of the caravan. We've had several hit just this week."

So this wasn't an immediate emergency; it was a serious situation.

Arthur and Brixaby exchanged a look, then Arthur turned back to Lopez. "Where is this road?"

The undersheriff blew out a breath in relief. "You're taking the assignment?"

"Of course. Why wouldn't we?"

"Well . . ." He rubbed his chin in thought and then shook his head. "I suppose it's different for you, seeing as you can just fly your beast out and back." He either ignored or didn't see Brixaby flashing his teeth at him for calling him a beast. Lopez went on. "Usually, adventuring groups want something a bit more solid before they agree to go out. I can't even tell you how far along the road you'll have to go. Here." He reached up to that odd ball of light that hovered over his right shoulder and then tapped it.

Immediately, the image of a map appeared in front of them.

Arthur's Counterfeit Siphon card immediately took note of the spell.

New Counterfeit spell obtained: Malleable Map
Remaining Time: 59 Minutes 59 Seconds

This was a Rare-level spell. It suddenly made more sense why an uncertain man like Lopez had been placed as an undersheriff.

At a glance, the image seemed to be an overhead illustration of the eastern part of the city and the walls. Lopez stuck his hand into the illusion, and with a widening of his fingers, the map expanded. Now it showed the full city and a larger part of the surrounding forest.

Lopez flicked his hand to the east, and the map shifted yet again to show more forest, and then a hatched-in area that was labeled *Scourge Country.*

Through that, several straight lines arrowed out in different directions. They looked a little like spokes on a wheel.

Lopez pointed to the thickest of the lines. "This is the main Interstate."

"Interstate?" Arthur repeated. He did have a good grasp on the language, but some phrases still threw him.

"Yes, from one city-state to the next. It's the most direct path out to Laredo, which most of the traders use. Most of our inbound traffic comes in through here. You'll know you've found it when you see the green flags."

Arthur nodded.

Lopez looked at him for a moment, as if he were chewing on his next words. Then he adjusted the belt on his pants, nodded to himself, and said, "You're new here, and I'm sure you've already been read the standard lecture, but I'll remind you *not* to harvest any scourglings on your own. Once they're slain, come back here and report. My men will ride out and do the official harvest. Then you'll get paid. Don't get smart and do it yourself."

"We would never *dream* of doing such a thing," Brixaby said, probably in a way that was meant to sound authentic, but it made Arthur wince.

"We know our duty," Arthur said.

"Safe travels, then." Lopez tipped his hat to him.

Arthur had a moment of fierce glee as he felt eyes on him while he remounted his dragon. The moment he was settled, Brixaby took off again, vertically. He knew even without the whoops from Lopez's men below that they made quite the sight.

Brixaby turned toward the east.

This side of the city was opposite from where they had originally come in, and the land was subtly different. The trees were thinner, more spread out, and broken by grassy hills dotted with beautiful blue flowers.

It made spotting signs of movement from the air easy.

"Out there . . . Are those scourglings?" Arthur asked, leaning forward with narrowed eyes.

He knew his vision was better than most thanks to his Master of Body Enhancement card, especially at night. But for extra-long distances, his human eyes could not compete with that of a dragon. He couldn't tell if the tiny dots moving across a far hill were deer or the enemy.

"Bison," Brixaby said. "Four of them."

Arthur frowned. Something about that bothered him, though he couldn't put his finger on what it was.

They were flying in the general direction of the wild bison, so Arthur put it out of his mind.

Instead, he accessed the Malleable Map spell for himself. He still had use of it for another forty-five minutes.

Too bad I don't have some sort of Master of Magic card, he thought. *Maybe that's what I need from the Dark Heart.*

It was certainly something that he wanted. But needed? That was a distinct difference.

A small ball of light appeared in front of him, which then flattened out into a map. However, it was different than Lopez's. This map had blank spots on all sides except for the direction they had come. Even then, the depiction of the city was full of holes.

"Looks like it's restricted to places we've already visited," Arthur said with a sigh, then on impulse, he mimed closing the map with both hands.

Sure enough, the display of light collapsed back into a bright yellow ball that was dismissed when he stopped concentrating on it.

"Perhaps you should take up a cartography skill," Brixaby said.

"I have a cartography skill," Arthur muttered. It had been one of his first. "Dannill did say that the Dark Heart is different every time it's delved. Creating a map as we go along might be helpful."

"Yes, I don't mind if we get lost as long as there are plenty of scourglings to harvest, but I would like to get out again with all my rewards." Despite his dark words, Brixaby sounded positively gleeful about the delve.

Repressing a shudder at the thought of being lost underground forever, Arthur patted his neck, then realized he'd lost track of the bison, but only because they were nearly on top of them.

"Brix, dive down a little. I want to take a good look at those."

There was definitely something off about the bison. Arthur only identified what it was once they got close enough to see the way that they plodded along, and, most importantly, how the grass moved behind them. As if they were dragging something.

The brown woolly fur obscured the harnesses still buckled onto them. But at least two of the bison were trailing the remains of leather straps and some of a wooden yoke.

These weren't wild animals. They had once been attached to a wagon, and Arthur suspected he knew what had happened to set them free.

These people didn't have dragon hives to protect them. In fact, due to the way that they cultivated the Dark Heart, they *had* to know that incidents like this were inevitable. And they did it anyway.

But another part recognized that he was looking at an opportunity.

"Brixaby, how much room do you have in your Personal Space?"

Brixaby looked down at the bison eagerly. "I have more room in my stomach."

"It would be a waste to eat them. Somebody lost these bison and would be interested in getting them back. I mean, if that person isn't already dead," he added with a wince. "In any case, those are trained to haul carts. We can sell them or give them to Dannill to sell."

Brixaby brightened. "Yes, very good. I have room in my Personal Space for all of them."

"Then let's make it quick." Arthur tightened his legs and took hold of one of the back-facing ridges.

Bison weren't sapient beings, and therefore didn't need to give permission before being stored.

Unfortunately, Brixaby was the only one quick enough to do what needed to be done.

Brixaby dived down low, and, spotting him, three of the bison started to lumber away. One, the largest and possibly the bull, turned around to face him with its massive head lowered.

Brixaby's lips pulled away from his teeth in a snarling grin. He lowered even further in a direct challenge, skimming so low over the meadow that his belly touched the top of the grass.

Just when it seemed the two were going to crash head-on, Brixaby beat his two top wings, which gave him just enough lift to sail over the top of the animal. As he did, he reached down and touched a claw to its broad back.

A moment later, the bison disappeared.

With an evil chuckle, Brixaby turned to the retreating bison. It didn't take long to catch up. They were too heavy footed to evade him. Another three taps, one right after the other, and all disappeared.

But as the last bison vanished, Brixaby staggered in the air so suddenly that Arthur was thrown forward and nearly lost his grip altogether. Somehow he managed to cling on, though one of the ridges had knocked painfully into his chest.

"Brixaby?" he gasped. "You okay?"

"I'm . . . fine." He coughed and shook his head, and quickly gained momentum again.

"What happened?" Arthur asked, and when the dragon didn't answer, "Brixaby?"

"The bison are heavy," he said shortly.

"So? You've hidden an entire other dragon in there. Digger wasn't small."

There was another short silence before Brixaby sighed, lowering his head in exasperated defeat. "I may not have had much success hunting yesterday," he muttered. "Deer look stupid, but they are fast, and they know the forest better than I do. I don't know how Joy managed to hunt so well back at Free Mesa. But," he added, "while I traveled, I came across something else: ruins."

Arthur got a bad feeling. "You mean you found some of the attacked carts?" Why hadn't Brixaby told him before?

"No, ruins. Buildings and odd . . . objects. I think they were for farming, because they were metal." Even while rapidly beating his wings, Brixaby managed to shrug. "They were old, and most have rusted, but I took the choicest bits. There was nobody around to stop me."

Arthur had become an expert at reading between the lines when it came to Brixaby.

"You filled up your storage space with metal parts, didn't you? Anything I can use?"

Brixaby shook his head. "Not right now, but perhaps later. I haven't had time to practice with my Combat Weaponsmith card, and perhaps I will make you some chainmail or something more interesting that will better fit your Metal Shot card." He turned his head and looked up at Arthur. "I had *intended* to keep it a surprise. We should be well armed when we descend to the Dark Heart."

"Well, consider me surprised." Arthur patted his dragon's neck, pleased.

Despite the fact his surprise was ruined, Brixaby preened.

They flew on, and soon they started to see signs of the deadlands up ahead.

CHAPTER 8

Brixaby suddenly dived, and for a terrible moment, Arthur felt his rear lift off the dragon's scaly neck.

"Brix!" he yelled, clutching desperately at the ridge in front of him and using the strength of his legs to pull himself back down.

Arthur couldn't quite catch what Brixaby called back to him, but it sounded something like, "If you fly with me, be prepared for surprises."

He managed to regain a firm seat before the dragon leveled out of his dive.

At least he got another **Dragon Riding** skill level out of it.

Skill level gained: Dragon Riding (Animal Husbandry/Dragon Rider
Class)
Level 19

Once his heart felt like it wasn't trying to leap out of his throat, Arthur snarled, "What was that about?"

In answer, Brixaby pointed ahead.

For a moment, Arthur didn't see what he'd spotted. The ground had become much patchier the closer they came to the deadlands. There were areas where, for no visible reason, the plants from the grasses all the way to tall hundred-year-old trees had yellowed and died. And other inexplicably dry spots, as if the water itself had been repelled from the soil. As they went on, these blighted areas became more common than the alive ones, and the spots that were still hanging on for dear life looked more sickly. To Arthur's eye, the deadlands were encroaching as the scourge-blighted soil poisoned the land.

Gazing ahead, he couldn't pick out much in the scraggly, half-dead weeds. This was one of those actively dying patches. That was until he glanced at the ground and saw . . . tracks.

Back when he was a child living in the borderland village, Arthur had been much too young to be allowed on the rare hunts when the adults snuck away from the village for a chance to bring home fresh meat. After that, he had lived in a city and so didn't have even the most basic of tracking skills.

But anybody with eyes could pick out the deep imprints in the dusty soil. And they were quite unusual.

"What are those? Birds?" he asked.

The tracks were three-toed, spread out. The smallest Arthur spotted was the size of his spread hand. The largest was the size of Sams's spread forepaw, which was pretty big, considering he was a full-grown yellow dragon.

And the more he looked, the more he saw. A sea of tracks, all pointed toward the deadlands instead of away from them.

"What bird lives on the ground?" Brixaby asked, shrugging under Arthur.

A bird that should not be, Arthur thought, which meant only one thing. "Scourglings."

Considering that there was a hot, dry wind blowing in from the direction of the deadlands, and no hint of dust had covered the tracks yet, they seemed fresh.

Arthur and Brixaby flew on, and the vegetation thinned out even more. The soil became rocky and hard, with no plants to help break it up. It took on a sort of bleached gray-white color that signaled there was no life to be found within.

The tracks faded away, as even the heaviest of the scourglings couldn't make an imprint in that soil. But they had all been aimed in a single direction. Following it, Arthur and Brixaby soon came to the road called the Interstate.

As Lopez had said, it was marked by green flags that stood about a foot tall and flapped in the dry wind. The green was weirdly visible against the gray-white soil.

The soil between the flags was so packed down that there wasn't a hint of a track, or even wheel ruts from the carts that must have passed by regularly. But the scourglings' tracks headed right for it.

Abruptly, Brixaby started to flap upward again at a sharp angle.

"What are you doing?" Arthur asked.

The dragon glanced at him in a puzzled way, as if he were just about to explain a very basic concept. "The sun is directly hitting the soil, and it causes the air to lift. Don't you feel it?"

"No," Arthur said, but then shrugged. In the air, Brixaby was the expert.

The dragon blew out an exasperated snort. "Observe," he said, and then positioned both of his wings on either side, close together, with a very slight overlap at the edges so that they provided more surface area. And though they were gliding . . . They were not falling. In fact, to Arthur's mild amazement, they seemed to be rising.

However, the process was slower than Brixaby liked, because he kept flapping his four wings to gain even more altitude. As they climbed, Arthur could see farther. The land had flattened out, and Arthur finally spotted dark dots in the distance, right on the edge of the horizon.

"Are those scourglings?" Arthur asked. "Or is that the oncoming caravan?"

"I think it's both," Brixaby said, and then swung his head around again, glancing at Arthur with a smug look. "You may want to hold on."

"Thanks," Arthur said dryly, then took hold of one of the ridges again and tightened his thighs. His legs were already starting to burn with the beginning of fatigue, and he expected he would be getting some kind of bonus soon from his Master of Body Enhancement card. Who would have known that riding a dragon would be a good workout?

Again, Brixaby dived, though this time he wasn't just falling with style. He was going for speed. And there was nothing that wasn't card powered in this world that could beat a purple dragon for speed in flight.

The wind screamed by Arthur's ears, and his eyes watered. He had to narrow them almost to the point of being shut, taking in the world through a thin bar.

I need goggles, he thought, mentally kicking himself for not taking the time that morning to outfit Brixaby with the basics. He doubted anybody in the city would have a dragon saddle, but he could have easily purchased some soft straps that would have been more appropriate. At least smiths and metal forgers often used eye protection for their craft, so he could start there for goggles. He'd remedy the situation as soon as he got back.

Through bleary, wind-induced tears, he saw the distant dots start to resolve themselves.

It was indeed a caravan—four wagons by the looks of it—and they were in dire straits. They'd stopped and grouped together in a tight circle, pulling the animals in and taking shelter themselves by using the wagons as a barrier.

A mass of at least thirty scourglings had circled around and were actively attacking the carts. These had indeed taken on a bird shape, though with strong legs meant for running, tiny flightless wings, and large heads that supported oversized curved beaks meant to tear and rend meat.

But because they were not truly animals—there was debate whether scourglings were alive at all—the feathers were displaced, knocked askew, and at a closer look, falling off, leaving weeping red welts. And even above the screaming wind, Arthur heard the terrible whistling that was the scourglings' cries.

They were flying in fast but still too far away to make a difference.

Arthur clenched his jaw when he saw one of the terrible bird scourglings leap up on top of a cart and lean down to pluck a person out from the center.

Other wagoners attacked the scourgling with what looked like spears and bolts of yellow magic. The scourgling fell away, but not before the unfortunate person was thrown outside the ring of carts. Arthur was too far away to tell if it had been a man or a woman, or even an adult. But they were dead seconds after they hit the ground as other scourglings set upon them.

Brixaby swelled beneath him. As they flew forward, faster than an arrow in flight, Brixaby let out his Stunning Shout. It was something more force than sound, and at this angle, straight on, it likely hit a few people as well.

Arthur saw bits of wood splinter and fly up from one of the carts.

But the Stunning Shout also knocked down a swath of the scourglings, including the biggest beast of the group, which stood at least ten feet tall.

"That's the one, the high ranker," Arthur said. "We have to kill that one first. Brixaby, give me some metal—anything I can send at it."

They had slowed only slightly from their long dive, just enough for his voice to be heard over the sound of the wind. But they were less than two seconds from being on top of the wagons, a handful of heartbeats away.

But of course, in Personal Space, time was meaningless.

Arthur didn't even see Brixaby flicker as he entered his Personal Space to gather from his metal hoard. In the next moment, he reached back to hand Arthur a handful of metal chips.

Arthur took them in his cupped hands. Activating his Nice (Metal) Shot card, he became aware of the metal as if it were a second skin. The chips flowed over the tops of his hands, wrists, and forearms, settling there like a thin coat of armor. But it wasn't armor. It was ammunition.

Arthur concentrated on the rows closest to his hand and charged them with as much mana as he could stuff into them. As Brixaby flew screaming fast over the scourglings, Arthur set the sharp chips flying, using his **Throwing Accuracy** skill and his Makeshift Weaponry card for every bit of advantage.

Anything that didn't hit dead-on bounced off the unusually toughened feathers and skin. Only one chip out of the dozen he launched made a difference, striking its eye. The scourgling staggered back with a whistling cry.

Then Brixaby turned about so fast that Arthur was in very real danger of being flung off his back. It took every bit of strength, as well as his **Dragon Riding** skill, to cling on.

But that quick maneuver had dumped his speed, and Brixaby came around for another pass, this time using his Stunning Shout at close distance.

Now it was Brixaby's turn to shine. He flicked his wings in a neat move that took him right above the scourgling. As he passed over, a twisted mass of metal seemed to appear out of nowhere and fell straight down on the creature.

The large scourgling stepped to the side, clipped, but it was still a heavy blow. The twisted ball of metal fell with a thud that shook the earth and did not bounce—two smaller scourglings were crushed where they stood.

I need to find out what else he put in his Personal Space, Arthur thought.

Meanwhile, the men and women trying to defend the wagons weren't sitting idle. Arthur heard a shout behind him. Turning, he saw one woman had taken a position on top of one of the wagons. This was a risky spot to be in, as she drew the eye of every scourgling. But she stood strong and straight, completely ignoring scourglings that were jumping up and trying to snap at her.

Her arms extended, and wind built up out of nowhere. A dust devil came down from the clear blue sky, picked up the scourglings closest to her, and tossed them away.

Unfortunately, that caused a huge amount of turbulence, which sent Brixaby careening to one side. The next Stunning Shout that he had been building up went wide.

"Stop trying to be helpful!" Brixaby yelled at her. Then, as an aside to Arthur as he fought to regain control in the sky, he said, "Is it time?"

"Yeah," Arthur said grimly. "Might as well see what happens." Brixaby would not be safe in the air with dust devils spawning out of nowhere. Time for plan B.

With a flick of his wings, Brixaby landed, and Arthur made an emergency dismount. The moment his feet hit the soil, Brixaby produced another object from his Personal Space—a bar of metal with crude runes carved up the side. Brixaby's enchanted object. As it had been originally based on Cressida's flame bear card power, it enhanced fire.

Brixaby activated it, and dark flames grew up and down the length of the metal as well as his spine. Void fire. He closed in on the large scourgling.

The creature was just as eager to engage. It staggered toward him, snapping a beak filled with razor-sharp teeth.

At the last second, Brixaby lashed out with the enchanted bar. It was an outwardly sloppy move, a little too wide, and the base of his claws brushed the scourgling's chest. This close, Arthur was the only one to see Brixaby yank back not a card, but a handful of card shards.

The scourgling acted as if it had been mortally wounded. It lurched backward, staggering, its whistling cry that of a dying animal.

Brixaby pounced on top of the scourgling and pressed the bar to its feathers.

It turned out, scourgling feathers caught fire very easily, and Brixaby's dark flame was particularly nasty.

Meanwhile, some of the minor scourglings, having recovered from Brixaby's Stunning Shout, made greedy lurches toward Arthur. He pelted those with metal shrapnel. Unlike with the larger scourgling, the sharp metal shrapnel proved fatal.

When he looked back to see how his dragon was doing, he saw that the large scourgling was completely aflame and had collapsed.

Nearer to the wagons, the dust devil was cheerfully doing its work, flinging the last of the minor scourglings here and there.

They had won, and the people from the caravan were starting to realize they weren't doomed. They cheered, but Arthur also caught some screams on the wind. A few people had climbed up on the wagon along with the dust-devil women and were waving to get his attention.

He jogged to them. "What's wrong? Is someone hurt?"

More shouts, all overlapping and confused.

Finally, a woman broke out from between the wagons and hurried to him. "Please, dragon rider, what about the others?"

"What others?" Arthur asked.

Turning, she pointed back up the road. "We'd heard this last leg wasn't safe, so as we were the best fighters, we took the first few wagons ahead of the rest. But when the attack came, the biggest beasts kept going down the road. These were just the small 'uns. Please, sir, our children are there!"

Arthur glanced back at the large scourgling, which was still cheerfully burning. With dread, he realized that while the thing was large, the size of its feet barely fit half of those largest tracks he had seen in the dust.

He looked at Brixaby. "The shards."

Brixaby understood immediately and snorted in disgust. "Uncommon."

The largest had been only an Uncommon, which meant that the minor ones had been Common.

There were Rare scourglings still up ahead.

CHAPTER 9

Arthur was torn. Time was of the essence, and he truly did not give one fig about the local rules about card harvesting . . . except that he knew *exactly* what would happen the moment he and Brixaby were out of sight. He had once been in the same place as these people.

A single card, even a Common one, could change the course of a life. Some of these people were showing signs of injury in the middle of the deadlands. Without a card in their heart deck, they might be dead men walking.

Even then, the pickings around them would be slim at best. The large Uncommon scourgling he and Brixaby had fought might yield a whole card.

He doubted the rest of the scourglings were good for anything more than Common shards. All combined, they might be enough to make a whole card. But if the officials from the city found out they'd been harvested . . .

All of this flashed in and out of his mind in a second. The wagoners were yelling at Arthur to hurry to the other caravan and the children there. Some were just outright demanding who Arthur was and if any other dragon riders were coming.

Arthur cut across them. "Who's in charge here?"

There was a brief silence as everyone looked around. Then one man, bearded and grim, stepped forward. "I was the assistant to the second-in-command, but both he and the wagon master are dead. I suppose that puts me in charge," he said matter-of-factly.

"Listen," Arthur said, "I'll go help the other wagons, but I'll be leaving these scourgling corpses behind. If you harvest them, then me and my dragon were never here. Do you understand?"

Thankfully, the man could read between the lines. His nose wrinkled, and he spat to one side. "Figures they'd have a card tax in this city too."

Arthur shrugged. The important thing was that the man understood. With the message given, he turned to Brixaby and called over his shoulder toward the wagoners. "We're faster than any cart. Don't go back. You may just get attacked again by scourglings. We'll be bringing any survivors to the main city hospital."

That caused a burst of commotion, some begging Arthur to save their children specifically.

As if he would leave anyone behind.

The moment Arthur was seated, Brixaby took off, buzzing straight into the air and then shooting down the road outbound from the city at full speed. This was no leisurely climb up into the heights only to drop down again. This was a purple at full breakneck speed. Straddling his back with no dragon saddle, Arthur was slightly intimidated. He crouched down low, both not wanting to create more wind resistance and suspecting he might actually get blown off if he tried to sit up straight.

Still, he was a little surprised at Brixaby's enthusiasm. His dragon didn't typically care for the plight of other people aside from Arthur and, occasionally, the riders of his retinue dragons.

When he said as much, yelling at full volume only to be barely heard over the shrieking wind, Brixaby curled his neck around to answer.

For once, his booming voice sounded normal through the wind. Arthur wondered if that was part of the reason why he was always so loud. Brixaby was built for speed in the air.

"I don't care if those people harvest Common scourglings. Let them have it. We have much more valuable prey up ahead—Rare shards." Brixaby punctuated this by removing the Uncommon shards from where he had stored them in his Personal Space. He crunched down on them, eating them like a child would a handful of stolen cookies.

That had been Arthur's plan. The wand let the city's administration know about unreported cards and shards in decks and extra storage spaces. But he was willing to bet they wouldn't check a dragon's stomach.

Uncommon shards didn't do much for a Legendary like Brixaby. But as the dragon crunched down, Arthur felt a ripple pass through his dragon.

Brixaby's speed increased just a tiny bit more.

Arthur grinned—or he would have, if he wasn't afraid of getting bugs stuck in his teeth. Instead, he just crouched down lower and tried not to get in Brixaby's way as he sped forward.

Finally, after a good twenty minutes of flying flat out, a dark shadow came into view on the horizon.

It was completely unmoving, and as they drew closer, Arthur worried that they'd arrived too late.

Sure enough, the dark spots resolved into a band of six wagons. By the looks of things, they hadn't even had time to circle around before they were hit.

Incompetence, maybe? They should have seen the scourglings coming. Maybe they'd been hoping for a last-minute rescue.

The rescue hadn't come.

The animals pulling the carts had been slaughtered, cut to pieces, and were already starting to rot, as if they had lain there for weeks instead of perhaps an hour. That was due to the scourglings—and the effect of the deadlands.

Most of the wagons had been knocked over, overturned, foodstuffs and basic supplies torn out and stomped on. Scourglings generally didn't eat food in the traditional fashion, though they certainly killed anything living. They were attracted to sources of magic: enchanted items, card anchors, and, of course, anybody who had cards in their decks.

Arthur saw evidence of that too. Several bodies—all adults—lay twisted and already decomposing on the soil. Their chests had been torn open to reveal the organs inside, as if the scourglings hadn't wanted to wait those extra seconds for death to take place before harvesting the cards. They had done it the fast way.

Arthur looked away, sick.

There was no sign of scourglings anywhere. They'd moved on.

"Is this the right caravan?" Brixaby asked, looking around. "Or do you suppose there might be more wagons up ahead?"

"Why do you say that?" Arthur asked.

"I don't see any child bodies. Or perhaps they were so small that the scourglings ate them whole," Brixaby added to himself.

"I don't think scourglings do that," Arthur replied. He looked around again, forcing himself to take in the scene without any emotion, much like how his dragon was. "Let's land and get a closer look."

Brixaby did, and as Arthur dismounted, he glanced down at the gray soil under his feet. Most of the wagons had been knocked off to the side of the road, and there were faint impressions of tracks here and there. Though the constant wind had already eroded most of them, and the tracks that were left were muddled and overlapping. Likely, the scourglings had moved up the road to the next set of victims.

He and Brixaby would have to hunt them down, or else no one coming into the city would be safe on this route.

Finally, reluctantly, Arthur turned to the destroyed wagons. "If there are any kids, they probably hid inside," he said quietly. "I should . . ." He took a deep breath, clenched his fists, and then let his hands relax. He couldn't let himself be overcome by this. "I should return the bodies to their parents."

Brixaby wiggled his head back and forth in a so-so gesture. "Yes, and also search the supplies. Do you think the scourglings left anything valuable behind? Pieces of metal, perhaps? Tools?"

"Brix," Arthur said, a little sharply. And while the dragon didn't look ashamed, he at least didn't continue. Arthur let out a breath. "Just . . . check the other wagons, please."

Arthur moved toward the closest wagon, which still had the remains of two bison yoked to it. The poor animals hadn't even had a chance to flee.

The door of the wagon was open, having landed with the door side up, and Arthur was able to hoist himself up. Bracing his knees on the side of the open door, he poked his head in.

All the contents were in disarray, and it looked as if a small scourgling had been inside to randomly rip things apart. But there was still a lot that was left untouched. These people hadn't been simply visiting the city. They were moving there, and they had brought everything of value with them. Their whole lives were stuffed into a couple of wagons.

And now the survivors in the first wagon caravan would have to start over again . . . if they could.

For a cowardly moment, Arthur wondered if he could pass the bad news along to one of the sheriffs to deliver to the other wagoners. Domingo or Lopez surely had given this kind of news before and would know how to do it with tact and grace.

But . . . no, Arthur supposed that this was part of his duties too.

Though . . . among the spilled linen, broken cans of food, metal tools—which he did not touch, as he didn't feel like being a grave robber today—there was no reek of rot and no sign of a body.

What happened to the kids? he wondered, repressing the shudder that wanted to race up and down his spine.

Maybe the scourglings *had* eaten them. There were no signs of them, no blood, and most importantly, no bodies.

Conventional wisdom said scourglings didn't eat small animals—or small children—whole. Then again, conventional wisdom also said scourglings didn't have the ability to plan. Yet the Mind Singer had built a pseudo-community within a hive she had taken over. She had even successfully farmed dragon eggs.

But baby dragons were born with full cards in their cores. Young humans didn't have that magic. They should be uninteresting to scourglings, except as something to quickly kill.

Maybe they all escaped? But running off meant traveling deeper into the deadlands, which would only make them sick, then kill them.

That was grim, but in Arthur's estimation, their best chance.

He and Brixaby needed to deal with the rogue Rare scourglings first to keep what happened here from happening to other wagon caravans.

Afterward, they'd do a wide sweep and see if they could spot anyone else in the deadlands.

Arthur was just thinking of chalking this up as useless and going back to Brixaby. There was nothing more to see here.

He had climbed down from the wagon when he heard his dragon call out, "Arthur, I am in need of your reading skills."

"Reading skills?" Brixaby knew how to read.

Curious, Arthur walked back from where he came and saw his dragon crouched off to the side of the road, puzzling over something in the dirt. As Arthur got closer, he saw someone had managed to scratch words into the nearly stone-hard soil. A knife lay to the side, discarded.

The wording was not written in their language, but in Texan.

"Someone hasn't been practicing," Arthur teased, bending down to get a closer look himself.

Brixaby grumbled something, but Arthur wasn't listening. His own reading skills for the language were still basic at level 5. It didn't help that the message had been scrawled in haste, which meant the handwriting wasn't easy to understand.

Arthur sounded out a few words, but when he got to the crux of the message, his heart skipped a beat.

Twenty survivors, coffin length down. 24 hours of air as of 13:30.

He had no idea what 13:30 was meant to mean, but . . . twenty survivors. The children had been *hidden*.

Arthur stood up. "Brix, tell me you have an extra shovel."

"Only because you insist on using them as weapons." The dragon reached into his Personal Space and handed Arthur a rather well-made shovel. Arthur spared a moment to look at it and note the stamp from Mesa Free Hive on the handle. Well, he couldn't criticize him for stealing. Arthur was the one with the Thief Class. And it was a really well-made shovel.

The spade end broke the hard crust of topsoil on the first try. "I think someone with an earth-manipulation card created a vault down there," Arthur said. "Coffin length down. That's six feet, I think? Help me dig."

Brixaby could dig, somewhat. Unfortunately, his claws were better at cutting through earth than moving it. While he could manipulate a shovel of his own, his shoulders didn't work the way a human's did, which meant he couldn't throw the shoveled soil out of the way. He was better at breaking up hard bits and shoving the loosened earth to the side.

It was left to Arthur to dig down. He did so desperately, aware he was soon hip-deep in soil that was poison to anyone without a card.

His imagination gave him vivid pictures of how it must be for the people down below: no card anchors to give them light. That would be a magical signature for the scourglings to sniff out. They'd be trapped in the dark in an increasingly stuffy hole, their only hope that someone would come and save them.

Arthur dug faster. Sweat poured down his face, and he received several levels in his **Shovel Proficiency** skill, bringing him up to level 16.

Six feet down, just when the top of the soil was over his head, the tip of his shovel scraped an area of earth packed so hard it was almost like stone.

As soon as he struck it, muffled knocking came up from below.

"Hold on!" Arthur called, driving the shovel into the packed earth. He guessed whoever created this had packed the earth here to keep the soil above from crushing the people below.

Brixaby, perched above, called down helpfully, "Arthur, hurry."

"What do you think I'm doing?"

"You may want to hurry *faster*."

Shooting his dragon an annoyed look, Arthur braced his boots against either side of the narrow hole. "Move aside! I'm going to break through!"

He brought the shovel down with all his strength, plus what his 20-Point Spree card could give him, focusing on his strength attribute.

The covering to the vault inside shattered like the shell of an egg. Relieved cries came up from below, and a slim hand poked out, reaching up.

"It's okay," Arthur said. "You're safe—"

The moment the word was out, a whistling cry cut through the air.

Arthur's head snapped up toward his dragon. Brixaby was looking out across the dead landscape, his expression grim. "I did warn you to hurry."

Arthur's mouth went dry. Down below, the cries of joy turned into wails of fear as they heard the whistles too.

Whatever Brixaby saw out there, out of Arthur's view, caused him to mantle his wings aggressively. "Rare scourglings."

"They're coming?" Arthur asked.

He shook his head. "They are already here, digging out of their own holes. They were lying in wait for this moment."

Arthur had been a fool. The Mind Singer had shown the ability to think and plan . . . and so had these scourglings. Much like Brixaby, their bodies weren't meant for digging. So they'd waited for someone else to do the hard work for them.

This had been a trap.

CHAPTER 10

W hat's going on?" a voice asked from the dark pit below. The arm retracted, and a face flashed into view. About Arthur's age, female, with accusing, suspicious eyes.

"What's happening?"

Arthur didn't answer. He levered himself up to the top to look out. There were several clouds of building dust in the medium distance, and from the middle of one, he saw a flash of a multicolored beak with a cruel curve at the end. Also, for some reason, daggerlike teeth.

The Rare-ranked scourglings were about four times the size of Brixaby, and there were a dozen of them. Too many to take on.

"Brixaby," he said, knowing he was about to ask a lot from his dragon, "I'll need a few minutes. Can you hold them off? Distract them?"

Brixaby snorted. "These are mere Rare scourglings," he said derisively. "I am a Legendary dragon. What do you think?"

Yes, he was a Legendary dragon, but one with only a few combat cards.

Though, even as he spoke, Brixaby activated one of those cards that he had not had the opportunity to use before. This was his illusion card.

Night-Mare Fire
Uncommon
Illusion
Upon activation, an illusion of flames will grow outward from the length
of the spine. While the illusionary night-mare effect is active, any sentient
being the wielder touches will experience a vision of their deepest terror. This
card uses mana.

Brixaby bellowed out a roar that was half a Stunning Shout aimed at the still-emerging scourglings. Then he barreled forward to meet them.

Trusting him to buy them time, Arthur dropped back down to the mouth of the pit.

"The scourglings have arrived," he said tersely. "I'm a dragon rider, and my dragon can hold them off for a couple of minutes, but we need to get you out of here."

Instantly, questions flooded up at him. "What? They're still here?"

"You don't look like a dragon rider."

"That's why we were hidden. What happened?"

Then the youngest voice asked, "Where are my mommy and daddy?"

Arthur winced and decided the best play was not to answer any of them. "I'm opening the mouth of this up so we can get you out. Move aside." Arthur counted to three and brought his shovel down again and again, feet leveraging him to the side of the hole so he didn't fall in. That was a lucky thing because now that the vault had been breached, its integrity was gone. It broke open easily.

Arthur reached into his Personal Space, grabbed a wooden ladder he held there just in case, and dropped it in.

Then he swiftly climbed down.

The vault below was just as dark as he had imagined, utterly pitch black except for the spear of light created by his opening. The air was stuffy and smelled of fear and sweat, and he could only dimly make out figures in the dark.

"I can get you out of here," he said.

Immediately, babble rose up from all sides. Each voice was heightened with stress, stress that only increased as Brixaby roared outside again.

Arthur knew how they felt, but he didn't have time for this.

"I can get you out of here," he repeated, raising his voice, "but I need your permission to place you in my extra storage space."

"What does that mean?" One of the figures stepped forward, the same girl he had seen earlier: tall and gangly, with a thinness like she had done a lot of grow-ing recently with not a lot of food. And her suspicious gaze swept over Arthur in a way that suggested she thought he was some sort of con artist. "What do you mean, 'store us'? Who are you?"

"My name is Arthur, and I am a dragon rider working with the city of New Houston," he said quickly. "But my dragon is not big enough to carry all of you. I can put you in a storage space. It won't hurt." He glanced up at the top of the hole meaningfully. "We need to hurry."

The girl sucked in a breath and looked very much like she wanted to say no, but the bellows from outside, as well as the distant stomping they could all hear through the earth, convinced her otherwise.

"Then save the youngest ones first. What do you need to do?"

"I just need your permission." Arthur turned to one of the smaller figures, which had resolved into a boy on the verge of teenagehood. "Do I have it?"

"Yes," the boy said, his voice cracking.

"Then grab my hand."

Arthur held out his hand, palm up. The moment the boy's fingers brushed his own, he disappeared as Arthur stored him in his Personal Space.

Alarmed cries rang out.

"He's all right," Arthur said.

"How do we know that?" the suspicious girl demanded.

Arthur's temper broke. "It's either this or you take your chance with the scourglings. My dragon is fighting for *you* to give me time to do this. If you want to take your chances by yourself, let me know right now, so I can go up and help him."

The girl stared at him for a moment, eyes narrowed. Then she nodded once. "I'm not dying in this hole." She raised her voice. "All right, everybody, get in line. This is how we get out of here."

One by one, the children and teenagers lined up. When they touched Arthur's hand, they disappeared.

A tiny girl, who seemed to be incredibly shy, sucked her fingers anxiously and needed to be talked into it by the suspicious girl.

Arthur bit back his frustration, but after a few moments, she extended a wet hand, and he stored her.

Finally, the last was the suspicious girl.

She looked at Arthur hard. "If you're betraying us, then I will find a way to kill you." She placed her hand into Arthur's, and she vanished with the rest to become a line item in his inventory.

Arthur's gaze swept around the vault once, but aside from a few supplies— water jugs and such—there was nothing left. He used the ladder to climb up, storing it again.

And just in time.

There weren't nearly a dozen Rare scourglings: there had to be hundreds of them.

So many that Brixaby had taken to the air and was harassing them from above.

The only reason none had bothered with Arthur and the kids was that Brixaby was doing his best to keep their attention. He darted in and out, dropping heavy metal on them from above and shouting with his Stunning Shout, which bowled over a few of them at a time. But as they were Rare beasts, they were made of sterner stuff. They didn't stay stunned for long.

In addition, most of them had to have cards and could fight back. As Arthur watched, horrified, one scourgling opened a beak filled with razor-sharp teeth.

Lightning shot straight up, and only Brixaby's quick maneuvers kept him out of the way.

No, Arthur thought, *this is impossible. Where did all these scourglings come from?*

There had only been a dozen or so dust clouds a few minutes ago. If the scourglings were smart enough to set a trap for them, why hadn't they overrun Arthur and Brixaby from the very beginning? Their numbers were overwhelming.

Even as his mind grappled in shock, he had his answer a few moments later. Brixaby flipped end over tail to change directions and fly in the opposite direction. As he did, he must have pulled a heavy metal spike from his Personal Space. He dropped it on a tight cluster of scourglings.

And the metal spike fell *through* them with a thump. The scourglings dissipated.

They're illusions, Arthur realized.

They didn't have massive numbers on their side. At least one scourgling was copying and recopying illusions—creating very realistic Rare-strength illusions. That meant they were obscuring which ones were real and which weren't.

Well, Arthur had an answer to that. Hoisting himself the rest of the way out of the hole, he stood up, activated his Nice (Metal) Shot card, and peppered the cluster of scourglings in front of him with metal shards.

All had their backs turned to him, watching the sky. They made for easy targets, and the vast majority dissipated as the illusion was broken.

From a crowd of seemingly twenty scourglings in front of him, only three were left.

Arthur grinned savagely as he ran straight toward the remaining scourglings.

The scourglings must have just realized that something was amiss. The shrapnel had barely penetrated their thick Rare-ranked hides, and it must have seemed an annoyance compared to the danger of the dragon above.

They had just started to turn when Arthur came upon them.

He phased through the first one, retrieving his ladder. Phasing out the other side, he left the ladder behind. The scourgling was instantly impaled and thrashed around, shocked and already dying.

That was a neat trick that he wouldn't mind repeating as many times as it took.

Turning to the next with a shovel in hand from his Personal Space, he phased through the next one—or at least tried to.

The next scourgling was like hitting a brick wall.

Arthur bounced back and caught a flash of savage satisfaction in its eyes. The scourgling turned to slash at him with razor-tipped wing claws. Somehow, Arthur managed to duck out of the way just in time.

He never even saw the third scourgling. As he ducked from the second and twisted, there was a flash of feathered claws and the smell of rotting meat.

Fire ripped through his chest from his left shoulder down to his bottom-right rib.

Instantly, he phased again. This had not been from the scourgling that had managed to harden itself against him. The savage toe claw had gone all the way through him and out the other side. He'd been hit, and hit badly.

Brixaby staggered in the air as if he had been struck himself.

Arthur sat down, hard. It hadn't been voluntary. He wanted to move, but every motion was agony.

His Phase In, Phase Out card was counting down.

Worse, the scourgling that had somehow solidified itself against him rushed at Arthur with open mouth and claws.

Just before it reached Arthur, Brixaby dropped straight down on its back and yanked the card right out of it. The scourgling fell.

Brixaby bellowed; his red eyes glinted like wet blood in the sunset.

Other scourglings had turned toward him. More illusions bloomed around them, making it feel as though Arthur was in a crowded room full of them.

But his eyes had locked on the one that had hit him—the one he knew for certain was real.

He could take it out.

At that moment, Arthur's **Pain Resistance** kicked in, and the lack of agony was a second shock. He was filled with new energy.

Springing to his feet, Arthur ran straight at the scourgling, which had backed up and tried to lose itself in the mass of illusions. But Arthur had never let his gaze leave it.

No more time for games. He had less than five seconds left of his Phase In, Phase Out card. He ran forward.

Once he reached it, Arthur dropped his phasing card. And for the first time, he accessed Brixaby's ability, Call of the Void.

His fingers brushed its chest, and he felt the card and a handful of disparate shards hovering around it. Arthur's hand closed, and he yanked back, taking the card with it.

The scourgling shrieked its last breath as it fell, bonelessly, to the ground. All the illusions shattered with it. Which was good, because Arthur's legs collapsed without him realizing it was about to happen.

Glancing down, he saw his entire shirt was soaked with blood. It was as if he had spilled red wine over himself. *Oh, I'm dying,* he thought. This was a wound far too grievous for his minor healing card. And he realized that if not for his **Toughened Skin** enhancement, the claw would have gone all the way to his heart.

I could almost thank Cousin Penn for that, he thought hysterically.

Brixaby landed next to him. He was unusually round, swollen up like a child's pig bladder about to burst. Standing over Arthur, he roared, swinging his head around to the oncoming scourglings. It stunned the closest ones, but the others that were incoming had only been knocked back.

The entire area had been cleared of the illusions, but there were still ten left. One had opened up its mouth again, and the lightning shot went wide as it was knocked back.

But that bought them a few seconds of time.

Brixaby growled but then turned to Arthur, nudging him with his muzzle. "Arthur, I must put you in my Personal Space."

Arthur nodded but didn't give his full permission yet. The world was starting to grow dark around the edges, as if a cloud had passed over the sun. He suspected it was his eyes. Through force of will, he made himself concentrate. "I took this card. Here." His mind was still fuzzy, and he tried to give Brixaby the Rare card he had pulled out. It must be some kind of illusion card; it would be valuable. For some reason, his eyes couldn't focus long enough to read the details.

To his shock, Brixaby knocked his hand away. "Arthur, give me your permission."

"I'll be fine," Arthur said. "You . . . you have to hide the evidence, hide the bodies . . . It's too good of a card to give to the sheriff."

"Yes, yes, I'll hide the bodies. Trust me to take care of it."

His dragon nudged him again, and Arthur, closing his eyes, gave permission.

Time did not move in Personal Space. Between one blink and another, he was out of the deadlands, and in the next, he was in a room.

And Brixaby was roaring, "Hurry up! Hurry up! Fix him!"

Arthur swung his head around, trying to get his bearings. He caught an impression of a white room, a glimpse of an outside window, which showed a sky that was orange with sunset.

"Hurry up! What are you doing? He's dying!"

I'm not, Arthur wanted to say, but it felt like he couldn't get a full breath into his lungs. The darkness on the edge of his vision was still encroaching.

He tried to sit up—not to be a difficult patient but because he felt like he couldn't breathe, and instinctively, he just wanted to get some air.

Hands pushed him back down, and a familiar voice said, "Oh no, you don't. Lay right there."

Arthur blinked up at a spectacled face. "Hey," he said, "I know you."

"No, you don't," Prince Marion said. "Healer," he called over his shoulder, "please hurry, he's almost bled out and delirious."

"Move aside," said a brisk voice.

A green light washed over Arthur, and finally, he knew no more.

CHAPTER 11

Arthur woke up.

Unlike when he had been put in Brixaby's Personal Space, he instinctively knew that time had passed and he had not been there for it. It helped that the window he'd first seen the sunset through was now curtained off and shut. A soft card anchor lit the room.

He heard his dragon snoring, loudly and enthusiastically, right beside the bed. From where he lay, Arthur saw the top of Brixaby's black spines rising and falling in time with his snores.

Only then did he realize that he wasn't in any pain. In fact, he was comfortable, lying on a mattress that was much softer than the one Dannill had provided for him. His once-bloody clothes had been changed, too. Now he was garbed in soft, though almost painfully thin, white clothing under the sheets.

Arthur pulled the neck of his shirt down and looked at his chest. The blood was gone, and so was the wound, save for a pinkish-white line that went from one shoulder all the way down to his bottom rib on the other side, crossing his chest. It was slightly puckered, but when he poked at it experimentally, there was no pain at all. It was like a wound that had healed a long time ago.

The sound of shifting on the other side of his bed caught his attention. Marion sat in a chair next to his bedside, glasses perched on his nose. Predictably, he was reading a book.

His friend hadn't changed much from when Arthur had seen him last. He had the type of face that was easy to lose in a crowd, with sandy-brown hair and unremarkable blue eyes. Long and lanky, he looked more suited to be a scholar than a fighter. That was a reason why Arthur had felt an almost instant kinship with him back at the hive.

Seeing Arthur looking at him, Marion gave an exaggerated sigh as if he were put out that he had to stop reading. Reluctantly, he closed the book.

"You're awake. I suppose that means I have to return to work," he said in a bored, cultured voice. "Your dragon insisted that somebody sit with you. How are you feeling, dragon rider?"

Arthur's voice was creaky. "What are you doing here?"

Marion blinked. "Oh, so you *do* remember me."

"Why wouldn't I?" Arthur tried to sit up but fell back down almost immediately. His arms were much more rubbery than he had anticipated and wouldn't hold his weight.

Immediately, Marion lost that half-amused look and rose to glance down at him, his hand hovering over Arthur as if wanting to check up on him but wasn't quite sure how. "Are you in pain? Should I call for a healer? Rosen insisted you were all healed, but with all the scourgling attacks, we've all been stretched thin. It's possible that they missed something—"

"No, I'm fine," Arthur said.

Marion looked at him doubtfully, then glanced at a secondary card anchor that sat on a small table next to Arthur's bed. This anchor glowed a steady blue. Arthur's best guess was that this card anchor had been tied to him as a visual representation of his health.

"No," Marion agreed reluctantly, "you don't seem to be ill."

"It's backlash from a card." Arthur sighed, raising his head and flopping back down on the pillow, annoyed with himself. "I used a boost from a card to increase my strength attribute by twenty points. This is what I get for pushing it so far." He closed his eyes for a moment, feeling tired enough to slip back into sleep, but he had way too many questions to allow that. He snorted. "You should have seen what happened when I used the luck aspect one time. The worst things kept happening to me all the next day . . ." He opened his eyes. "What are you doing here, Marion, and why do you think I would forget you?"

Marion shrugged, though to Arthur's eyes, he did look a little pleased that he had been remembered. "People of importance tend to forget boring underlings once they grow into power, and you are a Legendary dragon rider now."

"You've never been a boring underling," Arthur said. "You are a pr—"

Marion cut him off with a sharp shake of his head before he could even finish the word. "No, I'm not. You know better than most that I gave that up." His lips ticked up in a smile. "In fact, rumor has it that you met my father by blood."

Arthur noted the careful wording. Father by blood. Not king.

And it was true that Marion had given up his Legendary card that let him see five seconds into the future. It had been half a blessing and half a curse. And yes, Arthur had certainly met the king.

"You could've warned me about him," Arthur said wryly.

"I've actually never met the man myself. Was it that bad?"

"Yes," Arthur said flatly.

"Is that why you're here, across the world?"

"No . . ." He shook his head. "It's complicated."

Though, in his quiet moments, Arthur thought that meeting with the king had been the moment where his confidence in the kingdom had started to fracture.

"*You* still haven't answered any of my questions," he pointed out.

"Do me a favor," his friend said, "just call me Marion. As far as anybody knows, I'm just here for the Reshuffling, just like all the other foreign visitors." Marion shifted slightly, and Arthur caught a flash of a card-anchor tattoo on the inside of his wrist. According to Arthur's memory, that had been the one used for only one local language and for reading and writing.

That spoke more of Marion's current situation louder than anything else could. As a prince, he should have been able to afford the very best of the anchors, the ones that had every language known. Instead, he had opted for only one of the normal tattoos.

And he was here for the Reshuffling.

"You want to repair your heart deck," Arthur guessed.

Looking closely, he could see the faint signs of strain around Marion's eyes. His friend had refused to take back the Legendary card that had been in his heart. The hole left there would always be a permanent ache. Arthur suspected Marion had had his Legendary card from the moment he was old enough to accept a card into his heart.

People could learn to live with the pain of losing their cards from their heart deck—Arthur's father was proof of that. Some people became so inured to the pain that trading out cards from their hearts didn't seem to bother them at all. But those were hard men and women, and they usually existed without the capacity for empathy.

"Don't look at me like that," Marion said. "You have no idea what a burden that card was. I told you, now I can read books without knowing the ending, and I can talk to people normally, without knowing what they're going to say. But yes," he added, "I'm here to repair my heart deck—I'm hoping to start a completely clean deck. They say the Reshuffling has gifted many miracles, and if that's the case, I'm here to remake myself as a new man." He flicked his fingers around. "It's one of the reasons why I'm working at the hospital. I figured if I'm going to remake myself anew, I need to be a different man from top to bottom. So what can be more different than a former royal becoming a humble healer who deals with the sick and the poor?"

"I don't know," Arthur said, "you could be a former royal who cleans out the sewers for a living."

That got a flash of a smile from Marion.

"So you want to be a healer," Arthur repeated. He wished he could have said that he could easily picture that, but Marion didn't seem to have the personality for a good bedside manner.

"Well, I'm not a healer *yet*," Marion replied. "I'm only an attendant. Less than a nurse, even, since I don't have any training or any cards to help me out."

That got Arthur's attention. "You gave up *all* your cards?"

"Every single one," he said with a nod. "I had to afford the portal over here somehow."

Arthur's eyebrows rose. He was impressed.

If he were in the same place, he wasn't sure he'd be able to give up all that power voluntarily. That was a disquieting thought, but then he reminded himself that meant giving up Brixaby, too. That would be unthinkable.

He glanced over at his dragon to find him still gustily snoring away. Marion followed his look and stared at Brixaby for a moment, with an unreadable expression on his face, though Arthur was certain he caught a flash of envy. That made sense, considering that Marion, too, had been in contention for Brixaby's egg.

"I see that he managed to grow a little," Marion said. "He's definitely a purple, then?"

"Best as we can tell. He flies like one."

"They're usually so much more . . . happy-go-lucky." Marion tactfully didn't add that purples tended to be good-natured because they were very simple creatures.

"I didn't think we would see each other again," Arthur said.

"Me neither. When I heard there was a dragon rider in the city, I never would've thought . . ." Marion trailed off and shook his head. Then he looked at Arthur. "Why are you here? I rather thought that you would be ruling a hive by now."

"It's a long story—" Arthur started, but then stopped when Marion suddenly held up a hand. There was the sound of footsteps beyond the closed door. They waited as the footsteps grew louder, then left again. Just somebody passing by.

"Look"—Marion leaned in—"your dragon played the beast while you were unconscious and scared off all the doctors—even an overzealous sheriff that came to question you. But that's not going to last. Now that you're awake, they're going to want payment."

"Payment?" Arthur asked, puzzled.

"For healing. It's not free here. In fact, it's quite expensive. And you were gravely injured and needed the attention and mana of a single senior healer— they call them doctors here," Marion explained, shaking his head. "It will be two or three Rare card shards, at least. You're lucky that they didn't require the payment upfront. That happens sometimes, when somebody already has a bill they haven't paid from the last time."

"But if they're sick or already injured . . ." Arthur started.

Marion just shrugged.

Between paying for healing, government loans for cards, and the tax for scourgling harvesting . . . Arthur wasn't sure he liked the picture being painted here. "I can afford to pay."

"Can you? Because the sheriff seemed to be very concerned about any unauthorized harvesting."

Arthur groaned. "Did any of them scan me?"

"No, your dragon forbade it, though they insisted on scanning him, and he seemed to be fine, so they at least decided to wait for you to wake up."

That meant Brixaby must have eaten all of the shards they had collected. It also explained why he was so deeply asleep. Sometimes, when he ate a lot of Rare shards or a card, he needed to sleep it off.

That also meant they were down to only one card.

With a wince, Arthur pulled the illusion card out of his Personal Space.

Go Clone Yo'self
Rare
Illusion

This card grants the wielder the ability to create illusionary, noncorporeal clones out of him or herself. These clones will all be visually exact to the original. The number of clones depends on the amount of mana assigned to the task. These clones have the ability to act independently. However, they cannot exert a physical force upon the environment. When struck by an outside physical force, the illusion will be dispelled. The wielder may resummon the illusion at any time, at the cost of additional mana.
This card uses and unlocks mana.

"Marion," Arthur said, pushing the card at him, "I need you to hide this."

Holding his hands up, Marion took a step back. "You're seriously offering a card to a man who has none?"

That's right. Marion had no cards at all, yet he was working in a hospital with people who had been injured and were suffering from scourglings and attacks, perhaps even scourge-rot. That had to be incredibly dangerous for him.

Arthur's estimation of Marion went up another notch . . . though for a moment, Arthur considered letting Brixaby eat the card instead. He could imagine how terrifying his dragon would be with an illusion card like this, even only if he gained a portion of its power.

Arthur could consume the card, too. He had Brixaby's ability. But either option meant putting the card out of circulation forever.

He would do it if he had to, or if the right card came along. But he wasn't at that point yet.

"I trust you," he said, still holding it out to Marion. "And I know that I'm not in the position to ask favors of you—"

"Oh, please." Marion plucked the card from his hand and slid it into a wide pocket on the side of his pants as if he was not the least bit tempted. "You faced down my father to return my card to him. That meant he didn't send assassins after me. I do owe you something."

"Well, I was going to see your father anyway," Arthur said. But he was interrupted by a knock at the door. Neither of them had even heard the footsteps approaching.

Brixaby snorted awake, his head popping up and his lips lifting back into an automatic snarl, a snarl that died when he saw that Arthur was fully awake.

"How are you feeling?" Brixaby said, halfway climbing up onto the bed to get a close look at him. The frame groaned alarmingly.

"It looks like I'll have a scar, but otherwise I'll be fine."

The door opened, and an officious-looking man in a white smock and uniform strode in.

"I'll be the judge of that." Arthur didn't recognize his face, but he remembered his voice as the officious healer. "I'm Healer Rosen."

Sure enough, the man brushed by Marion as if he didn't exist, ignored Brixaby like he was no threat, and stood by Arthur's bedside to wave his hands over him. A blue mist, then a green mist, fell over Arthur—some kind of diagnostic card charm.

After a few seconds, Rosen grunted.

"You seem to be suffering from some kind of card backlash. I'm assuming it's an effect of whatever it took to get you out of that mess with the scourglings?"

"Something like that," Arthur replied.

"Well, whatever it is, you escaped by the skin of your teeth. And you have a whole pack of sheriffs waiting downstairs. I can't keep them away for much longer, now that you're awake."

"Arthur will not see them until he is fully healed," Brixaby growled, snaking his head around and glaring with bloodred eyes at the man in a way that made him look about twice as evil as normal.

Rosen gave him a look as if he faced down annoyed dragons every day. "Which, in my professional opinion, he is."

Then the healer turned to Marion with a scowl. "And what are you doing in here? Reading again?" he asked.

"I'm watching the patient," Marion said.

"Well, there are other patients you can go help with. Room three. Go."

Marion shot Arthur an apologetic look and made his way out.

Arthur struggled to sit up fully, and he needed help and the addition of some pillows. He'd like to blame the backlash on his 20-Point Spree card, but that had passed. Much of this exhaustion and weakness was natural from healing. He really wanted to sleep, but . . .

"Please send in the sheriffs. I need to speak to them. There are dangerous scourglings out there on the road."

"Says the dragon rider who came in half dead," Rosen muttered, annoyed all over again, as he shuffled out.

"Arthur," Brixaby said to him the moment the door was shut. "They will scan you for the card—"

"It's with Marion," Arthur said.

"And there is a matter of pay," Brixaby continued. "They wanted Rare card shards first before the healing would happen. Or an entire lesser card. I told them that I would simply kill them, harvest them, and then use their healing card myself to heal you."

Arthur pinched the bridge of his nose.

Brixaby gave him a look. "You should be proud that I did not reveal that I could have simply ripped out the cards without killing them. I was discreet."

"I suppose there is that," Arthur said, dropping his hand. "Good job, Brixaby."

He had meant it sarcastically, but the dragon preened as if he had just been given the highest of compliments.

A moment later, a small group of men and women in uniform tromped in, including, to Arthur's mild amusement, Oversheriff Walker with her two assistants.

The woman looked like she hadn't gotten any sleep. Considering it was likely the small hours of the morning, she may not have.

"Well," she drawled, stopping by his bedside, "I'd say that your first official mission was not a success. Give me a report."

Arthur scowled. "You could have gotten all of this hours ago from my dragon."

"Your dragon?" One of the sheriffs seemed taken aback.

"Brixaby is as intelligent as I am," Arthur said.

"And I speak much more eloquently," Brixaby rumbled.

Arthur continued, "There is a group of a dozen Rare-ranked scourglings hitting wagon caravans on the eastern Interstate. We managed to kill two—"

"Three," Brixaby corrected. "I killed one more after you were struck."

"Three," Arthur said.

"Are their bodies still there for us to harvest?" Walker asked, as if that was the most important thing.

Arthur gave her a look. "Those were *Rare-ranked* scourglings. They set a trap for us, so I suspect they are also intelligent enough to harvest the bodies of their own dead."

"That's convenient," she said, seeming skeptical. "Speaking of, let's get this over with." She nodded to one of her assistants who pulled out a wand and started to scan Arthur.

Arthur kept his expression calm. The wand beeped at the end, and the man frowned at it.

"No, there's no extra card signature, but there is something else . . ." He trailed off, looking perplexed. "Your life signature is . . . it's about twenty times what it usually is." He looked at Arthur, who was still sick in bed.

Life signatures? Then it hit him, and he was briefly ashamed he'd forgotten. "Oh, right," Arthur said. "Yes, I'm afraid there's something else that I need help with."

"Whatever it is, we'll come back to that," Walker said, and gave him a severe look. "You do realize that without scourgling bodies, you can't get paid. And as you're a contractor, not a city-state employee, we will not be covering the costs."

Her attitude annoyed him, but he had a good idea for revenge.

"How about a reward for saving survivors?" he suggested cheerfully. Then, before anyone could protest, he started to unstore the children from his Personal Space. One by one, they rapidly appeared in the hospital room.

The kids were shocked to find themselves in a room with a dragon, and were loud about it, even though Brixaby was on his best behavior and had pulled his wings in, and looked as least murderous as possible.

But they were safe, not underground anymore, and Arthur's Personal Space felt much emptier.

"I suspect you have some sort of assistance for the young—and a reward for us," Brixaby said pointedly.

The oversheriff looked as if she had just tasted something sour. Arthur, who after working as a leader in the hive was well aware of the ways of bureaucracy, knew he had just dumped hours of paperwork on her lap.

"Yes to both," she conceded.

CHAPTER 12

Come morning, there was a knock at the door.

Arthur snorted awake, confused, because he didn't remember falling asleep. Embarrassingly, he suspected he had slipped off while speaking to Brixaby. Hustling the displaced kids and annoyed sheriffs out of his room had taken some time, and he must have passed out right after.

Brixaby, who'd been sleeping by Arthur's bed, popped his head up with narrowed eyes to the door. "Who dares disturb my rest?"

A quiet yet firm voice on the other side replied, "Oh! I . . . Uh . . . Dragon rider? Are you up?"

Brixaby and Arthur exchanged a look.

"I don't sound like you," Arthur muttered, threw back the thin hospital blankets, and stood. He didn't realize until he was on his feet that he felt quite a bit stronger. That was good because he'd felt as weak as a kitten before.

. . . And he was back to being as poor as a stray cat.

All of the Rare shards that had been grudgingly awarded to him and Brixaby for saving the children had been instantly snapped up by the hospital as payment for his healing costs. Those had been incredibly excessive. In fact, he was certain that some of the fees had been made up on the spot. For example, having his own room for healing had been a Rare shard all by itself just for the night.

But as he had been trapped in a hospital bed, he hadn't been in a position to object. He was just glad Brixaby had eaten as many card shards as he had on the sly back in the deadlands, not counting the Rare card that was still with Marion . . . though he half suspected the prince would put it into his heart. The temptation to stop the ache must be terrible.

All this flashed through his mind as he stepped to the door. Opening it, he was surprised to see the suspicious girl from last night standing on the other side.

Now that he wasn't threatened by oncoming scourglings or suffering exhaustion, he had a second chance to look at her. She was tall for a woman, about his height, with dark hair and dark eyes, and a deep tan. It looked like she'd finally had some access to cleaning facilities because Arthur spotted freckles under the tan.

She was pretty, though in a completely different way than Cressida.

Even though her eyes were still narrowed in suspicion.

"Can I come in?" she asked, one step from a demand.

"Yes," Arthur said, "but just to warn you, my dragon is in here too, and he's very protective." A silent warning that she had better not threaten him.

She nodded once, and though her expression didn't change on seeing Brixaby again, there was a slight stutter in her step. She'd seen him last night, of course, but she likely had her hands full with all the crying, semi-hysterical children.

Closing the door, Arthur turned. "How can I help you?" he asked pointedly. That had been a trick he'd picked up from Valentina. Technically, as a Legendary rider, people should—and did—fall over themselves to try to "help" him and get into his good graces. So it put people on the wrong foot when Arthur asked if he could help them instead. It was a polite request to get them to forget whatever fluff they'd come up with to butter him up and get right to the point.

She took a breath. "I wanted to apologize for my . . . my attitude back in the deadlands," she said quickly, as if it pained her to speak the words. "You were a true hero, and I didn't think those existed anymore outside of children's stories. I thought you were working some angle, but I could hear the scourglings outside . . . and I didn't have much of a choice." Her chin lifted. "But I should have trusted you. You kept your word, and more. You got us all out to safety without losing any of the little 'uns, and I didn't think that would be possible."

While the words were pretty, it was all said quick and clipped, as if she hated every second of it.

"You're welcome," Arthur said, watching her. "I was glad to help."

She nodded once, as if having checked off a box from her list. "Also, I wanted to know where you bought your dragon egg."

There it was. The real reason why she'd come, he thought, stifling a smile.

"I didn't buy him—" he started, but was overridden by Brixaby.

"All of the highest noble scions and people of importance had come to witness my hatching. I merely picked the cream of the crop." He sat up to his full height of nearly six feet, his tail tucked primly around his claws.

"Yes . . . well," Arthur said, "that's one way to look at it." He looked at the girl. "I come from . . . well, we just call it the Kingdom, but you call it the Fabergé Kingdom. We don't buy dragon eggs—the dragons pick their riders." *Mostly*, he added, thinking sourly of the king's threats. He didn't expand on that, and just went on, quickly, to outline the system of dragon hives and how it was needed to take on the kingdom's scourge-eruptions.

Her eyes grew rounder as he went on, though it wasn't from fear; it was from excitement.

"When you go back, can I go with you?" she asked breathlessly. "I can pay my way, come then. In the meantime, I can help—whatever chores you need done."

Arthur hesitated. Brixaby extended his neck toward her. She backed up a half step before she mastered herself and stood still while he gave her a quick sniff-over.

"You have no cards. You'd be useless. Less than useless; you'd be a burden."

"This will be after the Reshuffling, right? I won't be a burden then. I'll have cards to my name, maybe even a full set of cards," she said boldly in a way that told Arthur she had no idea how extraordinary that was.

"Let's back up a step," Arthur said. "I don't even know your name."

"Soledad Boudreaux," she said. "If it helps, I come from the Boudreaux house in N'awlens."

That meant nothing to Arthur. "Okay, what about the kids? Your siblings. You'd be leaving them behind."

Soledad made an impatient gesture. "None of those littles are my siblings. I was just traveling with the wagons, and as the oldest unmarried girl, I was put in charge. But they're safe now. Most have been reunited with their parents—those who're left. And . . ." She shrugged. "The rest who lost both parents were put in city foster homes. I saw them last night. They're clean and will be well cared for and will probably be given cards when they're old enough. It's better than what any of them could have expected."

She seemed to be a hard person at heart, but it was something Arthur recognized. She was hard in the same way the borderland village families had to be in a place where death was common and kids were a burden until they were old enough to help out in the dragon soil fields.

He didn't necessarily like her, but he did understand her.

"So, you have nobody?" he pressed. "The kingdom I come from is across the world. You'd be leaving everyone behind."

"No, I . . ." She paused, eyes narrowing again. "I guess you're new here, so you wouldn't have heard. N'awlens was all run over by our Dark Heart. The authorities said they were keeping a close eye on it and were just waiting for it to ripen to its peak. Maybe they did and it just exploded before anyone could do anything. I think they were just drunk and corrupt," she muttered. "Not that it mattered. Most people lost everything."

Arthur winced. He could imagine it easily: an eruption right in the middle of the city and with no dragons to battle the scourglings back. "What happened after that?"

"It took months to knock it down, but the land is poisoned. It's pretty much turning into deadlands now. The rich got themselves out first, and whatever people were left tried to hang on . . . but we couldn't stop the rot. It's everywhere."

"No dragon soil," Brixaby muttered in his and Arthur's language.

Soledad went on. "Now, anyone who can load a cart is getting out. I said I'd keep an eye on all the little kids, and that's how I got my ticket out. Now I'm here, and it's time I start a new life. I got no one left back there—everyone who survived the Dark Heart started getting taken by the rot."

He'd been wondering what would send people across the deadlands. That would do it.

"I'm sorry," Arthur said. "I lost a sister to the rot."

She shook her head, rejecting all pity. "Yeah, but you can face down those creatures. I heard people talk. Those were a big pack of Rares out there, and you still got us all out. I want that. And I want to be able to fly."

She looked at Brixaby as if he were a useful vehicle instead of a living, breathing creature. He supposed that was fair. Brixaby was looking at her as if she might have a seed of usefulness to him, too. Buried way deep down below.

"I'm not saying yes," Arthur said. "Or even maybe. There are complications."

"Like what?" she asked.

"For one thing, I have no way of getting back to the kingdom right now. I'm hoping after the Reshuffling I'll be able to buy a portal back, if that's even possible." *If that's where I need to go next*, he thought. "For another, even if I could, Brixaby is only large enough to carry me. Though we might be able to arrange something else by then."

Brixaby added, "Dragons choose their riders, and they will not care about your sad story. They choose depending on if a card in your heart is compatible with their core card."

Arthur picked up his point. "So you may want to think about what kind of card you want, because that will determine the type of dragon. And you'll need to be able to speak my language because no one speaks Texan over there—"

He was stopped by a knock on the door.

"Now what?" Brixaby demanded. "More useless children come to beg their way into my retinue?"

"I won't be useless for long," Soledad said.

He narrowed his bloodred eyes at her. "We'll see."

The knock came again. Arthur answered it, figuring it was probably the healer come to check on him—and boot him out of the room now that he was on his feet again.

But he was surprised once more. It was Marion, loaded down with a tray overflowing with food. Arthur spotted at least two small round loaves of bread, one of which seemed to be cut out and stuffed with bean soup that looked thick enough to chew. There were squares of some crumbly yellow biscuits, and glasses of water that were worryingly brown.

"Came for lunch," he said, then stopped. "I didn't know you had company."

"A visitor," Arthur said, unsure if he should pretend he didn't know Marion or not.

Marion decided it for him.

"And who are you, then?" he asked, setting down the tray and adjusting his glasses to look the girl up and down.

"Soledad Boudreaux. Who're you?"

"They call me Marion," he said blandly.

"She's one of the"—Arthur started to say *kids* but changed it because Soledad looked close to his age—"survivors from yesterday."

"I heard about that. Sending wagons across the deadlands." He shook his head. "Perilous."

Soledad held herself tight as if bracing against criticism. "It's worse where I came from. You want my advice? You watch your Dark Heart here like a hawk watches a mouse."

"Oh, I'm assured that they are. But I think it's for greed rather than anything else," Marion drawled. "They want it right at the point of eruption—apparently when it's just stuffed full of magic." Then Marion noticed that both Arthur and Soledad were staring fixedly at the tray he'd brought. "Well, dig in. Try the drink first. They call it sweet tea here. I don't think it's good for your teeth, but I'm no healer yet."

Arthur broke the yellow cake thing first and gave half to Soledad. It was indeed a biscuit but incredibly sweet on his tongue.

Marion grinned at his expression. "Yes, they put sugar in everything here, even the cornmeal. I love it."

"Are you from another city-state?" Soledad asked. "You don't have cornbread there?"

"I come from the Fabergé Kingdom."

"Like Arthur?"

Marion glanced at him, then shrugged. "Yes."

"She wants to be a dragon rider," Arthur explained.

"Right now, she is cardless and wouldn't attract a Common yellow." Brixaby snorted. He slunk over and stole one of the round bread loaves and started tearing it up into easy chunks, popping them in his mouth as neatly as a person would.

"I don't care what it is, as long as it has wings and can fight," Soledad said.

Arthur, who'd taken up the other loaf and learned it was filled with something Marion called chili, like a bowl, took up a spoon then looked at her. "Maybe she'll get a red? They like to fight?"

He found Marion gazing at her speculatively. "I was always rather bad at guessing what people get, though I suppose she should aim for an elemental combat card." He explained for her benefit, "When a card—especially a first card—is inserted into your heart, you sort of grow around it."

That pinged something in Arthur's mind, but it was gone before he could chase it down.

"Well, that sounds like just the thing," Soledad insisted.

"Any dragon can fight," Arthur said. "I have a friend who has a pink meta dragon and . . . well, she has a poison aspect now, but she's killed more than Brix and me combined. I have another who has a yellow and can permanently blind you with some weird invisible light. There are a lot of ways to be dangerous."

"So you'd rather be a dragon rider than fight like the adventurers here?" Marion asked.

Arthur turned to him while Soledad shook her head. "How do they do it here?"

"Body-modification cards, for the most part," he said with an air of distaste. "Fairly extreme ones, too. Some of them are barely recognizable as human. They have to have specialist healers look at them when they're injured because their bodies don't even work the same way."

"I often think most humans could use some adjustment," Brixaby said, then clarified. "Though not Arthur, unless he gains wings. Though now that I can carry us both, that is less of a problem. Arthur, hand me a glass of that sweet tea. I will try it."

"Well, whatever," Soledad muttered over her own bowl of chili she'd taken. "I'd rather fly on anything, any color, than fight in the city-state way."

"Ah, yes, I've heard about the government card loans," Marion said with a wince.

She snorted her agreement.

"Fill me in?" Arthur asked. "I'd heard they pay a steep price, but is it that bad?"

"It's that bad," Marion confirmed. "Every child of age gets a card—it's a requirement not to get the rot around here, and you've seen the cost of getting healed up. But not only is the initial cost high, many people can barely read or write and don't understand what compound interest is."

"I don't know what that is," Soledad said, "but I don't like going into debt."

"Then you've got good instincts." Marion's voice was unusually warm. Arthur shot him a look and found he was gazing at Soledad again.

She continued, "Yeah, the cost for healing is crazy. They found rot spots on my lungs last night from the crossing. I had to pay four Rare shards to get it taken care of. I don't got it, of course, but they're going to give me three months to pay them back. Then the interest starts." She seemed more annoyed than concerned about this, but Arthur thought that might be one of the reasons why she was so eager to get out of the city-state.

Marion nodded. "I've heard that type of story before. Though," he added, "the pay for healers is quite good. That's probably done so they don't open their own practice and make a bundle just by charging a little less."

Arthur shook his head. "Healing is free where I'm from . . . unless you're born as a serf under an uncaring noble, then it's not available at all."

Marion gave him an odd look, but then shrugged. "Or you bond to some purple Common and you're relegated to a rescue squad for the rest of your life."

"They call those squads the Lobos back in my hive," Arthur said. "I never thought rescue duty would be bad."

"Good thing you ended up with a purple," Marion drawled.

Soledad's eyebrows rose, and she looked at Brixaby doubtfully. "Purple? You mean, the cracks between his scales?"

"I transcend purple," Brixaby told her.

"Brix is a little special," Arthur said.

"Which reminds me, now that you've eaten." Marion pulled out a thick envelope from his vest. The wax seal on the front was broken. "This came from the oversheriff. She said you need to see it right away."

Annoyed, Arthur snatched it from him. "Then why didn't you deliver it? And why did you read it?"

Marion didn't bother to deny the last part. "Healer's orders. Closing a wound like yours takes a lot of energy, and you needed to eat first."

"And the seal?"

Marion looked at him over his glasses. "I was curious, Arthur. You can't expect me not to read everything in sight."

Rolling his eyes, Arthur took out the message and read. It was short—the thickness of it came from the fairly expensive envelope and paper it had been printed on. He read through it, though it took him a few more seconds than usual to parse out the unfamiliar language.

"What is it?" Brixaby asked, when he could stand the silence no longer.

"It looks like the sheriffs are putting together a group of adventurers to take care of the Rares," Arthur said. "We're to lead them to where we were attacked."

"And, naturally, hunt for them ourselves," Brixaby added.

Arthur smiled tightly but didn't say anything as he folded the envelope. Soledad looked on with envy.

"Make sure you don't do it for free," Marion said. "Remember: everything has a price here."

"Oh, I don't intend to," Arthur said.

He already knew what he was going to ask Oversheriff Walker in return for going back out there again.

CHAPTER 13

A few hours later, fully dressed in his own clothes and feeling completely whole again, Arthur approached the sheriff's office. It was easy to spot, being one of the newest, largest buildings in the city capped with a gleaming dome of glass panels.

After a quick scan at the door to determine that yes, he and Brixaby still didn't have extra cards that they shouldn't, they were allowed to see Oversheriff Walker.

She sat at a desk, and judging by the dark circles under her eyes, she had not gotten any sleep last night. She glared as Arthur approached. "Don't tell me you rescued more kids between here and the hospital."

"Would it be so bad if I had?" he asked, sitting down, though she hadn't invited him to.

She gave him a baleful look, then admitted, "No, no . . . What you did was a good thing. A *heroic* thing. But it's a hell of a lot of paperwork for me."

Better doing paperwork on alive kids than dead kids, Arthur thought, but he knew when someone was sleep-deprived, they weren't thinking rationally. So he took a small measure of pity on her. "I understand you want Brixaby and me to lead the adventurers to the Rares."

"Yes," she said with a heavy sigh. "It seems that whatever you two did yesterday did not scare the blasted scourglings off for long. We've had reports of another wagon train completely decimated. At this point, we've sent word down the line to hold incoming wagons at the last oasis before the final push."

"Oasis?" he asked.

"There are a few spots along every Interstate where we've been able to keep the deadlands back. They're small, but people can usually stay there for a few days without getting sick. That way they can rest and refuel, but the clock is ticking. We need to make that road safe again."

Arthur nodded and then leaned forward. "In that case, I want a favor."

She gave him another sour look. "Other than your usual pay for killing Rares?"

"You just got finished telling me that this was an urgent situation," he said.

She considered him for a moment with narrowed eyes. "Well?"

Walker, he sensed, wasn't a woman who played poker. She wanted all her cards face up on the table. He decided to be blunt. "The Reshuffling," he said. "I've already secured two spots among the first to enter the Dark Heart, thanks to the deal I made with Dannill the merchant."

"Yes, I heard of that," she said with such distaste that it made Arthur think she had looked into that possibility as a juicy carrot to dangle in front of him.

"Well, I want to secure *more* spots. One for an assistant who was incredibly helpful to me at the hospital, and a secondary spot for someone of my choosing later." He intended it to be for Soledad. He just didn't want extra eyes on her before she had a card to defend herself. Marion was sneaky enough to take care of himself, card or no card.

He paused, then added, "As well as two secondary spots for people I choose in my future retinue."

Another lie. Those spots were for Cressida and Horatio.

"That's a lot of spots in the front," she said.

He shrugged. "You're about to receive a lot of Rare cards for our city."

She tapped her fingers on the table in a wave pattern. "So you need five spots in total?"

Actually, it was more like eight, but he didn't think she counted dragons as people, and he wasn't going out of his way to point that out to her. "That's correct."

"Done," she said, so quickly that she clearly thought she was getting the best part of the deal. It worried Arthur a little, but there was nothing else other than the payment that he needed. "You lead us to the Rares so we're not stuck on a wild snipe hunt through the deadlands, you'll get your reward—and your spots."

Arthur smiled. There were some odd things about the Texans, but as long as he wanted something they could sell to him . . . it wasn't too hard to get along with these people.

Brixaby had been remarkably quiet during the meeting and managed to keep his peace until he and Arthur were back in the air. Then he turned to his rider and asked, "How do you expect to find the scourglings?"

"What do you mean?" Arthur asked innocently.

His top lip ticked up in unconscious distaste. "They are very fast, mobile, and cunning. They are Rares, not idiots, and may have buried themselves again. Or set other traps."

All very good points. But Arthur smiled and patted his dragon's neck. "I have a couple of plans in mind. And if worse comes to worst, I suppose we could always level up tracking skills."

Brixaby snorted at that but knew by now when Arthur was teasing him. Showing unusual restraint, he changed the subject. "Fighting scourglings is all well and good, but after this, we should focus on the Reshuffling to come."

Arthur smiled. Brixaby might be a purple, but he was equally, if not more, intelligent than an average person, and he was more than capable of thinking ahead. More than that, he was growing up.

"I agree," he said. "Not to mention that Cressida and Horatio should be here soon."

"Well, I hope they don't arrive until we've had the chance to clean out this nest of Rare scourglings," Brixaby said. "It will be fun to greet them with Rare cards."

Sheriff Walker had given them the directions to where the adventurers were to gather up. Unsurprisingly, it was on the eastern side of the city, where the Interstate came to the wall.

Arthur saw several clusters gathered below, and Undersheriff Lopez walking among them.

Brixaby gave a snort of surprise, then quickly dived downward, not giving Arthur a hint of warning.

Luckily, Arthur was getting used to it and kept his seat.

Brixaby came in for a quick landing in front of one group in particular. "You!"

One man with pitch-dark skin, yellow slit pupils, and pointed ears smiled at Brixaby. "Do my eyes deceive me, or are you that itty-bitty dragon that was at Mesa Free Hive?"

He was also, Arthur saw on a second look, clad in very familiar-looking chainmail. And so were the people behind him, and if anything, they were all stranger-looking than the man in front of him. One was even covered in fur from head to foot.

"I am Brixaby," Brixaby said, "and this is my rider, Arthur."

"You know each other?" Arthur asked.

"Yes, I sold him chainmail once," Brixaby said, casting an eye over the chainmail the man wore. Then he admitted, "I suppose you are taking good care of it. I do not see too many rivets out of place."

"It has served me very well," he agreed, then frowned. "Though the Mesa Free Hive is not interested in trading for the next few weeks. Do either of you have something to do with that?"

Arthur sidestepped the question. "We're only here for the Reshuffling. You're an adventurer, then?"

"Yes, but we're not local here, either." He smiled, showing lengthened canines. "My name is Jon and these are my Lightning Cats, fresh from the city-state of Evanstown." That name invoked a few jeers from the adventurers who were eavesdropping.

Ignoring that, Arthur cast a quick glance over the rest of Jon's group. Cats was indeed the theme.

There was one girl who was dressed rather . . . skimpily, who smiled at Arthur when he looked at her. She clenched her fist and catlike claws came out, and she had catlike ears that swiveled here and there. One person had a catlike tail, though he used it to help search through a pack for something. A third draped herself bonelessly over the top of a boulder. She had no outright catlike features but still looked for all the world like a cat sleeping in the sun.

Body-modification cards.

"We're to be your guide," Arthur said, and at that moment, Lopez saw them and beckoned them over.

Arthur dismounted and left Brixaby to speak with Jon while he went to see the sheriff.

The cat crew were not the only ones who had chosen body-modification cards. He passed a man who had turned his right hand into a scythe-like blade, another who seemed to have living metal skin, and one with such large muscles that his head looked freakishly tiny in comparison.

He always found body-modification cards unsettling. Unlike body-enhancement cards, modification cards generally issued permanent changes on the wielder. Most were so extreme that the modifications themselves became fatal if the card was ever removed.

It was a subclass of card that was not often seen in the hives. In fact, body-modification cards were usually not generated within dragon cores, though no one knew the reason why. Privately, Arthur thought it was a dragon pride thing. Not many would accept extreme body modifications in themselves or their riders.

That meant that buying mod cards came from individual shards, or, commonly, from scourglings. They had no problem with different body types. It was one reason why body-mod cards were considered unlucky.

And unfortunately, since they were a permanent change to the body and not an active spell, charm, or even skill, he could get nothing from his Counterfeit Siphon card.

"So I see the oversheriff has convinced you to come," Lopez said, and presented his valuable map. "Let's sit down and talk. You can tell me where you last saw the scourglings. We can work out a search pattern from there."

"I can tell you where they are now," Arthur said.

All he had to do was think about those kids trapped underground in the vault and imagine all the wagon trains that had been decimated—the children orphaned and lives destroyed—and it became the thing he wanted the most.

Holding on to that feeling, Arthur used Brixaby's Call of the Heart card.

CHAPTER 14

Because Arthur could only access the Call of the Heart card through the link with his dragon, it required a different sort of effort. Something akin to the difference between Arthur simply walking from point A to point B and trekking up a steep hill where he had to check every position of his foot for accuracy.

However, Arthur made it work. As he focused hard on his desire to find the scourglings, a map bloomed up within his consciousness. But this was no ordinary map—it was created with the power of a Legendary seeking card.

With a mental image of the destination, as well as some of the surrounding areas, Arthur felt a tug at his heart pulling him in the direction as the dragon flies.

He lifted his foot as if to turn there before he caught himself. Resisting the urge, Arthur instead studied his new mental map.

"The Rares have stopped a couple miles northwest of the road—" he said, then corrected himself to use the Texan term. "I mean Interstate."

Sheriff Lopez's eyebrows rose. As a man with a map card of his own, he seemed to recognize the signs of someone else using one. Or at least, Arthur sounded so confident that he didn't bother to question him further. "How deep into the deadlands?" he asked, then added, "Can you see any signposts? They should be placed and numbered every half mile along the way."

Arthur concentrated again. The map was incredibly detailed, and he immediately spotted it now that he knew what to look for. "They're closest to signpost ten."

Lopez nodded sharply. "Half day's journey, then." He rubbed his chin. "But it'll be hard to call for help that far away if things go south."

"They'll be traveling on foot?" Arthur asked, surprised. "The city won't grant a portal?"

"No." Lopez gave him a sharp look. "Portals are restricted, and if you'll take a word of advice from me—if you have any portal power in your bag of tricks, keep it to yourself."

"I don't," Arthur replied flatly.

For once, Arthur was telling the truth: the closest card he had to any portal type was his Return to Start card. That was a teleportation card. Very different.

At least, that's what he told himself.

With another nod, Lopez raised his voice to be heard by his deputies. "Well, we have a solid direction. Let's get those scourglings cleared out."

The deputies turned to spread the word.

Lopez had told him half a day, but Arthur realized he hadn't accounted for how slow that would actually be.

None of the adventurer parties had horses. The bison the locals used to pull wagons were unsuitable for riding as well. Even those with body-modification cards didn't advance ahead of the main group. There was safety in numbers.

Arthur, who was used to the swift flight speed of dragons, now felt like he was leading a group of snails.

He tried to think about the silver lining: He and Brixaby had never focused on flight endurance. It seemed they would start now.

"I'm bored," Brixaby complained a couple hours later.

Arthur opened his mouth to reply when suddenly Brixaby shifted. It was a minute change. He'd been gliding, and right after the half eyeblink of time, his wings were held in a different enough position that they dropped a couple feet before Brixaby recovered.

Unsettled, Arthur clutched at his dragon's neck ridge. "Would you please," he said through gritted teeth, "stop dropping into your Personal Space while flying?"

Ignoring the comment, Brixaby handed up a stack of small- and medium-sized metal plates to Arthur. "Here. This is body armor. The larger ones go over your stomach and chest." He seemed particularly eager to protect the area where Arthur had been slashed.

Body armor. He should have thought of that before, but . . . well, he'd never been badly hurt fighting scourglings like that.

Activating his Nice Shot card gave him the ability to control metal an inch away from his body. He spent the next few minutes figuring out not only how to arrange the plates around himself, but to keep them in place. For now, he had to concentrate, but he thought with some practice it would become more automatic. Like muscle memory.

"This is a pretty good fit," he said, twisting one way and then the other before arching backward and bending forward. "It pinches if I have to bend too much, though."

"It is a first attempt," Brixaby said with distaste. "Give it to me. I will perfect it."

Arthur paused, concerned. "You shouldn't be putting in so much extended time within your Personal Space."

Though he suspected the dragon had a whole workshop in there. While he was happy for the armor, he didn't want Brixaby to be mentally exhausted for the upcoming fight.

"Tell me you haven't been doing the same," Brixaby challenged.

"I haven't been metalworking," Arthur said. "It's not the same."

"Hah." Brixaby rose up in the air a few more beats as if in victory. "What have you been doing?"

Instead of answering right away, Arthur glanced down to see how far the adventuring group had come. Their pace was . . . painstaking. They were just now reaching the edge of the deadlands.

"I've been reading some of the enchanting books we took from Free Mesa Hive," he admitted at last.

Brixaby perked up. "Anything useful?"

"No," he admitted. "They're all written in that old style that's hard to decipher, and I haven't found anything that could be directly combat related without first having a combat card. But," he added, "I did find some interesting ways to insulate structures."

He sounded disgusted. "Why would anyone care about that?"

"Not everyone lives in a cozy hive," he said. "Plus, with the right Common temperature-control card, I could use enchanting right away to make our own terrace cool in the summer, warm in the winter, and maybe even watertight."

"Hmm." Brixaby didn't sound enthused. Again, there was a stutter of his wings before he presented Arthur with a new set of segmented body armor. "Try this."

This time the metal pieces were arranged in overlapping horizontal strips, which provided more flexibility. They were also bound in the back by chainmail underneath. That took some of the strain from Arthur's Nice Shot card, as he didn't have to worry about keeping the plates correctly aligned in relation to one another.

"This is really good craftmanship," Arthur said, impressed. "More comfortable, too."

"It should be! I'm—" Brixaby abruptly snapped his jaws shut.

"What's wrong?" Arthur's gaze darted downward, worried something had happened. There was no change within the adventurer group—from this far up they looked like a dark group of ants crawling over the landscape. Checking his mental map, he made sure it still pointed in the spot. The Rares hadn't moved from it or come to hunt humans.

"I realized," Brixaby began slowly, and his tone was . . . odd. If it were anyone else, Arthur would have thought it was chagrin. "I never told you I reached level fifty in my **Chainmail Weaving** skill."

"What?!" Arthur's eyes widened in shock. His first thought was to wonder how long, exactly, Brixaby had been spending in his Personal Space. The second was guilt: He should have paid more attention to his dragon's advancement. "When did this happen? Just now?"

"Oh, back at Mesa Free Hive." Brixaby gusted a sigh. "I thought reaching level fifty would unlock something significant. But . . . I was mistaken."

That was a big admission coming from his dragon.

"And?" Arthur asked eagerly. "What happened?"

"I received three points in dexterity, two in wisdom, one in intelligence, and an additional twenty-five percent quicker reward for learning all skills in a Chainmail Class and any related body-enhancement skills."

Arthur's jaw dropped. "That's . . . amazing. Why do you sound like someone just died?"

Another heaved sigh. "Because I cannot progress further in my **Chainmail Weaving** skill until I get a class and level it up to the same level. *You were right*," he added in almost a snarl of frustration. "Classes are the fastest way to advancement."

Arthur sat back, thinking. There was a lot to go over.

Firstly, Brixaby, who'd been alive for less than a year, had already achieved bringing up a skill to level 50.

Arthur's highest skill—**Knife Work** at level 45—was nowhere near that and had only gotten there thanks to a couple years of working in various kitchens.

However, like Brixaby said, he had never focused solely on **Knife Work**, but all the related skills. His **Meal Preparation** was at level 39 right behind. And most of the other skills in his Cooking Class were around the same level.

In addition, getting the Cooking Class all by itself had given him 2 points in perception, 2 in dexterity, 1 in intelligence, and 1 in luck. As it was his only tier 2 class, he had it equipped almost constantly.

"Were those attributes you got permanent?" Arthur asked. "Or only when you're using the skill?"

"They are permanent," he said grudgingly.

Which meant once Arthur got the rest of his skills to the same as his cooking ones . . . his would be too.

"You know what this means?" Arthur asked, feeling poleaxed.

"Yes, there is much potential for gains." Rather than awed, Brixaby sounded grumpy. "But leveling up a class is so slow."

"Worth it, though."

"Yes, well, I have not received the class yet, though I have tried adding as many related skills as I can think of."

Arthur patted his neck, remembering how frustrated he'd been trying to get the last skills he needed for his Cooking Class.

"The only other class you have is Stealth, right?"

Cressida had that card now. Thanks to Arthur's Master of Skills card, both he and Brixaby had only needed to use the Stealthy Class card for a moment. It had been copied over, and then they were free to give it away. It was a powerful side benefit of having a Legendary card.

"Yes," Brixaby said. "But I don't collect skills haphazardly like you. I find it's much better to refine and focus on one skill at a time."

Again, Arthur patted his neck. No wonder Brixaby had sounded so disgruntled earlier. "Nothing wrong with broadening your horizons. And we have been going nonstop since leaving Mesa Free Hive."

Brixaby went silent for a moment as if mulling his words over. Then, finally, he spoke up. "Arthur, we are about to face the Rares again, which means there is a good chance we could obtain a Rare card. If you get the chance, you should consume one using my Call of the Void. You should have ten slots, like me. Why haven't you? Why are you ignoring such an advantage?"

Arthur winced. "You know why. I am . . . uncomfortable with permanently removing a card from circulation."

"Well, I am uncomfortable with my rider going into the Dark Heart unprepared," Brixaby snarked back.

The problem was, Brixaby had a point. And Arthur hadn't exactly opposed Brixaby consuming cards. He just didn't want to do it himself.

Using several cards of the same set multiplied their power. Destroying a card, and removing the capability forever, felt terribly wrong. He'd seen what happened with the rotted cards back in the scholars' guildhall. It had been a crime against magic—against the world—so severe that it had spawned the Mind Singer.

At the same time, Brixaby's method of consuming cards didn't corrupt the magic. It just removed the existence of it from the world forever.

But Brixaby was right. Arthur was ignoring a huge advantage.

"If I find a card good enough to take for myself . . . I'll think about it."

"Excellent," Brixaby replied, acting like Arthur had as good as agreed. For dragons, the decision was straightforward.

Arthur shook his head, then looked down to check the progress of the adventurers again. They hadn't moved as far or as fast as he had hoped.

"Let's move up ahead and scout out if there are any problems on their way."

"Scourglings we can kill, you mean," Brixaby said with an evil chuckle.

"That too," Arthur agreed.

Immediately, Brixaby began to flap straight upward. "Hold on tight. Rares might be able to recognize my shape in the sky, even from far away. It's best we make our profile as tiny as possible."

Back at the mustering point, Lopez had handed Arthur some odd thick glasses he said were "binoculars." They enhanced his vision without the use of a card or an enchantment. Arthur had no idea how it worked, but he suspected the thick glass bent light in some way.

Once Brixaby had climbed so high into the air that he could only make out the group of adventurers as a distant dark line, Arthur put the binoculars to his eyes and looked to the direction his heart was pulling him.

"Brixaby, move forward, just to the northwest."

"What do you see?" Brixaby called over the sound of the wind. The binoculars extended vision even farther than a dragon could see.

Arthur's eyebrows drew together. "This nest is bigger than what we were expecting."

And that was putting it mildly. A crack had opened in the gray-brown soil, and scourglings of all sizes and ranks milled around it. It shouldn't be possible, as nothing could live in the deadlands, not even scourglings, but the truth was right before his eyes. As Arthur watched, more crawled out.

This was a mini eruption, a fissure, and it was boiling up scourglings.

CHAPTER 15

Brixaby dropped down right in front of the adventuring groups, startling a few people.

Lopez and his men had been leading the way, with the rest ranged far to the right and left on either side. Arthur got the impression that healthy competition had turned to active dislike among the different adventurers, and the solution was to stay far away from one another.

Once he recovered from the shock, Lopez must have read the look on Arthur's face because his own expression went grim. "What's wrong?"

"Our scourgling problem has gotten bigger," Arthur said, and then started to describe the nest he'd seen. As he spoke, the adventurers crowded close to hear.

However, when Arthur explained that a fissure had opened in the ground, a lot like a mini eruption, he was interrupted by whoops of delight. Some people even took off their wide-brimmed hats and waved them in the air.

"This isn't a good thing!" Arthur snapped, shocked. "It's a precursor to an eruption."

All the way back, he had replayed Soledad's story of what happened in N'awlens over and over, and worried that these people were cutting it too close here.

But he might as well have been speaking to brick walls. Adventurers had already turned to their friends and were making plans with one another, discussing plans of attack and how to split their upcoming bounty. From the bits of chatter Arthur caught, responding to emergency situations paid more. Sometimes in entire cards.

Lopez gave a sympathetic shrug. "Things like this happen when the Dark Heart is almost ready for its harvest. It's just another sign we're nearly there."

Arthur gritted his teeth. "I get it's a good opportunity for shards and cards, but if those scourglings make their way to the city—"

"That's why we're here," Lopez said.

Someone called from the back, "What's wrong, dragon rider? You a coward?"

Brixaby's head snapped up toward the direction of the speaker and boomed out, "My rider is no coward! Say that again to my teeth!"

The heckler didn't speak up, but there were a few audible snickers.

Arthur kept a tight rein on his temper. "I'm not afraid to fight scourglings, but I've also seen what they do to people. They've destroyed incoming wagon trains up and down this Interstate—"

"Well, that's the risk they take!" someone else yelled. "No one said life was fair."

There was a difference between life not being fair and actively inviting a catastrophe, but the speaker's voice had come from a place where no one stood. Probably thanks to Brixaby's threat. Arthur suspected a wind card was at play, and he wasn't about to get into a shouting match with someone who wouldn't show his face.

Jon, who was in charge of the Lightning Cats, came up to Lopez. "Sheriff, may my group have permission to move forward? Many of us have speed enhancements." He looked at Arthur. "Since time is clearly of the essence."

Lopez took a moment to remove his wide hat and scratch a hand through his dark, sweaty hair before replacing his hat again. He nodded. "Yes, I suppose it's time."

That got another round of whoops, as well as groans from others who didn't have a way to outpace the others. There were a few men—and a woman or two— who had body modifications that were bulky and geared toward defense. They wouldn't be fast movers.

Lopez held up his hand, and the adventurers fell silent.

"You all know the rules: Kill as many as you can, but only tagged bodies get you the official credit. I need group leaders right here so me and my deputies can pass out the tags and log who gets what."

One of the men by Lopez pulled out a box full of organized paper slips, all with twine on the ends. The paper stacks were arranged in a rainbow of colors. As Arthur watched, he saw each group was assigned its own color.

The leaders each got their own thick stack and then turned to either pass them out to the rest of their party or kept them in their own possession, probably to tag the bodies themselves.

When the last group leader was assigned their tag and color, Lopez turned to Arthur. "You've done what you've come here to do by leading us to the nest, but I'd still like your help cleaning up if you can."

"Of course we'll fight," Arthur said, annoyed. It seemed Lopez was also mistaking his disgust for playing stupid games with scourglings as cowardice.

"We've very likely killed more scourglings than your adventuring groups ever have, combined. And we'll gladly kill more," Brixaby added.

"Good, because I thought this would go nicely with your dragon." Lopez showed Arthur a thick stack of deep purple tags. The color did pair nicely with the flashes of iridescent purple up and down Brixaby's dark scales.

Brixaby snorted and turned his head toward the direction where the Lightning Cats and other fast-moving groups had gone. Some of the Lightning Cats had gone down onto four feet in order to lope forward, which had been more than a little disturbing to watch. By now, they were distant dots along the horizon.

Lopez continued, "There still might be a little time before the Dark Heart is opened. If you can find any more of these nests for us in the future, I'm sure you'd be well compensated."

It was times like this that Arthur wondered if he was the crazy one for thinking cutting things so close was a stupid idea. Brixaby was looking excited at the prospect of eradicating more scourglings hideouts . . . but then again, he was a dragon.

To Arthur, these Texans were playing with fire.

Still, there was only one answer he could give. "Of course," he said stiffly. "I don't even want to think about what it will be like if one of these nests goes unchecked." He couldn't stop from adding, "I think you and the rest of the city government are taking this too lightly."

Lopez shrugged again. "Well, you haven't seen our adventuring groups in action, have you?"

That was fair. He hadn't. Grabbing the tags in poor humor, he threw them into his Personal Space. With a smile, Lopez tipped his hat and went on to speak with his deputies.

"Cheer up, we're going to be killing scourglings soon," Brixaby said. "And if this nest proves to be particularly virulent, perhaps we can wring more concessions from Walker. Plus," he added, "this will raise our popularity with the rest of the city, which means Dannill might pay us more, too."

That did cheer him up a little. But the feeling of duty he had from the moment he saw scourglings bubbling up from the ground so close to the city had a weight, which had landed full on his shoulders. Maybe it was a side effect from being a half-trained hive leader, but this . . . none of this felt good.

"Excuse me. Young man?"

Arthur glanced over and saw that an older man had approached him. He was a bit unusual looking in the normal Texan population, being tall and thin with hair that was either so blond it looked white in the blazing sun or so gray that it had turned white. His eyes were the pale type of blue that almost looked silver, and it was almost impossible to tell his exact age. "May I ask how big the nest is? And what is the distribution of ranks you saw?"

No one else had bothered to ask. They'd just wanted to be pointed in the right direction.

"I only saw Commons and Uncommons—perhaps three dozen or so. But my seeking ability told me that's the spot where the Rares are hiding, too."

"I see, I see." With a nod, the man reached into a leather bag tied to his belt and started pulling out long pieces of pipework with complex metal connections forged onto them. The absurd length of the pipes versus the smaller bag made it clear that this was a portable storage space. Though Arthur didn't see any runes around the bag.

Then, without comment, the man bent and started connecting the pipes in a way that made no immediate sense.

Brixaby tilted his head almost to the side to watch, oddly birdlike. "What are you doing?"

The man blinked up at them, then smiled as if he had just momentarily forgotten that they were there. "I'm afraid that while my cards are powerful, they do take a bit of prep time."

Then, to Arthur's shock, he gestured from his chest outward and displayed the images of two cards in his heart deck.

Maniac Kludger
Uncommon
Utility
The wielder of this card has an uncanny instinctive ability to join different machinery parts together to form an upgraded or new machine, tool, or part. The wielder has a 50% greater chance of having their creation work correctly the first time, even if it bends known physical laws. Seek additional cards in this set to add to overall inventive power.

Natural Mechanic
Uncommon
Utility
The wielder of this card has the instinctive ability to visually inspect broken mechanical objects, and understand how to fix them. The wielder has a 50% greater chance of their fix working correctly the first time, even if the fix violates several known common sense laws. Seek additional cards in this set to add to overall mechanical power.

It only took Arthur a moment to read through them: The nature of cards meant that they were displayed in his language rather than Texan, which he was still building skills for.

But already the man seemed to have forgotten him and was busy fitting the pipes into strange connections that formed a square frame. In the next moment, he pulled oversized wheels out of the small bag.

"Your cards are two of a kind?" Arthur asked.

"Oh, indeed." The man smiled. "I haven't introduced myself. Everybody calls me Claude the Kludge, due to the first card I had." He pointed to the Maniac Kludger card before dispersing the projection. "Anyway, yes, these are two of a kind. Did you see the last lines on the card description? That usually means there's a full set somewhere out in the world."

Arthur had something like that in his Master of Skills and Master of Body Enhancement cards. And so did Brixaby with his Call of the Void, and now Call of the Heart cards. But he hadn't known it meant every other card in the set was out there somewhere.

What if one card in his Master set was in the Dark Heart?

"You seem very free with your information," Brixaby said, narrowing his eyes suspiciously.

Claude shrugged. "I come from the icelands up north, you know? We have a reputation for being nice. Nice as ice." He laughed, though Arthur and Brixaby didn't. "Anyway, no one holds back card information—why would we? We're all paddling the same boat when it comes to the scourglings. I find the Southerner ways very stifling."

While Arthur appreciated his view, he wasn't about to share information on cards out of *his* heart deck. Instead, he asked, "What are you making?"

"This is a catapult. It's an ancient design, but it works well at killing scourglings from a distance. Back up a few steps, please," he said, though it would be easier for him to step back.

Brixaby moved a few paces, and Claude pulled out an odd contraption with two wheels connected by a frame and handlebars. He stood it up, and Arthur got the impression that he meant to ride that thing, only he had no idea how Claude could balance on it. "Another ancient device I've reworked again from old texts. A bicycle. Anyway, my tactic is usually to fire on the beasts from afar. Works great," he said, connecting the two devices with an odd rope that stretched and bounced back to a smaller length.

Arthur shook his head. He only had a bare idea of what he was looking at, much less how it could fire on scourglings. But perhaps this was all part of Claude's kludging power.

He glanced at Brixaby, who was watching the process intently, probably trying to pick up some crafting tips.

"Let's get into the air," Arthur said. "The first groups might be reaching the nest at any time."

Brixaby jerked in surprise and seemed to come back to himself. "Yes, of course," he said, then leaped into the air with enough force to threaten throwing Arthur off his seat before he buzzed forward into motion. But then the dragon curved his head back for one last look at Claude.

"Don't think about it," Arthur warned, though he was amused.

"I wouldn't take those cards from his heart with so many people around to watch." Brixaby sounded offended. "But if he happens to die . . ."

The first groups who had left were fast, but they were no match for the speed of a dragon in flight. Brixaby soon caught up to the leaders, and Arthur held him up for a few extra minutes to see how professional adventurers dealt with scourglings.

Brixaby grumbled, but Arthur could tell he was at least derisively curious.

Lightning Cats on four feet were eerie and terrible to look at, disturbing him enough that he focused on the others who still ran like humans. Though all of them wore chainmail of Brixaby's distinctive design—which had always looked delicate to Arthur's eyes and completely in contrast to the dragon's personality—they weren't slowed down at all.

Mentally, he started ticking off what he saw. Body enhancements to make them more animallike, speed-boost enhancements. There was also a slight distortion in the air building between the team members. He suspected it was mana. The start of a complex spell, perhaps?

As the Lightning Cats were in the lead, they were the first to reach the nest. The wavering in the air solidified and became a rain of lightning bolts that battered the first rank of Commons that hovered at the edge of the nest like guards.

A score of them died in an instant, and then the Lightning Cats were on the rest. Jon pulled a sword out of a personal storage space and began laying about. The sword must've had a poison aspect because even light cuts began to sizzle with foam, and the scourglings quickly dropped.

The girl who was covered with fur stood back up on two legs and gestured wildly with a closed fist. Ghostly claws extended out three feet, followed her motion, and cleaved a scourgling into three separate chunks.

But like an ant's nest that had been disturbed by somebody trampling on it, more scourglings boiled out. Several larger Uncommons were mixed in with the Commons. These gave the adventurers more trouble, though no one got injured. More Commons followed, and these were not of that odd bird shape. Instead, they were sort of small and monkey-like creatures with elongated ears that tilted out to the side, green-black skin, and razor-sharp teeth.

They could jump, too. Arthur saw one land on the back of one of the Lightning Cats before it was ripped away.

The Cats would've been on the verge of getting swamped, but more groups of adventurers arrived. One consisted of the extremely muscle-headed men, who waded through the fray and simply swung huge arms and oversized fists, pulverizing anything that they hit.

The leaders of each team followed their members, and Arthur saw them darting back and forth, tagging the bodies.

It was messy, but the adventurers were getting the job done. Unfortunately, the flow of scourglings out of the fissure didn't look like it would be stopping anytime soon.

"Where are the Rares?" Brixaby demanded, looking down eagerly.

Arthur quickly checked his internal map. "They're . . . everywhere," he said, looking down and squinting. He'd seen the size of the Rares. Nothing on the field approached that size. "I can't see them. These are all Commons and Uncommons."

"Perhaps they're invisible. One did have an illusion card. There may be more."

Arthur heard the question in his dragon's voice and smiled. "Why don't you give it a test?"

Buzzing eagerly to the side of the expanding battle, Brixaby blasted down with a Stunning Shout toward the edge of the group. His shout caught a couple of Uncommons and a cluster of three Commons that had been pushed to the side, but nothing else appeared out of invisibility. Brixaby blasted another group of Commons, just to be sure, peering down eagerly to see if anything would become visible again. But there was nothing.

Arthur shook his head. "Either you're not catching them or they're not here. I think they're underground."

By this time, even more adventuring parties were arriving, which was good because the flow from the fissure seemed to be never ending.

Arthur had to grudgingly admit that the adventurers were not doing a half-bad job. In fact, he noticed that the group leaders, who were tagging the dead scourglings, were pretty much ignoring the Commons and just focusing on the Uncommons. There was more than enough to go around, and no one wanted to focus on the small fry.

"The Rares are still here. Save your strength," Brixaby yelled, but if anybody heard him, there was no reaction.

A flaming fireball struck a cluster of scourglings, a fire that, when it hit, splattered like liquid and didn't seem to want to go out.

Arthur glanced over and saw, a quarter mile away, the small figure of Claude standing next to his odd machine. He had kludged an arm over the frame with a large cup at the top. Using a rope, he wound it down again, pulling something out of his bag to load it up.

"Keep an eye on that," he told Brixaby. "It's a machine, not a magical effect. I don't think he has any aiming skills attached to that thing."

"The day I get struck by something thrown by a human in the air is the day I return my wings," Brixaby said, though Arthur saw him turn his head slightly and keep an eye on Claude.

By this time, more Uncommon scourglings had crawled out of the hole and joined the battle, and some of the adventuring groups had to fall back, though they were still fighting and killing.

"Shall I join them?" Brixaby asked eagerly.

Arthur shook his head. "No, if Rares are out there, we need to save your strength."

His first indication that something was wrong was when he saw adventurers and scourglings start to stumble for no particular reason.

Dust rose from the ground, and Arthur couldn't figure out why because there wasn't so much as a breath of wind in the air. Then he realized what he was seeing.

An earthquake.

And that was when the ground fell out from under both scourglings and adventurers alike, plunging the whole fighting mass into a deep pit.

CHAPTER 16

As the ground collapsed, a cloud of dust rose up so thick that Arthur could not see through it. But he could hear growls, yells . . . and screams. Movement flashed—a shadow in the dust, and it was bigger than any of the Uncommons.

This was one of the Rares. There was no doubt. Once again, they'd set and sprung a trap for the adventurers, and now they were falling upon their prey.

Arthur's mouth opened to tell Brixaby to dive, but the dragon was ahead of him. His wings snapped shut, then they were diving straight in.

Arthur had to throw an arm over his eyes to protect against the worst of the dust. He had no resistances or even goggles to help.

Brixaby's eyes, however, were developed for flight. He could see where Arthur couldn't, so Arthur put all his trust in his dragon. Arthur couldn't see exactly what was going on. He pieced it together in flashes.

The two of them acted just like any purple pair in a hive: They were a rescue squad, pulling people out of danger.

But Brixaby wasn't even as big as Tess was when Arthur had been rescued as a child, and that caused problems. Brixaby grabbed a man under the arms. Wings buzzing furiously, he lifted them upward but only managed to scoot him out of danger. The tips of his boots skimmed over Uncommon scourglings, and it was a minor miracle he didn't lose a toe. Brixaby was forced to dump him in a relatively safer place that was thick with only Commons and none of the larger Rares.

"Let me off," Arthur said. "I'll help from the side."

Brixaby snarled in aggravation—he didn't like his rider being away from him in battle so soon after he'd been injured. But he couldn't yet carry Arthur and another.

He must have turned to fly out. It took Arthur by surprise since he'd completely lost track of where they were in the thick dust. But the next second, he was at the edge of the pit, and the air was clear enough to see in.

Arthur jumped off, landing hard and turning. He caught a glimpse of Brixaby's black tail as he turned back to the pit.

Then Arthur ran to help someone who was trying to crawl up the sheer side. Then another.

The screams below were mixed with scourgling whistles in a terrible cacophony.

It had been less than a minute since the pit had collapsed. It took that long for someone with a wind-type card to get their head back on their shoulders.

A stiff breeze came out of nowhere, and the dust was soon lifting and thinning.

Arthur was treated to the sight of his dragon's amazing agility. With no rider to worry about throwing off his back, Brixaby put all his flying skills and natural ability on full display. He practically flipped over from vertical to an immediate dive down to pluck someone out of the fray. Then claws sank deep into the unlucky person, and he immediately lifted and jinked to the side horizontally in a way that nothing but a four-winged dragon could do. A blast of fire from a scourgling below filled the air where he'd been a moment before.

Brixaby made a sharp V-turn, tossing the rescued person carelessly to the lip of the pit before diving in again.

The people he saved now suffered from wrenched shoulders, broken ribs and arms, and gouge marks from his rough handling . . . but at least they weren't being ripped apart by scourglings.

While the Rares had set a trap that had ensnared many people, some adventurers had survived. Notably, all the Lightning Cats, who had made it out of the pit in different spots and then regathered into a team to take down any scourglings that tried to climb up.

Arthur stood at the edge and did the same, using his **Throwing Accuracy** skill and Nice Shot card to pepper the scourglings below. He didn't kill any of them, except for the occasional unlucky Common, but he did provide a useful distraction.

Too bad he couldn't save everyone.

Brixaby dived toward a hugely muscled man who had been pinned by two Rare scourglings. He was a beat too slow, and it was doubtful he would have been able to lift the man's bulk or taken the time to explain he needed permission to store him. Arthur peppered one of the Rares with metal shrapnel that bounced off tough feathered hide. That Rare turned to hiss venom-green teeth at Arthur.

The second Rare, however, jumped on the unlucky adventurer and tore his heart out with oversized claws.

"No!" Arthur yelled, but it was too late.

The scourgling flipped the heart into its mouth, and the moment it was down its gullet, it began changing. Muscles bulged from its shoulders and legs as it took on the aspects of the body-modification card.

With a whistling shriek of triumph, it jumped high enough to easily clear the fifteen-foot-deep pit. It landed in the middle of a cluster of adventurers on the other side and started wreaking havoc.

There was nothing Arthur or Brixaby could do for them. Grimly, he focused again on keeping more scourglings from climbing the sides of the pit.

Sensing motion beside him, he turned to see Claude arrive. The fire-throwing frame was gone. Now he wore an odd contraption strapped to his chest with harnesses. It had a long metal tube with more tubes attached at random points. It looked so heavy and bulky that Claude had to lift it using the harness and keep it in place. A heavy metal barrel was strapped to his back, and when Claude moved, it sloshed.

Claude nodded at Arthur. "Different times call for different kinds of fire, don'tcha know?" Then he flicked something on the device.

There was a buzz, a pulse of mana, and then gouts of liquid fire sprayed from the muzzle of the tube onto the scourglings below.

"Silly of them to set up their own kill box like this," Claude commented over renewed whistling screams. Luckily for the few adventurers yet to be rescued, he aimed the liquid fire toward the thick clusters of scourglings. Since this was the heart of the nest, he had plenty of targets.

"That fire isn't going out," Arthur said, staring, a little dumbfounded.

"Not for a while, no. It's an alchemical invention—useful but dangerous!"

It may have been dangerous, and killed scourglings by the bucketful, but the nearby Rares could fight back.

"Duck!" Arthur pulled Claude down just as lightning flashed over their heads. It had been half aimed at them, half at Brixaby, who had swung neatly to the side at the last moment to avoid the bolt.

He dropped a half-unconscious woman in front of Arthur.

"This one is bleeding out," he said. "I'm running out of adventurers to save." Then he leaped into the air, flipped around, and headed back into the pit.

Bleeding out was . . . a kind word for it. The poor woman had lost both her legs and had horrific cuts on her torso. Arthur assumed she had some kind of vitality card to have stayed awake this long.

Arthur felt his breakfast threaten to rise up but battled it back down and crawled to her.

"Let me help—I can stop time for you. Give me your permission."

She just turned a shocked, blank look to him.

Desperately, he tried again. "Do you want to live or not?"

"Yes," she whispered.

He put his hand on her shoulder, which was probably the least bloodied part of her. In the next moment, she was gone.

And . . . oomph, there was definitely some magical weight to her. Either a heart full of Rare cards or a Legendary. Arthur could fit much more in his

Personal Space, but he felt the slight strain. Ever since stuffing so many of Mesa Free Hive's combat cards in his storage, he'd become more aware of such things.

"That's an interesting card," Claude commented. He'd become completely overbalanced and had to remove the heavier portions of his inventions to get to his feet again. As he stood, he once more removed the tank from his own storage space and strapped it back on.

Arthur's **Acting** skill made it so he didn't miss a beat. "Ultimate crafting card. And a metal-manipulation card to shoot the shrapnel."

"And a healing card, I see." Claude nodded with his chin toward his face.

On reflex, Arthur touched his forehead. His fingers came back wet with his own blood. Huh. He didn't know how that had happened. The cut was already half healed thanks to his Moderate Self-Repair card.

Turning back to the pit, Claude sprayed out more of that liquid fire. His tone was so casual it was almost academic. "Your cards seem to be all over the place. Let me guess, you shoved anything that looked useful into your heart?"

"Not *every* card," Arthur grumbled.

Just because Claude's liquid fire seemed to be so good at melting scourglings— even a couple of Rares had been caught in this last gout—he reached into his storage space and grabbed a packet of flour wrapped in thin cheesecloth.

Flour bombs had become his personal favorite.

He threw one down toward the burning scourglings. It reacted instantly to the fire, and a small explosion bloomed up, consuming several more.

"Oh, that's a fun idea," Claude said with approval.

The tide was starting to turn against the scourglings. As Claude had said, they'd made a kill box for themselves. Quite a few adventurers had fallen into the pit and died, but they'd gone down fighting. This had taken out more than a few Rares along the way.

Smart enough to make a trap. Dumb enough to trap themselves along with it.

The Mind Singer was a smarter scourgling, and able to think more steps ahead, but she also had mind-based power. Perhaps intelligence came along with that.

Or she was just older and these Rares had recently spawned.

Arthur had the uncomfortable feeling it was the latter.

And that made him wonder what else the Mind Singer, who was both older and more cunning, was capable of.

Either Brixaby had sensed the change or he'd run out of survivors. He started blasting down on the remaining scourglings with his Stunning Shout, either outright killing or disabling other scourglings.

The adventurers redoubled their efforts. One person had an interesting trick where they could temporarily maximize an object's size and weight. They tossed palm-sized stones into the air. Then, as the stones fell over the pit, they grew to an enormous size, smashing any unlucky scourglings they fell on.

Meanwhile, the Lightning Cats had formed up again into a pack and ran down any scourgling that happened to crawl out of the pit, either by slashing at it with ghostly claws or shooting it with their combined lightning attack.

Then there was the sound of trumpets from behind. Arthur turned to see that the last of the adventurers had arrived, along with the sheriffs, who brought up the rear.

"Better late than never," he muttered.

Claude looked around, saw the approaching group, and let out a long sigh. "I hate that guy. You're going to want to back away—far away—before you see what they're about."

"What do you mean?" Arthur asked, but Claude had already taken his own advice and was dismantling the liquid flame-throwing device on his back while backing up.

Other adventurers—and there were distressingly few of them; it seemed like the Lightning Cats were the only group without at least one missing member—also backed away. A few threw rude gestures at the incomers.

One of the new folk, a large barrel-chested, bearded man, started to glow green. He broke into a heavy-footed run straight toward the pit. Without pausing, he leaped right into the fray.

Instantly, the pit started to fill with green gas . . . and it was not by any means a small area.

Arthur caught a faint whiff of the stuff—astringent and sharp—and quickly backed away like everyone else.

No more scourglings crawled out of the pit.

Arthur waited a beat, then two more, before he let himself relax. The fight was over.

Now the cleanup—and card harvest—could begin.

CHAPTER 17

The problems started where they usually did: with greed.

While the toxic green gas appeared heavier than air and mostly stayed in the pit, looking like a pea soup, it took time to dissipate. Tendrils curled up over the edge, and no one risked going too close.

There was still a lot of work to be done, and cleanup to do. Many adventurers had died right after the initial pit collapse. But some had managed to find their way out either through card powers or through pure grit.

Either no one had brought a healer along with them or, more likely, those with external healing cards had died in the collapse. Arthur went from group to group, checking on the injured and seeing if any needed to be stored for their safety. Now that the adrenaline of battle was wearing off, some people had outright collapsed.

"Never needed a healer before," one man growled while he had a hand pressed tight to his stomach to hold the contents in. "Adventurers are supposed to be self-reliant."

"Take the damn out he's giving you, Jerry," his teammate said, then looked at Arthur. "How much you say the cost was?"

"One Uncommon shard." During the attack, time had been of the essence, and Arthur hadn't minded storing the initial dying adventurers at no cost. But a sure-fire way to get taken advantage of was to gain the reputation of providing life-saving services for free. He didn't want to be anyone's safety net, unconscious or not.

The man holding his own stomach in hemmed and hawed. His teammate rolled his eyes. "We'll be getting more than that haul from this mess, Jerry."

"Yeah, but I still got the healing fees. They can't just sew this up and call it good!" Jerry gestured downward.

Arthur let them argue back and forth. In the end, they agreed, but Arthur would only receive the payment once he delivered Jerry to the hospital. His teammate fixed Arthur with a hard look, and actual red light from a card spell flashed behind his eyes. "You'd better not screw us over, kid."

Brixaby bristled, but Arthur understood the man was worried. "Time will stop for him. He won't feel a thing. Besides," he added, "I want my shard."

A moment later, Jerry was stored in Arthur's Personal Space.

No sooner had he done that than someone jogged up to Arthur. He had vivid green hair, which had to be some sort of effect from a body-modification card, though Arthur couldn't tell from what. "You're the transport?" he asked, half breathlessly.

"For a fee," Brixaby growled.

"Emergency transport," Arthur clarified with a frown. "You look whole and healthy."

"It's not for me. I don't think we can get Cecil back in time to reattach his arm." The green-haired man turned and pointed.

Another man was walking up, and though he wore a smile on his face as if nothing was wrong, he was quite visibly missing an arm. Bandages covered the place where it had been, though they were stained bloodred. Seeing them stare, he raised the severed arm and used it to wave.

"He has a vitality card," the green-haired man explained. "He can make it back to the city worse than this, believe it or not. But regrowing an arm is more expensive than reattaching it."

Arthur had just finished quickly storing the still very cheerful Cecil when an uproar broke out at the side of the pit.

Glancing around, Arthur saw Claude, who had hung around nearby. He had been the one to slyly suggest a payment for transport to begin with, though he had not helped with the medical side of things. Instead, he had sat down to work on some sort of invention with a dozen moving parts that looked disturbingly like a spider.

Catching his look, Claude rolled his own eyes and returned his spider back to the bag. "Let's see what this is about." But judging by the exasperated tone in his voice, he already knew.

A few people had risked the dissipating gas at the side of the pit and were coughing between outraged yells. Hurrying over, Arthur glanced down himself.

The adventurer with the toxic gas had apparently not been affected by his card's power. And, by the looks of things, he had been busy. His brick-red tags were tied to every corpse that was bigger than a Common.

On top of that, he'd removed the tags of other teams and blatantly left them, jumbled up together, in a corner.

Now the toxic card user stood there, unrepentant, with his thick arms crossed over his chest. He smirked up at the gathering crowd.

"Sheriff!" Jon from the Lightning Cats bellowed. "This is theft!"

Turning, Arthur saw Lopez and his two undersheriffs had joined the fray.

Lopez took in the situation with a wary, unsurprised expression. He didn't answer Jon right away but turned to converse with his undersheriffs.

A drone of wings, and Brixaby landed next to Arthur, after having done a quick loop up top to confirm the situation. His top lip was curled in a snarl. "That man will not be keeping those riches for himself."

Arthur placed a hand on his dragon's neck. "Let's see what happens."

While he wasn't about to yell and rage like the others, he was aware all over again that he was an outsider to these people, and this process.

But he wasn't going to allow his rewards to be stolen, either.

First, he'd give the sheriff a chance to work this out.

A beat later, Lopez turned from his undersheriffs. He held up his empty palms, expression grim. "We have a tag system for a reason, people. The rules were explained to you all from the very start. The city developed the tag system to be fair—"

The rest of his words were drowned out by sheer outrage.

"There's nothing fair about this!"

"He locked us out of the pit with poison gas!"

"He's a cheater!"

Lopez's expression went hard. "Sometimes a battle favors one card user over another. You can call that unfair or you can call it bad luck. The next might favor you."

That didn't mollify anyone.

Claude gestured down toward a pile of creatures so burned it was hard to tell where one started and another began. "These creatures were clearly killed by my invention."

The toxic user leered. "I don't see your tags on 'em."

Lopez sighed. "The corpses down in the pit weren't the only ones."

It was true. A few, including the muscled scourgling, had managed to break out of the pit before being killed. That corpse seemed to be in dispute as well with two colored tags hanging off it—one yellow of the Lightning Cats and a green tag from another team.

Arthur frowned. He was surprised at how badly Lopez was bungling this. "Sheriff, you can clearly see that the other tags were removed while the gas was in effect. The only fair thing to do is to split up the pit among everyone."

Hearing him, the toxic man laughed. "He's welcome to come down and try."

"You don't want to make enemies here, Bradley," Jon warned.

"I ain't making enemies. Just getting my fair share. 'Sides, you can't say my powers didn't kill a good number here. I'm just asking for my fair share."

Jon waited a beat for Lopez to answer, and when he didn't, he spoke. "All of us fought to kill the scourglings. In the end, all of us were firing into the pit."

His grin grew wide. "But you can't prove what you killed, can you?"

Lopez watched on, his lips pressed into a thin line.

Unfortunately, Arthur could guess why he hadn't stepped in. It was the same reason why no one else had taken this into their own hands.

Bradley could easily fill up the pit with toxic gas. It hadn't taken him more than a few moments before, and by the confident way he stood, he had more than enough mana to do so again.

As for Lopez, while he had the backing of the city's government, he was well outside the borders. He must not have the combat cards to compete against adventurers. Finally, anyone who could bring loads of high-ranked cards to the city wouldn't be excluded from the Dark Heart.

Bradley extended his arms. "As for the tags, why, I just removed any that were placed by someone already dead. Can you prove otherwise?" A beat of silence. "Anyone gonna stop me?"

More silence.

Arthur glanced at the Lightning Cat group, who at least had ranged lightning attacks.

Jon caught his eye and shook his head. "He has personal shields," he said, and spat to the side.

Ah, so Bradley had tried something like this before.

Arthur grimaced and turned to Brixaby. "Whatever happens, stay up here."

"Ah." Brixaby sat back with a sound of immense satisfaction. It was almost a purr. His tail curled contentedly around his feet. "I was wondering who would take him out: you or me."

Arthur would rather take the heat of suspicion than his dragon.

He strode forward a few steps until his boots were at the edge of the pit. "You don't get to push people around because of the strength of your cards. Give people their fair share, or I'll make you."

Bradley laughed. "Oh, so the cowardly dragon rider speaks. You sure you don't want to just buy the cards off me? I'll give you a good price."

"I don't have to buy what's already mine," Arthur said.

Wisps of toxic gas came off the man. "Come down here and say that."

So Arthur stepped off the edge and into the pit.

CHAPTER 18

Arthur landed, with knees loose to absorb the impact, on unpleasantly soft ground. Wisps of toxic gas still drifted from the corpses, most of which were unrecognizable from the scourglings they once were. Aside from the effects of the toxic gas, the adventurers had thrown everything they had into the pit during that last final push, leaving behind a gruesome sight.

Bradley stood on the other side of the pit, hands on his hips, grinning broadly at Arthur. "Well, it looks like you have more balls than them up there, kid."

Arthur began to walk forward. Only patches of the ground were visible. Most of it was covered by corpses, often several scourglings deep. He didn't dare take his eyes off Bradley in case he pulled a trick, relying on his **Balancing** skill so he didn't misstep.

"You don't want to make an enemy here," Arthur said, his voice steady. "You'll still get your fair share, Bradley. But so will everyone else."

"An enemy of who? You?" Bradley laughed harshly. "Kid, you can't even get close to me."

A green, toxic-looking gas began to spew from Bradley as if he had sprung a leak.

Arthur continued to advance.

Bradley's grin widened, his teeth stark white against the billowing gas. "Your funeral."

Then the volume of gas doubled, rising to obscure Bradley completely. It thickened and built up, reaching above the height of a man. The message was clear: if Arthur got too close, there would be no escape from the toxin.

Arthur pressed on. He had various poison resistances, thanks to his experiments with odd plants for Flossie back in Mesa Free Hive, but they were mostly at levels 3 and 4. It was uncertain if any would counteract Bradley's poisons. No doubt those resistances would be getting a workout soon.

Not yet near the gas, Arthur's eyes were already stinging and burning.

As he moved, Bradley continued to spew out his toxin until it collected into a fierce-looking thundercloud. Above, the watching adventurers fell silent. Arthur felt Brixaby's gaze upon him, and though he didn't know if the dragon's look was one of encouragement or scorn for not having already killed Bradley, he knew Brixaby would step in if necessary.

The moment Arthur reached the halfway point in the pit, where retreat to the walls was no longer an easy option, Bradley made his move.

The green poison cloud, which had been building up like a thick wall, suddenly surged toward Arthur.

Above, people shouted curses at Bradley and encouragement for Arthur. Brixaby roared his support, drowning out all the rest.

Just before the toxic gas engulfed him, Arthur activated his Phase In, Phase Out card. It had come off cooldown sometime before, and he now had a full thirty seconds where literally nothing could touch him. He hoped that would be enough.

The cloud enveloped him like a suffocating blanket. All Arthur could see was a dim view of the sun above, and within moments that was gone. He was plunged into blackness.

Closing his eyes, Arthur focused on Brixaby's cards. Brixaby had often claimed he could smell the cards within people's hearts. Arthur always figured it was either an exaggeration or a scare tactic . . . but what if . . . ?

Brixaby's Call of the Void and Call of the Heart were part of the same set. Because of that, they overlapped and boosted each other's powers, similar to how Arthur's Master of Skills and Master of Body Enhancement worked.

Concentrating in a way he'd never thought to do before, Arthur began to sense something outside himself.

Card shards flickered with tiny motes of power from the corpses all around him. Stronger pulses came from the higher-ranked scourglings who'd had full cards.

Common cards felt like lit candles in the darkness, but they were outshone by Uncommon cards, which blazed like oil-fed torches. Those, in turn, were nothing compared to Rare cards, which were like a full moon casting silvery shadows across the land at night. His own Legendary cards, however, shone like the sun at noon on a clear day.

Each rank of card wasn't a simple step up from one to the next: it was an exponential leap of power.

In his mind, the pit transformed into a hilltop of glittering gems, each representing a card or a shard. It was nearly overwhelming, yet . . . barely manageable.

Most importantly, Bradley's three Rare cards stood out to Arthur like a lighthouse in a foggy night.

In his arrogance, the man had moved only about ten feet to the left, trusting that the obscuring toxic gas would hide him.

Arthur advanced straight toward him. Fifteen seconds left.

His plan was to use his Counterfeit Siphon card once he got within range of the man's aura, copy the gas, and somehow turn it against him. But when he got close and his Counterfeit activated, he was met with a surprise.

New Counterfeit spell obtained: Smoke Obscura
Remaining Time: 59 Minutes 59 Seconds

Smoke?

Was this a trick? Maybe Bradley's toxin was on a cooldown? No, Arthur's eyes had burned with the oncoming gas in a way it never would have with smoke.

It was possible Bradley didn't want that same toxin too close to his own skin. He'd used toxic gas on the outside of a ring to deter Arthur's attack, while pulling less-harmful green smoke to him.

As Arthur drew closer, he felt lesser, Common cards scattered throughout Bradley's body, likely stored in his card anchor. Bradley hadn't moved, either. Likely, he was just as blind as Arthur and was simply waiting him out. He didn't see him coming.

But he sure felt it when Arthur ripped three Rare cards right out of his heart.

Bradley's scream was unexpectedly high-pitched as he collapsed, and he immediately started choking in the dense smoke cloud.

Three seconds of his Phase In, Phase Out remained.

Arthur didn't have light to see the three cards he'd pulled, and his time was almost up. He shoved them into his card anchor. It wasn't his heart, so he didn't feel the description stamped on his soul, but he did at least get a notification of what they were.

Cards added:
Skin Shield (Rare)
Smoke Obscura (Rare)
He Who Dealt It (Rare)

Along with the cards' names came a tearing sensation in Arthur's arm, so intense that he cried out. It felt as though something was trying to burst outward from within, as if his flesh were parting from the bone.

Gritting his teeth and summoning all his willpower, Arthur fought through the agony and activated the Skin Shield card.

A warm blankness washed over his skin just as his Phase In, Phase Out reached zero and he rejoined reality. With Bradley's shield, the smoke couldn't touch him.

Bradley lay at his feet, choking, possibly also vomiting, suffering from the effects of the smoke and having the cards torn from his heart.

Arthur wasn't in great shape himself. He hunched over, clutching his arm as searing pain shot from his card-anchor tattoo to his heart.

It was all he could do to reach for the He Who Dealt It card which controlled the gas. As he'd suspected, he sensed that it was in a wide ring around the green smoke. Mentally, he grabbed it and pushed the gas farther out, dissipating it into something harmless.

The pain was so bad he thought his arm was trying to rip itself apart. He couldn't take it more than a few seconds—it had to be tearing itself from the bone. Arthur made himself take in a few gasping breaths, then held the last one. He yanked the three Rare cards from his anchor. Then, using a technique he'd never seen Brixaby do, reinserted them into Bradley's chest.

Dragons weren't usually known for giving power back, after all.

Bradley had gone limp and was unconscious. Using his good arm, Arthur grabbed him by the back of the collar and dragged him out of the smoke.

He didn't have to walk far, and the toxic gas beyond had dissipated entirely.

The moment he was visible, Brixaby dropped out of the air to his side, his buzzing wings dispersing a good deal of the smoke.

Exhausted, Arthur dropped Bradley on a mound of corpses and looked at his arm. It was completely covered with blood, though there was no open wound.

Now that the cards were gone, the pain had gone from a shriek to a bad throb. It could wait.

Arthur looked up at the high sides of the pit where the adventurers had crowded to watch.

"Anyone else?" he yelled out in challenge.

Brixaby reared on his hind legs and bellowed a roar.

No one challenged him. The gathered crowd of adventurers above responded with cheers, their approval echoing through the pit.

Good thing, because if anyone had taken him up on that, he would have had to send Brixaby after them. That wouldn't end well for that adventurer.

Arthur didn't let his relief show on his face. "We're going to be splitting these cards up, equally and civilly. And after that, we're going to get our wounded some care." He paused, waiting for objections, but none came.

Lopez, seizing the opportunity, stepped forward to take command. "Then you're clear to start the harvest. All cards are to be reported to me and my under-sheriffs in exchange for points. We'll hold an auction here."

That got another cheer.

Arthur wasn't sure what points meant, but he didn't have time to ask. Brixaby started nosing at his arm.

"This man hurt you?" the dragon asked in a low growl.

Looking down, Arthur saw he'd been wrong before: Skin was peeling away from the card-anchor tattoo as if it was going through a rapid sunburn. More blood was bubbling up from his pores near the ink, though it seemed to be slowing.

It hurt. A lot. But it was already much, much better than before. But it also wasn't healing, which meant his healing card wasn't taking care of it . . . and he knew the reason why.

He didn't dare show weakness now in front of the adventurers. With a quick shake of his head, Arthur turned away, feigning interest in a particularly gruesome-looking Rare scourgling.

"No, it wasn't him, Brix. I . . . I think I overloaded my card anchor. It's destroyed."

CHAPTER 19

Brixaby took a step back in shock, looked down at Arthur's bloody arm, and then narrowed his eyes.

"Let us talk," he said, placing one clawed hand on Arthur's shoulder.

Knowing he meant to draw Arthur into his Personal Space, Arthur nodded. They'd be able to talk as long as they needed to, and it would only seem like an eyeblink to people on the outside.

But the Personal Space card wasn't Brixaby's. It was Arthur's.

Fiery pain arched from his heart, where the card rested, down to his arm before coming back again. Arthur only kept from screaming because the air felt like it had been punched out of him.

He wrenched away, hunching over.

"Can't," he gritted out, breathing hard.

A few people glanced his way carefully, from the corners of their eyes, while trying not to look like they were watching too hard. Hopefully, they would just think that he had injured his shoulder fighting Bradley.

Arthur couldn't afford to be seen as weak.

"Arthur," Brixaby started to say, but Arthur shook his head.

"Can't use my cards right now," he said in a low undertone.

Brixaby's eyes widened. "This is unacceptable," he hissed. "The link between us is still strong. I can feel it. You must be able to use your cards. I will get you to a healer—"

Arthur breathed in and out carefully, mastering the pain. The intensity had gone down quite a lot. Now the connection between his heart and his broken card anchor throbbed.

He was likely doing so well because he had a few levels of **Pain Resistance**. Otherwise, that last move might have made him pass out.

He felt a bit of sympathy for Bradley for having three cards ripped out of his chest at once. But only a little bit.

"If we leave, we forfeit the cards," he said.

Brixaby's jaw snapped shut. He looked torn, though Arthur guessed he was leaning toward picking Arthur up and just flying off with him anyway.

Brixaby really, really loved new cards, but his ultimate loyalty was to his rider. Most of the time.

Too bad Arthur also really, really loved cards. Also, he knew Lopez's men didn't have the power to keep things under control. People had been cowed, thanks to Arthur's takedown of Bradley, but the moment Arthur left, the strongest would try to reassert themselves. And they'd likely kill any witnesses. Who would be left to say that a second wave of scourglings hadn't shown up?

No, Arthur could wait a bit to see a healer. The pain from his shattered card anchor wasn't getting worse as long as he didn't activate his cards.

"I want to see this through," he told Brixaby firmly.

The dragon hesitated for a moment, then let out a sigh, dipping his head. "Very well. But when we return to the city—"

"We'll go to the hospital," Arthur said. Marion would likely know someone who could see to the card anchor and would keep his secret.

Meanwhile, the adventurers who weren't actively harvesting under the sheriff's watchful eye—and a few who were—were giving Arthur and the still-unconscious Bradley glances.

One man in particular with a bald head and weird lips that were hardened into a point like the beginnings of a beak, approached the downed man.

He stared at him for a moment with greed in his eyes.

"He's still alive, then?" Something about the tone of his voice suggested he could easily change that if Arthur gave the go-ahead.

Arthur moved to stand between them. Though he didn't like Bradley, he'd worked hard to see the man at least come out of this alive. "He is."

The beaked man stared at him. Then, coming to a conclusion, he snorted. "Good. He owes me money."

"Then you can ask him about it when he wakes up."

The man snorted again, but then turned around and walked off. He walked like a bird, too, all stiff-legged and awkward.

"Pah, I would have very much liked those cards. Joy could have used the toxin, too," Brixaby said.

With a shake of his head, Arthur turned to him and spoke quietly. "I couldn't let anyone know what our powers are. Plus, Lopez and his men will be scanning everyone to make sure no one sneaks extra cards away. You think they won't notice if I suddenly have three more cards and Bradley has none?" That didn't even cover the fact he couldn't put those cards in his heart or shattered card anchor.

"Yes, yes, well, Lopez should give you all the cards you want for doing his job for him," Brixaby said, loud enough for one of the undersheriffs to hear.

Then he moved off to help harvest cards from the scourgling corpses.

Arthur stayed put under the guise of guarding Bradley. The truth was, he thought he might lose consciousness if he moved around too much.

Arthur kept his aching arm carefully at his side, resisting the urge to cradle it. Risking a glance down at the inside of his wrist, he saw that the ink from the tattoo was being ejected from his skin, forming pinpoints of black that smeared like blood. At least the bleeding had stopped, but what was going to happen to the cards within?

It took another solid half hour to harvest the rest of the corpses in the pit. They made a grim discovery of a layer of Rares that had been lying in wait, using the bodies of Commons and Uncommons to hide. They had died there, poisoned by Bradley's very thorough toxic gas.

Every scourgling—and there had been hundreds of them, including the Commons and Uncommons—had at least one card shard. Most had harbored multiple. And a smaller fraction of those had full cards. In total, there had been thirty-one Rare scourglings, and each of those had a full Rare card in them, along with several shards apiece.

It was quite the haul.

The full count came to ninety-five cards available for the auction. That meant there were more cards than people present.

Every adventurer would receive two Rare card shards as part of their pay.

Once things were counted up, Lopez explained the rules:

It was to be a silent auction, which Arthur had never heard of but didn't seem to surprise anyone else. Adventurers would write down their names and bids beside each card they desired. This transparency allowed everyone else to see everyone else's bid and to outbid one another.

As for what they'd be bidding? Each adventurer would be allotted ten points, and the bids had to be made in full points. No halves or quarters.

Some of the solo adventurers argued that it should be ten points per team because otherwise it let large teams, like the Lightning Cats, pool together their points.

Lopez firmly disagreed and said the rules were city standard.

Arthur was personally happy about that because it meant he and Brixaby would have twenty pooled points to work with.

The final rule was the hardest for him to swallow:

All bids were final.

The top bid had their points locked in, to prevent overbidding.

"You know the city-state rules," Lopez said, casting a stern eye around the adventurers. "If you're found to be overbidding with points you don't have, you forfeit all cards, and the city-state gets it to keep the next guy in line from overbidding. So, if you want that card, be smart. Any questions?" He didn't wait even a fraction of a second. "No? Then get to it."

That caused a few chuckles to ripple through the group, but most people were interested in what they were about to bid on.

Arthur was, too. And extra fortunately, Bradley had started to wake up. Arthur was more than happy to dump him, groggy and rubbing at his chest, on the undersheriffs, while he browsed the cards with Brixaby.

Trying not to clutch at his still-throbbing arm, Arthur and Brixaby moved through the crowd. By this time, his head pounded in sync with his arm, likely due to clenched muscles.

He'd hit **Pain Resistance 5**, which helped.

The cards themselves were wide ranging, and the majority held little interest for either of them. Especially the body-modification cards, which attracted the most attention from the others.

Arthur skimmed the cards, picking up titles and a few pertinent details. By the end, he'd sorted out a few favorites.

> **Thief Mask** (Uncommon) Created an illusion to change one's facial appearance into something else.

> **Compost Mage** (Uncommon) Could slowly turn organic garbage products into something edible . . . though not necessarily something tasty.

> **Right Back at Ya** (Rare) A kinetic shield that reflected physical attacks with equal force.

> **Frostbane** (Rare) Enabled the wielder to shoot off waves of frost. Enemies in close proximity had a high chance of frostbite.

> **This Is My Last (Shot) Resort** (Uncommon) Allowed for dealing an impossible or highly improbable critical hit on an opponent. 24-hour cooldown.

> **What Was Once Broken** (Rare) Could instantly repair broken non-mechanical objects. Skill-based card, though the mana required was fairly high.

Rainbow Knight (Rare) Absorbed spectrums of light ranging from 10 to 750 nanometers and could shoot them out again.

All Glory to the Seed (Rare) Could force-sprout any seed, even a dead one.

Speed Reader (Uncommon) Allowed the ability to read at an accelerated speed. Skill.

"No smithing, nothing to do with chainmail at all," Brixaby said with clear disgust.

Arthur wasn't feeling particularly drawn to any of them.

However, he thought Cressida might get some good use out of the kinetic shield, especially if it could stack with her mana shield. And Horatio might be able to do something with that light-based card. They could be nice gifts for his friends once they arrived from their long journey.

Feeling slightly better about his plan, Arthur decided to bid.

The bids themselves were tacked up to a board someone had pulled out of their spatial storage. Each card had its own sheet of paper, and there were plenty of slim writing tools to place bids. Several of Lopez's deputies stood by to watch the process and verify the points.

Right Back at Ya was the more popular out of the two. Someone had already bid four points on it.

The Last Resort card would have been useful to Arthur with his Nice Shot card, but it was too rich for his blood, already up to eight points.

No one had bid on Rainbow Knight, however. Even though it was a Rare card.

Arthur put down six points on Right Back at Ya and four on Rainbow Knight.

Brixaby was mulling over What Was Once Broken when Claude arrived, smiling, and placed a full ten points on it.

Brixaby showed the man his teeth but had only been feeling half-hearted about the card.

"Let us look at the body-modification section," he said to Arthur.

That was by far the most popular with all the adventuring groups, and bidding was thick and fast, with a few cards already on their second page's worth of scrawled notes. Teams were pooling together resources for the best of these.

A speed-enhancement card seemed to be the focus for many.

Arthur's attention was drawn away by Brixaby's sudden purr of delight. "Ah! This one. I will have it!"

Intrigued, he stepped over to read the card his dragon was focused on:

Scales as Hard as Stone
Rare
Body Modification
The wielder of this card will have any bodily scales turn as hard and impenetrable as stone, without affecting flexibility, weight, or movement. Stone scales will have normal resistance against temperature and will not change color.

"This is perfect for me," Brixaby exclaimed loudly. "Why was this made from a scourgling and not a dragon?"

"I kind of want to see the scourgling that this came from," Arthur said, amused.

They walked back to the bidding board, and Brixaby let out an indignant squawk. "Who dared put four points on my card?"

With a flourish, he picked up a spare writing tool in his claws and wrote down a bold 5.

The moment he did, the man with the weird beak-like lips approached, looked at the paper, and then bid eight points.

"You don't even have scales," Brixaby pointed out.

In answer, the man rolled up a shirtsleeve, which was covered in mottled skin.

Brixaby made a dismissive sound. "That is lizard skin, not scales. This card will not work for you!"

"Well, I don't see your bid to top mine," the man said.

Arthur frowned. "Brix—"

But Brixaby had already moved and wrote down ten points.

He turned back to the beaked man with a smug expression.

"That's fine. I didn't want it anyway," the man said dismissively, and then walked away.

Had Arthur's arm not been burning with pain, he might have face-palmed. The man had just clearly egged Brixaby onto spending all his points. Likely, he'd been seeking revenge for not being able to harvest Bradley's cards.

However, Brixaby seemed pleased with his top bid, so Arthur kept his thoughts to himself.

And with that bid, they had used all of their points.

"Let's go," Arthur started to say, gesturing toward an open area to wait.

Just then, a commotion broke out.

A small, skinny man, who'd been one of the few besides Arthur and Claude without visible body modifications, had obviously captured the attention of the wrong people. Arthur didn't see the actual theft, but the man was trying to flee straight across the flat plain.

Knowing he had zero chance to escape, Arthur stood back and watched the show.

The thief sprinted across the flat gray soil at normal human speed. There wasn't a sense he was using any sort of body modification.

Brixaby snorted in amusement. And even though Arthur was feeling completely lousy, he smiled, too. He was halfway rooting for the thief, despite himself. He'd always had a soft spot for underdogs.

And it was clear that the man had absolutely no chance of getting away. Two of the Lightning Cats, including Jon, were fast on his heels. Unlike the thief, they had enhanced speed. Jon pulled out in front as if he wasn't wearing a good thirty extra pounds of chainmail armor.

He caught up with the man in no time flat, but just as Jon reached for him, something interesting happened.

The fleeing man *shifted* his position in space. Somehow.

No, that wasn't quite right. Arthur had a hard time understanding what he was seeing. It was as if for a moment, the man grew impossibly, illogically, irrationally flat. He was as tall as he'd been, and the same width. But there was . . . nothing to him at all. Jon's hand fell upon his shoulder but had nothing to grip onto.

Jon fell forward, completely taken by surprise, and the man ran on. With his second stride, he popped out of his odd flat state and became normal again.

"What happened?" Brixaby asked. "Was that an illusion?"

"No . . ." Arthur drew out the word because he was unsure himself. "I think he shifted some aspect of himself. He had height, and you could see him from the side, but he just became flat." He shook his head. "I think he bent reality somehow or . . . put himself into another reality?" He shook his head again.

Now he was intensely curious about what kind of card caused that to happen.

Also, how anyone planned to catch him. Maybe something as extreme as hiding all of the mass in your body had a cooldown.

But the thief pulled the same trick again and again whenever somebody caught up to him. They'd reach out for him, and suddenly there would be nothing to hold on to. The thief became thinner than the finest piece of silk.

Despite every attempt to stop him, the thief was getting farther and farther away. Arthur was just starting to wonder if he should send Brixaby after the man and see if he could dodge a Stunning Shout. So far no one had tried a ranged attack, but that would be the next step.

Then, to Arthur's surprise, one of Lopez's men actually managed the trick. He was one of the few with a horse, and he rode up beside the man while twirling a loop of rope over his head. He cast the rope out, and as he did, it took on a white glow of a card power.

As the thief made himself thin, the air around him suddenly flexed. His condition reverted back to normalcy, and the rope settled over him, tightening over his arms and torso in an instant.

Brixaby rumbled in pleasure. "Nullification magic."

Arthur trusted his dragon's judgment, considering that Brixaby's natural magic was also nullification. He likely felt the power in that lasso.

The thief yelped and tried to shrug the rope off, but the deputy dismounted his horse in a flash. With expert movements, he twisted the thief up in loops. The thief soon found himself hog-tied and tossed over the horse's saddle, being led back to the auction.

Everybody cheered and then was treated to a show as the man was scanned for cards he did not have in his registry.

"The heart deck is clear, but you have five cards in your anchor, and only registered two." Lopez tsked. "Give them over. All of them in your anchor tattoo."

"But I only took three," the man protested.

This caused a minor uproar in the crowd. It seemed most people assumed the man had tried to sneak away one card, or maybe some shards. Three extra cards got on people's nerves.

Lopez was less than sympathetic. "You know the rules. You steal, you forfeit the whole shebang," he said. "Don't make us have to kill you for them. You know the city administration won't care, and you'll be dead even if they did."

He flicked open a knife that had rune etchings engraved on it. The few runes Arthur identified from his enchanting book suggested that it was a knife made to cut through all types of personal shields. A nasty piece of work.

Arthur winced and resisted the urge to rub at his own painful card-anchor tattoo. At least the thief had been fortunate enough—or smart enough—that he hadn't put the stolen cards in his heart.

The thief whined a little bit about this not being fair, but he must have caught the looks of the people standing around. No one was on his side, and by some dark expressions, they wanted all of his cards.

Finally, he gave in, allowed himself to be untied, and sullenly removed five cards from his anchor.

Arthur hoped one was the thinning card, but it seemed that one lived in his heart.

The others were very interesting, though, and quickly sent an uproar through the rest of the adventurers because three of them were body-modification cards. One was an inner healing card powerful enough to reattach limbs.

Arthur was interested in an academic sort of way, but far more interested in the thief's two non-body-modification cards. One was a Feather Fall card, which was useful for somebody who regularly rode a dragon. It would be like having his own personal safety device. The last card made his heart sink to his toes.

Endless Grindstone
Rare
Utility
The wielder of this card will be granted the ability to pick up new crafting skills at a vastly accelerated rate, with the chance to learn the basics of a new skill by casual observation reduced to one in three. The wielder will be able to learn these and previous skills 50% faster.

This card was perfect for him. But he had spent all of his points. And by the way everybody was gathered around the body-modification cards, no one would be outbidding him soon, freeing up those points again.

He was not the only one with this problem, and several yelled out to Under-sheriff Lopez to wipe all of the bids clean and restart the auction entirely.

"I wouldn't have bid if I knew there was a body-regeneration card on the line," someone said.

"Well, maybe you shouldn't have jumped first and thought later," a woman sneered at him, then went forward to the new bidding sheet and wrote down points for the healing card.

Lopez's expression was hard. "The rules were explained from the very start. In fact—" He would have said more but was drowned out by loud exclamations.

"That's not fair!"

"I bid before we saw these cards!"

"This is a conspiracy!" a third person yelled, without basis. But Arthur understood the sentiment.

I wouldn't have bid either if I knew there were better ones coming, he thought in frustration, looking back at the card. Everybody was so focused on the body modifications that no one had given the skill card more than a glance. Maybe Claude would understand the value of something like this . . . Or perhaps not. Did his kludging power fall under crafting?

Lopez had gone red in the face and raised his voice. "In fact," he said again, "to ensure there will be no more surprise cards, I'm ordering another rescan of everybody in the auction."

This quieted people down suspiciously fast, and a wave of angry grumbling went through the crowd.

Arthur suspected that the thin man wasn't the only one who'd kept extra cards while harvesting.

He didn't care. He was hurting, and now he was angry he didn't have a single point to put forward.

"I need that card," he told Brixaby.

His dragon growled under his breath. "If not for you, this silent auction would not be possible. You ought to have been awarded above everybody else."

That was a dangerous way of thinking, but Arthur didn't correct him because he was feeling sorely put out. He'd thought the same thing but kept quiet for the sake of peace. Now he felt like he was being cheated out of the card that was meant for him.

On top of that, more than a few people glared at Arthur, as if he were at fault for Lopez's hard-nosed decision.

Arthur was just sick of it. He wanted to go back to the city and get medical help for his card-anchor tattoo, then find a bed and sleep for a week.

But I'm not leaving without that card, he thought, and nodded to himself. He'd tried to be moral, but he'd reached his limit.

A plan brewed in his mind, and returning the angry glares with equal vengeance, he stepped up to be the first to be scanned for extra cards.

Brixaby, following his cue, was right behind him.

It was done quickly, and the undersheriff in charge of the scan nodded and recorded that neither Arthur nor his dragon had extra cards.

Seeing Arthur fall in line caused many other people to do the same. Arthur casually wandered back to where the cards were laid out, as if he was giving them an extra look. Still, no one seemed to notice or care much about the Grindstone card. Arthur suspected the crafting aspect turned people off.

Arthur mentally swapped out his classes, which was an aspect of his Master of Skills card. He swapped out Gambler for Thief.

He glanced at Brixaby, who was watching him curiously, knowing that Arthur was up to something but not sure what.

"Cover for me," Arthur said.

Brixaby didn't ask any questions, just subtly expanded his size, lifting his wings to provide more of a screen between Arthur and any watching deputy.

Turning, Arthur kept an eye on the people being scanned, using his **Acting** skill to keep his face neutral, even though his heart was beating hard and his arm throbbed worse than ever from unconscious tension.

Meanwhile, the atmosphere among the rest of the adventurers was turning sour, with more people objecting to being scanned.

So there wasn't too much of a surprise when someone tried to pull a trick out of desperation.

"Hey! Those two are swapping cards between one another," one man yelled, pointing. Off to the side, a man who had just been scanned was receiving two cards from a woman who was about to get in line. They were caught at the worst moment possible, with the cards visible between their hands.

And suddenly the crowd had a target for their anger.

A cry went up of "Cheaters!" Even though Arthur suspected a good handful were the pot calling the kettle black.

The crowd surged forward, quick to apprehend the two—and to get a good look at the new cards that were about to be put up for auction.

The two didn't even have a chance to try to escape before they were piled on. The deputies yelled out and rushed to restore order. For a few moments, it was a complete melee.

And Arthur knew it was his time to act.

He activated every relevant skill that he had, as well as concentrated on his Thief Class. Anything he thought would help, and there were a lot: **Stealth**, **Silent Movement**, **Heightened Awareness**, **Camouflage**, **Evasion**, **Deception**, **Concealment**, **Acting**, **Sleight of Hand**, and **Pickpocketing**.

To say that it hurt was a mild understatement. Waves of pain flashed from his arm to his very heart. For a wild moment, he had the urge to take a cleaver and just chop the limb off. That would be a relief.

Even Brixaby grunted, as if some of Arthur's soul-deep agony had reached out and touched him.

Arthur might've felt bad for it if he had any room in his mind for anything else. He had to clench his jaw to keep from screaming.

His **Pain Resistance** instantly reached level 6. That didn't take away the pain, but it gave him the extra edge he needed to work through it.

It was one of the hardest things he had ever done. Through watery eyes, Arthur took the two steps to the card. And under the cloak of all of his skills, he grabbed it.

He certainly couldn't put it into his card anchor, and he wouldn't risk shoving it into his heart. If they rescanned him, they'd know what he'd been up to. There was only one thing Arthur could do with the card. It turned out there was a point where he was willing to bend his morals, and this was it.

This is going to hurt, he thought, though he wasn't certain how he could possibly hurt any more than he already did.

Arthur consumed the card.

CHAPTER 20

Brixaby

When Arthur consumed the card, Brixaby felt nothing but pride that he was finally willing to embrace true power.

Well, there was the acute discomfort radiating from Arthur's side of their link. That wasn't exactly pleasant, but Brixaby knew he was only getting a small portion of what Arthur felt, so he could endure.

It lasted until the count of ten, right up until the moment every muscle in Arthur's body clenched up at once. The pain from their link sharpened. Arthur let out a strangled sound, and then he completely collapsed.

"Arthur!" Brixaby reached for him and managed to half catch him in his claws just in time to keep his rider's head from striking the ground.

"Arthur!" Laying his rider down, he frantically focused inward to check the link that tied Arthur's heart deck and his core.

The link was strong, and Brixaby let out a breath. Whatever was wrong with Arthur's card-anchor space had not affected his heart deck. The cards were whole.

That meant the rest of him would be fine, right? Brixaby didn't know much about how humans worked, but dragons were built around their core cards. It should be the same.

By now, the deputies had caught the two thieves and managed to restore some order. People had noticed there was something wrong with Arthur.

"What's wrong with him? Did something happen?"

Brixaby looked up to see Jon of the Lightning Cats had come over. That odd Claude man stood not far away, too, looking concerned.

Brixaby thought quickly. "He was more injured by the toxic gas than he wanted others to believe. It's caught up to him." Which irked him to say because Arthur had taken down that toxic gas man quite handily. Nearly as good as Brixaby would have, if had he done it.

Jon frowned. "We don't have any healers here—look at his arm. He's bleeding."

Jon bent down to check, but Brixaby would have none of that. He thrust his head forward, knocking him away.

"I will attend to my rider," he said, partially because he didn't want anyone who was unskilled in the ways of healing touching Arthur, and partially because he didn't want Jon to get a close look at Arthur's shattered card-anchor tattoo.

However, the catlike man was correct. Arthur's arm was coated in fresh blood. There was no visible wound: It bubbled up from his pores and wept openly close to his tattoo.

Concerned, Brixaby sniffed him over. Why wasn't he waking up?

He smelled only the mild iron tang of human blood, and . . . something else.

Startled, Brixaby flicked his tongue out to taste the air—not around Arthur's arm but the gray scourge-dust that it lay on.

There was something he had not noticed here. Something that should not be. Something . . . that would have to wait.

He leaned back and saw that he had attracted more of a crowd.

"I must get my rider to a hospital," he announced.

"Can't you store him the same way Arthur stored those other injured people?" the Kludger man asked.

Brixaby shot him a narrow-eyed look, disliking how observant the man was. He had correctly guessed he and Arthur could share the same card power.

"I need permission, and clearly," he said with a snarl that was half frustration, "Arthur cannot give it."

"The boy is breathing," Jon said carefully, "but if you two leave, things may get dicey around here."

As if Brixaby cared.

However, someone had called over the sheriff who'd been busy with the would-be thieves. Brixaby did not want that man to come over here because there was a chance he would notice that the Endless Grindstone card was gone.

Yes, they could scan Arthur and not find it, but it would not take a genius to put two and two together.

He looked at Jon. "You will guard my rider." Then he turned to stride back over to where the cards were being displayed for the auction. People quickly stepped out of his path.

Brixaby glanced over the cards, double-checked that he and Arthur still had the top bids for the three cards. Then he took them.

"Hey, wait a minute there," the deputy guarding the station said.

Brixaby ignored him as well. He turned to see Lopez striding up.

"What are you doing? Bad, uh, dragon! Put those down!"

Brixaby turned to him with a snarl, showing every one of his teeth. "People have had ample time to place their bids. If you had a brain cell under that overly large hat, you would conduct a second auction with the cards you just recovered, and all the other thieves you will find here."

Lopez drew up short and glanced at Arthur as if unsure if he was feeding lines to his dragon, unconscious or not. "This auction is over when I say it's over."

Brixaby drew himself up. He was not a large dragon, but his sinuous neck gave him height, and he took pleasure looking down his curved nose at the man. "The only reason you were able to do this is because my rider did your job. And now he has been injured for it. So *I* say when this auction is over."

Brixaby's Stunning Shout was a skill-based ability, and he had recently reached level 7. Each level allowed him a little more finesse and control over it. He added a touch of that shout to his last few words, and they rolled over the entire crowd.

All conversation stopped, and everyone's eyes turned toward him.

Brixaby held up the three cards. "These were won fair and square in your silly little auction. Who challenges me on this? Step forward!" he announced as he spread all four wings in an impressive display.

The humans exchanged looks with one another, and Brixaby almost hoped someone would step forward. He was exceedingly worried for his rider and wanted to take that out on someone.

There was a beat of silence then the Kludger man spoke up.

"What cards did you win?"

"Rainbow Knight, Right Back at Ya, and Scales as Hard as Stone." After Brixaby spoke, there was a noticeable relaxation among the others. They did not want those cards.

Well, they were fools, because he had clearly picked the best of the sorry group, and Arthur had chosen the second best for Brixaby's retinue.

"Fine. Take your cards and get out of here," Lopez said, as if he had to give permission. "And don't think I won't be reporting this."

"Do that," Brixaby said. "I will issue my report first. Do you think your words will fly faster than a dragon?"

Then, dropping back down to all fours, he deliberately shouldered past the man, knocking him down, and went back to his rider.

Jon stepped to the side to let him past. The Kludger, however, was looking back at the tables at the space where the Endless Grindstone card should have been. He was frowning.

Well, he might have figured it out, but as he had absolutely no proof, Brixaby didn't care.

Throwing the cards into his Personal Space to deal with later, Brixaby bent to carefully pick up his rider. Then he buzzed straight up, uncaring that the backwash sent scourge-dust everywhere.

Those people were not his problem anymore.

Flying like this was awkward and uncomfortable. Arthur's weight in his arms unbalanced him, and he had to beat his front pair of wings exceedingly fast to keep from falling forward.

But he was a purple dragon. He was built for agility and speed.

New skill gained: Flying Rescue (Flight Class)
Due to your card's bonus traits, you automatically start this skill at level 3.

"I have saved people before, including Arthur," Brixaby snapped to Arthur's ridiculous card. "Why did you not grant me the skill until now?"

Since it was a card, it did not answer.

Brixaby supposed it may be because a skill needed several repetitions to stick.

Brixaby flew toward where the sun was setting, following it and the smell of growing green things, which would lead him to the direction of the city. He set the fastest pace that he could. There was still an alarming amount of blood dripping off Arthur's arm, and he had not so much as fluttered his eyelids.

So Brixaby transferred his concern into speed.

Though he hated to admit it, he was also somewhat embarrassed. This was the second time in three days that he had brought Arthur to the hospital in dire straits.

If this kept up, people were going to think he did not take proper care of his rider. What would Joy think of him?

Once he reached the city, he located the hospital, which had a conveniently flat-topped roof on which to land.

Brixaby touched down. And, turning, he slammed his tail against the door that provided rooftop access.

It had been recently repaired from the other day when he'd done the same thing. But repairs could not hold against his might.

Unfortunately, the stairwell was . . . a tight fit.

He was forced to suck in his ribs and tuck his wings to fit in. After he reached the first door inside and knocked it open with the top of his head, he took a breath. And then with Stunning Shout–laden power, he spoke.

"Marion! I demand that you come tend to my rider at once!"

CHAPTER 21

Brixaby

So, you're telling me you do not have the skills to fix my rider?" Brixaby asked in a dangerous tone.

"What I'm saying," the healer said slowly, as if Brixaby were a beast and unable to understand, "is that we have given him several health potions, and cast several revitalization spells, but it appears this young man has shattered his card anchor. The trauma is in his *soul*, and that will take some time to recover from." He paused and then went on, again, as if Brixaby were slow. "A card anchor is not like a heart deck. It is only *attached* to the soul, not part of it. And he was lucky because this anchor was at least attached competently. But it's gone now, and unfortunately, I don't know the state of the cards within."

Brixaby growled under his breath and flexed his claws. He longed to rip out the Rare cards he felt in the healer's own heart deck, consume them, and then try to heal Arthur himself.

But he had been close enough when the healer cast the spell to copy them using his Counterfeit Siphon card.

The man had used a revitalization spell called Full Body Rebalance, which had visibly closed Arthur's remaining minor wounds, rehydrated him, and restored his natural energy.

Brixaby knew this much because he had cast it himself when no one was looking. Arthur still hadn't woken.

"Is he in danger?" Brixaby demanded.

"No," the healer said with clearly stretched patience. "As I *just* said, physically he is a healthy young man. But he must rest and recover from this ordeal to his soul. Hopefully when he wakes, he'll have the ability to reattach another card anchor. But that will require a heart deck specialist, which I am not."

"Then go fetch one," Brixaby said.

The man gave him a very unimpressed look. "Not until he rests. Now, while I'm sure your rider is very important to you, I have other patients to attend to—people *you* pulled me away from when you entered the hospital bellowing like the world was on fire."

Brixaby's bellowing had worked very well and gotten them a room immediately. The same room as last time, in fact.

Brixaby showed his teeth to the man. "Then if you are going to leave to attend to other patients, I insist that your assistant stay here and attend solely to my rider."

The healer's face scrunched up in distaste, but he nodded.

"Very well, then, but that will cost extra."

"I don't care about your costs," Brixaby said.

"No," said the assistant Marion, who had taken a seat nearby and was reading a book, "but your rider might."

The healer looked like he was getting a headache. "Marion, sit with the dragon rider, though by the first card in my deck, you could be doing more important things . . ." He continued grumbling as he made his way out.

The door closed, and Marion looked at Arthur, then at Brixaby. "So, what really happened?"

"What do you mean?" Brixaby snapped, wings flaring.

He shrugged. "It's just that with Arthur, things are always more than what they seem."

Brixaby hissed under his breath in irritation before he spoke. "My rider took on the duty of your so-called undersheriff to resolve a situation, but unfortunately, it damaged his card anchor."

"By overstuffing it with cards, right?" Marion shook his head and then pushed up his glasses. "That's the usual way it happens, and if people know that, they'll think Arthur was trying to steal extra cards."

"That is not what happened," Brixaby said quickly.

Marion shrugged and picked up his book, though Brixaby could tell he still had half his attention on the sleeping Arthur.

Brixaby looked down at his rider who was now cleaned of blood but was sleeping peacefully. This was becoming an unfortunate habit.

"You," he said to Marion, "will make my rider as comfortable as possible."

"He's sleeping. He couldn't be more comfortable."

"And when he wakes," Brixaby continued, "you will give him more of that food. Perhaps that chili in a bread bowl he enjoyed so much. And fruit. Fruit is good for humans."

This made Marion look up from his book. "You sound like you're leaving." He sighed. "You really are a dragon with a mind of your own, aren't you?"

"I have business," Brixaby said shortly. "Not that it concerns you. Your task is to ensure Arthur wants for nothing until I return."

"What busin— Never mind." He put down his book with an exasperated sigh and looked at Brixaby with an expression that Brixaby couldn't exactly read. "You know," he said, "I was once in competition for your egg."

Brixaby knew that already. Though his hatchling memories were blurry, he thought he had vague memories of Marion. Certainly a much sharper memory of the taste of the Time card he'd had in his heart. It was where Brixaby had received his danger sense.

"I would not have picked you," he said sharply.

"I didn't think you would. If I had wagered money on it, I would have thought you would take Penn Rowantree."

Brixaby sneered. "That *worm*? Never." Though, if he was being honest, he had thought Penn had been a slight possibility as a hatchling. But he had only been minutes old at the time and hadn't known any better. Arthur was a much better choice.

"The *worm* had one powerful card, true, but Arthur had two," he said with pride.

"Yeah, another secret he managed to keep from everybody." Marion frowned and looked at the door. "You know, the healer wasn't kidding. Another night in the hospital, me playing babysitter, and a heart deck specialist? This is really going to cost."

He made a dismissive noise. "Take care of my rider. I will take care of the cost," he said, then used his dexterous claws to open the door.

There were people in official uniforms standing not far away. From their sudden guilty expressions, it looked like they were mid-gossip. They saw Brixaby and quickly beat a retreat the other side of the hallway.

Brixaby again went to the stairwell and up to the rooftop. There were some men who appeared to be readying themselves to fix the door to the rooftop again, as it was off its hinges. One had his hand on the wall nearby and was visibly repairing the wood using a card power.

Uncaring, Brixaby started to push past them.

"Hey, now wait a minute here," one started to say. "You can't keep busting through this door. It's a safety hazard. Other people have to use it!"

Brixaby had never seen any other people come through this door, though he supposed that since this was a hospital, it might be better if the doors were not constantly broken open. "Then simply make this door larger next time," he told them, then paused to consider. "Actually, make it as large as you can because when I come back later, I may be bigger than I am now."

The man started to sputter something, but Brixaby shouldered past him again and banged the door open—which, as the hinges were currently being worked on, fell completely off.

Once out on the open roof, Brixaby immediately took off into the sky.

He gained more and more altitude, past where he thought he might ever take his rider. During his abbreviated classes back at Wolf Moon Hive, he had learned that unless humans had a body-modification card, they could not breathe the thin air as dragons could.

Unencumbered and riderless, he could climb as high as his four wings could take him. That way his form would be lost to those looking up from below. He would be tinier than the tiniest sparrow and unseen against the sky.

Up high, the sky grew curiously darker, and the great bright horizon beyond had a curve to it. He wondered vaguely if Joy and Sams would be visible beyond that curve, but as much as he focused, he could spot no signs of other dragons.

A whole kingdom without dragons. That was indeed a sad thing.

Once he had reached the appropriate height, he started toward the eastern Interstate. He kept an eye down and caught the slow train of adventurers and deputies making their way back from the scourgling nest.

He didn't know if the adventurers had decided on another method to distribute the cards after he and Arthur left, or if the sheriff had managed to keep his hold on power. Either way, most of the people seemed to be alive. He supposed that Arthur would be grateful to hear that, at least.

He felt another twinge of guilt that his rider was, once again, resting in the hospital. Well, hopefully this discovery would make Arthur happy when he awoke.

The former nest was easy to spot, looking like a darker crater on the featureless desert surface. Brixaby descended slowly, circling and looking around carefully for signs that any adventurers had noticed what he had and held back. Or that any scourgling had been missed.

His instincts were sharp and correct, of course. A Common scourgling, withered and wet with recent hatching, erupted out of the soil at the bottom of the pit as Brixaby watched.

It had barely taken its first glance of the sunset before Brixaby swooped down on it, bisecting it with his claws. He pulled out a Common card shard for his trouble. Flipping the shard into the air, he consumed it.

Now, Brixaby thought, throwing the carcass to the side, *how do I get down there?*

Unfortunately, without an earth card, it meant the hard way.

He hadn't picked up Arthur's knack of storing every conceivable item that might someday be of use into a storage space, but he had general tools. One of these was a trowel. Dragon wrists and shoulders did not work in the same way a human's did, so he could not dig and flip dirt over the side, but he could use his forelimbs and a tool to scoop.

He started at the point where the scourgling had crawled out, figuring that it had possibly made a path for him. They were already at the bottom of the pit, and therefore quite a ways from the surface.

Sure enough, several feet down, the hole opened into a wider cavern, and from it came the smell of scourge-rot.

Brixaby wrinkled his muzzle. It smelled too much like the free hive that had been taken over by the Mind Singer. But he sensed the presence of more shards down there.

This was what he had discovered when he had sniffed at Arthur's wound, the presence of shards, deep under the soil, lying in wait.

Brixaby kept on digging.

It didn't escape his sense of irony that had he been much smaller, squeezing into a small hole in the ground would have been no problem at all. On the other wing, he did enjoy being large enough to fly with Arthur.

Also, Brixaby fully expected that he would grow to an even larger—no, monstrous, no, stupendous size in due time, especially with enough cards to consume.

Brixaby continued to dig around the soil, cursing the fact that he lacked an earth card to expedite the process. Perhaps he should have stopped by the city to copy a spell from some kind of earth user.

Well, there was always next time. He doubted that this was the only nest in these cursed lands.

Eventually, by chipping away at the hard-packed soil and taking small breaks to breathe clean air—the smells coming out of the nest were truly foul—he widened the hole enough to peer inside.

"I need a light," he grumbled, reaching into his Personal Space for an oil-soaked rag and a torch. He was a dragon who had leveled up his chainmail skill to its maximum without a class. Of course he knew about using forges and how to start a fire.

With the lit torch gripped in his claws, he entered the depths. What he found was . . . interesting.

The scourgling nest was aptly named in every sense of the word.

He had dropped into a tunnel, its walls coated in a glowing blue light—some sort of mold that glowed dimly enough for him to make out shapes. There was no need for the torch after all. Quickly, he stuffed the lit thing back in his Personal Space, then looked around.

Clustered against the wall, resembling bunches of grapes, were wet ovals. He couldn't rightly call them eggs, for they lacked the appropriate outer shell. They were more like sacs, akin to frog spawn he'd seen a time or two in a pond.

Curiously, he reached out and skimmed the tips of his claws over the closest sac. It gave way instantly, and the half-formed creature inside tumbled out. It was so underdeveloped that it barely had a shape and died immediately. Brixaby drew out a Common shard from it.

"Interesting," he murmured, scaled lips curling back in an expression that was half snarl, half grin. This cluster was one of many in the tunnel.

The Mind Singer had farmed out dragon hatchlings for cards, and dragons newly born were far more self-aware than any of these scourge-spawn.

Perhaps it would be fitting, then, for Brixaby to return the favor.

CHAPTER 22

Arthur awoke with the strange feeling that everything under the surface of his skin was sore. Yet, as he shifted around in bed, he realized that it was deeper than muscle soreness. The odd, dull pain seemed to penetrate even past his heart.

Wait . . . he was in bed?

The last thing he remembered was the weird sensation of consuming the card. What had happened?

Even with his eyes closed, he must have made some movement or grimace. Or else there was an alert for when a patient returned to consciousness.

"Oh, good, you're awake," Marion's voice said with a very thick level of irony. Hadn't he said something like that before?

Opening his eyes, Arthur took a swift look around the room to confirm, yep, he was in the hospital. Also, Brixaby was nowhere to be seen. Though he felt the link between them was as strong as ever, so he wasn't overly concerned. He was probably just sleeping somewhere else.

From the dim light that filtered in through the window, it was just around dawn.

"How are you feeling?" Marion asked, this time putting down his book. He was probably concerned about Arthur's silence.

Arthur raised his hand. "I need a second."

Then, holding his breath—real and mental—he checked his version of Call of the Void.

Call of the Void
Legendary
Nullify
The wielder of this card has the ability to take another card of the same rank or lower from any deck. Once placed in a temporary deck, the new card's

aspects are slowly consumed and added to a list of ten removable/adjustable slots to grow the wielder's strength.
This list is not transferable and will dissolve upon the wielder's death or removal from the core.
This card is part of the Call set. Search out other cards in this set to add to your power.
Card Effects:
1/10
Endless Grindstone: The chance to learn the basics of a new skill by casual observation is 1:4, with a 33% overall accelerated rate of learning.

He had retained much of the card—not all of it, but the vast majority—probably because he had slept.

Wow, he thought, struck dumb. *This is really going to help.*

That was an understatement. This card represented a big boost to his already powerful Master of Skills.

Though he was struck with a pang of guilt that in doing so, he'd taken a card out of the world forever.

Maybe it would have been better just to stick it in his heart. Though, judging by how bad he felt . . . that would have been a very bad idea.

I'll just have to make sure I'm worthy of what I took, he thought, though it seemed like a thin justification.

Nearby, Marion was shifting around in his chair, looking more and more concerned with Arthur's silence.

Blinking, Arthur set aside the implications of the new boost in his skills for now and looked at him. "What happened?"

Marion's eyebrows shot up. "Well, your dragon said your card anchor was destroyed while fighting another card user, which is something I've never heard of before." He paused and added blandly, "The healer who attended you said it looked like your anchor was pushed beyond its limits to the point where it actually exploded. As I understand, the shrapnel hit your soul. So I'll ask again: How are you feeling?"

"A little like shrapnel hit my soul." Now that he was concentrating on it, his right side did feel worse than his left.

Lifting his arm, he looked at his card anchor. The skin had been cleaned of blood, but now only faint spidery lines remained of his tattoo.

"Don't try reaching for your cards," Marion said quickly, as if he'd read what Arthur intended to do. "Not until a heart deck specialist has examined you."

Heart deck specialist? That sounded serious, but also sort of interesting.

Arthur looked at him. "Can it be fixed? I've never heard of an anchor exploding."

"They do fail," Marion said, his tone grave. "Typically, the pain stops people from pushing them to explosion, though. Other failures usually happen when someone buys a cheap card anchor from some back-alley idiot or tries to do it themselves to save a few shards." He shook his head. "This isn't good, Arthur. The healer said it wasn't a coma, but it was close. You probably got lucky this time and didn't scar yourself, but only a specialist can say for sure."

"I . . . don't think I passed out because my card anchor exploded," Arthur admitted slowly, voice tinged with embarrassment. "I—well, I added something new to my heart deck *after* my anchor started to fall apart."

Marion exhaled sharply and then rubbed between his eyes like he was getting a headache. "You know, I had wondered if being a dragon rider would change you. If you'd become one of the elitists. But then I remembered all the stunts you pulled during that eruption. I think linking with Brixaby hasn't changed you one bit."

"Oh, ha-ha," Arthur said sarcastically, struggling to sit up. He managed it after a moment. "Where is Brixaby?"

"I'm not sure. He said he had some business to handle, and then he just left."

Either sleeping or trying to get his Chainmail Class, Arthur thought with fond exasperation.

"I'll have you know he made quite a scene coming into the hospital," Marion said. "Again."

Arthur shrugged at that because it was Brix. The dragon made a big scene when he couldn't get the right wellness on the meat he wanted.

"What happened with the rest of the adventurers?" Arthur asked. "Did they get back with the sheriff?"

"No idea. Though I haven't heard of any angry sheriffs beating at the hospital door and yelling your name, so they probably got back fine." Marion paused. "Soledad has found a position here, as a healer assistant as well. She checked in once or twice, and she wanted me to tell you that you were an idiot for getting hurt."

"She doesn't know what happened."

"She knows you took on too many scourglings at once and ended up back here."

"Brixaby and I already told you," Arthur said, annoyed, "it was another card user."

Marion looked unimpressed. "Yes, that's what you claimed. But what *really* happened?"

Arthur sighed. Okay, maybe Marion had a point.

"You know that in the kingdom there are people who stay on the outskirts of eruptions to see if they can hunt any scourglings that escaped the dragons or harvest dragon riders who fall?"

"I've heard of them. The vultures."

"Right, well here, there are no dragon riders. It's all vultures." He shook his head. "Someone with a toxic gas card tried to take all the spoils for his own, and the sheriff wasn't empowered enough to stop them."

Marion frowned, but he didn't look surprised. "Anyone who has any real power would already be an adventurer or a freelance crafter. Those with ambition but low or middling powers tend to go to government jobs."

"Which means the government here is barely in control," Arthur said.

Marion shook his head. "Maybe that's how it is outside the city, where there is no direct oversight. But make no mistake, Arthur, right now, the city's administration has never been more powerful. They get to lord access over the Dark Heart, and everyone knows it."

"That's another thing!" Sitting up straighter, Arthur grabbed his blankets. He sort of wanted to throw something. "Marion, we discovered a whole nest of scourglings. It was a fissure—practically a mini eruption—and I'm sure it led straight from the Dark Heart. They're flirting with a full-blown eruption here."

Marion's gaze snapped toward the window and the steadily brightening dawn, almost as if he was expecting to see a scourgling eruption at any point. It was peaceful outside, but his troubled expression remained.

"I confess that I haven't been able to get what Soledad said out of my head. What happened to her city . . ." He shuddered. "I don't miss my Time card. I really don't. But sometimes, I do wish I could still see the future."

Arthur nodded, feeling troubled, too. "I'd be happy if they opened the Heart tomorrow, but I'm still waiting for a couple of friends to arrive." He looked at Marion. "You're going down into the Dark Heart with me, aren't you?"

Marion seemed surprised. "You'd really have me?"

"Why wouldn't I?"

He put a hand over his heart. "Because I'm not a card user anymore."

Sympathy flashed through Arthur. He still felt lousy, but he couldn't imagine how having an empty heart deck must ache.

"You're my friend," he said simply. "I want you by my side. Also, tell Soledad she has a spot on my team, too."

"Wonderful, so you'll be carrying two deadweights." But despite Marion's words, his tone was unexpectedly light. Then he leaned forward and lowered his voice. "I still have the two you-know-whats."

The illusion card, he meant.

"Do you want it?" Arthur asked.

Marion leaned back with a deeper frown. "I don't know. My Time card was given to me because I was born . . . Well, you know the circumstances. But this time, I do want to earn my card. That was the whole point of this." He gestured around the hospital meaningfully.

"Think about it," Arthur said. "There's no rush."

"You think about it," Marion countered. "You're supposed to see a heart deck specialist today, and they are not cheap. That will be on top of another emergency visit and overnight stay." He sighed. "Arthur, you might have to sell you-know-what just to clear your debts."

CHAPTER 23

"Y ou are a very, very lucky young man," the heart deck specialist said gravely, looking down at Arthur through a pair of spectacles he had perched on the end of his nose. "I have seen a card-anchor failure of this magnitude kill people, or else damage their heart deck so badly they were never able to use a card again."

"That hasn't happened to me," Arthur said. He knew that for a fact, because while he was still weirdly sore in that indefinable way he couldn't quite put his finger on, it wasn't as bad as it had been even a few hours before. But mostly, it was that his Counterfeit Siphon card had copied several of the man's diagnostic spells—all Rare—that had been cast over him.

Unfortunately, because they were spells and not skills, he couldn't keep them.

But they had been copied just fine, and it felt like he'd be able to use them if he wanted . . . if he dared risk it.

Arthur had also been worried that the specialist would be able to sense the Legendary cards in his heart deck. If he had, though, he said nothing about them. In fact, all his attention was focused on Arthur's card anchor.

"No," the specialist agreed heavily. "As I said, you were unfathomably lucky. Though . . ." He had grabbed Arthur's arm upon his first examination and hadn't given it back yet. He bent down to examine the anchor so close that his nose almost brushed the inside of Arthur's wrist. "Unfortunately, it seems that the structural integrity of this card anchor is gone."

"Can you fix it?" Arthur asked.

The man snorted and straightened to look at him. "Fix it? No, the anchor is well beyond that. And I would recommend that you never add another one of these things to your body again."

"*Never?*" Arthur asked, his voice rising in an undignified squeak. He was glad that Marion had been kicked out of the room the moment the specialist entered.

The specialist gave him a hard look. "Card anchors are, as far as I'm concerned, a workaround to a perfectly natural and balanced system. Anchor failure is distressingly common—not that anchor salespeople will ever admit it. You should be happy with the cards you have in your heart—and from what I can feel from the power of you, you've got quite a lot. It must be nearly full." He reached out and poked Arthur on the chest, right over his heart. "My suggestion would be to develop these and stop worrying about what else you can collect."

"I'm going into the Dark Heart. I'll need every advantage that I can get," Arthur said firmly.

"For more cards, right?" The specialist rolled his eyes to the ceiling. "Don't get me started on that nonsense, either. People get themselves killed every single time. And for what? We have perfectly functional cards available for sale from the city. But no, people aren't happy with that. They always want *more.*"

The man's screed reminded Arthur of Red, his former caravan master. The man had very strong feelings about card users in general, and also thought that having cards went against the general order of the world.

Arthur hadn't listened to Red, either.

"What happens if I add another card anchor?" he asked bluntly.

The specialist scowled and then admitted, "It should be possible, eventually. Though I cannot recommend against it strongly enough. Give it a long rest before you do—as in a year, at least."

Arthur opened his mouth to object: *A year?!*

But the man spoke over him. "And if you don't listen to my good advice and do it anyway, then for the sake of your first card, add it to your *other* arm. Don't be an idiot and add it to your neck, your forehead, or wherever else your pigheaded generation thinks is 'cool' nowadays." He made air quotes around the word *cool.* "You're lucky you didn't lose your hand when your card anchor failed. Imagine what would happen if one on your neck exploded." His voice had risen to a near shout. "You'd lose your fool head, that's what! Or come away with brain damage. So put it on your arm or your big toe, and I hope for your sake it's the one you like the least."

Arthur nodded, figuring this was good sense. He wasn't sure how he'd look with an anchor tattoo in the middle of his forehead anyway.

"I can't access the cards inside my anchor. What's happened to them?"

"Well, now." The specialist leaned back in his chair and folded his hands in his lap. "That's an interesting question. Some scholars say that the cards will eventually be returned to the world. I think this has some merit, as every conceivable spell or magical ability has been put into cards, so it's reasonable to say nothing can truly be lost—"

"I mean," Arthur said dryly, "how can I get them back out?"

"They're gone, foolish boy," the specialist said harshly, taking Arthur aback. "They were likely shattered along with your card anchor and are now spinning off into the void or wherever it is all good cards go when they die."

"But—" Arthur sputtered. "But—"

"Better than rotting in your arm, I'd say. Card anchors are meant to shatter like that. At least, the good ones are." Seeing Arthur's stunned expression, his attitude eased. "I'm sorry. I'm sure that represented a good deal of wealth to you, but it's the risk we all take with card anchors." A bit of sarcasm crept back into his voice. "Surely the person who gave you the tattoo told you there were some risks involved."

"No," Arthur said. Then, "What other risks?"

"Well, what did you think would happen if, say, you got in a knife fight and the lines of the anchor were slashed? Or cooking? Yes, I see those little burn marks on your fingers. Or simple sun damage. Moles happen, you know."

Arthur was briefly struck dumb. "I never considered that."

"Well, maybe you should," he said shortly.

With a sinking feeling, Arthur was starting to understand what the specialist meant when he said he'd been very lucky.

He looked up at the man. "What now?"

"I can tell you that the worst has passed, and you should have access to the abilities in your heart deck. Though I would suggest waiting a couple of weeks to let everything settle down again."

That wasn't going to happen.

The specialist continued, "I would suggest you see another specialist outside of this particular hospital. He's a man who deals with the loss of heart decks, but I think his advice could help you, too. He also deals with the rearrangements of decks."

"Rearrangement?" Arthur asked.

"He'll explain it to you. Here, let me give you the address." He pulled out a bundle of loose papers, scrawled down the directions, and then handed it to Arthur. "Now, do you have any additional questions?"

Arthur shook his head. He just felt numb.

With a nod, the specialist let himself out of his room.

Arthur looked out the window, then down at the thin remains of his card anchor. He felt like he had just lost a few friends. Worse than that, he felt like he had *failed* people, including Valentina, who'd given him several of the cards in his anchor.

In some ways, he was going to have to start over from scratch. Though he knew he could do it, he certainly wasn't that young boy anymore from a borderland village, too naive to know what he wanted to do was too daunting to be realistic. But then, against all odds, he'd managed to anyway.

He'd managed it because of his cards.

It's not as bad as it could have been, he told himself. *It's my anchor, not my heart.*

Marion had given up all the cards in his heart and he was functioning just fine. His father had raised Arthur not only after the loss of his cards but also after he lost his wife and Arthur's sister.

Arthur could be strong. He could get through this.

But he felt the loss all the same.

With a sigh, he stuck the note with the directions in his pocket.

That was when Brixaby burst in.

"Excellent, you are awake," he said. "Have you paid the bill yet?"

"With what?" Arthur asked dryly, and made a show of patting his pockets. "I don't have any spare cards on me, and I'm not taking back what I gave to Marion."

Ignoring his sarcasm, Brixaby reached into his Personal Space and started spilling out card shards. There were dozens.

"Brixaby," Arthur said slowly, "tell me you didn't rob a card store."

The dragon snorted down his long nose. "Of course not. I simply went back to the scourgling nest and *properly* harvested it."

Then, to Arthur's amazement, his dragon explained how he had smelled the shards and had gone back to dig down to find scourglings and scourge-spawn developed enough to provide this bounty.

"No full cards, though," Brixaby admitted. "And only one Rare shard out of the rest."

"This isn't good," Arthur muttered, then checked himself. "I mean, you did very well, Brixaby. But the fact that scourglings are still developing underground on their own . . . I thought nothing could survive in the deadlands."

"I believe that the nest is being fed from the Dark Heart somehow," Brixaby said. "It is as if the Heart is a mushroom, and it is sending out spores."

That was much more poetic than Brixaby usually got. Arthur trusted his opinion, but . . . "But why the deadlands and not where there's still life?"

"Who knows? Now, tell me what has gotten you upset? Who do I need to kill?"

"No one," he said, because he knew Brixaby was not joking. "I just saw a card specialist, and the cards that were in my anchor . . . they're all gone. They were destroyed."

Brixaby snorted. "You can be foolish sometimes," he said grandly. "Show me your arm."

Hope lit like a spark from a dying fire. For some reason, he hadn't even considered he was linked to a dragon who could pull cards from people's hearts. Surely he'd be able to do the same for a card anchor.

Arthur extended his arm, palm up to his dragon.

Brixaby stared at it for a moment with unsettling concentration on his sharp face. Then he reached out with two pincerlike claws and . . . nothing.

He grabbed again, this time the tips of his claws lightly scratching Arthur's dead, scratchy tattoo.

Again, nothing.

That spark of hope began to dim.

"I can sense them. Barely," Brixaby said. "But there's not enough for me to grab onto."

"Do you think they're still whole?"

"I do, but . . ." Brixaby stared at his wrist with narrowed red eyes. "I cannot quite get a grip on them."

"There has to be some way," Arthur growled under his breath. Then he stilled as an idea struck him.

Brixaby noticed at once. "What is it?"

Arthur didn't respond. His mind was too full, racing with excitement. He hadn't thought of that particular skill in a while, not since he'd linked with Brixaby.

It was a ridiculous cheat. Too good to be true.

And yet . . .

Arthur placed two fingers on his broken card-anchor tattoo and concentrated hard on his **Card Shuffling** skill. He narrowed his focus to the task of withdrawing a card from the card anchor.

Slowly but surely, his fingers came away with the healing card, Moderate Self-Repair.

As he lifted it out, he felt as though something was physically removed from him. He lifted the healing card fully away, but as he did, he became unexpectedly out of breath.

"How did you do that?" Brixaby demanded, then sat back as realization dawned. "Of course. You accessed my Call of the Void card."

"No," Arthur said with a half laugh. He flicked the card at Brixaby playfully. "I used my **Card Shuffling** skill."

"That . . . that's ridiculous," Brixaby said.

But Arthur wasn't listening. He concentrated on pulling out another card: Mana Amendment. Then 20-Point Spree, Mana Vault, and The Perfect Snip.

Soon, all his cards not in his heart deck were spread out over the bed, and he was completely exhausted.

Other than getting the cards back, the only positive was losing Mana Vault didn't relock his mana away from him. He now had other cards that granted the use of mana such as Nice (Metal) Shot and Counterfeit Siphon.

However, Mana Vault allowed him a larger use of mana as he had consistently leveled that card up. Now all the progress was lost.

And his heart deck was nearly full.

Counterfeit Siphon was a card linked with Brixaby, and as far as he could tell, that was outside the heart deck. It didn't take a slot.

Out of the ones that did take a slot as individual cards were Nullify, which went with Return to Start; Charming Gentle-Person; Phase In, Phase Out; Hey Man, Nice (Metal) Shot; Subtle Influence, and Makeshift Weaponry.

Then his Mental Bookshelf, Eidetic Memory, and Personal Space were three of a kind, so they only took up one slot.

Lastly, his Master of Skills and Master of Body Enhancement were paired, giving him a slot.

Nine slots full. One free.

With a sigh, he gestured to the cards. "Brixaby, can you hide these? I think . . . I think I need to take a break."

Brixaby grumbled something under his breath.

"What was that?" Arthur asked.

"Why have you not developed a **Card Tricks** skill yet?"

"You mean, disappearing cards and then reappearing them like a street magician?" he joked.

But Brixaby looked completely serious.

Arthur took a breath, thinking. "When I discovered what it could do . . . so many things happened all at once. And your egg was found not long after."

"I see," Brixaby said. "Well, that is understandable, then. I would be much more of a distraction, and my ability comes from a card, which makes it superior overall. I doubt you could shuffle a card from someone's heart deck."

Arthur nodded and glanced down at the wealth in front of him. His cards, of course, but also the shards.

He looked at Brixaby. "There are more than enough shards here to form cards."

The dragon smiled evilly. "That was my thought, too."

CHAPTER 24

I'm sorry, sir, your bill is not entirely settled," the hospital billing lady said, sounding contrite yet painfully professional.

Word had apparently spread that Arthur was getting up to leave, because while the hospital billing lady who stood in the doorway was a diminutive woman, the two beefy guards at her side certainly were not.

Either they had chosen their moment well or were suspiciously lucky that Brixaby had taken himself to the rooftop to wait for Arthur's arrival.

Arthur scowled at her. "I was told that my earnings for helping the adventurers had already been confiscated and turned over to the hospital. That was two Rare card shards for myself and two for my dragon. Now you're telling me that you want more?"

"Yes, sir." She glanced down at her clipboard. "Your account indicates that you owe at least one more Rare card shard to settle the bill."

Arthur did have one more Rare card shard in his Personal Space, but he wasn't about to reveal that.

He considered for a moment. "What's the current exchange rate for Uncommon shards to a Rare?"

The woman nodded and quickly consulted a tablet that was etched with runes on the corner. Arthur saw that the numbers were constantly updating.

"It seems that twenty Uncommon shards equal one Rare at today's value."

Internally, he winced. Back home, it was about nine Uncommon shards to a Rare, depending on the shard. Corner pieces were much more valuable.

Things were getting more expensive in the city, and he suspected it had everything to do with the influx of visitors, all eyeing the Dark Heart.

The city set the prices of coins to shards and the rank value of shards. Unlike his home kingdom, those values changed day to day. Now it seemed they were getting greedy, knowing that the people inside the city had no choice but to pay.

But if he was being honest with himself, he knew he was getting off lightly. Sheriff Lopez had his private revenge by directing Arthur's pay straight to the hospital. But on the other hand, nobody had come to him for his official report, nor implied that he was in trouble with the authorities. Sometime after the heart deck specialist had left, a healer had even come in, very politely, to ask about the other adventurers that had been stored in Arthur's Personal Space. It felt to Arthur that they were waiting for the heart deck specialist to clear him before he was good to use his Personal Space card.

Arthur obliged and unstored them once there were healers standing by to take over.

Those poor men and women would have their own bills, and he did not envy them for it. They hadn't even gotten to participate in the silent auction.

So Lopez had his petty revenge, but it seemed to Arthur that they knew also to tread lightly around him and Brixaby. They were assets, and the city administration was also smart enough to know that both of them would make formidable enemies.

Last night, he and Brixaby had put enough shards together for two Commons and one Uncommon card. All were currently with Brixaby. None of the cards had been spectacular, and one had been a flat-out trash Common, but Arthur could probably use any of them to pay for his bill because full cards were certainly worth more than separate shards, with the exception of corner pieces. Arthur would much rather sell them to a card shop, or even a black market.

"Fine," he said shortly. "And Commons to Uncommons?"

"Eleven to one," she replied.

Arthur's jaw almost dropped. That was insane. It usually took around twelve shards to make a Common. It was almost as if the city was trying to force people to pay with full cards.

And there were still a few weeks to go before the Dark Heart opened. Things would only get more expensive from here.

He ended up paying in Uncommon shards, which pretty much cleared out the rest of his supply. But that was fine. He and Brixaby had a plan.

The lady counted them out, and the guards moved aside. Arthur rolled his eyes and left the room. Honestly, the presence of the guards was insulting, as if he would have tried to intimidate the woman.

In a foul mood, he stomped up the stairs a few levels until he got to the roof access. Brixaby was waiting out there, wings spread to take in the sunshine.

Arthur emerged, and Brixaby gave him a knowing look. "What delayed you?"

Arthur sighed. "It's a good thing we're going to refill our coffers."

"I don't know why you humored them. You are a dragon rider, and should be able to come and go as you please."

"Yes, but they might not heal me again, or you, if we snub them and then get hurt. Plus . . ." Arthur sighed and gave his real reason. "Brixaby, I'm tired of making enemies wherever we go. I am willing to play nice with this city's administration, at least until the Dark Heart opens."

"Yes, well, if you were playing *nice*," Brixaby said, giving him a significant look, "you would let them know about the bounty in the nests."

"I'm not that nice," Arthur said, and climbed onto Brixaby's neck.

They took off into the cloudless sky, and almost immediately, Arthur felt much better.

He'd been able to use his cards from his heart deck, just like the heart deck specialist said he could, but he hadn't been able to fully shake that odd feeling of soreness and discomfort. It was like an unreachable itch.

The specialist had mentioned that his soul had taken some damage, and Arthur hoped it was mostly superficial. How long would it take for something like that to heal?

Well, until he was certain, he probably shouldn't add any new cards to his deck. *And a year for another card anchor*, he thought with a sigh.

Brixaby had flown so high up that the city itself looked like a round bowl with a dark pit in the middle. Was it his imagination or was the pit . . . pulsing?

He blinked and shook his head. No, his eyes were playing tricks.

Reaching down, he touched his dragon's neck. Brixaby came to a stop in midair and hovered.

Arthur then focused through their link and accessed Call of the Heart, narrowing his desire to find more scourgling nests.

He and Brixaby had talked about this briefly. Brixaby had more experience with this sort of thing, and it was his card that sat in his core, paired with his Call of the Void.

But he had never canceled his previous query, which was to find something that they *needed*.

Cressida and Horatio were headed this way, guided by a map based on Brixaby's last search that led them here.

He and Arthur worried that if Brixaby searched out the nests themselves, it might interfere with that map.

So it was up to Arthur.

The response from the card was muddled at first, and the ache on his side and arm grew sharp with magical strain. Arthur refocused. It wasn't that his first question was too general, it was just that there were multiple nests dotted here and there. He could feel them through the seeker card.

That wasn't good.

Narrowing his focus even more to a needle point, Arthur concentrated everything he had on finding the closest scourgling nest.

Instantly, information flowed to him. "It's directly west," he told Brixaby. "Not too far away. Still in the deadlands, but within reach."

Brixaby took off with a buzz of wings, moving fast.

Arthur kept an eye on the ground, just in case someone had the bright idea to follow them. But Brixaby was moving so quickly that if anybody tried, they'd be very obvious matching them from the ground. Especially once they reached the deadlands, where there was nowhere to hide.

As they drew closer to the nest, Arthur saw there wasn't much to it. It was simply a hole in the ground with some tracks running to and from it.

Brixaby landed a little ways off, and Arthur carefully dismounted, bending to get a better look at the tracks. They were weirdly star shaped, but small, barely the length of his spread hand.

"Common scourglings, you think?" he asked.

"A minor nest," Brixaby agreed.

"Yeah, but there shouldn't be any nests at all." He stood with a sigh.

Brixaby rumbled in agreement. Together, the two of them approached the nest. Not a single scourgling peeked its head out of the hole.

"Do you think it's abandoned?" Arthur asked.

"No. They must sense the strength of our cards and are afraid," Brixaby said. "Allow me to demonstrate why they should be."

He stepped to the nest and inhaled deeply, his sides expanding. Then he stuck his head down the hole and unleashed the full force of his Stunning Shout.

Despite the fact that his head was underground and his voice was muffled, the shout's vibration resonated through the earth. Pebbles jumped and dust drifted upward, as if the area was experiencing a minor earthquake.

Suddenly, the ground forty feet to their left collapsed, creating a deep ditch.

Finishing his shout, Brixaby lifted his head, glanced at the newly formed ditch, and gave a swing of his tail that resembled a shrug.

They waited to see if anything would emerge, or if the rest of the ground would collapse out from under them. Commons weren't known to be smart enough to set traps, but Arthur didn't trust anything at this point.

But after a few minutes, there was no movement from the hole, and nothing further collapsed.

Arthur took out his shovel from his Personal Space and started to make the entrance big enough for both of them. Brixaby helped as best he could with a trowel and his claws.

"Too bad none of those Common cards were earth cards," Arthur muttered.

"You could not use them right now anyway," Brixaby said.

"I'm not waiting a year to get a new card anchor," he grumbled.

Eventually, the hole was large enough for both him and Brixaby to enter, if Brixaby kept his wings tucked tight to his sides.

Grabbing his sharpest kitchen knives and focusing on his **Butchering** skill, Arthur jumped into the hole. It was only about a ten-foot drop, and at the bottom, he found the bodies of several dead scourglings.

These weren't the bird-shaped ones they had encountered before. Instead, they resembled a disgusting type of mole, but hairless, with visible weeping sores and sharply pointed front teeth. They were visibly dead, with blood leaking from their ears, eyes, and mouths.

Arthur bent to harvest them and collected two Common card shards each from the first two, and one shard from the third.

Brixaby had described the nest he'd encountered before, and this looked very much the same. It was a tunnel tall enough for Arthur to walk in without ducking, if he kept an eye out for low areas. Along the sides and top were lines of the glowing blue luminescent mold, which provided just enough light to see by.

It also smelled even worse than Brixaby had warned him.

Arthur grabbed a rag from his Personal Space, soaked it in a bottle of vinegar he kept for basic supplies and disinfectant, then tied the wet rag over his nose. Vinegar wasn't exactly pleasant, but it was better than this.

"It might not be a good idea to stay here for very long," he said to Brixaby.

His dragon was busy wiggling down through the hole and snorted as he took in both the tunnel and Arthur's solution to the terrible smell. "I suffered no ill effects last time. It isn't like we'll stay here for months."

Not like those poor dragon mothers, Arthur thought, remembering the Mind Singer's hive.

Together, the two of them walked farther into the tunnel. Brixaby's Stunning Shout had shattered many of the egg-like sacs that clustered in bunches against the wall. Arthur busied himself with harvesting them and tried not to look at the dead infant scourglings too hard. All of the shards he collected were Commons.

There were a couple of adult scourgling bodies lying here and there, but to Arthur's eye, they didn't look particularly different from one another. There were a lot of eggs, but none of the scourglings looked pregnant.

How did scourglings even breed?

"What do you think?" Arthur asked. "Is there a mother scourgling? Or maybe a queen scourgling, like ants?"

"Who cares?" Brixaby said. "If there is a queen, I have killed it with my shout, or I will shout at it again and then kill it."

"Well, it's interesting," Arthur said. "No one really explores old scourgling eruption cones. Dragon hives are ancient. They've been cleaned out for centuries, maybe thousands of years."

"No one explores eruption cones because they are cursed places," Brixaby said with the logic of a dragon.

But he was right. Anywhere scourglings had concentrated would make people sick if they weren't carded. And if they *were* carded, they would be the first to be attacked if any scourglings were left. So exploring a more recent eruption cone was exceptionally risky.

Frowning, Arthur continued deeper into the tunnel. He passed more intact bunches of scourgling spawn, though none of the scourglings inside appeared to be alive. Nothing wiggled, and they all floated dead to the tops of their individual sacs. Brixaby's Stunning Shout had packed quite the wallop down here.

Was the mold growing brighter? It felt like it was, though it might be that his eyes were just growing more used to the dim light. Nevertheless, Arthur continued down the tunnel, deeper and deeper. No, the light was definitely growing brighter here.

"Arthur, you passed some without harvesting them," Brixaby said.

"I'll be back in a moment," Arthur called back.

He kept going. It felt like something was pulling him forward. No, that was too strong of a word. He felt like he was moving toward some larger core of power. The light was definitely getting brighter.

And at the very end of the long tunnel, he found a bundle of scourgling spawn that was significantly larger. It looked like half of the eggs were alive, as several creatures inside were twitching and wiggling, just visible within the thin coating.

Arthur pierced one with the tip of his knife, and a half-formed mole thing fell out, hitting the ground with a splat and dying immediately.

Bending, Arthur harvested it and came up with an Uncommon shard.

Around this bunch of spawn, the mold glowed brighter than ever. It covered the back wall entirely.

Frowning at the mold, Arthur muttered, "I don't understand . . ."

"What's that?" Brixaby asked, coming up right behind him and causing Arthur to jump. The dragon didn't notice and looked past him. "Understand what? That you found an excellent source of Uncommons here?"

"No," Arthur replied in frustration. "I don't understand why the nests are here at all. The sheriff said that new nests are an indication that the Dark Heart is ripening, so why aren't we seeing these nests in the regular land? *Nothing* grows in the deadlands, not even scourglings. But that's where these nests are."

Brixaby opened his mouth as if to reply, but then seemed to realize he didn't have an answer. "Does it matter? If these nests are indeed linked to the Dark Heart, it's good to plunder them while we can. Why are you overthinking it?"

"I just want to know why," Arthur said.

Brixaby looked at him for a moment, then shrugged, then started the grim work of harvesting the scourgling spawn.

Soon, the bunch yielded them thirty-five Uncommon shards, which wasn't a bad haul.

Brixaby looked back the way they came. "We should harvest the rest."

But Arthur was still staring at the mold splashed against the wall. "I wonder why it's brighter here," he muttered, and swapped out his knives for a pickaxe. He swung, using his **Pickaxe Proficiency**, and it bit in deeply. The soil crumbled away well when he withdrew the spike. The mold was a little brighter beyond.

Arthur swung again.

The soil crumbled away with each swing. He glanced back at Brixaby. "Keep harvesting. I'm going to see what's beyond this wall."

"More mold?" Brixaby asked.

Arthur ignored his sarcasm and swung again. After about a minute, Brixaby grew bored and went on to harvest the rest of the bunches that they had passed.

Arthur dug further, alternating between using the pickaxe and the shovel. He found that the mold actually went downward, and he followed it. After a while, he consulted a map he had stuffed in his Personal Space. Sure enough, this end of the tunnel pointed away from the city and the Dark Heart. So where was this line of brighter mold going? Maybe it led to another nest?

Arthur dug deeper. He felt like he was following a hidden path.

About five feet down and another five in, it occurred to him that maybe he should reinforce this tunnel to prevent a collapse. After all, the tunnel was already a good ten feet down by itself. That was a lot of soil that could come crashing down on him.

Just then, his next swing of his pickaxe struck something . . . different. Not as hard as a rock, but not soft, either.

Curious, he set the pickaxe aside and began to search around by hand. The tips of his fingers touched something different, something that should not be here.

"Brixaby, do you have a lit torch or something?" he called out.

"I'm surprised you don't, in your horde of things," Brixaby called back, but nevertheless returned with a lit torch in his claws.

Taking it, Arthur brought the torch close to the soil, brushing away more. Maybe he had struck a root? It seemed bigger than that, and what would a root be doing growing through the deadlands?

He brushed away more soil, then took in a sharp breath. "That's a scale," he said, shocked. "A *dragon* scale."

"What?" Abruptly, Brixaby was there, and Arthur had to shove his head back to get a closer look. He brought the torch down closer and brushed even more dirt away.

There were more scales, and each was large and well-developed. The sign of an adult.

"There's a brown dragon buried under here."

CHAPTER 25

At first, Arthur and Brixaby carefully dug around the corpse, wanting to keep as much of it intact as possible. But it became clear that there wasn't much they could do to hurt the thing. It was desiccated and mummified, dried out completely so that the scales were as hard as stone and the skin underneath tougher than boiled leather. Arthur had no chance of getting through it without a heavy-duty cutting tool—and no desire to do that.

Frowning, Arthur rocked back on his heels. "There's no smell."

Brixaby gave him and the vinegar rag tied around his mouth and nose a disbelieving look.

Arthur explained, "I mean, there is no smell of dragon death. It smells like scourge-rot in here, which is bad enough."

"Because nothing can live in the deadlands," Brixaby rumbled. "Even the insects that get into and rot corpses." He leaned forward and gave the corpse a good sniff-down. "Yes, this was once a Common dragon. I can still sense a visage of its power, though it was minor."

That twigged something in Arthur's mind. "This is a brown dragon."

"Yes?"

"The nest was filled with mole-type scourglings."

"Yes . . ." Brixaby said again, more impatiently.

"What if it's connected— No." Arthur shook his head sharply. "What if it's the reason why this nest is here?"

Brixaby narrowed his bloodred eyes at him. "You're suggesting dragons are the reason for scourge-nests?" he asked with an edge in his voice that said the answer had better be no.

Of course, Arthur plowed on.

"It's been bugging me why there are the nests here in the deadlands. If they're coming from the Dark Heart, they should be closer to the city, don't you think?

This dragon has been dead for a long, long time. Centuries, maybe. Any card that it had in its core would have long been rotted by now, but maybe there is enough magical residue left—just enough that it could be given a push or kick-started by the presence of a Dark Heart when it's at the top of its power."

Brixaby was silent for a moment, thinking about it. "What if the corpse was not the only thing that did not rot?"

"What do you—"

Arthur stopped as Brixaby reached forward and made a pinching motion at the corpse. When his claws drew back, it was with a card pinched between them.

But not any card Arthur had seen before. It was so thin that it was translucent, almost like the ghost of a card. The markings on it were long since faded, so that Arthur couldn't read a word or make out any of the pictures on the face. But the fact remained that whatever was left still implied that this was indeed a Common card.

Brixaby held it up for them both to see. As he did, sparks of dying power cascaded off the card. It looked like it was disintegrating in his claws.

"Brix—" Arthur started, though it was already too late. With a cascade of sparks like the magic inside was ripping itself apart, the card disintegrated into separate shards. Those shards were gone, faded away before they hit the floor.

The bioluminescent mold around them faded so only a hint of light remained.

The card was gone, and with it, the last vestiges of the dragon.

"It was a Common, very weak," Brixaby said dispassionately.

"That card shouldn't have been there—why didn't anyone harvest the dragon?" Arthur asked but saw Brixaby shrug in the dim light. "It was a Common. It should have rotted away ages ago, instead it fueled a scourgling nest—"

Arthur stopped. He and Brixaby looked at one another, and Arthur could see the same realization dawning in his dragon's eyes.

Arthur was the one to say it. "Which means that each nest we see has a dragon corpse under it."

"And this nest is merely a minor one and was barely able to produce adult Common scourglings," Brixaby said. "But the last one generated many Rares."

He and Brixaby traded another look, then immediately turned and started jogging for the entrance.

About an hour later, Brixaby was flying over the pit that was left of the Rare nest.

Arthur looked down and thought if he never had to see this place again, he could die happy.

The corpses of the scourglings looked exactly the same as they had before. Brixaby was right: the land was so devoid of life that there was nothing that could even rot the bodies, only dry them out. Likely, all those scourglings would remain there, in near-perfect condition, until the wind covered them with sand.

Brixaby landed nearby the hole he'd dug. "I will descend first just in case any more scourglings have spawned." He gave Arthur a look. "I refuse to bring you to the hospital for a third time this week."

Since Arthur was still somewhat soul-sore and also didn't want a third hospital trip that week, he agreed.

It didn't take Brixaby long to go down the hole. Once there, Arthur heard an annoyed grumble echo up from inside, though he didn't seem like he was in any particular danger.

Grabbing a ladder from his Personal Space, he headed down as well. Once down, he quickly saw what Brixaby was grumbling about.

Like the last nest, the walls were covered with bioluminescent mold. In one particularly bright patch, bubbles had started to form. Bubbles that he suspected, given enough time, would become ovoids and eventually . . . more scourglings.

"More scourge-spawn," Brixaby grumbled, reaching over and running his claws through the spawn to wipe it off. He then wiped his claws off in the soil. "This is a strong nest. It is already regenerating."

That was a concern, but Arthur had bigger worries. He moved through the tunnel system, noticing that it was larger and more well-developed than the last one. It even had some points that branched off into different areas of the tunnel system.

Any adult scourglings had been long killed, and they quickly destroyed any brighter patches that seemed to be recreating scourge-spawn. Unfortunately, the spawn was so undeveloped that it didn't give them any cards or shards.

"Brixaby, you said you found a Rare card in here? Where was it?"

"In the back," Brixaby said, "at the very end of the tunnel." He paused. "There was one branch that had collapsed completely, but there were only Common spawn points near it, so I did not bother to dig it back up."

"We'll try that next, if we don't come up with anything," Arthur said.

His heart was beating hard, and again he felt like he was on the verge of something big . . . But he wasn't quite sure what it was. Only that he was certain that this was the right track. It might be an echo from Brixaby's Call of the Heart seeker card pushing him forward. Or it might be destiny.

He felt like he was about to discover something vital, something grand. Something powerful.

Once again, at the very back of the tunnel system, they found the brightest patch of mold growing on the back wall. It had developed more scourge-spawn, too, but these ovoids were so developed that they had goo in the middle of them—a kind of proto-yolk.

Unfortunately, when they were destroyed, they didn't yield card shards, either.

Arthur took out his pickaxe and hesitated for a brief second, flashing to the idea of maybe farming these ovoids.

But . . . no. There were other nests, and if scourglings ever developed and attacked other people while he was farming them, he would be no better than the scholars' guild back at Wolf Moon Hive. No good came from farming scourglings.

With that thought, he dismissed the idea of easy riches and swung his pickaxe.

Just like with the previous nest, his pickaxe bit in deep, and found a line of brighter mold behind it. Arthur continued on, switching out the pickaxe for a shovel when he needed to take out bigger chunks at a time.

Brixaby helped by shoveling extra soil to the sides. He then got the idea of bundling up the growing piles into a tarp, storing it in his Personal Space, then going outside and dumping it.

Though this tunnel system was already below a deep pit, Arthur kept digging. Eventually, he received a skill for Mining, which was odd because he certainly wasn't doing it properly or looking for gems.

Also, it came with a surprising message.

New skill gained: Mining (Mining Class)
Due to your card's bonus traits, you automatically start this skill at
level 5.

Level 5, not level 3? That had to be an effect of the Endless Grindstone card he had consumed.

Previously, he would only start at level 5 if he either had somebody actively teaching him the skill or he had a lot of knowledge about it before.

That helped explain why he had gained **Mining** skill when he was barely digging.

Nevertheless, the next swing of his pickaxe dug in more deeply and easier than before.

Arthur grinned to himself, then checked his expression as he tasted scourge-dust on his teeth.

He spat to the side.

After a bit the soil changed and contained stringy, fibrous bits that looked like the remains of wood pulp. The fibers were so brittle they would crumble into dust at the lightest touch. Arthur bent to look closer. Some of the outlines of leaves lay darker against the soil.

"What is it?" Brixaby asked.

He shook his head. "It looks like ferns and big broad leaves, the type you see in a swamp, or growing around a lake. I saw something like this once when traveling with traders."

"This area is no swamp."

Arthur shrugged. "I guess it was a long time ago."

He continued digging down.

He didn't know how long it took him, and he was sore from his muscles to his still-healing soul. He also knew if he stopped, he wouldn't be able to start again until he had a good long rest, and perhaps a soak in a hot tub.

Even Brixaby was looking bored at transferring up extra soil. That was when Arthur's shovel finally struck something different.

Arthur fell to his knees and started digging with his hands. That feeling of being pulled forward, of being on the edge of discovery, only grew. He was frantic as he clawed away the soil.

Brixaby, who had just freshly returned from his last run dumping soil, gave him an odd look, but he helped out the best he could, though his claws were better at cutting through the tough dirt than actually moving it.

That was when Arthur uncovered the edge of a dragon's ridge—either one of the spikes that grew off the neck or a smaller one from the body. It was hard to tell.

"You have another torch in your Personal Space, right?" Arthur asked, breathless.

His dragon's answer was to grab one. Already lit, he brought it closer so they could both see.

The ridge gleamed silver in the light, weirdly clean for something that had been buried for who knew how long.

Silver. It had been a dragon of pure magic.

Arthur continued to dig around it with his hands, using the ridge as a guide to find the dragon's body. This was a mature beast, and the ridge itself was the length of Arthur's forearm, but finally, he reached the wide base and started to uncover the dragon's scales.

Arthur sat back on his heels. "Brixaby, can you feel . . ." He trailed off, almost too nervous and excited to finish.

"I can," Brixaby said, his head cocked. "I can feel its power, but it's indistinct. This dragon was a Rare."

"See if you can grab the card," Arthur said.

"Cards," Brixaby corrected. He reached down with clawed tips and then grunted in surprise. He came up with nothing but immediately tried again.

When he retracted his claws, this time, when he pulled back, it was with three ancient cards pinched between his claws.

Though they weren't translucent to the point of falling apart like the last one, they were still visibly damaged. Arthur caught sight of the Rare card titles, all written in the same flowing script:

Card Sympathy

Card Shard Insight

And the last and most startling:

Repair Cards

CHAPTER 26

None of the cards were on the verge of complete disintegration like the ones from the brown dragon, but warning sparkles drifted off them, indicating they were in very bad shape.

Arthur longed to study them but only nodded at Brixaby. "Put them in your Personal Space," he said, then after a glance at the silver dragon, raised a hand to rub his eyes. "I need to think, and I can't do that here."

"It reeks," Brixaby agreed.

Arthur shot his dragon a sympathetic look. He had his vinegar rag, but Brixaby had gone without, even though his nose was much more sensitive than Arthur's.

"Let's get out of here." Arthur took one more look at the dead hulk of the silver dragon, wondering if he was missing anything. But if there was, he couldn't see it. The dragon had been long dead. It wasn't going anywhere.

Maybe its rider is here lying along with him, Arthur thought with a reflexive shudder that went up and down his spine.

Collecting his tools, he turned and made his grateful way out.

Of course, the area outside the nest wasn't much better, with the scourgling bodies sometimes stacked on one another. Brixaby crouched in silent invitation for Arthur to come on board. As soon as he was seated, his dragon took off into the sky. Arthur ripped off the vinegar-soaked rag and stuffed it back into his Personal Space. Then he breathed the clean air.

Brixaby headed back toward the city and landed past the border of the deadlands. The sun was low in the sky, and hopeful crickets were peeping from the shadows made by clumps of weeds and bushes. It was peaceful here, and it helped calm Arthur's nerves. He hadn't realized how thinly they'd been stretched until now.

The fact was, every scourgling nest likely had a dead dragon under it, and those were only the ones that he knew about. Or the ones left that still had viable cards in them. Whenever that battle had happened, it had been long ago. The Dark Heart had gone through many different cycles, and Arthur guessed that those had depleted the strength of the cards inside the dragons.

The deadlands here were possibly an entire graveyard of dragon bodies.

Arthur shook his head. He didn't want to think about that right now. It was something that had happened long before he was born, something he couldn't change.

Though, he wondered if the city-state's administration knew about it.

If they do, I doubt that they care, he thought.

Then he turned to Brixaby. "Let's take a better look at these cards. Pull them out, one at a time."

Brixaby did, and Arthur was glad to see that his dragon was on the same page as he was, because he pulled out the most interesting card out of the three.

Repair Cards
Rare

Meta

The wielder of this card will be granted the ability and suite of basic skills in order to repair a damaged or malfunctioning magical card. When using any of these skills to repair a card, chances of spontaneous card fragmentation or scourge spawning are reduced by 25%. The skills granted are based on personality and ability in similar repair crafts. This card is skill based and uses mana. This card does not unlock mana.

Seek additional cards in this set to add to meta card knowledge.

Another skill-based card, which would fit nicely with Arthur's Master of Skills.

It was also the most damaged out of the three, with a faint translucent quality the others didn't have.

"Ironic," Brixaby said, "that this Repair Cards is in desperate need of repair itself."

Arthur slanted a smile at his dragon, then nodded at him. Brixaby put the card back into his Personal Space. Hopefully that would halt any further disintegration.

Taking a bracing breath, Arthur spoke what was surely on both of their minds. "That's not the only problem."

His dragon sent him a sympathetic look, which was another sign of his growing maturity. "You currently have no card-anchor deck to add that card to."

"I'm not sure that adding a currently disintegrating card *anywhere* into myself is a great idea," Arthur said.

Brixaby snorted. "But you would do it anyway."

"If I could, yeah," he admitted. There was no point in lying to his dragon. There was a reason why they had linked to one another.

"Okay," Arthur said, "let's take a look at the next card."

Brixaby brought out Card Sympathy.

Card Sympathy
Rare

Meta

The wielder of this card will be granted the understanding of magical cards on a fundamental and instinctual level. Every card has secrets that are not spelled out in the description. The wielder of this card will automatically be granted more insight into their own cards, and others that they see. The wielder will have unusual insight on how to best use compatible cards for the best effect.

Seek additional cards in this set to add to meta card knowledge.

And finally, the last:

Card Shard Insight
Rare

Meta

The wielder of this card will be granted unique insight on the nature of card shards on an instinctive level. The wielder will be able to position shards in the optimal position for the desired outcome when creating a card, as well as receive a 25% greater chance of harvesting a corner piece. In addition, the wielder will have a 5% chance of spontaneously harvesting a card shard of a higher rank rarity than a scourgling's baseline rank.

Seek additional cards in this set to add to meta card knowledge.

They only took a moment to read the final card before Brixaby put it back into his Personal Space.

"No doubt about it," Arthur said, "those are three of a kind."

Which meant that they would only take up one spot in his heart deck. But his heart deck was getting mighty full, with nine slots taken. And there was extra risk because of his recently destroyed card anchor. If he did this, he would have to be *absolutely* sure it was what he wanted.

"Well, while we're here, let's take a look at those other cards, too," he said. "The ones that we made from the card shards."

There were three Commons and one Uncommon. All were either useless or trash-tier cards, but then Arthur checked his assumptions. Was he becoming a card snob? Was there such a thing as a trash-tier card?

Effortless Paint Mixing
Common
Utility
The wielder of this card will be granted the uncanny ability to know the exact proportions of paint colors to mix in order to achieve the shade they wish. This card will not automatically provide the ingredients and dyes to mix.

Tracking Scent
Common
Utility
Once every twenty-four hours, the wielder of this card will be able to mark a target with a scent-based tracker. This tracker will only be smelled by the wielder and can be used to follow the target. This effect lasts three hours.

I Mustache You a Question
Common
Body Modification
The wielder of this card will be able to grow, on command, an impressive mustache. This is a skill-based ability, and the higher the skill, the fancier and thicker the mustache will be.

A Twist of Timber
Uncommon
Crafting
Using mana, the wielder of this card will be able to slowly twist, move, and distort wood out of its usual state into the artistic design of their choice. This altered wood will be resistant to rot, termite, and water damage. As all trees grow in their own time, the wielder of this card will also be granted with the gift of unusual patience.

Okay, maybe there *was* such a thing as a trash-tier card. He didn't know how anybody would find a use for the Mustache card. Except that any card in the heart, no matter how silly, allowed a person to travel into the deadlands without getting scourge-sickness. When he had been a child, he would've accepted anything into his heart to be a card user.

They also had the auction cards that they had won, and one more.

"Don't forget the toughness card," Brixaby said. "I have been hiding it on the rooftop terrace."

Arthur blinked and realized that he had indeed forgotten that card.

Alter-dimensional Tanky Constitution
Rare
Body Enhancement
*The wielder of this card will be able to move their physical body at will
into a dimension that is slightly more "real" than our own, with the effect
of hardening the body past most physical material penetration. This effect
also hardens mental and emotional resistances up to 50%, and counters a
variety of noncorporeal attacks. This effect does not use mana. WARNING:
.00001% chance wielder may become either temporarily or permanently
stuck in this alter-dimensional state, wherein the body will not be able to
properly absorb food or drink.*

"Well," Arthur said again, "that one's useful, but I'm not sure about that
drawback. We're getting quite the collection, aren't we?"

Sitting up, Brixaby curled his tail around his claws. He looked very pleased
with himself. "Indeed. Perhaps we should sell the useless ones to a card shop, or
trade them for others."

Arthur thought about it for a moment, then shook his head. "What are
the chances the sheriffs won't be watching for that exact thing? We could give
them to Marion and Soledad, but Marion hasn't even taken the illusion card."
He frowned. "Let's talk to Dannill and see if he's rented the rooftop terrace to
someone else yet."

Brixaby lifted his lips in threat. "He had better not."

"I'd started to wonder if you died," Dannill said to Arthur as he greeted him in
his shop, though the man was smiling as he said it, so clearly he hadn't been that
worried.

"I've been busy," Arthur said, not mentioning that he had been in and out
of the hospital . . . twice. Though, from Dannill's sly look, Arthur suspected that
the man knew.

"Well, you and your dragon have certainly made a name for yourselves," he
said. "People have started to call you the scourge of scourglings."

"Don't tell Brixaby that," Arthur said quickly. "Word of advice: Don't ever
compare a dragon to a scourgling to his face."

"It's all in good fun." Dannill must have caught the warning look on Arthur's
face. "But you are the expert on dragons. So, how can I help you?"

Arthur hesitated for a moment, weighing his decision. Then he nodded to
himself and drew out the Common and Uncommon cards from a leather bag.
He didn't want to put anything into his Personal Space that was that magically
heavy, so after he'd gotten them from Brixaby, he'd carried them by hand. And of
course, he held the meta cards back.

"I have a feeling that you could find some buyers for these."

Dannill's eyes widened, and there was a glint in them that was impossible to miss. "How did you get it past the sheriffs—" He stopped and looked around, though the shop was empty, and hustled Arthur into his office. Once inside, Dannill reached for a card anchor, and new runes glowed on the walls. "This isn't a setup, is it? You may be a powerful dragon rider, but I warn you, I have powerful friends in the city . . ."

"I have better things to do than set you up," Arthur said. "And if any of your 'friends' are interested, there's more where these cards came from."

The man actually licked his lips. "Let me see."

Dannill took the cards and looked them over, nodding to himself. He seemed to even appreciate the trash-tier card. Arthur suspected that in a place teeming with refugees and people looking for any advantage to survive in the Dark Heart, these cards would quickly find buyers.

"I can do something with these," Dannill said. "Now, what do you want for them?"

"Rent, the supplies we talked about, and most importantly," Arthur said, "a private workshop for Brixaby and I to prepare for the Dark Heart."

The Dark Heart would be opening soon, and they needed to be as prepared as possible. Plus, the small rooftop terrace was not going to fit Cressida, Horatio, and their dragons when they arrived. They would need places to rest, recover from their journey, and get ready for the Dark Heart as well.

Dannill's enthusiasm dimmed a touch, and he stroked his chin. "A workshop, eh? That will be expensive. Every day, more people are fleeing in, and there's less and less space in the city."

Arthur shrugged. That wasn't his problem. "Those people coming in will need cards, too."

"I'll see what I can do," Dannill said, which Arthur knew was as good as a yes.

Dannill started showing Arthur warehouses that could function as crafting spaces within a couple of hours. Unfortunately, none of them were perfect.

"Much too small," Arthur said, barely glancing at the empty room Dannill had shown him. It was about the size of his apartment he'd shared with Horatio.

"Well, no offense," Dannill said, "but your dragon doesn't require a lot of room."

No, he wouldn't, but Sams certainly would when he arrived. Arthur was still keeping that little fact under his hat, though.

Instead, he channeled his inner Brixaby and gave Dannill a hard look. "He may grow."

"Ah, well, this location is rather centrally located . . ." He trailed off at another look from Arthur. "But of course, you're a dragon rider, so I suppose that doesn't matter as much to you as it would to the rest of us." He hastily cleared his throat. "Come along, there is another option I have in mind."

The second one was an easy no as well. It was certainly larger, but . . .

"We need somewhere more private," Arthur said, casting a glance at the various crafters who were busily working in separate stations all around. While everybody certainly had room to expand, the noise of banging and item making created a cacophony. Arthur had to raise his voice to be heard and feared that if Brixaby tried to do the same, he might accidentally unleash his Stunning Shout.

Dannill seemed intent to put a spin on things. "I hear that many artists and crafters thrive when surrounded by like minds. Think of all that you could learn from one another."

"My dragon requires privacy," Arthur said. And so did he.

"Well, there is one more option . . . But it is right on the edge of town, far away from the Dark Heart."

"And closer to the deadlands," Arthur said meaningfully.

Dannill wasn't stupid. He'd likely guessed where Arthur had gotten his cards, so he brightened at that. "Okay, but renting it until the heart opens will cost you the Uncommon card all by itself."

"Let me see it first," Arthur said.

The last location was a large barn-sized building, with double doors big enough to allow a large dragon to walk inside. It still smelled faintly of animals, and Arthur suspected that it had recently housed woolly bison. But the floors had been swept clean of every bit of straw, and the walls and roofing looked solid enough.

"This will do," Arthur said with a nod. He only hoped it was big enough for everything Brixaby had in his Personal Space. The dragon had continued to be cagey about everything he had stuffed in there.

Dannill clapped his hands. "Excellent. What else can I do for you?"

Arthur fished in his pocket and pulled out the piece of paper that the heart deck specialist had given him. "I need directions to this location."

He hadn't told Dannill of the three-of-a-kind cards, only the trash Common and useless Uncommon. He wanted Repair Cards and the others as his own.

CHAPTER 27

Brixaby was overjoyed when Arthur showed him the barn, and only resented a little that renting it would cost them the Uncommon card.

Arthur also sold the Commons to Dannill for food, basic furniture to make the space comfortable, and more crafting supplies.

From the enthusiastic way Dannill agreed, Arthur suspected he was getting the better part of the deal. His **Haggling** skill didn't seem happy with him, either. But he didn't particularly care. Scraping up more cards was just a matter of him and Brixaby flying out to find more scourgling nests, collecting the shards, and putting them together.

Since they'd mostly be Common cards, it wasn't exactly an unlimited money scheme . . . but it would make them comfortable while they were in the city. As long as Dannill didn't get caught fencing the cards.

Brixaby quickly claimed the back half of the barn as his own, and immediately started unstoring things from his Personal Space.

Arthur blinked. "Why did you have a full furnace in there? You know you can't use it in your Personal Space, right?" The fact that time was frozen made something like using a furnace, which needed to have the temperature changed constantly, an impossibility.

Brixaby started to answer, but an even better question occurred to Arthur.

"Wait, how do you even *have* a furnace? Where did you get it?"

Brixaby looked at him like he was being a fool.

Arthur groaned. "Did you take it from Mesa Free Hive or Free Hive of the Waves?" He wasn't sure which was worse.

"When would I have had the time to properly loot the Free Hive of the Waves?" Brixaby asked with indignation. "It was all but destroyed by the Mind Singer."

Which meant he had stolen it from Mesa Free Hive. Arthur really should have kept a closer eye on him during that time.

On the other hand, no one had ever asked him about a mysteriously missing expensive furnace, so they'd gotten away with it.

It wasn't like Arthur hadn't come away with a few free items himself. He still had seeds from that very useful purple apple tree that provided temporary psychic-blocking abilities. So he stood back and watched as Brixaby started unstoring more and more objects. Enough to fill out the back half of the barn. There was everything from strange bits of metal objects, most rusted—though Brixaby must have seen some value in it—to more than his fair share of blacksmithing and chainmail-making tools. Most of the tools were in good repair and had other crafters' names stamped on them.

Leaving him to it, Arthur went to a shelf that had been built into a side wall and started to stack his own supplies, though he kept most of what he had in his Personal Space. He didn't like to be without any tools he might need.

It's not hoarding, he thought with a frown. *I'm just being practical.*

He thought about unstoring the turkey poults, ducklings, and baby chicks he'd had in a crate for the better part of a year . . . but they were better off in his Personal Space.

He turned to Brixaby to see the dragon still unstoring objects. "All right, I'm off."

Brixaby grunted. His claws were full of a long metal bracket, which had become bent over time. With a flex of his claws and a screech of metal, he straightened it.

With a fond roll of his eyes in exasperation, Arthur took off.

He didn't need Brixaby to ferry him back and forth as if he were his own personal horse. In fact, considering the fame that they'd gathered in the city, it was best that he didn't.

Instead, he walked the streets, enjoying the sights . . . if not the smells. It seemed that this part of the city didn't have someone with the proper card to maintain a sewer system. Also, from the thick scent of manure in the air, it was also close to the area where they stabled bison.

There weren't as many people on the streets, and those that were there had the air of being on business. There was none of the festival atmosphere he'd seen on the other side of the city when he'd first arrived.

Most importantly, the address of the heart deck specialist was on this side of town.

Arthur followed the messy map that Dannill had scrawled for him.

Within a few streets, he found himself in front of a storefront that had a curtain in place of a front door. There was no signage, but the little number on the side of the door was correct.

"Hello?" He peeked his head in.

There was no furniture in the room beyond, no desks or crafting equipment. Not even a bed. Just a colorful woven rug and a thin bearded man who sat cross-legged on it.

He completely ignored Arthur.

Arthur could feel a sense of power radiating off him and suspected he had the ability to throw anybody out that he didn't want to be there. The power was odd. It didn't have quite the flavor of a Legendary, but it was close enough to count. Maybe he was a Legendary with some sort of mitigating card?

The man continued to ignore him, so Arthur walked in and spent a few moments looking over the paintings that covered all four walls, and the ceiling. They were of cities, some of them fantastical with floating buildings and animals he had never seen before. Some sort of brown creature with a deerlike head but a long tail and two paddle feet. The scenes outside the cities mostly depicted people smiling, talking, crafting, and working in the fields.

There were no dragons in the sky, though he did see plenty of birds.

"You are the dragon rider."

Arthur turned at the man's voice. His eyes were still closed, though Arthur had no doubt the man had peeked at him.

"I am. My name is Arthur. Did the heart deck specialist say I was coming here?"

Eyes still closed, the man's lips peeked up at the corner. "Did he send you? Or did you come here of your own choice?"

Arthur hated it when people answered questions with more questions, but he decided to play along. "Both. I recently had an accident and destroyed my card-anchor deck. I was told that you could help."

"If you destroyed your card-anchor deck and still remain standing among the living, you might have already used up more than your fair share of luck." The man gave a sigh and opened his eyes. Even though he had a rather swarthy face, his eyes were a startlingly blue color. He stood in one swift motion and said, "Where was your card anchor?"

Arthur held out his arm and turned his wrist. The man caught it and spent the next few moments examining the thin, spidery lines that were all that was left of the tattoo. His brow furrowed. "Was the anchor empty when it was destroyed?"

Arthur hesitated for a moment, debating on what to tell him, and then shook his head.

"Have you heard of the **Card Shuffling** skill?"

"Ah, yes." The man exhaled. "You've mastered that skill, have you?"

Arthur jerked in surprise, and the man dropped his arm, giving him a gentle smile.

"I see it occasionally with craft masters, and those who use classes or bundles of skills in their work. They're able to bend the rules past what normal skills allow. It's a mark of proficiency and nothing to be ashamed of."

"I'm not ashamed. I'm just not used to people who understand how I use skills."

His smile deepened, now reaching his eyes. "What kind of a healer would I be if I could not diagnose my patients?"

"Which means that you have a card that gives you special insight into others' cards," Arthur said.

"No," he said, "I have *several* cards which give me such insight, and they are from the same set." He paused for a moment. "I suspect you know exactly what that means."

This was getting uncanny, and Arthur glanced toward the door, wondering if he should just leave.

"I should also tell you," the man said, "that I am bound by my own oaths not to discuss my patients' lives and medical conditions with others."

"Does that include the sheriffs?" Arthur asked pointedly.

"Is there a reason why the sheriffs would come sniffing around?"

Answering another question with a question. Arthur gave him a hard look.

This time the man gave in and answered. "They have asked before—not about you, but someone else—and what I can tell them is limited. They accepted it because they don't want to get on my bad side."

"Why not?"

"Because they use my services, too," he said. "I'm afraid I haven't introduced myself, which is very rude of me. But I admit, what I felt from you got me intrigued. My name is Ravi."

He held out his hand to shake. Arthur hesitated for a moment, again wondering if he should just walk out the door. But he had come here for some very important reasons.

"Pleased to meet you, Ravi," he said, adding in his mind, *I think*.

"Come, let us sit and talk."

Ravi had no chairs and simply sat on the floor cross-legged. Arthur did the same, facing him.

"Why have you come here, Arthur?" Ravi asked.

"Uh . . ." Hadn't he just told him? "My card anchor got destroyed, like I told you, and while I was able to retrieve the cards, I have nowhere to put them. I need to see about getting another card anchor, but the heart deck specialist said that he wouldn't recommend I get one for over a year."

"You don't strike me as the type of man to follow advice that you don't like," Ravi said.

Arthur thought of himself as somewhat cautious while Brixaby was the one who took chances. But thinking back on his life, and particularly the last few months . . . he had to agree.

He shrugged. "I guess I could get a card anchor in a place that is far away from my wrist, like . . . the top of my foot. Or even get a card-anchor bag, but it would still need a point of contact with the rest of my body, right?"

Ravi nodded, and Arthur continued.

"I guess I haven't done it because . . ." Again, he hesitated. This wasn't something he had been aware of at all until Ravi asked. "It feels like a really bad idea. Not just because I was told not to by a specialist, but I can *feel* it would be a mistake, deep inside."

Ravi nodded. "Your soul is telling you not to do it, and you are wise enough to listen."

"But I'm going down to the Dark Heart," Arthur said. "And I need those cards, and whatever else I can use to keep myself and my friends safe."

"You would not be the first person to have that problem," Ravi said.

Arthur stared at him for a moment, wondering if he would have anything else to say. Ravi just gazed back at him calmly.

"So what do I do?" Arthur said, after the silence became awkward. "Is there a card that functions as an artificial anchor?"

"Almost assuredly," Ravi replied calmly. "After all, there is a card for every spell, skill, or craft with a touch of magic out there."

That threw Arthur for a moment. "Magic? But my particular skill card doesn't allow for magical skills."

Ravi laughed softly. "Your skill card may not use mana or allow you to cast spells, but it is most assuredly magical, and not mundane."

They were getting off topic. "So what do I do?" Arthur repeated.

"There are several options open to you," Ravi said. "You could, of course, wait. You are young and the Dark Heart will have another cycle or two within your lifetime. Likely more, with the way it has behaved. And since you're a dragon rider, it would be easy for you to flit off to another city-state"—he twinkled his fingers in the air—"and find another Dark Heart that is ripening. There are adventurers who make their whole career out of plundering Dark Hearts. Then in a year, you may get another card anchor, though there is no guarantee that one may stick for you. It depends on the scarring to your soul. Though, by the fact that you seem to be whole and healthy and sane, I do have high hopes that won't be an issue."

"I don't want to wait," Arthur said. "What else?"

"Well, as you said, there are cards available that function as additional storage space for the heart deck. But as you can imagine, these are high ranked, enormously expensive, and likely kept a very deep secret."

Arthur perked up. He might be able to find something like that using Brix-aby's seeker card.

"The problem with that, of course," Ravi continued, "is that your heart deck is not only almost full, but incredibly cluttered and disorganized."

That brought Arthur up short. "It's not disorganized."

"I can feel that you have at least two pairs in there, and you just stuck the rest in willy-nilly, didn't you?" Ravi said.

"I like being a generalist."

"Well, it means that you have nearly filled up your heart deck slots. I suspect you'd be the type to get your hand on an additional heart storage card, if one existed. But make no mistake: That would be a false heart deck." The gaze that Ravi gave him was unexpectedly severe. "There are consequences for having something false within your heart."

Arthur opened his mouth to ask a question, but then realized he already knew the answer. "The cards in your heart deck become part of you."

"Yes, and people do not think of those consequences before they shove in the first card they can lay their hands on," Ravi said.

While Arthur could agree with what he said, generally, he couldn't say that he actually regretted his own path. He had added cards to his heart like Return to Start, which had a serious double-edged sword effect, and the Charming Gentle-Person card, which gave him extra points to his charisma.

Those seemed silly at first glance, but both of those cards had helped him immensely. The Return to Start card had saved his life several times, and though he didn't think of himself as charismatic, he did have to deal with people on a daily basis. Being slightly more likable in their eyes helped smooth the way.

He certainly didn't regret his two Legendary cards. As they were a pair, they acted as one and took a one-card slot in his heart deck. It was the same thing for his three of a kind. His Personal Space had come in handy too many times to count. And he relied silently on his Eidetic Memory card to instantly recall things that he had read. Meanwhile, the Mental Bookshelf card helped tie the three together and allowed him and Brixaby to actually go into his Personal Space.

No, he had no regrets for that. Or any of them.

"I can't undo what I've done in the past," Arthur told him, "and looking back, I'm not sure that I would. The cards in my heart have made me the man I am today, and I like that man."

To his surprise, Ravi's smile grew brighter. "Good, good, this is exactly the mindset that you will need."

"What do you mean?"

"The third option," Ravi said, "and the one I feel would be best for you. But in order to do it, you must be open to exploring your own heart deck and be comfortable with the truths that you may or may not uncover there."

"Explore my own heart deck?"

"Yes, to rearrange it," Ravi said, "and make room for more cards in your heart."

Arthur stared at him for a stunned second. "You're not talking about a card to add more cards? Just . . . more space in my heart? That's possible?"

"Oh, indeed," Ravi said. "In fact, that's where my specialty lies. Usually, I help people process the grief of losing cards. Together, we work toward readying that person to accept more cards into their heart. But occasionally, there is someone who, for one reason or another, needs more cards in their heart and can't—or won't—use a card-anchor deck. The process is not easy, but you're in luck because it does usually require the Dark Heart."

It finally clicked for Arthur. "Because the Dark Heart bends rules."

Ravi smiled again. "Much like a skills master, yes?"

A while ago, Arthur was asked what he truly wanted from the Dark Heart, and other than a general desire for more power or a way to defeat the scourglings, he hadn't been able to find an answer. Now, a whole new possibility opened in his mind. "You're saying that the Dark Heart can allow me to add more cards to my heart deck? How does it work?"

"No one knows how it works, exactly. And it is certainly not an outcome that is guaranteed. What I can do here is prepare you and your mind. It is said that those who delve into the depths of the Dark Heart have exposed their soul, and their greatest wish is granted. But what you want and what you *need* are sometimes different." He paused, letting that sit for a beat before he went on. "What I can do for you, Arthur, is help prepare you and give you the right mindset that you will need to delve into the Dark Heart, and perhaps have this rule bent or even broken for you."

CHAPTER 28

Skill level gained: Meditation (Insight Class)
Level 15

Ironically, that notification broke through Arthur's concentration and shattered his meditative state.

He grimaced, opened his eyes, and checked the time on the simple sand hourglass he had set by his side. He'd been down for an hour this time. That was a new record. When Ravi had first started teaching him, he'd barely been able to sit still for more than five minutes.

Arthur had not had much opportunity in his life to actually sit down and do nothing. So focusing on his inner self had been a brand-new task for him. And not necessarily one that he had taken to easily.

Healer Ravi had given him his first lesson that day Arthur had visited him. And because he was being taught by a teacher, he had started his skill at level 7, thanks to his various boosts.

He suspected it was only because of his new Grindstone card ability that he had been able to increase it by eight more levels within a few days. **Meditation** did not come naturally to him. But as he leveled, it certainly was getting easier.

The goal was to get his **Meditation** skill up as high as possible because only once he had started to master it would the rules be able to be bent. And if he focused on them the right way, he might—*might*—be able to use the Dark Heart to twist those rules into expanding his heart deck.

Arthur had just never thought that sitting still for so long and concentrating on his inner self would be so much work.

And he also knew himself well enough to know that now that he'd broken out of the meditation, he wouldn't be slipping back into it anytime soon.

Getting up and stretching, Arthur went to the ladder that had led up to the roof of the barn. He climbed down and, as he came around, the distant sound of a hammer striking against metal from inside grew louder.

There was a reason why he hadn't tried to meditate inside the barn. Brixaby did not craft quietly.

He found the dragon at an anvil, beating on a red-hot piece of metal as if it owed him money. The dragon had a haggard look about him, indicating that he had spent a lot of time in his Personal Space already. Arthur suspected that he was only crafting on the outside because he had a massive headache from overuse.

His quest to get his Chainmail Class—or at least a Blacksmithing Class—continued.

"Any luck?" Arthur asked.

"No, I still require a skill to acquire my class," Brixaby muttered. "Perhaps two skills. I do not know what I'm missing." He cast an evil eye at whatever he was trying to craft. It looked like a long red-hot piece of metal without any particular shape, but Arthur knew better than to ask a crafter about a project that was unfinished.

He hated to see Brixaby hit a wall. The easiest solution was to apprentice him to a blacksmith. But this city was not like the hives, and people were not used to dragons here. None of the blacksmiths would agree to teach him. Not even when Arthur said that Brixaby would work for free, bring his own supplies, and even, somewhat desperately, when he offered to pay for their time.

And the blacksmiths certainly weren't interested after Brixaby threatened them for saying no.

While having a dragon apprentice would be a novelty, it seemed too many people thought of Brixaby as an animal and were afraid that their reputations would suffer.

Plus, the Dark Heart was slated to open within the next two weeks at best guess, and every crafter was running at full steam in order to fill in commissions or get themselves ready for their own dive. No one had time to teach.

Arthur hesitated. "Brix, I know we talked about this—"

Brixaby cut him off. "No, you are busy with your own projects."

But Arthur continued anyway. "I could go to the other side of the city where we haven't asked around yet. I might be able to apprentice myself. Then I could teach you—"

"It would not be the same," Brixaby said. "If I am to learn, it will need to be from a master."

Arthur wasn't entirely sure about that, but he could also recognize that Brixaby had his own pride. "All right," he said, "but we're still going to the library later. Maybe there's some technique books or something."

"That is acceptable," he said shortly, then turned and continued hammering away.

Watching him, Arthur doubted that Brixaby had a shape in mind. His dragon seemed to be taking out his frustration on the metal.

Arthur turned to his side of the barn, knowing a lost cause when he saw one. And he felt for Brixaby. Sometimes getting a class could be as easy as finding the appropriate card, like when Arthur had gained his Stealth Class. And sometimes it could be accidental, like how he had acquired his Thief Class.

But sometimes . . . classes could be elusive. He had banged his head against the wall for months trying to get his Cooking Class when he'd been a kid. Though the hard work had been worth it. He'd gotten it as a Tier 2 class, which had given him greater benefits.

Blacksmithing might be the same, which was why Brixaby was having so much trouble with it.

Speaking of the Cooking Class . . .

Arthur walked to his new stove, installed only three days ago. It was an amazing device, the best that they could find using Common shards they had gotten from clearing out another scourgling nest. It ran on mana instead of coal or wood, which meant no additional fuel to worry about. And the flame was weirdly clean, with no additional smoke to taint the meal. Even then, it didn't require nearly as much as it did for a spell.

Unfortunately, while Arthur still had access to mana thanks to his Counterfeit Siphon card, his regenerative Mana Vault had been in his card anchor. He didn't dare use mana that wasn't earmarked for combat.

So he'd had to buy chips of crystallized mana, which was an invention in the city-state that he had not seen anywhere else. One chip lasted him a good hour of stove time, which wasn't bad. It was amazing how many problems could be solved by buying his way out of them.

Another thing the city had were magical spices and ingredients with different enhancements.

Surely the herbalists here didn't use dragon soil like Mesa Free Hive did to mutate the herbs, but however they cultivated them, they had more of a selection than he'd ever seen. Those, too, were expensive.

But expensive exotic food gave him more experience.

Arthur had been looking forward to this all day and had used it as a reward. Now that he had finally broken through to level 15 in his **Meditation** skill, he deserved that little reward.

He was going to make chicken soup.

But not just *any* chicken soup.

He started with the chicken, which had been stored in his Personal Space a few moments after it had been butchered by the vendor. The man claimed that it had been raised on enhanced corn and grains. Arthur had taken a good look at the chicken feed, noting that it boosted vitality. Hopefully that would transfer to the chicken as well.

Brixaby, of course, pointed out that if that were the case, eating *humans* who had just eaten magically enhanced food would also provide a boost. Arthur had ignored him.

Using his **Butchering** skill, Arthur prepared the carcass, plucking the feathers and setting them aside in his Personal Space. He didn't know when he would need chicken feathers, but one could not be too careful.

After gutting the chicken and giving the entrails to Brixaby, he set it to boil to cook the chicken and start the broth.

Then he worked on the vegetables: cloves of garlic, which were supposed to have a boost in energy; an onion, which was bright red instead of yellow and was said to ward off infections; two carrots to boost physical integrity; celery stalks that were supposedly good for the eyes. He also added normal peas and lentils because he liked his chicken soup as thick and nourishing as possible. Plus, he got good prices for them.

The rosemary was particularly interesting as it was enhanced to be healthy for the skin. The vendor who sold them said that it was good for ladies' oils and that Arthur should give it to his girlfriend. Then he had winked.

The thyme, unfortunately, was just thyme and not anything interesting.

He chopped up the ingredients, using as many fancy cuts as he possibly could. Because his **Knife Work** skill was high already, he suspected he would have to chop something truly extraordinary to keep it leveling. But every little bit helped.

Arthur had made chicken soup many times during his work in kitchens before he had linked up with Brixaby. It was soothing, and he almost found himself slipping again into a semi-meditative state as he worked. However, it was never a good idea to daydream when using knives and while around an open flame, so he didn't let himself drift off completely.

When the ingredients were all prepared and there was nothing to do but wait for the broth to continue simmering, Arthur sat down and tried to get back into his meditative state. He found himself entering it quickly, but he had trouble staying in it, the smell of the cooking ingredients itching at his nose.

Pushing that to the side as best he could, he focused on his Master of Skills card, and thought, for a moment, he could sense something *more* about it. Almost like he was aware of it in a way that he hadn't been before. But when he tried to analyze it, that feeling went away.

With a shake of his head, he stopped trying to meditate and got up to check on the soup.

Finding it still bubbling away, he pulled out a deck of cards and worked on his shuffling. Brixaby had been right: He had long overlooked that skill, too.

He knew the chicken soup was ready when Brixaby finally broke off to come have a hopeful sniff. Arthur offered him a bowl before he tried it for himself.

Thanks to enhanced chicken soup, you have received a temporary minor healing boost.
Time Left: 59 Minutes 59 Seconds

"Did you get that, too?" Arthur asked.

"Yes, minor healing. The soup is good, but it needs a bit more salt." Brixaby was a big fan of salt—it likely went along with his taste for raw meat.

"It is not as good as a healing card," Arthur said, "but every little bit helps."

That said, he started ladling it out into portions, using extra crockery he had purchased on the cheap in town, and storing it in his Personal Space. He planned to repeat the process later and perhaps boil down the broth to a jelly. It might become more effective that way.

He had just turned to Brixaby to ask him how he was doing when the shadows seemed to deepen subtly on the walls. Arthur tensed, and he noticed Brixaby did too, fire springing up and down his ridges as he activated his Night-Mare Fire card.

Suddenly, a serpent made of shadow detached from the far wall and slithered across the floor straight to Arthur. His heart picked up its pace.

"Cressida?" he asked, glancing at the door as if he expected her to come striding in. That was her snake, an effect from her Slithering Shadow Sender card. She was sending a message to him. About time.

The serpent raised its flat head and hissed out in Cressida's voice, "We are crossing the deadlands, three days out. Reply if you can. Let me know if you're safe."

Arthur almost drew from his now-precious store of mana. Yes, he wanted to save it for combat emergencies, but this was more important.

Then a thought struck him.

"Wait!" He reached into his Personal Space for his final mana chip and flicked it to the snake, which snapped it up.

Concentrating on the image of Cressida in his mind, he said, "There may be scourglings running wild in the deadlands. We're in a city called New Houston. Message me when you get within view of it, and Brixaby and I will meet you." He paused. "I've missed you."

He felt a little silly, but before he could think too hard about what he'd said, the serpent went flat again and retreated into the shadows. In a moment, it was gone.

He exchanged a look with Brixaby. "Three days."

"Excellent," Brixaby said. "I will need to continue my crafting so I can show Joy and Sams how much I have grown."

CHAPTER 29

Arthur and Brixaby waited at the border between the living land and the deadlands.

Pacing back and forth, Arthur absently shuffled a deck of playing cards in his hands. Over the last few days, he had increased his **Shuffling** level to 19. His most recent trick he'd mastered meant he could now effortlessly bridge out cards from one hand to another without dropping one, and while keeping track of where the most important face cards were placed. He was still working on the numbered cards.

That shuffling technique had become part of his muscle memory. Since he hadn't received a new level in the last few hours, he suspected that he'd have to start working on some tricks.

It didn't help that this particular deck of playing cards was brand new, with a waxy slipperiness under his fingers.

Brixaby watched him with undisguised curiosity, likely since Arthur had caught him sneaking away his last deck of playing cards and trying to shuffle them himself. Unfortunately, his claws got in the way, and he had bent or punctured a good deal of them. That was why Arthur's playing cards were brand new.

Brixaby's claws could be worked around with enough skill levels, but he didn't seem interested. Instead, he had grumpily gone back to his smithing.

"Shouldn't you be meditating?" Brixaby asked.

"Can't," Arthur grunted. There was no way that he would be able to calm down enough to try to get into a meditative state. He glanced to the sky for some sign of Cressida and Horatio and their dragons . . . but there was nothing.

He didn't say as much, but Brixaby could easily read him anyway. "I believe that's exactly what meditation is supposed to solve, was it not?"

"I don't see *you* doing meditation," Arthur shot back. "Don't you want to increase the size of your secondary core?"

Brixaby snorted. "My secondary core will grow naturally as I mature. Already, I believe that I am nearly ready for a third card." He paused and cocked his head at Arthur, the toes of his front paw tapping against the ground in thought. "Do you believe meditation would increase my cores further?"

Arthur shrugged. "The Dark Heart bends rules. Who knows what would happen?"

Brixaby let out a pensive growl, then shook his head and sent his own long, lingering look out to the sky. It was a stark blue color, without a hint of any dots among the horizon. "Perhaps you should check your Call of the Heart again."

He had asked Arthur this about ten minutes before, and ten minutes before that.

Arthur had sent his message back to Cressida three days ago, saying that they would go out to meet them once she and Horatio were in view of the city, but once the day arrived, neither one of them wanted to wait.

It was worse for Brixaby because Horatio and Cressida were using his map of the Call of the Heart to find their way here. He did not want to drop that query and try another one, which could possibly leave Cressida and Horatio stranded.

So it was up to Arthur. Nodding, he stilled his fingers, placed his playing cards back in his Personal Space, and closed his eyes to check again. Casting his heart out toward the two was much easier than finding scourgling nests. Probably because a part of Arthur was still disgusted at the thought of scourglings and didn't really want to focus *any* part of his heart on them.

But Cressida and Horatio? He wanted to see his friends . . . and he especially wanted to see Cressida.

He hoped that deep down inside, Cressida wanted to see him just as badly. *I should've put them in my Personal Space and taken them with me*, he thought. *Between me and Brixaby, we could've fit Sams and Joy, too.*

But he hadn't known what he would be facing at Wolf Moon Hive when he had returned.

There had been every possibility Whitaker and his entire retinue would have been waiting on the other side of the portal to arrest Arthur. Or Whitaker himself might have tried to challenge them to a fight. Arthur had full confidence in Brixaby's abilities, but Crag, Whitaker's orange dragon, was wily, and Whitaker had had years to accumulate powerful cards.

Or, in the worst-case scenario, Whitaker could have easily contacted the king for backup. After all, if he suspected that Arthur had gone rogue, then reaching out to the king would be the next step.

It was that last possibility that had frightened Arthur the most.

He had no chance at all against the king's Mythic-level dragon, and the king was notoriously . . . changeable.

The last time, Arthur had barely escaped by the skin of his teeth. If the king had come, he'd have very likely died. And with Cressida and Horatio locked in his Personal Space, they would never have come out again.

He couldn't risk it. And at the time, it seemed better that they travel separately.

Granted, none of his fears had been validated. Whitaker was either lazy or an idiot and had assumed that Arthur would come to his call. Or perhaps he was wary of the dying Valentina.

Either way, it was over and done with. Arthur had escaped, he was nearly reunited with Cressida and Horatio, and he didn't want to dwell on the what-ifs.

Pushing regrets aside, Arthur focused his Call of the Heart on his two friends.

Instantly, a map appeared. Arthur frowned at it. It looked like they were still in the same spot, about three hours out or so, by a normal dragon's flight time.

But they'd been there the last two times Arthur had checked, too.

At first, Arthur thought maybe they had taken a midday break.

The sun was high in the sky, and it was not only hot but incredibly humid around New Houston.

But they'd be in the deadlands. Unless they found one of the oases, there was nowhere to rest.

"So?" Brixaby asked.

Arthur shook his head. "According to the map, they haven't moved."

Instantly, the dragon became more alert. "Are they in trouble?"

"I don't think so," Arthur said. "They know how close they are to us, and I think if they were in real trouble, Cressida would send a message."

Why hadn't she sent back a message in the last two days? Hadn't she missed him as much as he missed her? Was she mad at him for sending her on a long journey? Maybe she and Horatio had come to some kind of understanding?

Again, he pushed those thoughts away. They would only drive him crazy.

"This is unacceptable," Brixaby said. "I could be crafting right now." But that didn't seem to be what was really bothering him. He broke off and paced back and forth, tail whipping the air behind him with irritation. "Joy is not a dragon to dally. Neither is Sams, though with the heat . . ." He shook his head again.

Abruptly, Arthur made a decision.

"I'm tired of waiting. Let's fly out to meet them."

Brixaby perked up, and they spent the next couple of minutes collecting items and storing them in their Personal Space. After all, Arthur wasn't going to wait around without a nice chair if he could help it. Brixaby had, for some reason, packed his entire furnace and some smithing tools. Though, like Arthur, had been fretting and hadn't used it.

It wasn't long before they were ready to go. Arthur cast the Call of the Heart one more time just to double-check. The dots that designated Cressida and Horatio still had not moved.

"Let's get there fast," he told Brixaby as he climbed on and took hold of the neck ridges. He still hadn't gotten a proper dragon saddle for Brixaby. But with his **Dragon Riding** skill almost to 20, he wasn't sure there was much of a point.

Though, he did pull out goggles for his eyes that were on a stretchy strap that fit snugly around his head. It was amazing how fast one's eyes dried out when on the back of a dragon.

Brixaby immediately leaped into the air, and Arthur hung on, keeping as low as possible to present less wind resistance.

For the most part, Brixaby saved his breath while he flew and only used a mental thought to ask if Joy and Sams had moved.

Each time, Arthur reported that they still hadn't.

And every time, Brixaby put on even more speed in the way only a purple dragon could.

Arthur's estimation of three hours had been a little on the conservative side. At almost two hours on the mark, they started to see dots in the distance. But not just two dots. There were more—large blobs that resolved into clusters. Considering they were still over the deadlands, Arthur knew that these were not birds.

"Flying scourglings."

Brixaby had been flying quickly before, but now Arthur felt him activate his **Flying Sprint** skill. Arthur was rocked back but managed to hang on as they shot through the air faster than an arrow leaving a bowstring.

Soon, the dots resolved themselves to more detail. Joy and Sams were easy to pick out, especially Sams with his larger shape. They were both surrounded by a cloud of scourglings. Bright light glittered off Cressida as she activated and deactivated her mana shield to keep the worst of the flock from her.

And Sams intermittently glowed like a shining star as he activated some of his light-based powers, though Arthur knew that the real devastating card he shared with Horatio was some kind of invisible light that couldn't be seen with the naked eye.

Scourglings fell, broken from the sky, but there were many more where they came from.

Despite the fact that they had to have been fighting for hours, the two dragons didn't seem to be faltering. From a distance, it appeared they were keeping their heads above water. The problem was, for every enemy that was knocked down, another was quick to take his place. There was a long line of scourglings stretching back into the distance.

Arthur guessed they had tried to get away, but the scourglings were nimble, with razor-thin wings that lent them speed. Perhaps they had chased the dragon pair until they were finally forced to take a stand.

Arthur felt Brixaby swelling underneath him—not with anticipation, but with a Stunning Shout.

Arthur touched his neck. "Be careful, you don't want to hit our friends."

"I know what I'm doing," Brixaby grumbled. "This is a skill, and I have been leveling it."

However, he deflated again and held back for a few minutes, until they got so close that Arthur could see the details of the scourglings. They looked like grotesque, fleshy cranes with webbing instead of wings and a hammer-shaped head instead of a normal elegant form. Of course, when they opened their terrible beaks, they were filled with teeth.

That was when Brixaby opened up *his* terrible jaws and let out his Stunning Shout.

With Brixaby's head pointed forward, Arthur wasn't subject to the force of the shout, and he didn't hear it, either. Instead, he watched as it rippled through the air. A distortion that looked like an upside-down crescent headed straight for the messy flock of scourglings with Cressida and Joy in the middle.

Arthur's hands tightened into fists, but there was nothing he could do. He had no ability to call the shout back. All he could do was watch and trust in his dragon's judgment and skill.

Brixaby had aimed rather well—that crescent of force hit the bottom of the flock of scourglings that surrounded the dragon, shearing them off quite neatly before rolling outward.

The crescent expanded as it rolled outward and struck Sams's part of the flock that was encircling Sams and Horatio, cutting off a neat third of the scourglings before they could react.

It seemed like time stopped as all the scourglings, plus the dragons that they had been attacking, turned to look at the newcomers.

Joy gave a glad cry. "Brixaby!" And without further ado, she folded her wings and dived into the hole in the flock that Brixaby had created.

The scourglings whistled in outrage and immediately flew after her, but Joy had already gotten a good head start on them. She flew straight toward Arthur and Brixaby. Had she gotten bigger over the last couple weeks?

And was Cressida wearing plate armor?

The next moment, an enthusiastic pink dragon reached them and enfolded her wings around Brixaby in midair.

"Brixaby!" she cried again. "I missed you so much!"

CHAPTER 30

Pink wings enfolded Arthur and Brixaby from all sides, one wing with a trace of green in the membrane.

But what concerned Arthur more was the dropping sensation in his stomach and the feeling of weightlessness. The dragons couldn't fly clung together like this. They were falling.

His yell of alarm was echoed by Cressida, whose voice sounded muffled, either from her armor, the wings, or distance.

Of course, Brixaby's objection was the loudest, though completely unheard by Joy, who was busy babbling.

"I haven't seen you in so, *so* long! It's been forever, and we went through *so* many horrible things. And there weren't even any other dragons other than old Sams, can you believe that? None that were alive, anyway. Whoops," she added, slightly chagrined, "we're falling."

In the next second, the dragons separated. Brixaby righted himself, buzzing to regain his equilibrium.

Arthur looked around, but though it had seemed like they had been falling forever, in reality, it had only been a couple of seconds. They were still high in the air, the flat, gray, featureless landscape of the deadlands still far, far below.

Unfortunately, the incoming flock of scourglings was nearly upon them.

With half an exasperated roar, Joy extended her poison claws—claws that were lengthening. It seemed that sometime during their trip, she had absorbed the Sharp as Nails card into her secondary core.

Brixaby, too, swelled as he prepared his next Stunning Shout. He was forced to swallow it down a moment later as Joy barreled in his path to throw herself at the scourglings.

Arthur made a note to work on that. This was his retinue, and they would have to learn to work as a team.

That was for later. Now, they had scourglings to kill.

Arthur pulled sharp metal bits from his Personal Space. With a moment of thought, he started circling them around both arms, prepping them to fire.

Curiously, it was harder to move the shrapnel around his arm with the damaged card anchor.

Not having time to think about the implications of that, Arthur switched the metal around so that they circled his torso instead. As long as they were within an inch of his body, it was good to go.

Unfortunately, shooting them out as he normally did used a lot of mana he could no longer spare. But Arthur had already thought of that.

He used his fine control of the shards to spin faster and faster around his body until they were a blur. Then, once he was within range, he simply let one fly free.

This method didn't exactly allow for precision targeting, but there was a whole flock of scourglings in front of him. He just made sure not to send them in Joy's or Sams's general direction.

The scourglings were Commons, and if he was able to strike one at center mass, they fell immediately. Otherwise, the wings made good targets. The membrane was thin, and any hole quickly opened wider. Then the scourgling just fell to its death.

Meanwhile, Sams glowed brightly, so bright that for a moment, he was like a second sun in the air. Scourglings whistled in pain and rained down around him.

Then the yellow dragon made his way toward Arthur and Brixaby. Sams was old enough and wise enough to keep out of the way of Arthur's shots.

Horatio, who also wore metal armor, though without a helmet, yelled, "It's past time you showed up!"

Grinning, Arthur threw him a rude gesture.

However, the flash that he had seen of Horatio showed that his friend looked more hollow-cheeked than usual. Stress, or not getting enough to eat?

More scourglings were inbound, flying in a line from the distant nest.

Leaning down, Arthur spoke to Brixaby, who gleefully relayed his orders in the minds of the others.

Keep flying toward the west. We'll outpace the reinforcements soon.

Both Cressida and Horatio raised fisted hands in the hive signal of acknowledgment.

They continued fighting as they flew, though Arthur and Brixaby seemed to be what had turned the tide.

Fewer and fewer scourgling reinforcements were appearing, until the steady stream became a trickle.

Brixaby had swelled and turned, ready to finish off the rest of them, when Joy shouted, "Brixaby! Don't!"

Immediately, he deflated and looked at her. "What is wrong?"

"I only need five more to finish my quest!"

Brixaby swelled again, though this time it was indignation. "I didn't get a quest!"

"Well, you weren't here when the fight started, silly!" Joy called back as she flew past him. Conveniently enough, there were only five more scourglings left in the air, and they looked exhausted from having chased the dragons so far.

One light scratch from Joy was enough to quickly spread the poison through them. They fell with foam coming out of their mouths.

Arthur frowned. "Do you think her quest told her exactly how many scourglings she'd be fighting today? Or do you think that it updated when the nest stopped sending reinforcements?"

"Her card is a meta ability," Brixaby grumped. "Who knows." But he was more concerned with other issues, yelling at Joy, "What was your reward?"

She gestured to the ground, which was peppered with scourgling bodies. "All of these Common shards, of course!"

Sams snorted a pointed protest.

Quickly, Joy amended, "Well, of course we'll share. It would be totally unfair of me since you guys don't have quest cards."

The dragons landed, and the riders were able to reunite properly.

Horatio was first, deftly unhooking himself from his professional, high-grade dragon saddle. He hit the ground with a clank of armor and ran over to Arthur, pounding his friend on the back. "Glad to see you. I was starting to think you wouldn't show up."

Arthur frowned up at him. At first, he thought it was the armor, but while they were both on the ground, he wasn't so sure. "Aren't you too old to still be growing?" Horatio was now at least a head taller than him.

He grinned down. "Are you sure you haven't shrunk?" He reached out as if to ruffle Arthur's hair like he was a kid, but Arthur deftly ducked away.

Close up, there was no doubt: Horatio's cheeks were sunken in, like he had missed his fair share of meals. His lean face gave him a more stretched look, and his dark hair looked stringy and unwashed. The patchy beard he was trying to grow didn't help.

Then Cressida was walking up to him, having dismounted Joy. Arthur went to hug her, and she him, but then there was a terrible awkward moment where they both paused and hesitated, almost as if realizing that this might be too much and they weren't sure how to treat each other.

Then, pressing her lips together in a thin line, Cressida closed the distance. Arthur was happy to envelop her in his arms, even though her armor smacked hard against his chest. She smelled like sweat from the long fight, but with a unique sweetness that was all her.

"I missed you," she said.

He leaned back, grinning, he knew, like an idiot. "Me too. Uh, I mean, I missed you, too."

He caught Horatio rolling his eyes at both of them.

Meanwhile, off to the side, the dragons were starting their harvest of all the scourglings they had downed. Thankfully, Sams and Joy didn't seem interested in denying Brixaby his share, and Brixaby wasn't trying to assert his authority of being a Legendary by trying to grab theirs.

"If you're here," Cressida said, regaining Arthur's attention, "then the city isn't far away?"

She almost sounded desperate.

"No, not at all. It's about three . . ." He thought for a moment, remembering that the dragons would be tired, and therefore a little slower. "Maybe four hours away." He pointed back the way he and Brixaby had come.

"There are people there?" Horatio said, almost inanely, or so Arthur thought until he clarified, "Still alive?"

"Yeah, of course," Arthur said. "Why?"

Cressida and Horatio exchanged a glance.

Then Cressida said, "Then that would be the first undestroyed city we've seen this entire trip."

There was a beat of shock.

"Explain. No, wait." Arthur hadn't failed to notice that Cressida's face, too, looked lean. Definitely missed meals, then.

He pulled out chicken soup bowls, still steaming, as they'd been put into his Personal Space piping hot. By the way his friends' eyes went wide, he knew he'd made the right choice.

Horatio took his and then grimaced, looking over his shoulder back at the dragons. "We were counting on hunting on the way, but it was mostly deadlands, and even the small patches of live land didn't have much life to it. So the dragons had it worse. I can see Sams's ribs."

This was an exaggeration. Sams did look a little leaner than last time, but Arthur didn't begrudge Horatio. He would be upset if Brixaby was infrequently fed.

Cressida, too, was looking at her bowl with a guilty expression on her face, like she was starving but didn't dare eat it. "Joy's had it worse. She hit another growth spurt on the way here."

And of course, the dragons couldn't eat scourglings.

"Don't worry about them," Arthur said, then unstored half a haunch of bison. It was already butchered, the skin and fur cut away. It was also at least two hundred pounds, so it thumped loudly to the dusty ground.

Arthur looked down at it with a wince. "Sorry, I forgot, I don't have anywhere to cook it." It wasn't like there was dead wood lying around for a fire. Why hadn't he stored logs in his Personal Space?

"Cook it?" Horatio said with a laugh.

Arthur looked up to see his friends giving him an amused look. Oh, right. Well, he was used to cooking meals for Brixaby.

"Joy won't be picky." Turning, Cressida called out, "Joy, come over here, dearest, and see what Arthur has for you!"

Immediately, Joy's head popped up as she sniffed the air. "Meat? Fresh meat?"

Arthur unstored another entire bison leg and thumped it not too far away. He'd nearly made Dannill cry with his requests for dragon supplies, but he hadn't regretted it for a moment.

Joy and Sams started on the bison while Brixaby looked over them with an air of mild superiority as he drank from his own bucket-sized portion of chicken soup.

Arthur encouraged Horatio and Cressida to drink theirs, too, as it had the added effect of mild healing.

Joy ate happily and only looked up long enough to ask, "This is very good, but do you have the head that goes with this cow? I'd love to crunch down on some brains."

"It's a bison, not a cow," Arthur said. "But no, I don't have a head."

"Bi-son." Sams said the word slowly, testing it out. "That would explain the gaminess to the meat." He crunched down, snapping the femur in two before eating it whole, bones and all. "Not that I am complaining."

Arthur winced and turned back to his own meal. When feeding dragons, he found, it was best not to *watch*.

"Tell me about your journey."

Cressida explained. "Arthur, these cities were huge. Bigger than the hives. Bigger, I think, than the central cities back in the kingdom."

"Weird buildings, too," Horatio added. "They weren't eruption cones, but they went just as high as some of them—at least the ones that were still standing. All glass and steel, it was crazy."

"And it was empty?" Arthur asked.

"All on dead land," Horatio confirmed. "Not a damn thing growing anywhere. I almost thought it was a scourgling city, except for the nasty skeletons."

"And the dragon bodies," Cressida added quietly. "Too many to count, and a lot of them were . . . pretty small."

"Hatchlings?" Arthur asked.

She shrugged. "No, they were old enough to fly. Some were in the buildings, even. And they didn't upset Joy like a dead hatchling would."

Brixaby perked up. "If there were dragon bodies, what happened to the cards?"

"No." Horatio shook his head. "No, these had been dead for a long, long time. More than decades. Centuries, probably."

"But if they were in the deadlands—"

Arthur stopped Brixaby with a shake of his head.

Cressida noticed and started to narrow her eyes at him, but Arthur caught her gaze.

"Later," he said.

She looked at him for a moment, then shrugged and continued hungrily digging into her soup, dipping a handmade dumpling that Arthur had added. The dumplings weren't made of any extraordinary ingredients, but they did taste very good and went nicely with the richness of the broth.

Horatio continued. "The cities were . . . weird. There were all sorts of machines everywhere, all rusted out. I have no idea what they used to do, and the signs were all in a different language." Horatio shrugged. "Some of the letters looked a little like ours, but—"

"No, they speak a different language here, and have a different alphabet, too," Arthur said. "Don't worry, I'll get something for you so you can understand it. It's kind of like a card anchor."

Cressida's eyebrows rose, but then she nodded and returned to their story.

"Well, the cities weren't completely empty. That's where we found some of the armor, and I was able to scrounge a better saddle for Joy off one of the dragons. She'd outgrown her old one."

He looked, and Joy was indeed wearing a different dragon saddle, with an odd black material that wasn't quite leather. But he couldn't tell much more about it without closer examination.

Setting his now-empty bowl aside, Horatio sat down on the scourge-dust, stretching out his long legs. "I have to say, I'm not too much of a fan of this part of the world from what I've seen of it."

"You're just sitting on the dirt?" Cressida made a face.

"I'm carded, aren't I? I'm not catching anything from this."

"Yes, but it's scourge-dust. It's gross."

Arthur grabbed a picnic blanket from his Personal Space and set it down. Horatio rolled his eyes at him but shifted to sit on the blanket.

The dragons, unfortunately, were too large for the blanket, even Brixaby. But they settled down nearby, resting. Brixaby pulled out a few buckets of water.

"I usually use these for dowsing fires, but this will do nicely."

Joy and Sams sucked down the water so greedily that Arthur felt bad.

"Tell me about the city we're about to see," Horatio said.

So Arthur took the time to explain what he knew of the city of New Houston, and most importantly, of the Dark Heart.

Horatio and Cressida's reactions were exactly as he had hoped—both horrified and fascinated, leaning more toward horrified.

That was a relief because with everyone else looking forward to it opening, sometimes he felt a little crazy for thinking that the Dark Heart was a bad idea.

"This is worse than playing with fire," Horatio said, shaking his head. "There's nothing good about dealing with scourglings."

"Yeah," Arthur said. "From what I understand, other cities nearby have been overrun by letting their Dark Heart erupt. There are no dragons to deal with scourglings in the middle of a city. And from what I can tell, the deadlands here are trying to encroach on what they have left." Arthur shook his head. "If it were my city, I'd make changes."

"It *could* be your city," Horatio said.

"H," Cressida said, and it took Arthur a moment to realize that was her nickname for Horatio. An immediate flare of jealousy flared up in his chest, hot and bright. But the next moment, he was able to rein it back.

He shook his head. "No, I might be a Legendary, but I'm not here to take over the city. Besides, I guess the Dark Heart isn't all bad. It's already given me some gifts. Brixaby?" He waved to get the dragon's attention. "You got the—"

He stopped as Cressida reached out and grabbed his arm. "What's this?" She turned his hand over and caught her breath at the look of what was left of his card anchor.

"Oh, yeah," Arthur said. "I sort of blew up my card anchor."

"You *what*?" Horatio scrambled over, then let out a low whistle when he got a look at Arthur's arm. "I'm surprised you still have that hand."

"Yeah, well, that's another reason why I'm not ready to write off the Dark Heart. It brought me here because it's what I *need*." He went on quickly, "But that's not all I found."

"What else?" Cressida asked.

"Scourgling nests," Arthur said. "And what lies at the heart of them. As soon as your dragons rest a bit, I'll show you."

CHAPTER 31

Arthur was barely able to keep the smile off his face. "But first, I have some welcome home gifts for the both of you."

"So, this city of yours is going to be our new home?" Horatio asked, but he and Cressida had sat up at Arthur's words, interested.

Brixaby, who'd been half paying attention to the humans' conversation, came over. With a flourish, he pulled out two cards from his Personal Space.

"You should be grateful that I did not eat this," he commented offhandedly. "They were rather magically heavy to carry around."

"They can't be heavier than all those combat cards you carried from Free Mesa Hive that one time," Joy said.

"Yes, but that was briefly and during battle. These have sat in my Personal Space for some time, tempting me . . ."

Ignoring the byplay, Cressida and Horatio sat forward eagerly.

Cressida halfway reached for the card. "Is that . . ." She glanced at Arthur. "Are you sure?"

"Well, it's not like I can put them in my card anchor." He meant it as a joke, but there was a note of bitterness he hadn't planned for.

Cressida shot him a sympathetic look. Horatio, meanwhile, had no trouble plucking the card from Brixaby.

"Rainbow Knight?" he said doubtfully, but then his skepticism cleared up as he read on. "Wow, Sams, what do you think of this?" He turned the card to his dragon so he could read it.

Though Arthur knew what the card said from before, his **Reading** skill let him scan over it again at a glance.

Rainbow Knight
Rare
Combat Support

The wielder of this card will be able to collect all spectrums of light from 10 to 750 nanometers from artificial and natural sources. This light will be stored in a light well with a meter accessible from the wielder's card deck dashboard. Light collected from natural sources such as fire or sunshine will naturally be more potent. Once collected, the wielder may be able to emit that light again at will. Note: This card can only collect visible spectrum light and does not include any heat generated by light.

"I have seen something like this before," Sams rumbled. "For farmers who wish to grow plants and such indoors. They go out and collect sunlight, come back in, and release it in an otherwise dark room. It is usually paired with a card anchor."

"Hang the farmers," Horatio said. "We can use it. Too bad about the heat, but you can add that, can't you?"

Sams snorted his agreement. "Yes, add it to your heart deck."

"Go on, Cressida," Joy said from the side. She was bouncing from foot to foot, and now that she'd grown larger, she made the pebbles around her dance with her excitement. "What's our new card? I want to see! Is it powerful?"

Cressida read the card to her, though Arthur already knew what it said. He knew it by heart.

Right Back at Ya
Rare
Combat Defense

Using mana, the wielder of this card will be able to form a shield around themselves and their allies. The exact size of the shield will depend on the quality and amount of mana, as well as the skill of the wielder. When defending against physical attacks, this shield will reflect a portion of the energy directly back at the attacker. The amount reflected is proportional to the user's skill, the amount and quality of mana, and the strength of the attack. This is a skill-based card.

"A skill-based card?" Cressida breathed.

"Yes!" Arthur couldn't stop his grin. "So the more you use and exercise it, the greater control you will have. In higher levels, it may use less mana. Of course," he added eagerly, "that means at first it might be mana hungry, but I think if you practice some and level—"

"Arthur!" She laughed, placing her hand on his forearm. "I know what a skill-based card is. I am just amazed. My current mana shield isn't skill based."

"Oh. Of course." He snapped his jaw shut and ignored Horatio's smirk. But he still couldn't keep down his enthusiasm. "That's another thing—I was hoping, based on your mana shield, that the two might share some synergy. I don't think they're part of the same set . . ." He waited for her to shake her head to continue. "But they still might combine to two of a kind if there's a lot of synergy."

"There's only one way to find out," she said, and added it to her heart deck, to Joy's cheers.

Cressida closed her eyes for a moment, but the smile that bloomed over her face told Arthur that there was indeed some synergy.

"I can't wait to try this," she said.

"You'll get your chance soon," Arthur promised. "I want to show you something special about the nests."

"Ugh," Joy complained as they flew. "We're going back the way we came. I know we're collecting the shards we missed, but seeing the same land again is sooo boring."

Brixaby turned toward her, but Sams spoke up first, in a low-measured tone. "As I understand it, we are to destroy the place that spawned those scourglings to begin with." He paused to curve his big yellow head around to check with Horatio, who nodded at him. Satisfied, Sams turned back. "Dragons should never let scourglings live and should always destroy them at the source."

"I guess," Joy said. "It's just boring, and I'm tired."

Arthur suspected that the last complaint was the real reason Joy was in an unusually grumpy mood.

It had taken longer than he liked for her and Sams to say that they were ready and able to fly again. They had truly been close to their last legs during that fight and were more exhausted than they had let on to their riders.

If it were up to Arthur, he would have let them rest the entire day—deadlands or not—or had Brixaby carry them in his Personal Space. Joy, at least, would fit.

But Cressida and Horatio knew their dragons and insisted that they were ready to go. Arthur had to trust their judgment.

Part of it was that they'd been properly horrified by the existence of the nests, and even more so that the city-states not only knew about them but used them as a bellwether for their Dark Hearts.

"No wonder you said the deadlands are expanding around here," Horatio said, spitting to the side. "What else do they expect to happen?"

Cressida had wrinkled her nose at the spit but agreed. "I never imagined there could be so much dead land. I mean, I've seen it on maps outside the kingdom, but here . . . there is no kingdom. Just little oases of life. I can't believe they'd be foolish enough to threaten that."

"The people here call the Dark Heart opening a Reshuffling," Arthur said. "There's a lot of power and cards to be gained—enough to completely upend the workings of an entire city."

"Like a boy from a border town getting a Legendary card?" Cressida asked.

"Something like that."

They knew they were getting within range of the nest when the flying Common scourglings came after them again.

The real danger these presented was if a flock overwhelmed a single target.

But the vast majority had been decimated by the last fight. The scourglings came at them in dribs and drabs and were easily killed by Sams or Brixaby, who was more than happy to level his Stunning Shout ability on more pinpoint targets. Joy took care of the very few that got close.

Even better, they followed the ragged line of scourglings straight back to the nest.

Commons weren't the most intelligent.

The nest was a thick crack in the ground, and from up high looked like a scar on diseased flesh.

As the dragons drew close, a final burst of about two dozen scourglings emerged. Most of these were knocked out of the sky by a flash of light from Sams.

Arthur made a mental note to ask Horatio what his dragon's cards were, exactly. Now that they were an official retinue and were going to go into the Dark Heart together, he needed to know his team's strengths.

A few of the scourglings escaped the blazing light and circled around at different angles. Brixaby swelled, preparing his shout. Joy flexed her claws.

"Wait!" Horatio yelled. "Let me!"

Then he activated his Rainbow Knight card.

It was pretty obvious that was the card because the air around Horatio seemed to twist all out of proportion, and colors briefly became inverted and then . . . odd. It was like looking into the depths of a glass prism built by a merchant of fancy gifts.

His head was red, shading to yellow at the neck, then green, blue, and finally purple at his feet.

"Aw," Joy said. "It's very pretty!"

Suddenly, all the colors bled into purple and then seemed to vanish.

Arthur remembered that Horatio, for some reason, often described their invisible light card as purple.

No sooner had he thought that than a fully visible purple beam shot out farther than any of their attacks had before—farther, even, than Brixaby's Stunning Shout.

It split into several mini beams, striking every single scourgling.

The air, which had been full of whistling shrieks, suddenly went silent except for the occasional thunk-thunk-thunk of falling bodies hitting the ground.

No more scourglings came out of the nest.

"Wow." Horatio turned to Arthur, grinning. "That worked even better than I had hoped. Great card, Art!"

Arthur waved an acknowledgment back and tried not to feel a little bitter that his friends could add cards to their decks while he was stuck without a card anchor.

"I could have done the same, had I shouted," Brixaby grumbled.

Arthur patted him on the neck.

The three dragons circled the nest opening a few times just to make sure the fight was done. When nothing more emerged, they landed.

The crack itself was large and deep enough that no one could see to the bottom. But it was too small for any of the dragons, even Brixaby, to get in.

"We'll be fine. They're just Commons." Arthur pulled his ladder out of his Personal Space. "Why don't you three dragons harvest the scourglings we just killed, and we'll clear out the nest?"

He dropped the ladder and moved to descend, but Cressida stepped up. "I'll go down first."

"What? Why?"

She gave him a fierce look. "You're the one who gave me the new shield card, remember? Horatio got to test his, and now it's my turn."

He winced, but he agreed.

Cressida leaned over to look down the crack. Then she summoned Wicker and one of her water cranes. They both slipped down the crack, and Cressida followed.

She didn't use her shield on the ladder, but it was possible using it would give her trouble while interacting with outside objects.

It only took a few seconds, but it felt like forever until Cressida called back up. "There were a few scourglings down here, but the area's clear now. Hurry, while it's safe to come down."

"Me next," Horatio said, pushing past Arthur and giving him a jaunty smile. "You do want to see down there, right?"

"There's glowing mold," Arthur complained, but Horatio was already halfway down the ladder.

Arthur followed. On his way down, he heard an odd pulsing thud, like a heartbeat.

At the bottom, Horatio activated one of his light abilities, as light seemed to diffuse a few inches off his skin. And even though there was glowing mold, it did give Arthur more visibility.

Like the others, this nest was arranged into corridors.

And Cressida was under attack.

. . . sort of.

The rhythmic pulsing sound was coming from newly hatched scourglings—still wet from their ovoids—throwing themselves against her shield.

She must have had her new kinetic shield up, because it had a different hue, redder than the blue of her mana shield. More importantly, the scourglings bounced back every time they threw themselves at Cressida. Awkward and ungainly on the floor, with only the use of their hind feet and wing arms . . . they were a little pathetic.

Meanwhile, Cressida stood strong in the middle of the corridor, protected by the shield.

Horatio glanced pointedly at Wicker and the water crane, which stood to either side behind Cressida, watching but not engaging with the attacking scourglings. "Are you going to let them fight?"

"In a few minutes," Cressida replied. "I'm trying to get some easy levels for my shield."

Arthur smiled. *That's my girl.*

But the smell down in this nest was just as awful as the others. Arthur quickly fished around in his Personal Space for more rags to soak in vinegar and tie around his mouth and nose. He gave one to Horatio as well.

With a frown of concentration, Cressida lowered the back half of her shield to allow Arthur to pass one of the rags to her.

Meanwhile, Horatio bent and squinted at the wall. He held out his hand, and abruptly it was perfectly illuminated, showing more proto-ovoids growing in clusters that Arthur hadn't seen.

"So this is how baby scourglings are made, huh?" Horatio asked.

"Yeah, but here's a fun trick." Arthur grabbed one of his butcher knives and stabbed the tip into the largest ovoid of the bunch. From the partially developed scourgling inside, he harvested a Common shard and flipped it to his friend.

Horatio caught it, eyebrows lifting in surprise. "Wait . . . do you know what this means?"

"Yeah, we can farm scourglings . . . or we could if it wasn't like playing with fire."

"Acid fire," Horatio grunted, then turned to Cressida. "Are you going to let those poor things bash themselves to death?"

"Poor things?" she repeated.

Horatio shrugged, but Cressida seemed to think he had a point. Lowering her shield, she sent Wicker forward.

The three scourglings that had been attacking her were by then too exhausted to move out of the way of the flame bear. They fell to one swipe of his paw.

"Send Wicker and your crane down the corridor," Arthur said. "Have them kill the scourglings but leave the egg sacs. We can harvest them ourselves."

Cressida suddenly grinned at him, feral and beautiful at the same time. "Watch this."

She clapped her hands, and with a crackling roar from Wicker and a gurgling cry from the water crane, the two elemental beings rushed down the corridor. Just as they got into a good clip, they merged into a gout of steam that continued with rolling momentum past where Arthur could see down the way.

Pained scourgling cries echoed back to them. From the gust of heat that blew back at them a few moments later—uncomfortably hot but nowhere near what the rest of the corridor got—Arthur realized Cressida had created superheated steam.

"The steam dissipates too fast out in the open," Cressida explained as if reading his thoughts. "But they're really good in enclosed spaces."

With that, she started walking down the hall, resummoning her elemental creatures and sending them along for another steam bath.

Horatio leaned close to Arthur. "Don't tell her I said this, but your girlfriend can be a little scary."

Arthur grinned.

They cleaned out the nest rather quickly, it having spent its best fighters in the aerial battle.

Cressida and Horatio seemed glad of the shard harvest . . . but not so much when Arthur pulled out a shovel at the end of the tunnel.

Thankfully, the dragon corpse wasn't buried too deep down. It was a purple—an unusually large one.

Seeing buried dark purple scales made a lump grow in Arthur's throat. He quickly used Brixaby's Call of the Void to harvest its remaining card.

It was so rotten that he could only read the rank—Common, and that it had something to do with flight. It was also actively disintegrating.

With a wince, he stored it in his Personal Space, where it sat like an uncomfortable lump against his soul. He would to transfer it to Brixaby as soon as possible.

Horatio stared. "That shouldn't be possible. It's been dead for how long? That card should be gone."

"That's the thing," Arthur said. "It's buried in the deadlands. Nothing about this dragon's corpse is rotting. Well, not much."

Cressida had seemed too shocked for words but finally gathered herself again. "Arthur, that card is disintegrating! And you . . . you just put it inside yourself."

"Time doesn't move in my Personal Space—"

She spoke over him. "The last time someone played with disintegrating cards, it spawned the Mind Singer! I haven't forgotten that. Have you?"

Arthur let out a long breath. No, he certainly hadn't forgotten what had happened under the scholars' guild—or completely forgiven himself over it. Especially not after seeing what had happened to the free hive . . . and those poor hatchling dragons.

Even Horatio looked uneasy.

"It's safe," Arthur said.

She crossed her arms. "For now."

"Yes, for now. But there's something else. Brix and I have gone through other nests, and one dragon buried below had a trio of cards. One of those repairs other cards."

Horatio made an appreciative sound. However, Cressida narrowed her eyes as if she knew there was a "but" coming.

And of course, there was.

"The repair card is in need of repair too, but if I *can* fix it . . ." He waved his hand around. "Think about it. How many times were you and Horatio attacked on the way here? All those different scourglings came from nests, and all of those were powered by disintegrating cards."

Cressida and Horatio exchanged a look.

"We were attacked more the closer we got to here," Horatio said. "But sometimes there wasn't a day that went by when we didn't see a scourgling."

"Think about how many cards that represents." As Arthur talked, his voice grew faster as he became more excited. "These are ancient cards. They haven't been active in the world for generations. Who knows how much power they represent—how much opportunity! And right now, they're just rotting away into scourglings. Everything around here is!" He smacked the side of his hand against the tunnel wall in emphasis. "We shouldn't let them just die!"

"Arthur," Cressida said quietly. "If you wanted more cards, you could always just go to a shop. Why is this so important to you?"

"Because . . . because . . ." He sputtered for a moment. He couldn't put his mixed but suddenly desperate feelings into words.

Until in the next moment, he could.

It was as if something unfurled in his mind. He knew himself and could see the motivations behind his own muddled feelings better.

"You know what Brixaby's power is. For him to gain more power, he has to eat cards."

And I've done the same, he thought with another surge of guilt, thinking of the Grindstone card.

If he had a chance to go back in time, he probably would have still absorbed the Grindstone card. But still, removing something from the world didn't sit right with him.

With a final burst of clarity, Arthur blurted, "What if Brixaby is a card destroyer . . . but I could somehow bring cards back into the world?"

Skill level gained: Meditation
Level 20

He had gained several levels in **Meditation** . . . without meditating. Or had he?

The next alert was more surprising.

New skill gained: Self-Insight (Self Class)
Due to your card's bonus traits, you automatically start this skill at level 5.

CHAPTER 32

Arthur, pal . . .” Dannill gave Arthur a smile that managed to barely remain on this side of smug. Barely. “What you’re describing—a card that stops card disintegration? Never heard of it. I don’t think it’s possible.”

“Of course it’s possible,” Arthur said, frustrated. “Every spell, charm, or skill has its own card.”

“Well, if it was . . . you wouldn’t find it in a store. That’d be a Legendary-level card, and you don’t find such a thing in a store.”

Arthur wanted to snap back that he knew more about Legendaries than Dannill, but he held his tongue. He’d had a frustrating morning after he returned to the city with Cressida and Horatio, clandestinely going through the city’s card shops. The shelves were bare, and he hadn’t found anything stronger than a Common. But he’d held out hope because Dannill had back channels that Arthur didn’t.

Dannill slowly shook his head and, as if he had read Arthur’s mind, said, “This close to the heart opening, there’s not much left out there but scraps. Everyone who can get their hands on a card is buying, and that was before the latest influx of refugees.” He paused. “You have heard the news, right?”

“News?”

Dannill nodded. “The city government finally got off their useless behinds and reevaluated the heart. They figure about a week or so ’til it’s ripe now, but everyone knows that date seems to be accelerating closer and closer. We could only get a couple hours’ notice, so make sure you’re ready and you got your team all set.”

Accelerating. And if they misjudged the timing, instead of the heart opening, they could have an eruption on their hands.

Arthur shook his head and wondered if he should take Cressida, Horatio, and the dragons and just dive into the damn thing before it burst.

Dannill didn't let him respond and swung back to Arthur's original question. "Now, if you want something reasonable, I hear tell of a Rare portal card that might be floating around . . . for the right price. It's one of the very few Rares left in the city. Unless"—he eyed Arthur—"you have one to sell to me? People have noticed you've been gone the last couple days . . ."

Trailing off, he looked at Arthur hopefully.

Arthur ignored that, and the mention of the Rare portal card. More than one card shop owner had mentioned it as well, and he'd gotten details. It was a short-distance portal spell that only carried the wielder. Great for relocating yourself during combat but useless for his needs.

Instead, he fixed Dannill with an unimpressed eye. "Why? Who's been looking?"

"The usual. Undersheriff Lopez, Oversheriff Walker. They realized we have a business connection, so when they couldn't find you, they came asking like I'm your minder."

Arthur wasn't surprised by that. He also didn't fail to notice that Dannill kept trying to change the subject away from the card he wanted. He considered for a moment, then, with a wince, activated his Subtle Influence card. He kept a light touch on it, however, just to add emphasis to his words.

"Dannill, finding that card is really important to me. If you have any type of . . ." He struggled for a moment. " . . . meta card that fixes other cards, I want to know about it."

There was no indication Dannill had been influenced other than he seemed to take Arthur's words more seriously. "So do I, kid. I'll put the word out. Just don't expect anything. But what about our sheriff problem? Right now, they're asking for your help kindly. But with the Dark Heart opening soon, that means more scourglings on the loose . . . and I thought you had a soft spot for refugees."

"I do, and I can help," Arthur said firmly. "But not for free."

"I'd say that's between you and the sheriffs—"

Arthur cut him off. "I'll need at least three more whole bison this week, and at least that each week going forward."

Dannill gave him a sharp look. "Three more? No offense, but your dragon ain't bigger than a small horse. Does flying really cost that much energy?"

"It does," Arthur replied. "But they're not all for him."

He turned and pointed back to the barn. One of the double doors was thrown open, and as if on cue, Sams's head poked out. The big yellow dragon looked around, probably trying to see where the noise of conversation had been coming from, as Arthur had met Dannill outside to let the dragons rest.

Larger than Joy, he'd had a difficult time fitting through the barn doors last night. While inside, he had to be wary of his wings and tail to not knock over any of Brixaby's furnaces.

"Well, I'll be dipped in bison manure," Dannill muttered. He stared for a moment, then took off his wide-brimmed hat and stared for another few seconds like that would help him see. His grin widened. "Now *that* is a dragon!"

Arthur ignored that. "And there's a second one in there, so you can see why I need the—"

"A whole team of dragons! And their riders, too, I expect?" Dannill turned to him. "What's the other's color? Is he as striking as that yellow fellow?"

"She's pink," Arthur said.

Dannill practically rubbed his hands together. "That will work well for the girls. Perfect! I don't suppose you can convince them to fly around the city a few times? Make themselves be seen?"

"Get me enough to feed them," Arthur said, though privately he didn't think he would be able to stop Joy and Sams once they had rested. "I assume you'll cover the fines for disrupting the city?"

Dannill's eyes glittered. "There's a difference between official attention and unprofitable attention. Let me handle the sheriffs and officials."

Good enough. He took Dannill by the elbow and started leading him in the direction of the barn. It wasn't hard. Far from fearful, the man was enthusiastic, talking about quick-run paintings and possibly stuffed animals if they could manage it in time for the heart's opening.

Arthur guessed he had already made a good deal of profit from Brixaby's likeness.

He spoke up to get the man back on track. "One more thing. My dragon rider friends are going to need your services . . ."

Cressida was not happy about getting a tattoo.

"It *has* to be permanent?" She frowned. "I've always avoided those."

Dannill, ever the salesman, had a good command of their language—he would not be a language merchant otherwise—and jumped right in.

"It won't hurt a bit, young lady. We have a specialized numbing gel, and I'm nothing but scrupulous with sanitation. You'll heal up quick."

Her frown deepened. "I'm not afraid of pain, *sir*. It's the look. It's one thing to get a card-anchor tattoo, but there are ways around that." She unconsciously touched the pocket where she kept a fancy purse she used for her own anchor.

She was a nobleman's daughter and had particular ideas of what was proper and what wasn't. Arthur personally couldn't care less, but it wasn't his body on the line.

Of course, Dannill had an answer for that, too.

"My tattoos are flexible enough to be almost anywhere on the body that's not visible. The back of the shoulder, perhaps, where it will be covered up by a shirt, or a leg. And of course," he added, "I do have female artists to do the task. Your comfort is paramount."

Horatio watched this byplay with his arms crossed. He snorted at that last bit, sounding like his grumpy dragon. "Put it on my forehead for all I care. Not being able to talk to people gets old fast. You don't want to go out shopping and get swindled, do you, Cress?"

Arthur jumped in. "Joy will be upset if she can't talk to people. You know that."

Her expression smoothed. Reluctantly, she nodded.

Arthur worked out the payment with Dannill, taking care of the cost with Common shards. In this case, Dannill preferred shards to cards because he had clients who wanted to put them together themselves.

"Superstitious," he said with a shrug.

Joy woke up soon after and guzzled down two large barrels of water before she was ready to fly. Horatio offered Dannill a seat on Sams to transport the man back to his store. Dannill was delighted.

"You aren't going with us?" Cressida asked Arthur, noting he was not moving to join them.

He glanced at Dannill, then decided he didn't care if the man knew what he was up to. Chances were, he somehow already did. "I need to see that heart deck specialist."

Though he was powerfully curious about how Dannill planned to tattoo dragon scales for Joy and Sams, he felt a strong draw to see Ravi. It was as if his new **Self-Insight** skill was whispering that he was on the cusp of something important.

"All right," Horatio said easily. He mimed a punch at Arthur's shoulder. "Don't wait up late for me. After I can talk to these people, I'm going to see those sheriffs." He glanced at his dragon. "Sams and I want to target practice on some scourglings—we'll be in tip-top shape for when that heart of theirs opens."

Cressida tilted her head in thought. "Does this place have a scholars' guild, or perhaps a conservatory for knowledge? I would like to know if they have anything about the abandoned cities we saw on the way here."

Dannill smiled at her. "Oh, a historian, are you? Yes, I can point the way."

Arthur wasn't sure he liked the proprietary way he gestured her toward her own dragon, but he trusted Cressida enough to handle herself.

After seeing them off, he said goodbye to Brixaby who, of course, was still at the smithing forge, and then set off to Ravi's small shop.

"Level twenty already?" Sitting cross-legged on the floor in his office, Healer Ravi gave Arthur a long look as if he was concerned Arthur was making it up. "It seems you do have some talent in this area after all."

It wasn't talent. Arthur was certain it had everything to do with his Grind-stone card. Well, that, and a lot of focused practice.

"I've always worked better under a deadline," he said, shifting uncomfortably on his seat. Why didn't this man have chairs? "But there's more. Most of the time, when I hit twenty, I'm awarded by either an advancement to the skill or attribute points. This time, there was nothing."

"Nothing?" Ravi asked, eyebrows rising. "Nothing at all?"

He shrugged. "I did get a skill in Self-Insight, but that's separate . . . isn't it?"

"Perhaps, perhaps not. But you should not so easily discount the gift of insight, Arthur."

"But the Dark Heart will be open soon, and I need those cards that were in my card anchor."

Ravi hummed. "Is that truly what you need?"

He started to answer, stopped, then frowned. "What do you mean?"

"That is something only you can answer, not me."

Arthur let out a breath in aggravation.

"But," Ravi said, "perhaps there is a way I can speed things along."

Arthur leaned forward.

The healer smiled. "For a price."

That price, of course, was an Uncommon shard. Arthur paid the equivalent in Commons and Ravi took him to another room. This one was more colorful than the last, with complex geometric patterns on the walls, ceiling, and floor, as well as the thick scent of some spicy incense.

Again, there were no chairs. Instead, Ravi sat across from Arthur on small square pillows.

Ravi began. "I have taught you about meditation before, but this time I will lead you into guided meditation, which may be a deeper experience." He paused. "While in this state, some people gain insights about themselves that may be uncomfortable. If this happens to you, I suggest you do not fight it, lest you break yourself out of the deeper meditation."

Arthur hesitated. This was sounding close to what he'd seen some confidence men pull on marks in Wolf Moon Hive's city. People would claim they had cards to see the future, to speak to the dead, or forecast if a relationship would succeed or fail.

Of course, if they did truly have cards like that, they'd be working for the high nobles, not in the poorer districts in the shadow of a dragon hive. But those who believed never saw it that way.

"You're not going to serve me special tea, are you?" Arthur asked with suspicion.

Ravi smiled. "No, none of this is hallucinatory. But some people, especially when they are at war with themselves, may suddenly *see* more vividly. Are you ready for that?"

Arthur wasn't sure, but he straightened his spine anyway. "I'll do whatever it takes to prepare for the Dark Heart."

"Very well, then. Take my hands."

New Counterfeit spell obtained: Induce Deep Spiritual Self-Awareness
Remaining time: 59 Minutes 59 Seconds

Ah, not a skill, then, but a spell. Interesting how Ravi had neglected to mention that.

Not a confidence man, but not exactly honest, either.

However, Arthur could feel that this spell would only work if Arthur allowed it in. He had a measure of trust for Ravi, and he had ways of defending himself. So he relaxed his mind, ensured all his mental shields were down, and allowed the spell to sweep over him.

"Fall into meditation," Ravi intoned. "Focus on your heart deck."

Suddenly, Arthur was no longer sitting in the overly colorful room. He was now standing in darkness.

He was also aware that a part of him was "outside," still in his body. He could feel the pillow under him, his hands lightly clasped with the healer's to provide the link.

It was a lot like being in his Personal Space. This was a journey of the mind and not the body.

And he had the feeling that if things went terribly wrong, he could wrench himself out of it and return fully to his body at any time.

Though it was velvet darkness around him, he felt pulled forward.

Arthur walked, and in the curious way of dreams, he realized the pull wasn't any intuition of his own, but from the connection he always felt between himself and Brixaby's core.

Specifically, his Call of the Heart.

And why not? It was a seeking card.

The pull led him smoothly forward without a stumble. Around him, he heard a rhythmic thumping of a heartbeat.

Was that his heart deck?

When his straining eyes perceived a faint illumination ahead, the thumping picked up its pace.

He fell into a jog, and the glow ahead suddenly jumped into bright focus.

His Master of Skills and Master of Body Enhancement cards stood tall, bright, and glittering like two unmovable pillars inside his heart. But beside them, ghostly in outline, were three additional spaces for cards.

Arthur stared at them, feeling the pull not only from the seeking card, but a kind of wistful sense of incompleteness from his two other cards.

"You'll never complete your Master set, traitor."

Turning, Arthur took an involuntary step back as he saw his cousin, Penn, standing close enough to punch.

He stood, confident, in fine nobleman's gear with the house crest of Rowantree on his tunic, which glowed almost as brightly as the cards. And his face was twisted in hate.

In the twisty way of the mind, he was now positioned in front of the faintly glowing Master of Combat card.

Penn's eyes flashed. "Betrayer."

"Yes." The word came through a dry mouth. "Yes. I had to lie to you, and you tried to take Brix away from me."

"You'll never have what I have!" A sword appeared in Penn's hand, and he charged forward in an attack.

New Counterfeit skill obtained: Decisive Strike (Sword)
Remaining Time: 9 Minutes 59 Seconds

Arthur reached into his Personal Space for the first thing he could find and came out with a shovel.

Desperately, he used Decisive Strike himself, adding it to his Makeshift Weaponry card's abilities. The spade end parried the edge of the blade, sparks coming off, and deflected it just enough that it missed Arthur.

Undeterred, Penn struck again.

New Counterfeit skill obtained: Vital Thrust (Sword)
Remaining Time: 9 Minutes 59 Seconds

Again, Arthur parried, though the sword edge nicked the outer side of his arm. It was a shallow cut, mainly due to Arthur's Toughened Skin body enhancement. Ironically, one he had gotten from Penn.

Penn drew back for another attack, but that gave Arthur the moment he needed to swing the shovel at him like a club.

Penn seemed to reel out of the way. But suddenly, Arthur had picked up that trick, too.

New Counterfeit skill obtained: Dodge (Defense)
Remaining Time: 9 Minutes 59 Seconds

And he had more.

Grabbing a handful of metal shavings, he threw them at Penn with an enhanced effect from his **Throwing Accuracy** and Nice Shot card.

The bits peppered Penn's face and torso. He roared in rage and came at Arthur again, swift and striking. This time, Arthur had to use the stolen Dodge and leaned on his **Balance** skill to stay light on his feet.

They went back and forth like that in a strange sense of time that could have been seconds or an hour.

Arthur had the feeling that if this were a real fight, his shovel would have been chopped into pieces long ago. Perhaps it was an effect of the mindscape or an aspect of his Makeshift Weaponry card, but he was able to hold on.

He was also growing tired of this.

Penn closed in, and Arthur did too, catching the base of the sword right above the guard against the wooden stick of the shovel. With his other hand, Arthur grabbed Penn's wrist and held him in place. To his surprise, he was able to do it. Was he stronger than Penn, or was it because this was all in his mind?

Penn growled in his face, less human and almost like a scourgling.

"You have Master of Combat," Arthur said. "But I have Master of Body Enhancement and Master of Skills." He flexed his **Meditation** skill, somehow redirecting it from an endless fight that would only bog him down to something more productive.

Penn shattered and blew away like he was made of fallen leaves on a windy autumn day.

Arthur looked at the place his cousin had stood, lips pressed together tightly.

Ravi mentioned he might have to face inner truths. This was one that Arthur had been dodging: Penn was not done with Arthur, and Arthur still had business with his cousin.

With that thought in mind, he glanced back up to the shining pillars in this heart. His Master of Skills, which had been with him the longest and he knew so well. His Master of Body Enhancement glowed nearly as brightly . . . he sensed it was still settling within his heart.

Beyond sat Master of Combat, which was so dim Arthur could barely make out the letters.

Beside that stood the two empty cards.

He looked around for more inspiration, perhaps a glimpse of the other cards he knew lived in his heart. Or was there a spot he could push out and expand for more space?

"If I can get them fixed, is there room for that meta card trio?" he asked. But that was the wrong question, wasn't it?

"What do I need?" he asked instead. That chimed right because that was going to be what the Dark Heart would ask him.

And it was one of the most important questions Arthur could ask himself.

He started listing off the things he knew. "I need a way to defeat the scourglings, to keep what's happened here from happening to my own kingdom. I need to advance and grow stronger because while I might be a Legendary, I'm not strong enough yet. And"—he added the revelation he'd had only yesterday—"I need to find a way to balance Brixaby's natural destruction powers. I can do that through those meta cards, I think, but I need to repair them. So how do I do that? How do I do everything? Ugh! Is it even possible?"

He held his head, but no new inspiration struck him.

Slowly, Arthur lowered his hands and really took in what his heart deck was showing him. His Master cards.

"No, this isn't one separate question . . . it's three. It's everything. I need something that does it all."

Distantly, he felt notifications crash in, but he ignored them.

Every card in the Master set flashed as if his words had been a key that had just unlocked something in him.

He had found the right question to ask.

"It all comes back to cards. I need to find the next card in my set."

As he spoke, he reached out and touched his awareness to Brixaby's seeker cards.

One of the empty spaces flashed into light again. Just the title, but it was enough.

Master of Cards.

And Arthur knew what was waiting for him down in the Dark Heart . . . if he dared to delve deep enough to find it.

CHAPTER 33

Brixaby

With one final ringing blow of the hammer, Brixaby finished the kite shield he was working on.

Lifting it in his claws, he bent his head close to look it over. He tried to take it in objectively, like a master of the craft would.

It was too small for him, much too small for any dragon to use. There were a few extra dents he could not fully manage to knock out, and it still needed to be fitted with a strap suitable for human arms. The metal was well forged, though it lacked any fancy designs that would have made it more pleasing to look at.

All in all, it was good apprentice work.

Brixaby set it down, rumbling in discontentment. Then he checked for new notifications from his rider's Master of Skills card and found none.

That rumble became a growl.

"Why have I not received a skill, or at least a level, for this?" he demanded to his rider's annoying card.

Of course, it gave no answer.

"Bah!"

Brixaby knocked the shield aside, and it clattered up against a pile of other discarded weapons that had failed to gain him any levels. His pile was beginning to grow large.

Another source of his discontentment.

With irritation, he swung his head around to see what everyone else was up to. With the Dark Heart opening soon, all would be busy bettering themselves.

That was when he realized the barn was clear of others. He was completely alone.

How in the world did Sams manage to squeeze himself out without Brixaby noticing? Though, after a moment's thought, Brixaby concluded that he had been so focused on his own crafting—specifically, seeking a suitable class so he could continue to advance—that he had taken no notice of what else was going on. And why should he? It was beneath him.

With a long sigh, he turned back to the shield and picked it up again for another examination. He had to understand where he was going wrong.

At least tossing it away hadn't caused another dent. Brixaby's **Metallurgy** skill was up to 15, so he knew how to mix metals for the greatest effect.

There were no other flaws in the shield he could see, other than it was very plain. In fact, he was simply not enamored with making it. He'd only done so because actually creating weapons was by far the best path to weapon smithing.

But his pile of discards said otherwise.

Tossing the shield back on top of the pile, he wandered out of the barn through the back door.

The moment he was outside, his attention was caught by the sound of crunching bone. He came around the corner to see Joy sitting in the bright afternoon sun and gnawing on a bison femur. The bulge in her stomach spoke of where the stripped meat had gone.

Upon seeing him, she dropped the bone. "Brixaby! There you are!"

"I have not gone anywhere," he grumbled, "though it seems others have."

"Yeah, I just came back. Cressida is off at that library thing. Don't tell her I said this, but researching sounds so boring. Hey, Brix," she suddenly added. "Look what I got!"

And Brixaby's mind stuttered to a halt as she swished her tail at him in a very fetching manner.

Then he saw the mark a few scales shy from the tip of her tail. It could almost be considered a spot or a blemish, but aside from her green forearm and the veins on that side of her body, Joy was almost eye-blindingly pink.

Brixaby bent to look at it. "One of Dannill's language tattoos. He was able to apply the ink directly to the scale? What happens when you shed it?"

"Then I'll have to get a new one, but tails don't shed very often, or get hurt a lot in battles. That's why I chose that spot. It hurts less than putting a needle in a toe, too. I think it's pretty. Don't you?" She went on before Brixaby could answer. "Cressida wasn't happy about getting a tattoo, so she had hers put on the back of her shoulder where people wouldn't see it very often. And now I can talk to everyone!" Joy finished happily.

"Yes, but that does not mean anyone here will have anything worthwhile to say to you."

Something in his tone must have caught her attention. She squinted at him. "Are you all right?"

Part of Brixaby was obscurely annoyed, and he almost asked if she had been swishing her tail that way around Sams. Then he remembered that Sams was quite old, and not a Legendary dragon like Brixaby. Besides, it did not matter.

So he moved to another subject that was annoying him. "No, I am not all right. I have . . ." He grimaced. "Failed to obtain a Smithing Class."

She cocked her head. "Why do you need that? Remind me."

"Because I have a weaponsmith card, and Arthur has another in weapon improvisation—they're linked, you see. I could create things for him, and I am certain they would become twice as strong. We need every bit of strength we can get for the Dark Heart. Yet with all these advantages and my constant practice, I am unable to gain any sort of official class in smithing." He snorted in disgust.

"Oh!" she said brightly, nodding. "I'd be happy to help!"

"Excellent." He rocked back on his haunches, and they stared at each other for a beat.

Annoyed, Brixaby narrowed his eyes. "Well? Will you not give me a quest to solve this?"

"Oh, silly, you know I can only kinda guide a quest, but only when the quest agrees. Most of the time it's random, even for me." She paused for a moment, scrunching her face in concentration. A moment later she opened her eyes and shook her head. "Sorry, I didn't get one right now. Did you?"

"No."

He knew that had been the case before Joy and Sams had left on their journey, but he had hoped she had some sort of growth or breakthrough on the way here.

Casually, Joy reached over and grabbed the bison femur bone, cracking it with her jaws and licking out the marrow.

Brixaby watched with mild distaste. Raw meat was fine for some occasions, and he would still like to know the thrill of hunting and eating his own meat, but on balance he preferred his meals cooked. "You know, bone jelly is better for you."

She spoke slightly slurred, as her tongue was busy trying to get out the rest of the marrow. "That would take hours."

"Why are you so hungry? You just ate that entire leg."

"Ugh." She threw the now fully stripped bone away in disgust. "It was so terrible. Horatio has his Second Helpings card that doubles things, right? We thought that would stretch the supplies. But it turns out that the food it creates doesn't actually do anything for you. He couldn't figure out why—our riders kept saying something about material and not vitamins. Do you know how terrible it is to eat and eat and still be hungry because your body doesn't get anything from it?"

Brixaby blinked. "I suppose . . . not," he acknowledged. Joy would have had it slightly worse than Sams, too, as she was going through what Arthur called a growth spurt. Then, remembering something, he pulled out a roasted mutton that had been marinated with spices. "This was one of Arthur's previous experiments. It does not have the healing powers of his chicken soup, but it should at least be filling."

Joy squealed in happiness and immediately tore into the roast. Between bites, she asked, "So if you still need a class on weapons and stuff, why don't you just find a teacher?"

"Bah, I have already approached many of this city's so-called 'best' blacksmiths. No one will take me as an apprentice. They do not know what to think of dragons, and see us as curiosities." He hated to admit the next part, but it came out anyway. "Perhaps . . . I should have been more general and not worked only on chainmail when I had the opportunity to learn in the free hive."

She shrugged. "Okay, but why do you want a weapon-smithing class? I know you have the card, but you don't need the class for the card, do you?"

"No," he admitted. Embarrassment warred with the need to be truthful with his friend. More important, Joy was someone who had a quest card, and therefore possibly some meta insight.

"I do enjoy blacksmithing, and especially creating chainmail pieces. It is . . . pleasant to make myself and others look good as well as protect my rider."

"Sure," Joy said, then paused to swallow a large chunk of meat. "That's what dragons and riders do—we protect each other. That's what makes us good partners. But, Brix, have you ever made anything for yourself? Not for combat," she said when he opened his mouth to point out he'd just mentioned the chainmail. "Not for any kind of fighting or to level up or to grow stronger . . . but just for yourself?"

"Of course I have—" he started to say, then stopped.

Had he? Without the secret intent of leveling up a skill? He couldn't remember anything off the top of his mind.

"What does it matter?" he asked instead.

She didn't answer right away, peering off into the distance. Brixaby turned his head to follow her gaze but saw nothing except the backside of the barn. Annoyed, he was about to ask again when she spoke.

"You know, when we came here, we flew over a lot of cities. All were dead and forgotten—it was very sad. But sometimes we'd stop in them and look at some of the weirder stuff. There was one place . . . Cressida said it looked like a park for people to gather. Except that it was filled with metal art. Very twisty. It looked like . . ." She couldn't quite find the words and instead swayed her head back and forth in a wavy pattern. "Only there were dozens of them, and when the sun was angled just perfectly, their long shadows created pictures. It was trees and humans playing and throwing balls to one another in grassy fields. Even though the metal didn't look like any of that."

"Trees and grassy fields." Brixaby snorted. "What a boring thing to spend your time on."

That seemed to snap Joy out of it. She looked at Brixaby. "Well, if you could create something like that, what would you create?"

Brixaby knew immediately. He would create the best thing ever, which of course would be a dragon in flight. He could imagine it now.

In fact . . . it was easy to imagine Joy that way, fully grown and majestic, as any dragon in his retinue should be. Her wings would be curved to catch an oncoming breeze, and there would be a particular flirt to her tail . . .

Brixaby's eyes narrowed. "I will return," he said shortly, and went back into the barn and to his forge.

He assumed that Joy would understand his need for privacy and requirement to work, but less than two hours later, she popped up at his forge, asking what he was doing.

Brixaby looked down at the lumpy thing he was trying to twist into shape using tongs. "I am creating a sculpture of a dragon." Though right now it was extremely rough and didn't have nearly the graceful form he could see in his mind's eye.

In fact, it looked a bit like the real Joy, who was a little awkward and ungainly in dragon adolescence.

She blinked. "Which is the head and which is the tail?"

"This one, of course!" he said, and then on second thought admitted that she may have a point. "I will put some teeth on it."

He went to do just that. Then, after using a mallet to pound in some sharp metal, he had to admit that the overall form looked much more like a proper dragon.

For extra inspiration, he put in sharp claws. Those were much like Joy's own, too.

Joy murmured in appreciation and flexed her own claws.

"There," he said, and was somewhat satisfied with his own first effort.

New skill gained: Metal Art (Artist Class, Blacksmith Class)
Due to your linked card's bonus traits and class, you automatically start
this skill at level 5.

New Class!
Blacksmith Artist (Tier 2 Crafting)
It takes knowledge of fundamental skills to start down the road of any
craft. But to truly begin to master a craft, one must show a dedication
to art as well as utility.

As Blacksmith Artist is a crafting class, individual skills maintain their own levels and are not rolled into an overall average. In addition, relevant skills are split into synergistic subcategories:

Metal Artistry

Forging

Metal Weapon Work

Metal Utility Work

Add more skills within this class to create more subcategories.

All new skills within this class start at level 5, and experience is gained 15% faster in addition to existing card's bonuses.

When equipped:

+3 to Stamina (+ additional 20% to heat resistance at the forge)

+2 to Dexterity (+ additional 3 when using weaponsmith crafting-specific tools)

+1 to Intelligence

+1 to Luck

Do you wish to equip Blacksmith Artist (Tier 2) now?

CHAPTER 34

Arthur could barely wait to get back to the barn and tell Brixaby all that he had discovered.

He found his dragon excitedly talking to Joy. His bloodred eyes were bright, and his chest was puffed out with pride. Turning, he saw Arthur and boomed out, "Arthur! Let me tell you about my grand accomplishments!"

"Oh?" Arthur came over and glanced around. It seemed that Brixaby's metal refuse pile, which he did not allow anyone to touch or even look at too closely, was bigger than usual. Also, he'd been working on an unusual piece over by his anvil. Was that a flat outline of a duck? A duck with teeth?

"Did you have a breakthrough with your weapons?" Arthur asked, hoping that awkward metal silhouette wasn't supposed to be a dragon.

"I finally acquired my first class!" Brixaby let out a roar of delight that literally shook the rafters and sent dust sprinkling down on them. "It is a marvelous one! Fit for me. Tier two!"

And Arthur was momentarily distracted as Brixaby went through the benefits and attributes of his class. He wasn't exaggerating . . . They were quite good. Even better in some ways than Arthur's only tier-two class, Cooking.

He was briefly . . . Well, jealous was too strong of a word, but *envious* that Brixaby had happened upon something so productive. Other than his Stealth Class, which he had gotten by way of a card, when was the last time Arthur himself had gained a class?

Uncomfortably, Arthur realized that unless he focused more on his skills, he was in danger of falling behind his own dragon. As usual, he was stretching himself too thin.

But it was hard to feel overly worried when he thought about his own news.

His expression must have given it away because Brixaby finally stopped his boasting and gave his rider a knowing look. "You have a secret you wish to share? Did you finally expand your heart deck?"

"Ohhhh." Joy swung her head around to him. "Did it hurt?"

"No, it's not about my heart deck," Arthur said. "But I think I found something just as good."

Then he told Brixaby briefly about what he believed was waiting for them down in the Dark Heart. He didn't care if Joy knew, as she was part of the retinue. Besides, her little squeal made Arthur grin.

The slits in Brixaby's eyes actually expanded and contracted several times in excitement.

"If this is true, we should gather my retinue and go down there now. Why are we waiting for it to open?" He looked around wildly as if hoping Sams and Horatio would show up at any second so he could order them to accompany him. "We have three strong dragons . . . even if two are slightly underfed for the moment. No one would dare stop us!"

Arthur shook his head. "Let's say we do that. We'd still have to battle our way back out. And at that point, it would be against an entire city who thinks we're cheaters, right after the Reshuffling has distributed powers right and left. No, Brix," he added sternly when the dragon opened his mouth to argue. "It's not worth it. That card is ours. We're going to get it and we don't need to cheat to do so."

Brixaby grumbled, wings slumping.

"Besides," Arthur added, "don't you have a new class to explore?"

That did it. Brixaby perked up at once. "Yes, very well, but woe to anyone who picks up that card before us!"

Arthur didn't disagree.

Cressida and Horatio came in later in the evening, both with their own tales to tell. Cressida apparently had a relaxing, though not particularly fruitful, time in the library.

"Their scholars' guild, which they call a public library, is four stories tall and full of books," Cressida said, "though the history section is less than two shelves. Most was about this city and written in the last few decades. So I asked a worker—a *librarian*," she added carefully in the new language she'd acquired, "and he said that this city is one of the largest holdouts on the continent . . ." She paused for dramatic effect. " . . . from the time before cards."

Arthur and Horatio glanced at one another. Off to the side, Sams and Joy were eating yet another bison lunch, and Brixaby listened nearby while fiddling and twisting a metal wire into an odd shape.

"Time before cards?" Arthur repeated slowly. "There was a time before cards?"

Cressida nodded. "Apparently, it was a magicless time."

Horatio asked the next logical question. "So how did they fight scourglings?"

"They would have had no dragons," Brixaby said with authority. "We are created with cards in our cores."

"We did see a lot of machines in the abandoned cities," Horatio said, and Cressida nodded. "They're all sort of rusted out now, but maybe that's how they kept the scourglings at bay . . . Well, right up until they couldn't."

Arthur shuddered, glad he lived in the here and now when things made sense. "Anything else, Cressida?"

"No, but I'll be going back tomorrow," she said with relish.

With a nod, Arthur turned to Horatio. "It looks like you and Sams had fun."

Horatio's shirt was spotted with scourgling blood that smelled fairly rank. He grinned. "Those sheriffs practically cried with joy when they saw me and Sams fly up. Apparently, a bunch of Uncommons were really ripping at the northern wall."

Brixaby's head whipped around to him. "They did not tell us they needed our assistance."

"Yeeaah, well, I got the feeling there's a bit of distrust there, and no offense, but knowing how you two operate, I can see why." Horatio held up his hand to forestall any argument. "I'm only the messenger here, and it wasn't like the wall was about to be breached—they were only Uncommons—so it wasn't an emergency. They definitely appreciated the help, though."

With that, he held out his other hand and showed off five Uncommon shards.

"That's good, but you would have gotten more if you were hunting scourglings with a hive," Cressida pointed out. "I'm sure you killed more than five scourglings."

"I did, but there's such a thing as ingratiating yourself with the locals," Horatio replied. "Besides, all that practice helped work out a couple of kinks in the new light card—"

He started to say more but stopped as the door to the barn creaked open.

Everyone turned, tense. Was it thieves? One of the undersheriffs? Some government officials who didn't appreciate dragons in the city?

Marion popped his head in, saw Arthur, and said, "Oh, this is the place. Your directions were a little unclear."

In all the news, Arthur had forgotten that he had invited Marion and Soledad for dinner and plans. He hurried to welcome them in, and introductions were made all around. Though, of course, Horatio was already aware of Marion from his time in Buck Moon Hive.

Cressida nodded to them with the dignity of a former noblewoman.

Soledad's eyes, however, were all for Joy and Sams, the latter of the two who took up fully half the inside of the barn. "These are your dragons?" she asked, eyes wide as she gazed at Joy. "Oh, she's so beautiful. She's a she, isn't she?"

"Of course I am," Joy said. "You can tell girl dragons from the shape of our head." She turned hers to the side. "Not as wide, and if we have horns, they lie flatter. How do you know Arthur and Brixaby?"

"Me and the people I was traveling with were caught out in the deadlands." She turned to give Arthur a smile that was only slightly sarcastic. "They're proper heroes."

"I assure you, I did most of the work," Brixaby said.

Arthur caught Cressida giving Soledad a long look, but he couldn't dwell on it for long as he had a dinner to put together. Thankfully, pulling already pre-pared meals out of his Personal Space didn't take long. Soon, the humans were sitting at a cluster of chairs around a rough table. The dragons ate on the other side of the barn, as no one wanted to be splashed with flying bits of bison. Even if Brixaby's portions were cooked, he wasn't always the cleanest eater.

Arthur waited until the meal wound down before he spoke. "So, now that we're all here, I wanted to talk about the heart. Assuming you two still want to join us?" he asked Marion and Soledad.

Soledad sucked in a breath. "Yes, of course. But why would you have us? We're both cardless, so it's not like we can be of any use."

"It's a Reshuffling. You're not going to be useless for long there. I'll need a good, solid team." He looked at Marion. "Do you still have that illusion card?"

Marion nodded and brought it out of a pocket with a slightly pained look. He showed it around.

Go Clone Yo'self
Rare

Illusion

This card grants the wielder the ability to create illusionary, noncorporeal clones out of him or herself. These clones will all be visually exact to the original. The number of clones depends on the amount of mana assigned to the task. These clones have the ability to act independently. However, they cannot exert a physical force upon the environment. When struck by an outside, physical force, the illusion will be dispelled. The wielder may resummon the illusion at any time, at the cost of additional mana.
This card uses and unlocks mana.

"That's a good one," Cressida said. "If you don't mind me asking, why haven't you used it?"

He sighed. "It doesn't exactly fit my build."

"You don't have any cards, from what I've heard," Horatio said bluntly. "You don't have a build."

Cressida elbowed him and spoke to Marion in a kinder voice. "What do you want for your build?"

Marion seemed to hesitate for a moment, almost as if expressing his wish was embarrassing. But he must have found his inner strength because he lifted his chin. "I want to heal."

"Well, even as a healer you're going to need some way to defend yourself. Making multiple copies of yourself is a good way to confuse your enemies." Horatio jerked his chin at Soledad. "Or give it to her."

"I don't know if that's what I want, either," Soledad said.

Exasperated, Horatio threw his hands in the air. "It's a perfectly good card. I'll take it, then."

He reached out, but Marion jerked it back on instinct.

Horatio grinned at him. "Gotcha."

"H, that's no way to treat a prince," Cressida said.

But it was Marion who spoke. "I'm not a prince any longer." His eyes, however, had not left the card.

Arthur had kept quiet during this little exchange, but he had to ask. "Is it because it's not a Legendary card?" He spoke gently, not trying to shame Marion. Honestly, he wasn't sure if he could stomach a Rare card if he somehow lost his Legendaries.

A flicker of pain crossed Marion's face. "No, that's not it, either. I suppose . . . while I don't regret my choice, I do always live with the constant reminder that my card is gone. If I put another one in my heart, I want it there forever. I'll never take another card out of my heart again, so I must be completely sure I want it there."

The table fell awkwardly silent.

"Okay," Arthur said with a nod. "Well . . . think about it. You'll have a week or so according to the best estimates. Maybe less. And that's why I brought you all here today." Arthur looked around at all of them, making sure to meet every eye. "We're going to be a team down there. And yes, it may be rough. Brixaby and I plan to go down to the deepest part of the heart and get the most powerful card we can get our hands on. That means we're going to need to trust one another. I'll lay my cards out on the table if you guys will, too. At the very least, we'll need to know each other's major abilities."

Horatio and Cressida looked slightly uneasy. Though they were part of Arthur's retinue, people did not just give up the secrets of their powers on a whim.

Soledad snorted. "Well, that's easy. You know I don't have any cards."

"That's not all," Arthur said. "I've heard a few times that the Dark Heart focuses on your needs. So we'll need to hear them, too."

"Easy again," she said, crossing her arms over her chest. "I want to stop the damn heart from erupting fully, and I want to kill scourglings. I figure the best way to do both is to get a dragon."

Cressida made a surprised sound. "What kind of dragon? What rank?"

"Best and most dangerous I can get," she said immediately. "A real scourge-killing menace. I don't give a fig about the color, but I want it to be as powerful as possible. Rare."

"Rares are born every few years in the hives," Cressida said. "You may have to wait."

Soledad narrowed her eyes as if challenged. "I can do that."

There was a strange, unfriendly tension between the two of them, but Arthur couldn't figure out where it was coming from. He started to speak, but Marion beat him to it.

"As we've already discussed, I don't currently have a card." His eyes flicked down to the pocket where he'd stored the illusion card. "But I'd like to think I would make a good healer. Perhaps even a research healer. I want my life to mean something."

Horatio spoke up next. "Me and Sams have light-based combat powers. There are more colors out there than your eyes can pick up. Some of them get real hot, and they can blind or burn without you even seeing them. What do I want?" He shrugged. "To get stronger, I guess. Maybe collect more cards on the way."

Soledad jumped in. "That's not good enough."

Horatio bristled, but Cressida rested a hand on his arm. "No, she's right, H. Tell them what you told me on the way here."

He cast a dark look around at everyone, but then in a switch of mood, shrugged. "I thought I had made it when I linked up with Sams. He was my father's dragon, and carrying on his memory and being a dragon rider was all I wanted. But afterward . . . there wasn't much to do. It was a triumph, but an empty one. We were still low ranked in Buck Moon Hive and set to be that way for a long time, 'til I got 'seasoned.'" He made air quotes around the word. "I didn't like the idea of struggling for decades just to get some respect or join some jerk's retinue—no offense, Arthur. I just wanted to be a good dragon rider. But . . . killing scourglings is an endless grind. You wait around until the erup-tion, beat them back, and then go on with the rest of the day or week. I wanted it all to mean something. I wanted to know there's an end to the war." He shrugged again. "I know it's all kind of scattered, but it comes to the same thing: I'm tired of feeling like I'm running in place."

Arthur had no idea his friend had been going through all of this, and he felt bad he'd never asked.

I need to be a better leader, a better friend, to my retinue, he thought.

Cressida's power and wishes for the Dark Heart were all more straightfor-ward. "I use mana shields and have fire and water elemental summons. Joy has poison in her claws if it comes to close combat. She's meta, which means she has flashes of insight that come as quests, so if she tells you to do something, then do it." This was aimed at Marion and Soledad. "As for what I need . . . Well, I need to make Joy stronger, to make her the truly spectacular dragon I know she's growing up to be. I want her to have all the best opportunities possible. It's what she deserves."

And abruptly, Arthur was the only one who hadn't spoken.

"First, my needs. I was given a hint of what is down there, waiting, if we can delve deep enough. It's a Legendary card in the same set as my existing cards."

Horatio whistled.

Marion nodded. "A Legendary trio. Suddenly I understand why we're so far away from my father."

"Legendary? And you have two of them?" Soledad looked at Arthur like she'd just discovered he could grow an extra head.

"Yes. No one knows about that in this city other than you guys. So needless to say, I'd appreciate it if you kept that to yourself."

Arthur took in a breath. He'd asked everyone to lay out their powers, but as the leader, he had to do more.

So without further ado, he reached to his chest and projected Master of Skills and Master of Body Enhancement for the room to see.

CHAPTER 35

The moment of silence while everyone read over Arthur's Legendary cards felt both weighted and stretched.

Arthur felt as exposed as if he had removed all his clothes and then asked his friends to look for flaws on his body.

In a way, it was even worse than that. His deepest truths were finally exposed for all to see. These were cards from his heart, a portion of his soul laid bare. Which was why it was so monstrous during the occasions he'd seen people trade heart cards for objects or money.

Cressida was the first to finish reading. Silently, she nodded to him and leaned back. She didn't look surprised because he had told her the nitty-gritty details during their time together at Mesa Free Hive.

Horatio was next. He shook his head, catching Arthur's gaze and rolling his eyes. He, too, knew the broad strokes of Arthur's secrets, though perhaps not to this extent. "That is a doozy of a card pair. And that second card . . . So what are you? Stronger? Smarter?"

"I'm getting there. When I get a physical body-enhancement skill up to level twenty, it usually provides some benefits." He glanced at Brixaby, who was having his own side conversation with Joy and Sams. "My Master of Skills provides classes for clusters of skills, and those give extra attributes, too."

Soledad whistled. "Reminds me of a saying my dad used to say: Born on third base."

"Whose base?" Horatio asked her.

She shrugged. "Don't know, but it means born lucky."

"I grew up in . . . well, I guess you could call it a prison camp," Arthur said. "Getting my Master of Skills card was the first stroke of luck I ever got."

"Well, it looks like you saved up all your luck for that moment."

Though Marion was likely the fastest reader of them all and had seen a glimpse of Arthur's cards before, he was the last to look away from Arthur's projected cards. "Either one of those are Legendary cards fit to be assigned to a prince or a princess."

Arthur stiffened and resisted the urge to cover his heart with his hand. But Marion wasn't voicing a threat, just an observation.

Marion continued, all of his attention on Arthur. "But you don't act like you have these cards. You've had Master of Skills since you were twelve? So that's five, six years? Seven?"

Arthur started to answer, but in his usual irritating way, Marion spoke over his reply.

"I know that skills take some time to ramp up from novice to journeyman to master, but I'll be perfectly frank, Arthur: It feels like you haven't been using your cards to your best advantage."

"What do you mean?"

He waved a hand backward, indicating the past. "I've seen you fight. It was luck that got us out of that hive's eruption."

"I can't use combat skills," Arthur said. "That's another card—Master of Combat."

Marion drawled. "Yes, the one your cousin has."

That sent an unpleasant chill down his spine. "Yes."

Marion nodded, then picked up a corner of crusty bread and flicked it at Arthur's head.

Arthur shifted out of the way before it hit. "What was that for?" he asked, and at Cressida's irritated look for making a mess, bent to pick up the crust from the floor. It was half stale and no good to eat, but no need to attract mice.

"Why didn't you catch it?" Marion asked. "You do have a catching skill, right?"

He shook his head. "I have a juggling skill."

"Show me."

Horatio grinned. "He juggled up a storm back when we were both nobodies in Wolf Moon Hive. He was one of the best bartenders you'd ever seen. The tips were crazy."

"Can we get back on track?" Cressida asked, looking between them all. "We should work out some plan for delving into the Dark Heart."

Marion held up a hand as if asking for patience. "This is part of a plan. Arthur, show me your juggling."

Privately, Arthur agreed with Cressida, but there was no harm in a little fun. In fact, he decided to show off a bit and picked up a few differently sized mismatched objects. He used the bread crust as well as a graphite writing stick that sat nearby, and Marion spotted him a copper coin. He tossed the crust and the coin in the air, followed by the stick.

It had been quite a while since he last did this—since before he'd known of Brixaby's egg. By all rights, he should have been rusty. But that was one of the benefits of using card-based skills. He didn't forget or backtrack.

Yes, his skills were a little slower to ramp up, as Marion said, but those levels represented knowledge and experience. He didn't lose those.

He'd gotten a few tosses in when Marion threw another copper coin at him. Arthur smoothly caught it and incorporated it into his juggling. When he glanced at his friend, he saw Marion frowning.

"You caught that just fine, but you said you don't have a Catching skill?"

"Well, this is part of juggling, isn't it?" With a flourish, Arthur flipped all the objects in the air and caught them one by one. "See?"

"But why don't you?" Marion asked.

Arthur paused. "I just don't get skills for everything I do. Like sitting in a chair or grabbing something."

"But why not?" he pressed.

Horatio made an annoyed sound, and Cressida looked irritated by what she clearly thought was a waste of time. Soledad, however, leaned forward.

"No, he has a point. Grabbing for something and pulling it to you isn't just something you do—little children can grip almost straight out of the womb, but they have to practice grabbing with intention."

"I'm not a baby," Arthur said.

"No, but you're being obtuse," Marion countered. "You know what she means."

He supposed that he was. Arthur frowned, thinking about it. "I guess it's all about intention. When I first got the card, my dad had me learn my letters and reading, but he mentioned I had to do so with intention. I guess that is the difference between a skill I level up and something I just . . . do."

"I still don't see why this is important," Horatio said. "What would grabbing do for him?"

Marion had an immediate answer. "Maybe increase his finger strength if he was holding on to a ledge. Especially paired with his Master of Body Enhancement card." Then, without warning, he threw another copper coin straight at Arthur's head.

Arthur caught it. "If this keeps up, I'll be rich."

"Did you think about catching it?" Marion asked.

Embarrassed, Arthur lobbed the coin back to him. "No, do it again. It may take a couple of repetitions for the skill to activate."

Horatio snorted.

"Before we all start throwing things at Arthur," Cressida said, "can you please explain why you're fixated on catching something, specifically? Because I'd rather we be taking this time going over strategies of the Dark Heart."

Marion adjusted his glasses, then nodded. "Because our fearless leader cannot combat dodge, and while he might be catching a coin now . . . what if he can soon catch a thrown fist? Or an arrow headed for his throat?"

Cressida's mouth clicked shut, and she looked at Arthur with raised eyebrows as if asking, "Is that possible?"

Arthur frowned. "I would have to get the skill up pretty high."

"Then no time like the present. Everyone: Start throwing things. He's a Legendary card user. He can take it."

Horatio visibly perked up, and even Cressida smiled. Soledad was the first to throw a balled-up paper. Arthur caught it just in time and braced himself for the hail that was to come.

They didn't let up on throwing things at him until he had reached level 7 and finally called for a halt.

Arthur pointedly asked Cressida to explain to the group what she knew of a dungeon. It was the closest thing to the Dark Heart that they had dealt with.

Horatio knew the theory behind dungeons, vaguely, and Marion knew a bit more. Though he had never experienced one.

Cressida looked surprised. "Surely you were trained in a dungeon, seeing as you were . . ." She paused, seemingly torn about whether bringing up that he was former royalty was rude or not.

Marion understood. "My card was neither combat-based or leveled up with a skill. There was nothing I could do to improve its function—only learn to endure it. You have no idea how constantly seeing into the future can alter your sense of the present. Anyway," he continued before anyone could find something to say, "my sister, Echo, was constantly in and out of dungeons. I have heard her stories." He nodded to her. "I would appreciate your input, Lady Icehouse."

Horatio groaned. "Don't call her that. You'll give her a big head."

"That is my name," she said tartly. "I may be a dragon rider now, but I will not forget my roots as a noblewoman."

He smirked in reply but didn't answer back. It seemed that riling her up had been the goal. There had been no heat in either's words. Horatio and Cressida had formed a sort of friendship while traveling here, but to Arthur's eye, it wasn't a particularly warm one.

Shaking off the teasing, Cressida put her hands on her knees and straightened her pose in what Arthur thought of as a teaching pose. "Dungeons are extradimensional pockets created by card wielders called dungeoneers. As Pri—" She caught herself. "As Marion said, most of them are used as training grounds. Let me tell you about the two I've been in . . ."

She spoke for a good length of time, though it was nothing she hadn't told Arthur before. He was able to add some examples of the second wave-type dungeon he'd been a part of as well.

Cressida finished with a sigh, shoulders sagging. "But dungeons are created by people, and the Dark Heart isn't." She looked at Soledad, the one native to this land. "Right?"

"I've always been told it's the heart of a former hive," Soledad said quietly. "I've never been in one either, but from what I've heard, there are levels, usually three, and sometimes more. Each takes you deeper, and within these levels are challenges."

Arthur exchanged a look with Cressida. That sounded a lot like a dungeon.

Soledad went on. Her gaze was fixed to the middle distance, eyes haunted by something they couldn't see—likely the destruction of her former city. "The deeper you go, the harder it is, but the greater the rewards. People say it's the Dark Heart's way of killing those who get too close to the center. And they say the farther you go, the more the rules of the world change. Sometimes they're broken completely."

"Give an example," Marion said.

She shrugged. "I've heard of mana becoming unlimited, and someone who uses a lot of their mana finds that their overall pools or regeneration have increased. Nothing's changed on their cards, but maybe their regeneration has tripled. Or they go to a level where everything weighs the same—like you have the weight of an apple, but you can't move smaller objects because you have no force behind it. And you get a gravity card out of it. Some people tell of finding cards that fit exactly in their heart to fill the holes of what was lost. They come out, and they're not in pain anymore." She didn't quite look at Marion at this last bit, and Marion showed no outward reaction other than to go very still.

"So it's always good?" Horatio asked, naturally skeptical.

"Unless you're killed, or the Dark Heart ripens before people can harvest all the magic out of it. But . . . the heart messes with people's minds. Sometimes people go down as teams only to be pitted against one another, only to then find out it was a fake and the fight was an illusion. Or worse, they thought they'd killed someone only to find out they'd murdered someone else."

So you can't trust your senses down there, Arthur thought with a frown.

Soledad continued, "Two people can delve the heart together and have completely different experiences on the levels. There ain't no rhyme or reason to it, except . . ." She swallowed. "People say what you face down in the Dark Heart, it reflects what's in your real heart, too. That's why you gotta go down there with a focus on what you need from it." Her gaze drifted to the dragons. It was clear that concept would be her focus.

Everyone went quiet as they took in her words. Finally, Marion spoke.

"Does the heart only reward people with cards and abilities? From what I understand, dungeons can occasionally reward mana-created objects."

She shrugged. "Never heard of that, but it's the heart. Anything is possible."

Horatio let out a long sigh. "Which means that there's no point in making a specific plan other than 'come back out alive.'"

Arthur gave him a sharp look. "You don't have to go in if you don't want to."

"I never said that. I'm just being realistic."

And unfortunately, he had a point. "Our plan should be to stick together—if the heart will let us." He looked at Cressida. "There may be information in the library about previous delves."

She brightened. "I'm sure there has to be something."

"It will go faster if you offer the librarian a bribe," Marion said, then seemed surprised when everyone looked at him in surprise. "What? I came to this city knowing nothing. How do you think I found the resources to acquire the language and a job at the hospital?"

"Well, that's where Sams and I come in," Horatio said. "If we need shards for bribes—well, there are scourglings right outside the walls for the killing. Hey, Arthur," he suddenly said, "catch." And he flicked the rind of a fruit right at Arthur's forehead.

Arthur caught it just in the nick of time. He sighed. "Guess I know what I'll be doing: leveling."

If Arthur thought that the previous few days were busy, it was nothing compared to his schedule now. He was running on full steam. If he wasn't busy finding and storing away anything and everything he thought might be of use in his Personal Space, he was cooking and trying to prepare supplies for the delve.

That wasn't easy, as prices for food in the city were sky-high as the last of the people hoping to delve into the heart flooded in. Enhanced spices with magical effects were even more expensive. He quickly became glad that Horatio and Sams went out every day to hunt and harvest scourglings. Arthur even directed them to lower-level scourgling nests so they could clean those out.

Arthur used his few moments of downtime to continue leveling his **Meditation** skill. He didn't receive any new insights, like with Ravi's guided meditation, but he found the action relaxing, even restorative, as if he had taken a satisfying nap.

And, of course, he always had to be on the lookout for someone throwing something at him. His **Catching** skill was leveling quickly, and he surprised himself, and Horatio, after hitting level 12. Horatio had just lobbed a green crab apple his way. Arthur snatched it out of the air, and without even thinking about it, rolled his wrist and sent it back in a way that the apple kept its momentum. Now his **Throwing** skill came into play, and he nailed his friend dead center between the eyes. Luckily, it hadn't been a hard throw.

Arthur hadn't laughed so hard in weeks.

Meanwhile, Brixaby's enthusiasm for smithing, and specifically chainmail making, had been entirely reinvigorated. While he occasionally went with Horatio, Sams, and Joy on a scourgling hunt, he was more likely to be found at the forge.

The first thing he made was another chainmail glove for Joy to fit over her venomous forepaw. Her recent growth spurt had strained the previous one to the point that links were about to snap. The new glove was butter soft and the links so small and even that there was no danger of the links catching on even scratchy fabric. Joy hugged him again, much to Brixaby's embarrassment.

Cressida researched at the library and returned to the barn every night with tales of previous Dark Heart openings. All were varied. One that stuck out in Arthur's mind was an endless field where people had to fight others and scourglings for loot.

But many coming from the depths of the Dark Heart refused to speak of their experience and returned fundamentally changed from the men and women they had once been.

While this was going on, Marion and Soledad returned to their work at the hospital. From there, Marion was able to keep an eye on the talk of the city and occasionally pass purloined herbs to Arthur to add to his recipes.

Between all that, Arthur only got a few hours of sleep at night.

Finally, on the fifth night after their meeting, two full days before the Dark Heart was supposed to be ready, sirens rang through the city.

The Dark Heart was finally ready to be delved.

CHAPTER 36

It was that strange hour past midnight where it was so early it was late, and so late it was early. There was no hint of dawn or even a fresh morning breeze. But sirens screamed through the city, fed by giant card-anchor horns on top of buildings. Every bell was set to ringing, too. No one could possibly sleep through this, and every living soul who was old enough to have a card in their heart was out of bed and rushing up the steep hill to the middle of the city.

With the streets choked with people, no one, not even vendors greedy enough to try to make a final profit, was silly enough to bring carts pulled by beasts of burden with them.

The crowd became a mob as they got closer to the gates that barred the Dark Heart. People were shoulder to shoulder, all pushing forward but with nowhere to go. Finally, the pressure grew so much that even the gates that held them back were starting to groan and strain, even though they were reinforced with card powers.

Of course, Arthur and his retinue didn't have to worry about any of that. They simply flew over on their dragons. To Arthur, the many people carrying lamps and portable lighted card anchors weaving their way up the hill looked like a glowing snake.

He caught flashes of oval faces turned up toward them at the sound of flapping dragon wings. He could only imagine their feelings as the dragon riders cut in line.

Arthur called to the others. "There's no way Marion and Soledad can make their way through this. Go to the hospital and get them both—they live at barracks there. I'll make sure our place in line is secure." If there was going to be a problem with the city authorities keeping their word, Arthur wanted first crack at them.

Cressida and Horatio lifted their arms to ensure that they heard, and their dragons peeled off, flapping toward the east side of the city.

Brixaby buzzed on, and people shouted in anger as he flew over the top gate.

There was a wide strip of empty land large enough for a dragon twice the size of Sams to land. Brixaby, with his small size and pinpoint flying ability, had no issue. He took the opportunity to circle a couple times.

Beyond the land was a sharp drop-off to the pit of the Dark Heart. The purple-black pulsing heart sat far, far below. Arthur could feel power washing off it in a sensation that raised the hair on his arms and the back of his neck.

"This feels very much like an eruption," Brixaby growled.

Arthur took a second look, alarmed. He could see in the dark better than most, thanks to his Night Vision body enhancement, but he double-checked anyway. "I don't see any scourglings coming out. Do you?"

"No." The word came out through clenched teeth, and Arthur felt Brixaby was tense under his seat. No dragon liked the feeling of a scourgling's power nearby.

The few clusters of officials gathered below didn't notice Brixaby at first, as his dark scales blended in with the sky. Only the constant buzzing drone of his wings gave him away, and now those were obscured by the alarms and frustrated people shouting on the other side of the gate.

But they noticed when Brixaby descended vertically into the light and landed a few dozen feet from them.

Oversheriff Walker peeled off from the others and strode up. Wisps of hair escaped from under her wide-brimmed hat, making her look slightly harried. "Arthur, the heart isn't open yet."

"I'm just ensuring my place in line," Arthur said. "Remember our agreement."

Her scowl deepened. "I wouldn't go back on that, but this is not the front of the line." She pointed over to the gate. Through it, Arthur saw arms sticking out of the slats as people literally reached for empty air. "That is."

"You want my dragon to push his way through there?" Arthur asked dryly. "And the people I have with me?"

"What other people—" She stopped and rubbed her face. "No, no, I remember now. I suppose those are the other dragon riders I've heard about? The yellow and the pink?"

"Yes."

Walker shook her head and muttered, "I don't know whether I should be upset about that or not." Though she seemed to have dropped the idea of Arthur somehow moving Brixaby behind the gate.

"What do you mean?" Arthur asked, then paused to rest a comforting hand on the side of Brixaby's neck. The dragon had turned his head with his full attention to the pit of the Dark Heart and was growling low in his throat.

"He senses it, doesn't he?" Walker asked. "We nearly . . ." Trailing off, she glanced over her shoulder back toward where other officials were gathered. Then she looked back at Arthur. "I trust you to keep this to yourself and not spread rumors, but the heart has ripened before we thought that it would."

No kidding, Arthur thought. The last he'd heard, they were to have half a week left at the very least . . . and that had already been an accelerated timeline.

She nodded once, sharply. "This is going to be chaotic. It's very, very close to an eruption." She licked her bottom lip. "We need the elite adventurers and anyone else worth their salt to delve in and take as much power out of there as possible. The experts say that will release the magical pressure that's built up. I trust that will be something you'll be willing to do."

Walker had always struck him as a hard woman, but now he saw real fear in the back of her eyes. There was a good reason for it. If the Dark Heart exploded into a full eruption in the middle of the city . . . instead of collecting treasures, these people outside the gates would be fighting for their lives. There was no dragon hive to call to help, and from what Arthur now understood . . . no other reachable city-state to call for backup.

Not to mention that with so much scourgling activity, the deadlands would be encroaching yet again. Perhaps, like with Soledad's doomed city, it could poison the land here completely.

"Of course. I'll do what I can," Arthur said. "My retinue—the other dragon riders—will be here soon."

"I'll be glad to see them, even if other people won't be." She hesitated for a moment. "Word of advice, Arthur: Watch your back. There's no such thing as murder in the Dark Heart."

He nodded grimly, and she stepped back to confer with other leaders. Many had concern etched on their faces. A few, however, looked jubilant. He guessed those were the ones who had the same mindset as Whitaker: more interested in power than the implications of what would happen if it all went sideways.

"I don't like this," Arthur said.

Brixaby hadn't stopped growling all this time, but at Arthur's words, he turned his head to him. "What else?"

Arthur nodded to the leaders. "The Dark Heart is way, way ahead of schedule. Look at their faces. Most of them were taken by surprise."

"Yes, it is ripened. I knew that already," he said impatiently.

"Brix," Arthur said. "Eruptions are happening more frequently back in our kingdom, too."

The dragon's growl cut off, and he tilted his head in thought. "Our kingdom is all the way across the world."

"I don't think it's a coincidence." Arthur straightened in his seat. "Though even if it is, it's not going to change a thing for us. We're going to take whatever we can from the Dark Heart and leave nothing behind."

He didn't particularly care for Oversheriff Walker's warning about murder in the Dark Heart—especially as the dragons would be large targets.

Then again, dark deeds were pulled during eruptions back home, too. One of Arthur's first glimpses of a fighting dragon had been during the assassination of a poor pink and its rider. That was how he got his Return to Start card. Speaking of . . .

"You got the key point set for Return to Start?"

"It is set at the same location as last time," Brixaby said. "If the worst happens, I would rather find myself outside of the city rather than appear possibly surrounded by enemies inside the city."

So he had caught the sheriff's warning, too.

Arthur nodded. "If something happens and your life is in true danger, I want you to activate it and get out of there. Even if it's without me."

Brixaby was shocked. "I am *not* leaving you!"

"The Return to Start card is in my heart, so as long as you can activate that, you know I'm safe. But that's the same reason why you need to escape first. If I die, you'll be trapped in there."

Brixaby growled under his breath, but Arthur sensed he would obey. Most likely.

In the next moment, he tilted his head to the sky. "Joy and Sams have arrived."

Sure enough, Arthur soon heard the sound of flapping wings and alarmed calls from the guards. Brixaby's appearance had made them pay attention to what was going on above.

"Hold your fire!" Sheriff Walker called.

Sams and Joy came swooping over the tall buildings that made up the barrier to the Dark Heart. Neither one could hover the way Brixaby could, but they had their own ways to land. Sams, the more seasoned flyer, circled the heart a few times to dump speed and altitude before he came in. Joy, who was smaller, only had to circle once. She had Marion and Cressida on her back. Horatio had Soledad.

The moment Sams landed, Soledad vaulted off the dragon's neck. Her dark eyes were bright, and she was the first to speak. "Did you see that crowd out there?" She shook her head in amazement. "Guess knowing you has already started to pay off."

Dismounting, Arthur walked up to meet them. Everyone looked tense but ready to go. His focus was on Marion, though. He looked a bit pale about the lips, and on seeing Arthur, reached into his jacket and pulled out several small thumb-sized vials.

"Healing potions, brewed by the hospital's alchemists," he said under his breath. "I got enough for everyone to have two."

Arthur's eyebrows rose. "You paid for these?"

"Don't be an idiot." He cast a worried look over at the cluster of sheriffs nearby, as if concerned they would sense his misdeeds and arrest him on the spot. "I think I got away with it, but just in case I didn't . . . I'd better come out of here either with something valuable enough to keep me around or something expensive enough to sell."

Nodding, Arthur tucked the vials into his Personal Space. "Well, good news. I've been told by the oversheriff to take out as much as possible from the heart."

"No kidding?" Horatio drawled. "I was going to come all this way just to leave some good cards behind. Glad someone cleared that up."

But Arthur's attention was still on Marion. He seemed different, and it took him a second to figure out why. Ever since becoming a dragon rider, Arthur had been trying to pay attention to how people with different card ranks *felt*.

Dragons could sense this instinctively, with Brixaby knowing almost immediately at a glance what dragon was a Common, Uncommon, Rare, and so on.

It was more nebulous for Arthur, but now he sensed Marion had a new weight about him. Not physical, but magical.

A Rare power.

"You used the clone illusion card?" Arthur asked.

Marion gave him a sickly smile. "I guess I'm all in now."

"I suppose you are," Arthur said, relieved. The illusion card could not replace the Legendary that Marion had given up, but he wasn't looking for a replacement, just a fresh start.

Clapping him on the back, Arthur moved on to quickly check in with Cressida and Horatio. They had dismounted their dragons and were doing last-minute adjustments to their dragons' gear. Unlike Arthur, they both had dragon saddles and were making sure everything was in order. Both looked tense about what was waiting for them in the pit, but he didn't see true fear in their eyes. Once they were done, his retinue gathered around Arthur.

Oh no. Are they waiting for a speech?

Brixaby took that moment to shoulder his way into the group. "Now it is time for me to gift you what I have been working on. You may thank me for it profusely."

And then he pulled out . . . metal ingots that were sewn to bright fabric straps.

For a moment, Arthur wasn't exactly sure what he was looking at. The fabric straps weren't even pretty, which was weird because since receiving his class, Brixaby's work had taken an artistic slant.

Then he spotted the runes that were inscribed on the ingots . . . runes that looked familiar to him, as he had read many of the same books that Brixaby had.

"I have been working on my enchanting," Brixaby said with chest-puffing pride. "Here, this is yours." He thrust an ingot that was sewn to a pink square of fabric at Cressida. Arthur assumed that the pink was for Joy, as Horatio received a garish yellow one.

"Thanks?" Holding it like it was a dead thing, Horatio seemed uncertain.

Cressida shot him a look and said, more emphatically, "Thank you, Brixaby. Um, what does this do?"

"Tie it to your arms with the ingot side down so that it touches your skin. Arthur, you may help them," Brixaby told them grandly.

He was in quite a good mood, so Arthur trusted him and did as he was told. He was as professional as possible but noticed Cressida's skin was soft under his fingers.

"What does it do?" Cressida asked again, once it was on. "Is it another fire enhancer, like you made in the Mesa dungeon?"

"Indeed, though that was only a first attempt! Think of this as an elemental focusing device, like how a glass lens can focus light. Yours is a fire enhancer and a water enhancer, for your summons," Brixaby said, then he paused. "Perhaps using them both at once may result in more steam, I don't know. But it will not likely be dangerous."

Before Cressida could reply, he turned to Horatio. "You may find that yours will enhance light even more than your current Rainbow Knight card. Apparently, it may also function with temperature. I'm not quite sure yet."

Arthur expected Horatio to snark something in his typical way, but he just looked interested. "Temperature isn't a type of light, but it may be a type of energy. Sams and I argue about it."

Arthur jumped in. "Brix, how did you connect the enchantment with a card?"

"I have been working with Joy and Sams," Brixaby said, which wasn't a real explanation at all. Translating that into guilty-dragon speak, those two had been up to something. He only hoped Brixaby hadn't been accosting people, plucking cards out of hearts, and then quickly returning them again.

Arthur waited for a beat, but Brixaby quickly changed the subject. Now there was definitely a guilty look on his face.

"I attempted to make a Stone Skin enchantment, much like my new card, but the chances were high that you wouldn't have been able to breathe or move, and possibly your heart would have stopped. Had I had another week, I am almost certain that I would have cracked it."

That was a disappointment, but Arthur didn't let it show on his face.

"I'm glad that you've found a way to protect our retinue," he said, and he was even gladder that Brixaby had at least been able to put the Stone Skin card in his secondary core. The core was still developing, as Brixaby was still growing, so it hadn't been a certain thing.

Instead of dwelling on disappointment, Arthur focused on what he did have. He had the cards still in his heart, and he had his friends, and of course, his dragon.

That had to be enough to face the Dark Heart, right?

But Brixaby didn't leave him completely empty-handed. He was, after all, a blacksmith. He pulled a fine metal chainmail shirt out of his Personal Space to present to Arthur. It was a fine silver with gold edging. The best part was, Brixaby had found a way to fashion bits of razor-sharp shrapnel all over the shirt. The threads securing them were brittle enough for Arthur to pluck one free with a sharp tug. With his Nice Shot card, he barely needed to. He had full control over them—his own arsenal.

Arthur quickly put it on and activated his card to control any jingling so he didn't sound like ringing bells whenever he moved.

There was movement from the group of leaders. It seemed that the sheriffs were getting ready to finally open the gate. Everybody scrambled to their dragons.

A man that Arthur didn't recognize but who the sheriffs all treated with deference, stood before the gates and spoke. Even the crowd quieted to hear.

"Welcome, all, to the seventeenth opening of New Houston's Dark Heart! Now, a couple of quick rules: As soon as these gates open, everybody's to follow that path—" He pointed, and the sharp footpath that rounded the interior of the pit blazed to life. "No pushing, no shoving. Grab what you can and come back rich!"

The crowd roared in approval, and from the sound of it, the cheers were taken up by the crowd behind them—back and back through the city as people realized they were about to be admitted.

With that, the gates opened, and people surged in en masse. They would have crowded around the dragons, but Brixaby, Joy, and Sams had gone to the very edge. From there, Arthur saw the footpath that ran around and around the edge, like the cuttings of a screw. It was large enough for two men to walk shoulder to shoulder, though there were no handrails.

But the dragons didn't have to worry about *walking* a path.

The crowd rushed forward. At the front, Arthur saw a few people he recognized. Jon and some of his Lightning Cats, Claude the Kludge, and a few others who had survived the Rare nest. He heard Horatio hail some of the others, too—acquaintances he'd made while fighting scourglings over the last few days.

Cressida caught Arthur's eye and leaned toward him. Arthur leaned toward her as well. Joy's shoulders were wide, and all they could do was brush their fingers together before they had to lean back. But it was enough. A silent wish for good luck.

Before the first of the crowd could reach them, the dragons launched themselves into the pit, back-winging to keep from hitting the steep sides. Sams had the worst of it, but he was experienced enough to keep his wings from brushing the edges. Brixaby, of course, had no problem buzzing straight down.

As he did, the sense of power grew stronger and stronger, until it was like they were slowly sinking through not air, but thick liquid.

But as far as they descended, the pulsing heart still seemed to be the same distance away.

You can't trust your senses down here, Arthur reminded himself.

Screams and shouts came from above. Brixaby looked up and then jinked to the right as someone fell past him from above—the man reached for Arthur's leg, fingers brushing, but couldn't get a grip. In a flash of a second, he was below them, still falling.

"Brix!" Arthur yelled, though he wasn't even sure what he wanted from the dragon. The man had fallen too fast, and even if Brixaby dived now, he would be too late. Arthur looked up, and to his horror, saw the man wasn't the only one.

People had ignored official warnings to descend in an orderly fashion. Of course they had. There were untold riches in the Dark Heart, not to mention the press of thousands of others behind them. Several adventuring teams were at a full-on sprint, circling around the downward path, and those that were slower were being overtaken.

And the path was only wide enough for two men shoulder to shoulder.

"Look out!" Arthur yelled, seeing a woman tip over the edge. She tried to drag the man who had shouldered her off the path down with her, but with a vicious shove, he pushed her away.

Arthur couldn't ask Brix to save her. He was too small to carry two riders, much less catch someone falling at great speed with the weight of Arthur already on his back.

Joy and Sams, however, could.

With a snort of annoyance, Sams shifted the angle and beat of his wings to catch her on the main sail of his wing on the downstroke. Thankfully, his wing membrane was not as delicate as it looked. The woman struck hard and rolled, unresisting, to a lower level of the path on Sams's upstroke. She looked stunned.

Arthur saw her sit up, though, cradling her arm and looking dazed.

Joy caught the next with her claws, though she was careful to mainly use her nonvenomous, ungloved arm. She easily flipped the shrieking man to the path at the side. The fallen people now had a lead on the others . . . if they weren't too injured to move.

They continued downward, and still the Dark Heart seemed no closer.

Then, without warning, something from the outside seized Arthur's mind.

Instantly, he threw up every **Mental Blocking** skill he had, including his area-of-effect shield to protect the others. The shields and skills shattered in a way that even the Mind Singer hadn't been able to do.

Then again, the Mind Singer was only a Rare power. In the second before Arthur's mind was completely rolled over, he recognized Legendary strength.

A thought shook his mind, coming from everywhere at once, from the outside and the inside, too.

What do you need?

Somehow, Arthur was able to gather his scattered thoughts enough to answer.

The Master of Cards, he thought, focusing on that shining image he'd seen while in guided meditation.

He thought he heard a laugh. **We will see.**

Suddenly, Arthur was no longer on Brixaby's back. He was standing somewhere else entirely.

CHAPTER 37

The world revolved around Arthur. Or maybe he was the one spinning while the world remained still. Lost, disoriented, and confused, the only thing he knew for sure was that he was no longer sitting on Brixaby's neck.

The first things that finally came into focus were the classic scents of frying garlic and mushrooms. Then, in the next moment, he found himself standing nearly nose to nose with a brick wall that radiated heat.

He took a step back. No, it wasn't a wall, it was a brick oven. A huge contraption he'd seen in a few high-end kitchens with brickwork extending to the ceiling.

"Brix?" Arthur started to turn.

Before he could, a voice shouted right behind him. "You there! Boy!"

Fully turning, he saw who—what—spoke and jumped back so fast that the back of his shoulders knocked against the uncomfortably warm oven.

Automatically, he reached for his Nice Shot card. To his horror, it wasn't available. Only a few bare cards were: Master of Skills, Charming Gentle-Person, and Return to Start.

He had nothing to defend himself against the scourgling in human clothing that stared down at him with an unimpressed gaze. It was shaped like a donkey. Though, like a scourgling, its remaining fur was thin and left patches displaying weeping sores. One long ear was half off and drooping over its—his?—face.

It raised a hoof hand, pointed at Arthur, and in a man's voice said, "Are you just going to lollygag around or are you going to work?"

"Work?" Arthur breathed.

Was he meant to kill this scourgling with his bare hands? He'd been through a dungeon before and knew he had to fight his way out. Where was Brixaby? Cressida?

Arthur's reply had been a question, but the scourgling took it as an answer. He waved at him with a hoof hand. "Then follow me. Let's see if you're worth anything."

There was a tail sticking out of workpants.

This was . . . very, very wrong.

A horrible thought seized Arthur, and he shot a quick glance at his own hands. Still human. That was a relief. But his hands were smaller, the skin a little brighter, and he was missing a few peppered burn scars that usually dotted his knuckles. These were still his hands, but younger.

Master of Skills, Charming Gentle-Person, and Return to Start were all my first cards, he thought.

This all flashed in and out of his mind within a second, then he moved to follow the scourgling. They moved through a professional kitchen that didn't look too different from the one in Barlow's restaurant back in Wolf Moon Hive.

Though the kitchen seemed larger than Barlow's in an exaggerated way because Arthur found he was shorter. He was maybe twelve or thirteen, he judged, thinking of his cards.

Glancing internally, he made sure his Cooking Class was equipped. Strangely, his other classes like Thief and Gambler were all locked, even though he'd had them as a kid.

What in the world was going on?

There were other cooks in the kitchen, including a crab-type scourgling that, horribly enough, seemed to be making a seafood stew.

The other cooks glanced at Arthur, though only in mild curiosity, like anyone would when seeing a new face in the kitchen.

The donkey scourgling stopped at the last workstation in line at the back. There was a cutting board, a set of knives—only some were appropriate for chopping—and one whole side piled high with vegetables.

"Now, let's see what you can do with this." Despite the fact the scourgling had a hoof for a hand, he grabbed a knife from the block. It made sense in a dreamlike way. He handed it, handle first, to Arthur.

Taking it, Arthur wondered if he was meant to stab the donkey with it and harvest its cards. Then he took a closer look and frowned. "You want me to . . . chop the vegetables?"

"No," the donkey said dryly, "I want you to sing a tune. Keep us all entertained while we fix your meal."

The casual disrespect in the kitchen—the way it acted like a boss—struck a reflex in Arthur. "No, Chef. I only meant this knife isn't appropriate."

The donkey's eyes narrowed. One was weeping pus. "How so?"

With his free hand, Arthur pressed the tip down, and it bent, flexible as a green twig. "This is a fillet knife. I could carve a fish with this, but not carrots."

The donkey said nothing but half stepped back and gestured to the block. "What would you use?"

Arthur replaced the fillet knife and instead picked up a good straight-edged paring knife. "I'd use this for peeling and segmenting smaller vegetables and fruits. And a heavier weight knife, like this medium weight here, with the thick heel"—he pointed to the base—"for the harder stuff."

New skill level: Knife Work (Cooking Class)
Level 46

Arthur flinched slightly at the surprise notification. **Knife Work** was a higher-tiered skill, and he rarely got a new level in it, much less so easily.

The donkey didn't seem to notice his flinch. "Hmm, not a complete idiot, then." He gestured to the pile. "Get to work. I want all these prepared for the dinner service."

Arthur glanced at the pile. It was truly random, with carrots, peppers of all varieties from sweet to hot, root vegetables including squash, carrots, and potatoes in several colors. There was celery, cucumber, tomatoes of several shapes, florets of broccoli, lettuce, onions, and more.

He glanced at the chef. "Is there a way you want them prepared? For a particular recipe?"

The long donkey face gave no expression that he could read. He only tossed his head, knocking that revolting hanging ear out of his eye. "Use your best judgment."

This, he thought, *was a test*. Arthur nodded and got to work. He still wasn't entirely sure if he was meant to fight or not—he'd keep a hand on a knife just in case.

Then he took one of the carrots, peeled it, and started to neatly julienne the pieces. As he did, he glanced around to see if there was any sign of his friends or Brixaby.

Wherever they were, they weren't in the kitchen. He only hoped that whatever test they were facing, they were okay.

"This has to be some sort of a joke," Horatio grumbled.

"Be calm," Sams advised.

"You be calm. I'm perfectly calm. We're just light-deck specialists who are stuck in a never-ending dark room. What's there not to be calm about?" But he could hear the peevishness in his own voice. Horatio made himself stop. "Sorry, Sams."

"Thanks to your Rainbow Knight card, are we ever truly without light?"

As a matter of fact, they probably weren't. Did Arthur even know the value of the gift he'd given to them? Well, if he did, Horatio thought that he still would've done the same thing. Arthur could be nice like that.

And his dragon was turning into an enchanter, of all the ridiculous things.

"All right, all right." Sams was right. Just because his eyes didn't see, that did not mean it was truly dark. There were bands of light that went beyond what dumb human and dragon eyes could pick up.

Horatio activated his Rainbow Knight card. Sure enough, he felt power trickle in through what he liked to think of as the slow low light, even though he never said as much out loud because it didn't make a lot of sense. It was light so red that he couldn't see it, but it was still there.

Thanks to his Rainbow Knight card, Horatio could gather it. Then, with a push through Brixaby's ingot thingy, he raised his palm and let out a beam of light in the visible spectrum.

Sam snorted in approval.

They stood next to a wall. One that Horatio was certain hadn't been there a moment before since it felt like they'd been walking for at least a half hour before this.

The walls had squares all over it. And by "all over it," he meant thousands of squares. Each was a different shade.

"I don't suppose we could use the Flash Fry card to get through this," Horatio said.

That was the card that he and Sams had created together on their linking.

Flash Fry

Rare

Elemental Manipulation

The wielder of this card will be able to condense a beam of light that is hot enough to burn.

It was a simple description for a Rare card, which meant it was ridiculously effective. No catches, no weirdness like with his Second Helpings card, which made food . . . but not necessarily nutritious food.

Plus, when Horatio used Flash Fry with his Ultraviolet Light Manipulation card, that beam of light became invisible to the eye.

Unlike material objects—or a few people he could name—light wasn't complicated. Yeah, Horatio liked light a lot. And he liked it better that his dragon had a whole lot of light-support cards stuffed in his three cores.

Sams was old enough to be wise and had been high ranking in the hive when he'd been linked to Horatio's father. So it wasn't too much of a surprise when he looked at the wall and said, "We should not blast past this. We should solve it properly."

"Properly?" He remembered something Cressida said during their conversations over the last few days. "So you think this is like a puzzle dungeon. Ugh." He made a sound of disgust. "I always hated puzzles—always lose the pieces."

Sams, used to his complaining, ignored it and pointed one claw to the middle of the wall. "See this? Middle green, as you see in the midrange of the visible spectrum. And here, perfect ultraviolet purple. Do you think you can copy these exact shades with your Rainbow Knight card?"

There were literally thousands of shades, but Sams had pointed out the exact midranges of each band. He was just that good.

Horatio squared his shoulders. He had to work to be a rider who could match his dragon.

"Let's find out."

He lifted his hand and accessed his Rainbow Knight card. With Sams's help through his own light modification card he had, they made it the same shade of green that was shown on the square on the wall. A beam shot out and hit the square dead on.

The green faded and turned dark. Then Horatio turned his attention to the next square, which was a touch lighter in color.

Unfortunately, a few squares down the line, he got a little sloppy and accidentally swept the green beam of light over a blue square, which was a row lower.

A buzz filled the room, and then the darkened completed squares all lit back up.

Horatio winced. "Guess I gotta start over. Say, what are the chances we put in all this effort and the wall drops, only to show a bunch of scourglings or something horrible waiting on the other side?"

Sams snorted and took a long look around through the darkness. "It doesn't seem like we have much of a choice but to move forward."

That was true enough. "All right, let's start with the middle green again." Because there was nothing stopping him, he stepped close to make sure his light beam hit accurately. "This is going to take all day . . ."

If Cressida didn't have to see another wave-type dungeon in her life, she would die happy.

And she didn't care what other people said, this was absolutely a dungeon. A twisted scourgling version of a dungeon, but one all the same.

She really hoped Joy was okay.

But she couldn't think much about that as she sent her fire bear summon, Wicker, forward to kill another scourgling that came at her from over the top of the left-side hill.

She'd arrived in the valley between two identical earthen hills. Sometimes the scourglings, which had the shape of giant centipedes that scuttled in the dust, would come at her from both sides. Sometimes one at a time. Wicker was happy to maul them all, though her water crane was less useful because centipedes didn't have lungs and therefore couldn't be drowned.

Cressida was safe for now, but her mana would not last forever.

"Arthur, if I get killed in this stupid dungeon, I'm going to kill you," she muttered nonsensically to herself.

Then, deciding she couldn't stand here forever, she summoned her water crane again and charged up the right-side hill.

Three enemies immediately scuttled over the top and down to meet her. Cressida kept moving upward and urged Wicker and the crane together. They did so in a roiling burst of steam that cooked the three scourglings.

Cressida glanced down at them as she passed and was dissatisfied to see no glowing from their chests. This truly was a terrible dungeon.

Bracing herself to fight a boss or guardian at the top, her foot hit level ground and . . . the landscape changed.

Suddenly, she stood in calf-deep mud. The hills were gone, and she was in a swamp with lichen that hung low off dead trees.

"These pants cost two Common shards," she muttered, squelching forward.

But she wasn't alone in the swamp.

Several froglike scourglings the size of wolves started leaping her way. They didn't get stuck in the mud.

When Cressida reached for her shields to protect her, she found that her pool of mana had mysteriously refilled from one landscape to the next.

Mana doesn't work like that, she thought, then remembered the conversation she'd had with that girl who'd made eyes at Arthur—Soledad.

Rules changed in the Dark Heart.

The issue was, the moment the shield was up, all the scourge-frogs in the immediate area seemed to be alerted by it. Dozens of big, moist, rotting frogs jumped at her from all directions. Hitting her shield like that would drain her mana down to nothing.

So Cressida resummoned Wicker and the water crane, focusing the effort through the enchanted ingot Brixaby had given her.

Wicker burned like a white light. The water crane was enhanced as well, with particles of ice reinforcing its daggerlike beak and wings. To Cressida's shock, she saw it drill straight through two of the frogs, mid-leap.

The water where Wicker stepped boiled. He made short work of anything attacking him as well.

With her summons for protection, Cressida squelched toward a glimpse of dry land she could see ahead.

"This had all better be worth it," she muttered.

CHAPTER 38

Brixaby

You want *my* art?" Brixaby roared at the top of his lungs.

It was a pity he was currently without his Stunning Shout ability, but that hardly mattered. He would be perfectly happy to kill without it.

The scourgling in front of him opened up its jaws as if to answer, but Brixaby lunged forward and ripped the shards in its heart out anyway. The fact that the thing was wearing clothes and speaking meant nothing, other than it was slightly less convenient to harvest the body.

Brixaby had found himself in a foundry and surrounded by scourglings. As a dragon, he knew exactly what to do next.

The fact that the thing had spoken and asked Brixaby to create something . . . well, that was an insult that he would not take lightly.

More scourglings, all shaped like stags with pointed antlers, came at him with blacksmithing tools raised.

Brixaby buzzed into the air. The foundry's ceiling was high enough to account for the high temperatures of the forge. This gave him enough room to get some altitude and maneuver.

Picking his target, he shot down and tore shards out of his next victim, all the while avoiding strikes from hammers and improvised tools.

Though not all of them.

One beefy scourgling brought down a mallet on Brixaby's side—it bounced off, and Brixaby felt only pressure instead of pain.

A swift check to his core showed his Stone Skin card had activated.

And strangely, he now had access to his Stunning Shout ability through his Call of the Void card.

It seemed the moment Brixaby had chosen to attack the scourglings, the rules changed.

Brixaby flew into the air again and did a flip, just to annoy his attackers. They didn't know it yet, but they were already dead. Brixaby only had to decide when.

"I will make art . . . of your shards!" he yelled. "I will build a monument to myself and all dragonkind. Come at me, scourglings!"

The creatures obliged, and more poured in through the doors of the foundry.

Brixaby's danger sense kicked in, and he jinked out of the way when one dared to flick molten glass up at him. Naturally, Brixaby retaliated by grabbing an anvil out of his Personal Space and dropping it on the foul scourgling's head when it went back for more glass.

He snatched a pair of tongs out of the air that another threw at him. Hmm. These were of exceptional quality.

Since these were most certainly stolen from real blacksmiths, as no scourgling could create anything of value, Brixaby tucked the tongs away. He did the same to any other tools he could catch.

In between, of course, he went back to harvesting shards.

He only hoped that wherever Arthur was, he was having just as grand a time.

"I don't like this," Joy muttered to herself. "This makes me not happy-happy—" She stopped, catching herself from her double-speak. That was something she used to do occasionally when she'd been a tiny hatchling and felt unsure of herself, back when she wasn't as big and strong, and before she got her venom.

Joy hugged herself, careful as always that her poison claws didn't prick past her scales, then settled back on all fours. She looked down one empty hallway that seemed to go on and on, leading into darkness, then to the other.

"Hello?"

Her voice echoed back to her. "Hello, hello, hello, hello . . ."

Joy sighed. She always had someone to talk to, whether it be Cressida or Brixaby or Sams, or friendly people on the street, or unfriendly people, or people who didn't know they were about to be friends . . .

But now, for the first time in her life, she was truly alone.

She hoped Cressida was okay. She hoped Brixaby and his rider were okay. She hoped—

Cutting herself off from that line of thought, she instead said aloud to the empty hallway, "You know, for a heart, you don't have a lot of kindness."

Then she chose to walk down the hallway behind her. Choosing to go forward would be too obvious.

She expected to have mean scourglings jump out at her at any moment. That's why she kept her chainmail glove off, just in case.

But nothing really happened. Just a lot of twists and turns and empty slate hallways that were always partially lit even though there wasn't a light source. There was a ceiling up on top, so she couldn't even fly out. She just had to walk.

For the first hour, Joy sang to keep herself occupied. Then she grew bored of that. What was the point of singing if there was no one else to sing with?

She made turn after turn, with no idea if she was getting closer to her destination or farther from it. She didn't even know where her destination was.

Finally, she stopped at yet another T-section. "Have I been here before? Oh, maybe I should have been marking along the way. Oops." She used a nonvenomous claw to scratch out an *X* on the wall.

Then she continued. Turn after turn. No end in sight.

What had Cressida called one of these? Not a maze. A labyrinth, maybe?

Though she marked her turns, she never came across the same one again.

Finally, Joy stopped. "Um, quest card? Do you want to give me a hint?"

She knew better than that, of course. Her card didn't work on command, but she was out of ideas.

Well, except for one.

She'd seen Brixaby's rider doing his meditation thing. He was trying to change the size of his heart deck. Could she maybe access her quest better by doing the same? Or at least find an answer within herself?

Instead of moving forward or singing or talking to herself, Joy sat on her haunches, slowed her breathing and just . . . tried to be.

Her thoughts, which always bounced from one subject to another without any care, became quiet.

Finally, she opened her eyes.

"I want to go right," she said, without really knowing why except that taking the next right-hand path really seemed to be the right idea.

"Ha. I'm hilarious."

Nevertheless, there was a new hallway to the right only a few steps away. One she hadn't noticed until now.

She took it, and to her surprise, the next hallway wasn't all boring and empty. A chest sat in the middle. It had all sorts of pretty jewels encrusted on top, and though it was weirdly too heavy for Joy to pick up, the top opened on a hinge.

Inside was an entire flank of raw bison meat, nice and bloody, just the way she liked it. As well as a bucket of water. It was one of those weird storage things where the items seemed tiny on the inside but became regular sized when she pulled them out.

"Ohh! I was just getting hungry! Thank you!" Happily, Joy dug in. After she was done, she closed the top of the chest with a pat, then continued down the hallway.

When she came to another turn, she sat down and thought.

"Nope. But I'll take the next left, I think."

That decision seemed right. Something was building in her chest, and she wasn't quite sure what it was. But the nameless feeling had given her food, and she was certain that it was bringing her close to Cressida, too.

Joy continued on.

"I said I wanted a dragon!" Soledad yelled to the empty air.

The only answer she got were the shrieks of murderous, seagull-type scourglings, the far off yowls of large mountain-lion-type scourglings, and the whistling howls of wolf-type scourglings. Luckily, the last two were still in the thick jungle up the slope and rarely came down to the beach where she stood.

With a sigh, Soledad flicked another perfectly cute newly hatched turtle—which was certainly not the dragon hatchling she'd focused on when the Dark Heart asked what she wanted—into the roiling sea in front of her.

In the sky above, a big counter rolled over from 401 to 402 turtles saved.

Then Soledad turned from waves and went up to the beach, where more adorable turtle hatchlings were struggling out from under the sand. Did turtles bury their eggs there? That seemed to be a stupid idea.

Especially as the moment they emerged, seagull scourglings dived and plucked them from the sky, and mountain lion and wolf scourglings, slavering and half rotted, darted out of the jungle to grab mouthfuls at a time.

At least the predators didn't seem to notice her at all. But they were so numerous that without Soledad's help, not one of the baby turtles would make it to shore.

When Soledad had picked up a handful and flung them into the water, the counter started to tick up.

She'd heard of point-based challenges before, so it became a mad dash to try to save as many turtles as possible. It could be worse. This could be a match to the death, and her without any cards at all. Only . . . it seemed there was no end.

The sand sucked her down with every step, and soon her calves were burning. By the time she reached six hundred hatchlings saved, she didn't care how cute they were anymore. She just wanted this to end.

If I had a card, I could be faster. I could be doing this better— "Oh, go away!" she yelled, batting away a seagull scourgling that had swooped for a hatchling she was trying to pick up.

So far, she'd avoided trying to fight any of the scourglings for fear they'd turn on her. But frustration had her swing wide, and she accidentally knocked the thing out of the air.

It whistled in rage and tried to right itself. Soledad had grown up in a city being slowly swallowed up by dead land. She knew what to do.

Before the seagull could come at her, she stomped down on it. Hard.

When she stepped back, she saw its chest had begun to glow. Quickly, she snatched out the shard.

A whole card shard? Just for a lousy seagull?

Soledad stuffed the precious shard in her pocket, then remembered the original challenge and quickly grabbed up an armful of turtle hatchlings. They netted her ten more points.

But none would get her actual shards.

When she returned to the beach, she paused to grab a big stick from the edge of the jungle. It had a bulbous end on it, like a club.

Then she stood on the other side of a large tree trunk and waited for one of the wolves. Without her helping the turtles, their numbers increased, and the wolves closed in.

Stepping from behind the tree, Soledad brought the club down on the head of the closest. It struck off to the side and turned to her with razor-sharp teeth sticking every which way from its unnaturally large jaws. She struck it again and again until its chest began to glow.

The rest of its pack was too busy gorging on turtle hatchlings to notice—or care—until Soledad chased them away. She used the bottom of her shirt to scoop up the remaining hatchlings and return them to the water. Only then did she harvest the wolf.

Four shards.

She couldn't tell if they were Common, Uncommon, or what. And she suspected that would be determined based on how many hatchlings she saved.

With a grin, she remembered Arthur's words.

"I need to take everything I can from this place," she said to herself. "That means harvesting the predators, too."

It didn't seem like this challenge had a mind to end anytime soon. Maybe she'd come out with enough shards to make a full set. Wouldn't that be a kick?

Marion couldn't look at the faces of the people he was stitching together anymore. They all had the features of his friends and family. Their voices, too. Especially when they cried out in pain.

He didn't even know where he was, except that it was in a healer's tent that was placed outside of a disaster zone . . . A disaster that left people bloody, with pieces taken out of them, as well as broken bones from impact injuries. Most of them were actively bleeding out.

The Dark Heart sure had a way of surprising him. When it had asked him what he needed, naturally, Marion focused on his desire for a healing-type card. This was where it plopped him.

Not hard to understand the challenge here.

On the other hand, there was no fighting, no puzzles to solve, and no thought other than assessment, triage, and getting the person as stable as possible before moving to the next.

"These people aren't real, these people aren't real, these people aren't real," he told himself, which was easy to say because while their faces and voices came straight from his memory, their bodies were clearly not human. Some kind of scourgling? Though the rot or the weeping sores didn't seem to bother them as much as the injuries did.

He didn't have time to think about that.

Because the Dark Heart hadn't granted him any additional cards or powers for this challenge, he just had himself and his skills—apparently, he was the lone person in this entire disastrous scenario who knew how to fix other people. At least the hospital tent was well stocked with basic healing implements: bandages, fire-sanitized needles, clean thread, and freshly boiled water to irrigate wounds.

No healing potions. That would have been too easy.

So he did what he could with one patient after another. And occasionally, he would lose one.

He tried not to think too hard about that and just moved to the next patient, and the next . . . and the next.

But as he continued in an endless stream, something odd started to happen. Marion didn't know if there was a pattern emerging that he was subconsciously picking up, if he was getting more experience, like people who had cards that leveled did, or if it was something deeper.

Sometimes he would experience flashes of what was wrong with somebody, even before he got a good look at the injuries. And sometimes he would know, without knowing exactly how, when a bone was perfectly set.

This wasn't anything that he could pinpoint or replicate on demand, but as the challenge wore on, patient after patient, with faces he couldn't stand to look at, he learned to lean into that feeling.

It was miserable work. But at least there was this: every new patient was a surprise.

After years and years of seeing the immediate future unfold in front of him with no surprises at all, Marion found he could grit his teeth and bear it.

Even unpleasant surprises were better than none at all.

Arthur had been cutting vegetables for hours. He should be feeling fatigue, but his **Knife Work** skill was advancing spectacularly fast—he hit level 48. Soon, Brixaby would not be the only one with a level 50 skill.

Knife Work had been one of his very first skills. It felt right that it would be the one to hit that threshold first.

At this point, it felt like his knives were floating through the vegetables. Even though he was currently without his Toughened Skin attribute, there was no chance he'd cut himself.

The pile of vegetables to his left seemed to be completely endless. He experimented on them with every trick he could think of, mincing, chopping, rough cutting, straight cuts, julienne, even some fancy diamond cuts and making roses out of radishes. Anything to challenge his skill.

If he were in the real world, he'd need more. He knew it. After all, it had taken him years to get to his level. Yet, in the Dark Heart, his skills continued leveling at an accelerated pace.

With all this, he got no direction from his odd co-workers. It took a few hours before he finally accepted that they weren't going to kill them. In fact, they only interacted with him when somebody from one of the stations came over to collect the next of whatever he had just finished.

Arthur continued his cutting, but at this point, it had become so easy that he had to struggle to keep his mind on task and not wander to other places. So it was with a complete shock when he looked down and realized that he was cutting into a scourge-infected carrot.

The signs were subtle, bits of blackness that were not quite mold and were certainly not dirt.

Arthur stopped and stared. Then he looked at the pile he had just completed before: a colorful variety of bell peppers.

Well, I am cooking for scourglings, he thought. But memories of his childhood friend, Ernie, dying of food poisoning reared its ugly head.

And he realized with a sickening swoop in his stomach that he'd been so busy at fancy cuts he had neglected to *look* at the food closely.

In fact, the bit of celery he'd minced up before the bell peppers had just been taken away by the crab-like saucier who managed the soup station to Arthur's right. Glancing over, Arthur saw that those pieces, too, had bits of infected scourge-rot on the perfect cubes. And the saucier was about to tip the plate right into the soup.

"No," Arthur yelled, and grabbed a jointed arm. The crab click-whistled something at him and tried to knock him away with a giant pincer arm, but Arthur was prepared for that, ducked in close to position himself in between him and the soup, and pushed him away.

The chef walked over in a huff. "What is going on here?"

The saucier turned to him. "This boy is trying to push me off my station."

Arthur simply pointed. "The celery's rotted, Chef."

He looked, and his long face wrinkled before he gave the saucier a hard look. "You didn't see that?"

"I trusted the prep—"

"You always look at the ingredients you put in your own food." Then he turned to Arthur, and Arthur braced himself to be yelled at.

"Well, if you think you can do better, you're in charge of the soup." Then he paused. "Good job catching the rot."

And with that, Arthur's **Knife Work** skill jumped two levels:

Skill level gained: Knife Work (Cooking Class)
Level 50

Congratulations! For reaching this milestone you have been awarded
the following:
+3 Dexterity
+2 Wisdom
+1 Strength
+25% quicker learning in all Cooking Class skills.
+25% quicker adaptation to all Cooking body-enhancement skills.

Pride flushed through him in a rosy glow, but he had no time to revel in his accomplishment or wonder what a Cooking body-enhancement skill was. Nor did he receive the warning Brixaby had about his skill no longer advancing due to a lack of a class, because of course Arthur had long ago gotten his Cooking Class.

Suddenly, in the odd way of dreams, Arthur stood in front of a roiling kettle of boiling water. The saucier was gone.

Arthur stared blankly for a moment, then looked to the chef.

"What am I to make?"

"You're the saucier, aren't you?" the chef asked, and Arthur was certain he saw a gleam of challenge in his eye.

Of course, Arthur already had ideas in mind. He took a moment to look at his new workstation: Again, the ingredients seemed endless, though he also had meat along with vegetables.

He started cutting into a cut of beef and got a level in his **Butchering** skill. Then he sautéed the first few cubes to make sure that they were browned. When he dumped them into the soup, he received a surprise.

New skill gained: Saucier (Cooking Class)
Due to your card's bonus traits, you automatically start this skill at level 5.

Arthur had been working in kitchens for years and had been frantically cooking chicken soup for his friends to act as a poor man's healing potion.

He'd never gotten the **Saucier** skill. He'd always thought of creating sauces and soups as part of his overall **Meal Preparation** skill, but he must have been wrong. Was the Dark Heart plugging up holes in his education?

And now he was starting to see a pattern. The next workspace was strictly for butchering, with whole carcasses hanging nearby, some with skin. The next one after that seemed to be for standard entrees, then the desserts.

It seemed he was to level up the workstations one at a time.

And when he reached 50 in all his cooking skills . . .

He was excited to see what a third-tier class looked like.

CHAPTER 39

Time lost meaning to Arthur as he slowly moved through the workstations, one by one. From sauces, he moved to butchering and then to entrees. None of the stations were easy, and all had their individual challenges and hidden traps to avoid.

A few times more, he caught other signs of scourge-rot on the food that he was working on. But also, while he was at the butchering table, he encountered new animals and fish—some that had poisonous parts to avoid.

For that, the chef gave him additional material in a scroll to study. Mostly, however, Arthur focused on his ever-advancing **Butchering** skill to tell him what parts would be safe to eat and what wouldn't. The combination of gut instinct and experience his high-leveled skills gave him was becoming increasingly invaluable.

Trying to pass the entree station had him studying a recipe book that was not so different from the one he had used at Barlow's. Only, this book had ways to help him increase his **Cooking Intuition**, too. Each recipe had portions that were flat-out missing. A few of them had ingredients listed in proportions that either were so under or over that they would ruin the entire dish.

Also, he encountered unfamiliar terms here and there that he had to puzzle out, despite his **Language Proficiency** skills. He suspected those had been made up by the recipe writers to confuse people who were not supposed to have the book.

However, every time he successfully navigated through one of the hang-ups or outright traps, he received a bonus of a few levels in that particular skill.

But that wasn't all.

While at the workstations, he was forced to cook using wildly different methods, from roasting several dishes in stoves that all required different but precise timing to frying food in hot oil. He even had to cook on an open flame while managing the temperature so that it didn't char the food.

He must have messed up one time without knowing how or why, because suddenly he found himself pulled from the entree workstation and sent to the dishwasher's sink. There, he was faced with pots and pans that had been piled up nearly to the ceiling.

At first, Arthur was frustrated, but soon he realized this, too, was an opportunity to advance his skills. He'd been a dishwasher for years in various kitchens and already had his **Dishwashing** skill at a fairly high level 23.

But now, keeping in mind what Marion had told him about his **Catching** skill, Arthur fully concentrated on his task. To his surprise, he immediately gained a new skill in **Scrubbing**. And it was one that he quickly started to level, as well as his current **Dishwashing** skill.

It might be silly, a grown man focusing on leveling **Scrubbing**, but he didn't care. He was going to take everything that the Dark Heart would give him.

Besides, finding new and interesting ways to clean pots and pans that had been sitting too long and had food practically glued to the bottom also helped his **Tidying** skill. That was one of the first skills he'd acquired as a boy, and now it started to shoot up in levels, too.

By the time the last of the pots and pans were dealt with, and he'd cleaned out the sink for good measure, his **Scrubbing** was up to a respectable level 25, **Dishwashing** was at 38, and **Tidying** up to a staggering level 47.

He was reassigned to the entree station and began working with renewed vigor. As he did, he took special care to clean up after himself while concentrating on his **Tidying** skill. He wanted it to pass level 50.

The station that threatened his completion of the challenge was Confectionery and Bakery. Arthur had never excelled at desserts, and no matter how high he got his **Baking and Cooking** skills, he could never make caramel without burning the sugar. While he could produce functional cakes and cookies, decorating them to perfection required an artist's touch, which he lacked. His were good enough without that extra something that made them extraordinary.

He didn't have an artist's soul—not like Brixaby with his blacksmith artistry skills.

However, even if he didn't have a natural talent for desserts, and his chocolate work was more functional than inspired, he was determined to brute force his way through it. By the time his **Confectionery** and **Baking** skills reached the midthirties in rank, he let those skills carry him through.

He'd been working on the stations for . . . how long had he been here? Certainly more than a few hours. It might even have been days at this point.

Nothing changed in the kitchen: no staff changeover other than when Arthur took over a new workstation. The orders kept coming. Yet he didn't feel the fatigue he knew he should have been experiencing. Not even mental fatigue. He didn't start making careless mistakes, and not once did his knife slip while cutting.

The Dark Heart was providing him with as much time as he needed to complete the challenge. Considering how much he was leveling, he wasn't in a hurry to end the process.

He still couldn't help but worry about how Brixaby and the others were faring in their challenges. Were they also working in their versions of kitchens?

No . . . no, that would be silly.

Arthur shook his head and dismissed the thought, then continued to create small, delicate tarts to an acceptable standard.

Mindful after his time at the dishwashing station, he took a few minutes after he was done to clean up the mess.

This time he was rewarded with a new skill.

New skill gained: Kitchen Organization (Cooking Class)
Due to your card's bonus traits, Endless Grindstone, and unique
practice location, you automatically start this skill at level 10.

Starting at level ten? That was quite the jump. Was it because of his Endless Grindstone card, something the heart was doing, or—

That thought was cut off a moment later as he received another notice.

Skill level gained: Tidying
Level 50
Congratulations! For reaching this milestone you have been awarded
the following:
+2 Wisdom

He smiled to himself, and on a whim, started some heavy meat dishes. Those would require a lot of processing of fresh carcasses that had come in. His **Butchering** skill was so close to level 50 that he could practically taste it.

It took him roughly another hour, which was so quick that it was almost unheard of. Yet in his challenge, it felt natural.

By combining **Butchering** and **Meal Preparation**, he was able to level those two skills up together side by side.

Skill level gained: Butchering (Cooking Class)
Level 50
Congratulations! For reaching this milestone you have been awarded
the following:
+1 Strength
+1 Dexterity

Skill level gained: Meal Preparation (Cooking Class)
Level 50
Congratulations! For reaching this milestone you have been awarded
the following:
+2 Dexterity
+2 Intelligence

The real surprise came with the next announcement.

Alert: Class upgrade! (Cooking Class)
Cooking Class has upgraded to tier three!
You have the knowledge and passion to not only learn the fundamental
skills of your craft, but have shown a willingness to truly master your
skills and push the boundaries of your art.
All new skills within this class start at level 10, and experience is gained
25% faster in addition to existing cards' bonuses.
New subcategory added: Kitchen Sanitation which includes the
Dishwashing, Scrubbing, and Tidying skills.
Bonuses to attributes are now permanent and no longer need to be
equipped to be active.
+5 Perception
+5 Dexterity (additional 3 when using kitchen tools)
+4 Intelligence
+3 Wisdom
+1 Luck

But it was the next notification that truly took him aback.

*Any skill over level 50 in the Cooking Class may now be enhanced by
magical aspects.*

Arthur blinked at the notification. "But," he said, speaking aloud, "my Master of Skills card doesn't allow for magic-based skills. So what does that mean?"

As usual, there was no answer.

Could it be that he didn't know his Master of Skills card as well as he thought he did? That was both a frightening and reassuring thought.

Then he thought about his Nice Shot card and the fact that his **Knife Work** skill was up to level 50. Now that had some possibilities to it . . .

But before he could truly mull that over, he realized that the kitchen around him had gone quiet. Looking around, he saw that the world was starting to dissolve around him from the outside in, like a version of tunnel vision. Arthur took an involuntary step back as the world grew dark and close, like he was the only thing left that was solid.

And before he could worry about what he would be facing next, the world where he'd spent an endless dinner service was gone. Abruptly, he found himself sitting at the base of Brixaby's neck.

His dragon twisted hard under him, half barrel-rolling in the air in shock. Arthur yelled and had to lean hard on his **Dragon Riding** skill and newly enhanced strength attributes to keep from being flung off.

"Brix!"

Brixaby righted himself almost instantly, nearly throwing Arthur off the other side.

But he wasn't the only one who had reacted sharply. Their whole group had been thrown into confusion.

Above them, Joy yelled, "Finally! I'm out of those horrid hallways!"

Meanwhile, Sams seemed to have briefly lost altitude and was quickly flapping his large wings to stay up in the air. He'd come perilously close to falling straight down on Cressida and Joy.

"We're back!" Horatio yelled. "How long were we gone?"

A little dazed, Arthur looked around. He couldn't quite shake the feeling he'd just reentered a memory of something that had happened a few days ago. But no, the challenge was fake and this . . . this was real.

They were still descending into the pit of the Dark Heart.

Oh no, he'd taken so long in his challenge . . . had he somehow held up the rest of the retinue or let too many adventurers into the heart ahead of them?

Arthur glanced up and saw that there was still a crowd of people descending the circular pathways. In fact, it looked like they hadn't advanced at all from the last time he'd seen them.

It was as if no time had passed at all.

What was more, it seemed the sheriffs had finally started to restore basic order in the pushing, shoving group, along with some conscientious adventurers. One of Jon's Lightning Cats caught a young man who'd been wobbling close to the edge.

Meanwhile, Arthur's own retinue was still yelling back and forth to one another, with Marion and Soledad adding their voices.

"Joy, dear," he heard Cressida say, "did you get a card, too—"

"Cressida!" Arthur cut her off and pointed up at the descending crowd meaningfully. "You don't want your voice to travel."

She gave him a sharp look but then nodded, looking chagrined.

Arthur glanced down. The Dark Heart lay just as deep under them as before, as if they hadn't traveled at all. It had to be an illusion.

"Keep sinking," he told Brixaby. "Nice and steady."

Brixaby nodded, though he seemed unusually twitchy and kept staring closely into the deeper shadows. It was almost as if he expected something to leap out at him, though he seemed to be looking forward to the fight.

What had gone on in his challenge?

Arthur intended to find out soon, and only hoped that his dragon had benefited as much as he had.

Brixaby sank lower and lower within the pit, the other dragons back-winging after him. Still, they didn't seem to be getting any closer to the pulsing center of the Dark Heart.

Then, suddenly, Arthur found himself somewhere else entirely.

He stood in the middle of a green field of ankle-high grass with hills surrounding him. A cloudy blue sky arched overhead. Though it was just as bright as midday, there was no way anyone could mistake it for being outside. The sun was entirely different. It had been replaced by a pulsing Dark Heart.

And this time, Arthur had arrived with the rest of his retinue.

CHAPTER 40

Looking around, Arthur's gaze first fell on Cressida. Unlike him, she'd arrived standing next to her dragon and not astride. She met his gaze and said, "I think this is the first chamber."

"Chamber?" he repeated, though immediately his mind went to the hearts and offal of the animals he'd prepared for cooking. It was messy business, but one did not get to level 50 in **Butchering** without dealing with inner organs.

Cressida started to answer, but Soledad spoke first. "I've heard of this before from people who've delved into Dark Hearts. It's a sort of staging area—a place where we go to take a load off, rest, and prepare to face harder challenges."

"If this is the staging area, what was that all before?" Horatio asked.

Soledad started to answer, but this time Cressida interrupted her, while throwing a pointed look her way. "That must have been a preliminary. I think it was meant to see if we were ready for the rest of the challenges—or to prepare us somehow." She looked around. "Did you guys get earth challenges, too?"

"Earth challenges?" Arthur started to ask, then shook his head. "No, never mind. It looks like we're the first here, but I don't think others will be far behind. I don't want to be caught here talking. Let's see if we can find a shelter or somewhere that's more private to talk."

"I can help with that," Marion said unexpectedly. Then, four exact versions of himself seemed to step out of him and run in different directions, each toward a separate hill.

"Oh, is that your new card power?" Joy asked.

He nodded and pushed his glasses up his nose. "Yes, my illusionary clones."

Sure enough, one crested a hill to the south, turned, and waved to get their attention before he poofed out of existence. One by one, the others shook their heads before also disappearing.

"That way, I assume," Marion said, nodding to where the one that had waved had been.

It was a short enough distance that all started walking without remounting the dragons, though no one spoke. All seemed to be in a pensive mood, lost in what they'd see in their own challenges.

Near the top of the hill, Brixaby took it upon himself to buzz ahead. He returned quickly. "There is a shallow cave on the other side."

"Good, it won't hurt to have some kind of shelter."

Unfortunately, when they got there it was more of a divot than an actual cave. Sams could only stick his head in.

There was also a blank card floating in the middle of it. It glowed faintly green at the edges.

Arthur exchanged confused glances with the rest of his group, then reached out to grab the card. Before the tips of his fingers could close on it, a message flashed in his mind.

Do you wish to claim this territory for your party?
Yes/No

Couldn't hurt. "Yes," Arthur said. And when he grabbed the card, the edges glowed blue.

Instead of a description or a rank, all of their names appeared on the card in a list.

"I've heard of these." Soledad leaned over to squint. "This is an inclusion list. As long as you hold the card, no one but the people—or dragons, I guess—who have names on the list will be allowed to enter."

Horatio threw a disgusted look at the shelter. "Enter what? It's like two feet deep at most."

"We don't have to stay here, but I think we should take a moment and talk." Arthur looked around at the others. "I take it you guys didn't get the kitchen challenge, either?"

They threw him baffled looks.

"No!" Brixaby puffed out his chest. "I was dropped in a blacksmith's foundry and fought scores of scourglings until there were none left. They were attempting to trick me into forging weapons for them, but I know what to do with scourglings when I see them. And I took shards from them all!"

From his Personal Space, he grabbed a clawful of shards and held them out for the others to see. But they were unlike any card shards Arthur had seen before. They were oddly blank, but in a way that was more than surface deep. It was as if each was an absence of power that was waiting to be filled. Arthur couldn't tell if they were Common, Uncommon, Rare, or just fancy pieces that were meant to look like shards.

"Those were the same type I got," Soledad said.

Arthur took a good look at her for the first time since coming here and saw that the pockets of her trousers and the bag she'd slung over her shoulder were bulging. In fact, several seams on the bag had split.

Soledad continued, "Only, mine wasn't a blacksmith foundry. I had to save turtle hatchlings—scourglings were the predators. That's where I got the shards." She smiled ruefully. "I thought I was working against a timer or something, but when I'd saved a thousand hatchlings, the challenge ended."

Am I supposed to understand what any of that means? Arthur thought. *Turtle hatchlings?*

"I wish I got some shards," Horatio grumped. "Me and Sams were put in a puzzle challenge—we had to complete a wall of light by matching the different frequencies. Well, it would make more sense if you had light cards." He waved a dismissive hand at them. "It took us forever—felt like days."

"Yes, but the amount of practice did you well," Sams said. "Your sensitivity to the different spectrums of light has grown by leaps and bounds."

"Yeah?" Joy perked up. "I got stuck in a really boring hallway maze that went on forever and ever, but then after a while I calmed down and sort of listened to my inner voice. I didn't get any cards or shards, but a sort of . . . intuition? Like I was practicing something that I already had, but it became really good in there."

"Intuition?" Brixaby repeated. "Does that have to do with your quest card?"

"No! Well, I mean, kind of? But it's not really in the description," Joy said, which of course didn't help.

"Wait, so am I the only one who got a card?" Cressida asked.

Immediately, all gazes turned to her. Arthur noted that most were jealous.

Marion sheepishly raised his hand. "I got a card, too."

And now that Arthur was paying attention, he saw his friend was radiating quiet pride. From his heart, he projected an Uncommon card.

Healer's Instinct
Uncommon

Healing

Upon visual inspection of individuals, the wielder of this card will be able to instinctively know if that person is sick or injured. As this card does not use mana, the information may be indistinct. Exact diagnosis will depend on the wielder's education and experience in the healing arts. As experience grows, the wielder will be able to make diagnoses with greater accuracy.

Brixaby made a noise of delight, and for a horrified second Arthur worried he was going to take the card for himself. But his dragon was looking down at his own chest. "Yes, I see . . . now that I look, I realize that I have gained a new addition to my Call of the Void list."

"What?" Arthur swiftly glanced at his own list. The only thing there was his skill grind. He refocused on Brixaby. "What did you get?"

The dark dragon tilted his head. "It is called Berserker's Rage."

"Ohh, that sounds powerful," Joy said. "What happens when you use it?"

"I do not know. But I could try it out—"

"No!" everyone said all at once.

Grumbling, Brixaby visibly backed down.

Glad to have dodged that, Arthur turned to Cressida. "You said you got a card?"

"Yes, I did." Like Marion, she was quietly happy, and for some reason sent a smug look in Soledad's direction. "My challenge was . . . odd. At first, I thought I'd entered a wave-type dungeon again, but the moment I started to beat the enemies, the location changed. I got sand, a swamp with a lot of mud." She looked down at herself and grimaced in memory, though there wasn't a speck of dirt on her. "Then the side of a rocky cliff, and it went on like that. Eventually, I realized that every location had to do with different aspects of Earth. And once I figured that out, I knew there had to be more to the challenge. I started to look around more carefully rather than just fighting scourglings. And on the next location change, I found a card just sticking out of the mud."

Then she projected the image of her card out, too.

Earth Hedgehog
Rare
Summon

The wielder of this card will be able to summon a semitransparent hedgehog companion three feet in length. When directed, this summon will be able to throw spikes toward enemies. These spikes are not poison tipped (unless the wielder pours poison on the summon ahead of time) but have barbs at the end, which will make removing them a challenge. Spikes may pass through allies' defenses. When the summoned is killed, it may be resummoned within the same hour with the use of mana. The amount of mana used during summoning will determine how many spikes the hedgehog will be able to throw, the range, and overall accuracy.

"I guess I'm keeping up with my animal theme," Cressida said with a wry smile.

"Interesting. Is that a matched card to your current set?" Brixaby eagerly asked. "You could have three of a kind."

She shook her head. "No, they're from different sets. Just a similar theme. But I think the hedgehog will pair nicely with my shield."

"Can I name him?" Joy asked. "Ohh, can I name him Prickly?"

Cressida hesitated. "Let's get to know him first."

"Arthur, what did you receive?" Brixaby asked. "Another card?"

"Ah, no." He resisted the urge to rub the back of his neck. He had nothing to be ashamed about. "I was put in a scenario where I was able to increase my Cooking skills." He hesitated, having the feeling that Brixaby had been given a very similar challenge, only at a foundry instead of a kitchen. But while Arthur had gone with the flow and completed the challenge, Brixaby had decided to fight.

Meanwhile, everyone was giving him very unimpressed looks.

"You increased your Cooking skills?" Horatio repeated flatly.

However, Joy was enthusiastic. "Then you learned to cook some more stuff? Did you bring back anything tasty for us?"

"Well, no, I didn't . . ." That hadn't even occurred to him. "I didn't have access to my Personal Space, and some of the food was scourge-rotted anyway. But it wasn't just my Cooking skills." He glanced at Brixaby, hoping he'd understand. "I was able to increase my entire Cooking Class to tier three and got several of my skills up to level 50. That gave me attribute bonuses."

The last part finally seemed to have an impact on the rest of the group. At least, the ones who knew what attribute bonuses were.

Brixaby understood quite well and actually staggered back a step. "That is quite impressive!"

"Well, I'll take your word for it," Soledad drawled. "But if I'm hearing y'all right, none of this is game-changing. It's just a taste of what the Dark Heart can offer us."

Arthur nodded. "Let's continue on and stake out a cave or somewhere big enough for all of us to fit. It's important we have somewhere safe to return after a challenge. Then, we're going to delve the Dark Heart for real."

CHAPTER 41

They made the decision to trek over the hills on foot because Joy and Sams were both subtly grimacing and stretching out their wings when they thought no one was looking. Back-winging was an unnatural position for most dragons, and doing so for a long time while descending the pit had threatened to strain muscles.

Not every dragon can be a purple, Arthur thought with a hidden smile.

But also, they didn't want to overfly any possible reward. After hearing how Cressida had found her card, all were mindful that the Dark Heart could hide cards anywhere.

Besides, the landscape was pleasant, and despite the fact that the sun was definitely not a sun at all, it was a nice temperature.

As they topped the next hill, Arthur took a look back toward the way they'd come. Other adventurers were now popping into existence in the same location they had. Most took off running in different directions.

Arthur saw Jon's Lightning Cat group do just that, and they were so fast that they disappeared within moments.

But others took the opportunity to launch instant surprise attacks.

Thankfully, the people who had made it down to the staging area first tended to have powerful cards and knew how to use them. So it wasn't a case of the strong beating up on the weak. Most people could defend themselves.

No one went out of the way to approach Arthur's group. A few people crested the hills and pointed in their direction, but no attacks were thrown their way.

"Might be the three dragons we have with us," Horatio snarked, noticing the attention as well. He threw a sarcastic wave their way, and the group eyeballing them quickly went back down the other side of their hill and out of sight.

Brixaby buzzed up in the air a few dozen feet to watch them go before sinking down again. "What a shame. If they are afraid to fight us, then what chance do they have of defeating the Dark Heart?"

"They don't want to defeat it," Arthur said quietly. "They just want to take enough to be considered rich when they get back home."

"Bah. They think too small!"

As they walked on, the landscape subtly changed to become drier, then rockier. But now the areas between the hills were woven with occasional freshwater streams.

Arthur took the opportunity to fill a few empty buckets he had in his Personal Space with fresh water. Of course, he already had barrels locked away, but when dragons grew thirsty, those barrels emptied fast.

They passed dwellings that were both familiar and unusual. Some were no bigger than huts, others were cottages in good repair or decrepit. There were stick-built homes of unusual design with high-peaked roofs, a large door on the side big enough to fit a small dragon, and windows that didn't look like they'd last against a scourge-eruption. They even passed by a multistory castle that didn't look too far off from the type nobles used back in Arthur's kingdom . . . except for the fact that the masonry was crumbling.

All had one of those blank cards hovering near the entrances, ready for someone to claim it.

Arthur didn't consider any to be suitable for their needs until they came to an unusual structure which was tucked in a valley between two sharp hills. Soledad called it a pavilion. It had a large red roof held up by pillars, and no walls at all. The floor was smooth, dark slate. But the structure was large enough for three dragons Sams's size to shelter under.

Cressida made a face but then seemed to accept they wouldn't be staying somewhere fancy anytime soon. "I suppose because there are no walls, we'd see someone trying to sneak up on us."

"Yeah! That's super convenient!" Joy said, enthused.

"I have bedrolls in my Personal Space," Arthur said.

Cressida smiled. "Of course you do."

But as they walked closer, they found the card to claim the territory was nowhere in sight. However, there was the outline of a trapdoor in the slate flooring. It was so heavy that it took Arthur and Marion heaving to lift it, but once the stone was up a few inches, it slid easily to the side as if under some kind of card power.

Below was a stairway that led down. And at the bottom hovered a territory claim card.

Marion gestured grandly. "After you, fearless leader."

Arthur gave him a look, but since he was the one who would take the card, it made sense for him to go first. With a light touch on his Nice Shot card, he descended the stairwell.

Nothing jumped out at him from the dark, and though he couldn't see a thing, he had a feeling of a large space beyond.

Then he reached out and grabbed the card. A message flashed in front of his vision.

Do you wish to switch territories?

Yes, he thought back.

Well, that solved one question: Someone could only hold one territory at a time. Not that he was interested in hoarding shelter from other people.

Instantly, he sensed that the card he'd carried from the shallow dugout disappeared from his pocket. Meanwhile, the new one he'd just acquired filled in the names of everyone who stood in the pavilion—his entire retinue.

Your territory is now claimed.

"All clear. It's ours now," he called, and pulled a lit torch from his Personal Space. Arthur cast it around, blinking in surprise.

The others except for Sams and Joy joined him, and they set off exploring.

The underground was indeed a massive area, so much so that it was a pity that none of the dragons except for Brixaby could fit down the stairs.

One corner of the area was filled with two rows of bunk beds. There were at least forty beds in total. Another wall had a fancy sitting area filled with over-stuffed cushions and comfy furniture. The next held a grand fireplace that would provide both light and heat at night.

The last wall was . . . odd. A bright banner stretched over it proclaiming LEVEL 1, and beyond stood three doors, each with their own labels:

PUZZLE, UNITY, COMBAT.

One by one, they all came over and stood facing the doors.

"This must be how we start," Arthur said. It was obvious, but he wanted to break the silence. "It makes sense."

Horatio turned to him. "We're in a weird underground house in the middle of nowhere. How does any of this make sense?"

He shrugged. "There are only so many territories—the heart only allows one person at a time to claim one—but you saw the crowds lined up to get down here. They're all going to be taken fast. Then it's going to be a fight to hold on to them. But until then, we have access to the next levels of the Dark Heart."

Soledad frowned. "That really shallow cave didn't have anything like this."

"But we didn't explore it, did we?" Marion answered reasonably. "For all we know, it had a false back wall that led to something like this."

"Who cares?" Horatio said. "We're here now. Let's see what's behind these doors." With that, he strode toward the one labeled *Combat.*

"No, wait!" Arthur said, but Horatio had already grabbed the handle.

Just as quickly, he yanked his hand back, hissing in surprise and shaking it out.

Soledad took a half step toward him. "Are you okay?"

"He's not hurt," Marion drawled. "Just suffering from a case of stupidity."

Horatio shot Marion a dark look but turned back to them. "Got a message that only the territory holder can assign the party, whatever that means."

"Then it's up to me." Arthur took his place, and the moment he drew close to the door, he felt a low buzzing sensation from the territory card, as if it was seeking his attention.

He flipped it over, and lines appeared as if freshly inked on the back side.

Level 1

Assign your party members.
Puzzle:
Combat:
Utility:

And in a line next to those choices was everyone's names, including Sams and Joy. He supposed they were counted since they were in the territory of the pavilion, even if they weren't downstairs with them.

Turning back, Arthur flashed the card around so everyone could take a look. "I'm thinking combat, right?"

"Of course," Cressida said.

Horatio nodded. "Sorry, Art, but not all of us can be faffing around in the kitchens."

"You worked in kitchens with me for years!"

"Yes, and I graduated from it."

He smirked and gestured up to Sams, who was crouched at the mouth of the stairwell along with Joy. Both dragons were looking down. Meanwhile, Brixaby had long ago come down and was busy poking around the bunk bed's metal framing for some reason. Though Arthur could tell he was listening.

Arthur, knowing Horatio was just poking fun at him, ignored him and instead looked around. "What does everyone think?"

He got nods and firm looks from everyone, even Horatio, who seemed to realize this was not a moment to be sarcastic.

Privately, Arthur suspected that this level would be every bit as hard as the wave-type dungeon that he, Brixaby, Cressida, and Joy had barely completed. He told himself they were more prepared this time.

Arthur nodded once sharply. "All right, when we go in, we're going to take up defensive positions until we know exactly what we're facing. Marion and Soledad, I want you to go up and get back on Sams and Joy. They're your best protection until you get combat cards, and since their names are included, I think they'll just be added to the challenge even if they can't fit through the door. Cressida, be ready to snap up your shields at a moment's notice—"

"Wait!" The shout came from Joy. She'd stuck her neck down the stairwell, all of her suddenly intense focus on Arthur. He got the impression that if she could have reached out and shaken him, she would have. "No, I don't think you should!"

"Should what?" he asked.

"Don't go through the combat door!"

Everyone had various reactions to that, but Horatio's was the loudest. "I am not going through another puzzle challenge!"

"Joy, dearest," Cressida said on a sigh. "You and I would do poorly in a utility challenge."

"I, too, wish to fight," Brixaby said.

Arthur shook his head. Even though in his heart of hearts, he did feel a twinge of regret. "Everyone's right. We need to grab strong cards and abilities from this place, and combat is the fastest way."

"You guys aren't listening to me!" Joy said. "I really, really feel like Arthur should go into the utility challenge. Just him."

This time, the loudest objection came from Brixaby. "No! He doesn't have access to his anchor cards. He will be completely helpless!"

"Well, not completely," Arthur grumbled. Though his heart did pick up the pace at Joy's suggestion, and it wasn't fear: He would rather face a utility challenge.

Sams rumbled. "What prompted this, Joy? Did you receive a quest?"

Joy stomped her foot so hard that dust rained down on the humans below.

"No! That's not it at all. It's . . . it's really hard to explain. Remember I told you that I had to practice my intuition back in the first challenge? So, this isn't something I can put a claw on. But I really, really, really feel like it would be a mistake for Arthur to come with us. He should go to the utility door! Sorry," she added in Arthur's direction.

"This is ridiculous," Brixaby growled. Then, just as quickly, "If Arthur chooses utility, I shall, too."

"No."

Arthur surprised himself with his own vehemence. Even Brixaby drew up in surprise.

"No," Arthur said again. "We need all the combat advantage we can get, and Brix, you have combat abilities. Your Night-Mare Fire, which you can't even use with me sitting on you. Not to mention your Stunning Shout, and now you have that card that makes your scales harder. No," he said again. "You need to be in combat. And my strength . . . it's always been in utility." He cocked his head, coming to a slow realization. "Maybe it's time that I learned to embrace that."

"That's what I was saying! Why doesn't anyone listen to me?" Joy whined.

Cressida stepped forward, her brows knit with concern. "Are you sure?"

"I don't like you going to a place where I cannot help you," Brixaby added.

"I'm sure," he told Cressida, then looked at Brixaby. "And you will be helping me. I'm wearing your anchor, remember?"

He looked around. No one seemed to be happy about this, and on one level he understood: He was supposed to be their leader. That meant being with them.

But at the same time, he wasn't looking for a consensus. In his heart, he knew Joy was correct.

"Brix, I'm going to depend on you to be the leader while I'm gone," he said. "I know you'll fight whatever you see in there, but think of the rest of the retinue, too."

"Of course I will," Brixaby said, looking slightly offended.

But everyone else seemed a touch relieved.

Arthur continued, "Joy has a point. My goals are to increase the size of my heart deck and find Master of Cards. That's a utility card. I have to do this."

"What about him?" Horatio jerked a thumb at Marion, who'd been quiet this entire time. Now that Arthur looked at him, he saw that his friend seemed torn.

Arthur shook his head. "He won't get a better experience of being a healer than while in a battle situation."

Marion's shoulders sagged, though he nodded in agreement. He just didn't like it.

Brixaby growled. "If you get into trouble, if you get hurt, you had better use your Return to Start card."

"Yes, then I'll come back through the Dark Heart and return here," Arthur agreed. "Though it might take some time. I'll be at the back of the crowd."

"Then pull rank!" His dragon was exasperated. "Should the worst happen, your job as my rider is to return to aid me."

Nodding, Arthur patted his dragon's shoulder.

Then he turned and looked at the doors. Now that everything had been decided, he could feel that they were more representations of a door than actual portals. Something to trick someone who didn't hold a territory card.

And sure enough, above the middle Utility door was a divot that was the perfect size and shape of his card.

It appeared the Dark Heart had been listening to their conversation as well because when he glanced at the card, he saw that his name was the lone one under the utility list. Everyone else was under combat.

"All right. Good luck in there," Arthur said to the group.

Then he stepped forward and reached to press the card to that divot.

There was a burst of light, and Arthur concentrated fiercely on his primary goal: Master of Cards.

A voice whispered in his mind.

How will you be a Master of Cards when you don't even know how cards began?

And with that, he was pulled away.

CHAPTER 42

The next thing Arthur knew, he was surrounded by complete chaos. He blinked and found himself standing outside, taking in a lungful of fresh air scented with pine and the cold sharpness of snow. Then, suddenly, he was jostled from behind. To keep his balance, Arthur reached out and caught himself on another person, but they were unsteady, too, and the two of them stumbled into another. Somehow, Arthur and the man managed to keep their feet, but it was a close thing.

He was staggering forward, pushed from behind by a crowd of people who were all running down an extremely hard-packed road of dark, smooth stone with lines separating the middle. The panic and despair in the air was so thick that he could almost taste it, and the scourgling whistles from behind him were so loud that he could barely hear himself think. More people knocked against him, blinded by fear, and not paying attention to anything other than the need to get away.

If not for his dexterity and strength attributes, he might have fallen. And if he fell, he would have been trampled.

The moment he caught his balance, Arthur half turned to glance behind him. Then he knew why the crowd around him was so frantic.

What could only be described as a wave of scourglings galloped at them, not far down the road. There were so many, he couldn't even tell for certain what shape they were, and they seemed to move as a mass. More scourglings were coming out of the thick pine forest behind them to join the mass and run the humans down.

Men and women dressed in randomly patterned green-and-gray uniforms screamed out orders to the fleeing people and pointed what had to be weapons at the scourglings. The weapons boomed—sharp reports that threatened to deafen Arthur further. The projectiles were so fast that Arthur couldn't even see them. Some kind of card power? An enchantment?

The front scourglings fell as they were struck, tripping up others behind them, but there were always more to replace them. It slowed the mass, but not by much.

The fleeing crowd passed odd machinery, dead and broken on the road. They were some sort of cart, only made of metal with seats in the middle. In desperation, some people climbed in a few and seemed to be trying to get them to move, though nothing happened.

Other people were pushing carts full of children and the elderly who could not run as fast as the rest of the group, but these had their limits, too. The crowd parted around one woman who stood behind a wheelbarrow. Three children sat within, clutching a blanket and looking terrified.

"I can help," Arthur said, slowing. "What's wrong?"

"I don't know!" She was half frantic. "The front wheel is so wobbly. I think the axle thing in front is broken. Do you know how to fix it?"

Arthur frowned. He didn't have a lot of mechanical skills. "Do you have a part?"

Her answer was a stressed-out laugh. "Do I look like I do? This was all I could grab from the house. There wasn't any warning!"

She went on, but Arthur was focused on the problem. Bending, he saw the pin that connected the axle with the wheels had snapped. It was metallic and oddly made, in a way he'd seen carved into wooden screws . . . but how in the world did someone manage that with metal? Did these people do everything with metal?

He did have a piece of kindling in his Personal Space made of hardwood that would fit in the hole. It was tapered wider on one end and hopefully wouldn't fall out. Switching them out, he tossed the snapped metal screw in his Personal Space to show Brixaby later. Maybe it would give the dragon some ideas.

New skill gained: Basic Mechanical Knowledge (Engineering Class)
Due to your card's bonus traits, you automatically start this skill at level 5.

The piece of wood wouldn't last long, but it was better than nothing.

Their salvation was visible a half mile down the oddly packed road. The sheer face of a mountain stood at the end, and the crowd flowed through a pair of large steel doors, each bigger than the size of the barn. Unless the scourglings were the burrowing type, they should be safely protected by steel and rock.

He took one end of the wheelbarrow, and the lady took the other, and they pushed and ran. Arthur found that he could run faster than her—as well he should, with his **Running** skill. But it seemed that, too, would be increasing in this challenge.

Skill level gained: Running
Level 26

It's a utility challenge, he thought grimly. *And this time I'm not limited to kitchen work.*

More people in uniform screamed at them to hurry up. Looking back, he saw other guards were starting to retreat, still firing their weapons.

The delay had cost him a little time, and the double doors were starting to creak shut as he and the woman approached. Before they stepped through, Arthur took one last glance up. The sky was bright blue and empty of dragons.

It seemed they'd be facing this scourge-eruption alone.

Once inside, Arthur turned and watched the last few people stagger in. To the guards' credit, they were the last in, firing toward what had now grown to an unending wave of oncoming scourglings. This wasn't a combat challenge, but Arthur wondered why no one was using any other card-based powers to protect the group. There were no earthen barriers, no shields, illusions, lightning, or even a single sword or edged weapon visible.

If this was reality and not a challenge from the Dark Heart, Arthur would have stepped in with his Nice Shot card—

Wait.

He stopped that thought in surprise and looked down at himself. Then he staggered back a step with a stomach-dropping sense of shock. His hands weren't his own. They were bigger, the skin older and weathered like a middle-aged man, with more hair on his arms. He reached up to his face and felt a beard, where he had always been clean-shaven before. And running his hands over his head, he found a bald spot.

He was not wearing his own clothing. His shirt was a lightweight white fabric with N-A-S-A written in Texan on the front. His pants were of a thick blue fabric. Most importantly, the armor Brixaby had crafted for him was completely gone.

But a quick check through his heart deck showed him that at least he had access to all of his cards, including his Master of Skills and Master of Body Enhancement. He didn't know what he'd do without those.

"This isn't real, this is a challenge," he told himself, and turned to watch the last of the guards retreat while firing at the oncoming mass of scourglings. There wasn't time to grab any of the shards from the fallen beasts. The moment a scourgling was down, it was rolled over by the rest of the wave.

The double doors were still rumbling to a close. Then, three feet from shutting completely, they ground to a halt. Alarms blared, and people yelled.

"What's going on?!"

"Doors are jammed! I'm doing a reset. Hold on!" A nearby man pounded an odd machine with lighted squares. Were those words on the screen?

Arthur desperately wanted to look, but his eyes were drawn upward to the gears and lines that ran to the double doors. His **Mechanical Knowledge** skill was new, but it still provided him a little insight where he'd had none before. The main line was attached to a pulley system that, when tugged, would help shut the door.

"We can push it closed manually!" he said, pointing. "Someone grab that line! You! There! Grab the one on the other door. Hurry!"

Skill level gained: Leadership
Level 26

He was always glad to level that one up.

A man objected. "It has to be thousands of pounds!"

"And if we don't do something about it, there will be thousands of scourglings in here," Arthur snapped. "Hurry!"

"They're coming!" a woman shrieked.

Her fear seemed to spur on the rest.

And suddenly Arthur had more hands trying to help than he knew what to do with. There was some shouting, a little pushing, but within a few moments, enough people were hauling at the line that, with a groan of metal and a squeal of gears, the door started to move.

The same thing started to happen with the other door, though it was slower to close. The group might have figured it out on their own, but seeing death rush at them from less than a hundred yards away had numbed people's critical thinking.

Meanwhile, the guards kept using their weapons through the shrinking gap. The noise echoing in the chamber was enough for Arthur to feel deafened.

It wasn't quite enough to hold the horde back, and some scourglings raced in front of the others to get to them first. One snaked a too-long forearm through the gap between the doors and snagged a guard. His friends started shooting at it. With a whistle of rage, the scourgling fell back.

The first door was shut. Arthur yelled at everyone to help with the second door, though he couldn't hear the sound of his own voice between the whistles, the shooting, and the screams.

But something must have gotten through because he received another notification of a **Leadership** and **Mechanical Knowledge** increase, and people rushed to help with the pulley for the second door.

Within moments, it, too, was closed.

The doors were so thick that the moment the second clicked shut, all sounds from outside were cut off.

There was a moment of darkness, and then lights—probably from a card anchor, though Arthur had never seen anchors burn so bright and regular—came up.

Someone nearby gave a nervous chuckle. "That was like a zombie invasion, man! Wild."

Arthur wasn't in a good mood. He scowled. "Why didn't anyone put up shields?"

The man who stood next to him mopping his forehead clear of sweat suddenly stopped and stared. A half smile quirked up at his lips, and he gave an uncomfortable chuckle. "What? Like *Star Trek*? All shields to full?"

"That's *Star Wars*, damn it," someone else said.

With a squawk of outrage, the man turned to the other speaker, leaving Arthur baffled. They were speaking Texan, he was certain of it, but he had understood none of that.

Turning, he looked around until he saw the woman he'd helped with the wheelbarrow. She was not far away and was busy calming her kids. Nearby, a helpful guard was directing her to move down farther into the tunnel with the rest of the civilians.

The woman spotted Arthur's approach and straightened to smile up at him.

"Thank you for your help back there. I don't know what I would have done if we didn't get a move on."

He nodded. "I was happy to help, but if you don't mind me asking . . . What cards do you have?" It was a rude question, but considering he had just helped save her children . . .

She was silent for a baffled moment. "Credit cards?" Then she started patting her pocket. "Oh, of course. A payment, but . . . I don't think that will work, and you know, cell phone towers have been down. So, it's not like I can Venmo you."

Again, Arthur didn't understand what she was saying, but he shook his head. "No, no, no payment needed. I think I misunderstood. Thank you." Then he walked away to a clear area of the room, leaving her staring after him. He needed to think.

He wasn't an idiot. He remembered the Dark Heart's words to him. It challenged him to learn how cards began. So had it really dropped him in a reproduction of an ancient time before cards? In some other man's body? He looked around at the people. They just seemed . . . normal. A few of them were heavier than he was used to seeing, dressed oddly, and the room was full of strange blinking card-anchor lights—but then again, they wouldn't be card anchors, would they? How were they getting lights on command without cards?

None of it made sense. He was told not to trust his senses in the Dark Heart. Who knew how much of this was real?

"Hey." He turned as someone touched his arm. It was one of the guards in the mottled uniform.

"You didn't hear the announcements? All scientists are to gather together at sublevel two." He glanced at Arthur's shirt meaningfully. "You *are* a scientist, right?"

There was only one answer he could give.

"Yes, of course," he said, and got a skill level in **Acting**. This was going to be beneficial if this kept up like this. Nowadays, **Acting** was almost as hard to level as **Leadership**.

"What's your name?" the man asked.

"Arthur."

"Well, Dr. Arthur," the man said, "come this way. After that FUBAR situation, we're going to need all hands on deck, am I right?" He laughed, but there was a note of strain to it.

"Uh, sure," Arthur said, and had no choice but to follow.

He and the guard walked out of the room and into a smaller corridor. More of those not-quite-card-anchor lights were up on the ceiling, casting a harsh glow. After a few twists and turns, they descended several stairwells. Arthur wondered how deep these people had dug into the mountain.

Suddenly, the guard opened a door into a large room. Other people milled about, most with anxious expressions, but there was more than enough seating for everybody.

"Got another one for you, General," the guard said. "Came in with the last of the civvies."

The man he spoke to nodded. Then he called out "Everyone, have a seat!" before striding to the front of the room.

He had the air of a stern leader and wore a guard's uniform, though his shoulders were decorated with different medals.

"The whole compound has been secured, and just in time. But I'm afraid we don't have any good news for you. Satellites work, but almost all other communication is down across the board. These things chew on wires and anything else they can get ahold of . . ."

"How long will we have electricity?" someone asked.

"We have enough fuel, and most of this facility is powered by geothermal heat under the mountain. But unless we can get some air support, I think we're going to be here for the long haul."

"What are these things?" a woman called.

"I've heard them called the scourge of the world," the general said, "and they seem to be spreading, too." He clicked something in his hand.

A map came up on the far wall. Arthur was torn between amazement at the ability to do this without a visible card anchor and confusion about what the map was meant to portray. It was all unfamiliar to him except in broad strokes. He had no points of reference, so he wasn't entirely sure what he was supposed to be looking at. A village? A country? But there were several lands portrayed. Was that water between them? Was this . . . the whole world?

If it was, it made the dots of red that started out small but were quickly spreading all the more ominous.

"These goddamn things are spreading like a virus," the general growled. "We can kill them just fine, and as far as we can tell, they're staying dead, so I don't want to hear a single zombie joke. But somehow they're breeding faster than we can make bullets." He paused to let that statement sit. The moment stretched, and Arthur gave a slight mental nod to the man's **Leadership** skills. He knew how to keep people on tenterhooks.

"So," the man drawled out after what felt like an age and a half. "The sixty-four-thousand-dollar question is: What are these things? Some new biogenetic mutation?" Another weighted pause, and he screwed up his mouth slightly like he didn't enjoy what he had to say next. "Aliens?"

For some reason, all eyes turned to Arthur.

He shifted in his chair, a little confused. Even the general was giving him pointed attention.

"You got an opinion on that, NASA?"

Oh. The shirt he was wearing.

Arthur didn't know what the man meant by alien, so he spoke the only truth that he knew. "Well, scourglings erupt from the ground, don't they? From nests?"

And they can be spawned by rotting cards, he added in his head. He didn't say it out loud because he still hadn't seen any indication of card use from these people.

The general's face twisted again. "Scourglings? Maybe workshop that name." Then he turned away.

"So, they're popping up like daisies. *Outstanding*. As you can guess, your goal today, ladies and gentlemen, is to find out how to stop these things. Because they're killing anything they come across: people, livestock, crops. We're going to be looking at widespread famine if we don't get a hold on this ASAP."

The best way to kill scourglings was by using dragons, but there hadn't been any mention of those so far. Besides, people on this continent didn't have them anymore. Maybe he should raise his hand and tell them to look toward the Fabergé Kingdom?

But something told him that would be a bad idea. What did the Dark Heart want him to do?

He hadn't forgotten that whisper of a challenge before he'd entered this place. This seemed to be a representation of the past. Was it trying to show him how cards had come to be? As a need to control scourglings?

But that didn't quite fit. Card shards were found *in* scourglings.

What was the answer here?

People seemed to take the general's words as an order, and the meeting was breaking up. As it did, a man with curly dark hair and glasses approached Arthur. There was something about his demeanor that reminded him of Marion. He was scholarly.

"You're one of the latecomers, right? The last of the evacuees before they shut the doors?" He continued before Arthur could answer, a lot like Marion as well. "Glad you made it. I'll show you down to the labs so you can see what we'll be working with."

With a nod, Arthur rose and followed him down through several blank and impersonal hallways. The illuminated blocks of light on the ceiling were quite interesting—not card power either, he supposed. He kept an eye on it as the man chatted about things Arthur didn't understand . . . right up until the moment that he did.

"Wait, you said more subjects? You mean . . . you have scourglings here? With us?"

He nodded. "Yeah, the army guys were happy to kill 'em, and some of the corpses are pretty fresh. Not that you'd be able to tell from the smell. I assume biology isn't your thing. You're more of a physics guy, right?"

Arthur didn't know what that meant, but he nodded since the man seemed to expect it.

"Well, at least you know your way around a lab. At this point, we need as many outside opinions as we can get." He gusted a sigh. "I'm not afraid to tell you that we've hit a bit of a wall."

As he spoke the last line, he shouldered open a door.

They came to a large room that was filled with . . . Arthur wasn't even sure what he was looking at, at first. There were water barrels everywhere up on tables, except they were made of fine translucent glass.

And floating in each of them was the corpse of a scourgling.

Even though they were kept preserved in liquid, it still smelled faintly of scourge-rot.

These people are insane, he thought. *If they're uncarded, they're breathing that stuff . . .*

But they didn't know, did they?

Then his attention was caught by another scourgling corpse—fresh, by the look of it—laid out on a table.

It had the rough shape of a squirrel, only without fur, plenty of weeping sores and teeth that sprang out of its muzzle in every direction like a bristle brush.

And its chest was glowing. This scourgling was unharvested.

CHAPTER 43

Brixaby and the rest of his retinue emerged into the clear open air, very, very far away from the ground.

Brixaby gave a squawk of surprise that he would later insist was merely an exclamation and certainly not a yelp like a new hatchling. Quickly buzzing his wings, he situated himself upright in the air. Sams and Joy, both being larger with a greater wingspan, took longer.

Unfortunately, when the Dark Heart had taken them to the challenge, Cressida and Horatio had been standing near Arthur and had not been astride their dragons. So they continued to fall.

"Cressida!" Joy tucked her wings and dived, completely ignoring Marion, who was clutching onto her neck for dear life.

Sams did the same, diving after the flailing Horatio.

That was right and proper in Brixaby's opinion. No dragon should ever be expected to care for some random person over their own linked rider.

But Marion was not experienced in dragon riding, and though Joy was doing nothing more than diving, he managed to slip off Joy's neck.

With a roll of his eyes, Brixaby sprang into action. He didn't simply dive—he buzzed his wings and flew down, even faster than a normal dive.

Just as Joy swooped neatly under her rider and allowed the woman to cling onto her saddle and pull herself aboard, Brixaby caught Marion under the man's arms. He was heavier than Arthur, which made it a struggle to zip back up out of the dive, but at least Marion wasn't screaming. Much.

However, there was no question about letting anyone else aside from Arthur ride him. Swooping back up, Brixaby neatly dumped Marion on Joy's back before he turned to check on Sams's extra passenger.

The yellow dragon had caught his rider. Somehow, Soledad had managed to hang on the entire time, probably because Sams had a much wider neck.

Only then was Brixaby able to take a proper look around. They were still very far up in the air—he didn't know why the falling humans had screamed so much—and the blue ocean extended as far as he could see. The only spot of land was an island nearly directly below them. Green and lush, it was dominated by a volcano.

And that volcano appeared to be erupting with scourglings.

"Oh, I just got a quest," Joy said, a moment before words bloomed into being in front of them, as if a large, invisible painter had taken a brush to the sky.

New Quest: Cleanse The Island
Defeat enemy scourglings and save the island.

Joy scoffed. "*I* was about to say that, Mr. Dark Heart. Anyway, we need to clear out as many of the scourglings as we possibly can, without letting them destroy the island first."

Then she paused, frowning, and became unusually silent.

Cressida touched her neck. "What is it?"

"I don't know," Joy said. "I just don't have a good feeling about that volcano down there."

Brixaby made a dismissive sound. "Of course you don't. It is erupting with scourglings. This is a grand challenge fit for dragons."

"I agree," Sams rumbled.

All this time they'd been talking, they had been in a spiraling dive. The island, which at first had seemed tinier than a foreclaw, was growing larger and larger. This would be quite the space to defend, which was a good thing in Brixaby's opinion. That meant there would be a lot of scourglings to kill.

"What are your orders?" Sams asked.

Brixaby felt a rush of pride that *he* was to lead his own retinue in a proper battle. However, that pride was mixed with a little regret and irritation that Arthur was not here to share this moment with him.

"Kill as many scourglings as you can, and harvest everything," Brixaby announced, and saw dragon-ish grins on Sams's and Joy's faces. Cressida and Horatio looked enthusiastic, too. In fact, the only one who seemed a little ill was Marion, but that might be an aftereffect of falling several hundred feet.

Brixaby went on. "I, of course, will attack from the air. Sams and Horatio, use your light to burn anything on that western slope there." He pointed down to the rockier side of the island, which was free of the lush vegetation. That meant there would be less places for any scourglings to hide. "Joy and Cressida, sweep the jungle. Seek out the higher-ranked scourglings and poison them."

"It looks like they're chewing on the vegetation for some reason," Joy said, squinting downward. "When they're not setting it on fire, they're just . . . chewing it down to the bare earth.

"Excellent," Brixaby said, pleased. "That will make it easier for you to find them." Then he looked at the two riderless humans. "You two: try not to slow us down or die. That would be most inconvenient."

The girl scowled at him, and Marion threw what had to be the worst salute ever.

But Brixaby was distracted a moment later when Joy flicked her tail at him.

She was looking at him with concern. "Brixaby, I want you to be very, *very* careful. I don't have a good feeling."

He scoffed. "I will be victorious—I mean, we will *all* be victorious, and will return with many shards! Now, follow me!"

It is a shame, he thought as the dragons dived to meet their enemy. *Arthur is really missing out.*

An hour later, Brixaby was still having a grand time. He had positioned himself near the mouth of the volcano, which was as close as he could get while avoiding the hot poisonous gasses.

He was currently practicing interesting ways to kill scourglings as they were thrown free.

Most were the nonflying type, and as they were ejected upward, they unfurled themselves in midair in preparation for a landing. This was when they were the most vulnerable.

Brixaby used any number of offensive capabilities to kill them. His personal favorite was his Stunning Shout, which paralyzed or knocked them unconscious and kept them from landing correctly. The splat sound when they hit the ground was most satisfying.

His Night-Mare Fire had a very similar effect, which put stunning fear into the heart of any being he touched while using it. However, he had to be careful using that effect, as he could not use it when Arthur was aboard.

Occasionally, he would simply take out several weapons to test on scourglings from his Personal Space. He had forged several swords and affixed different basic runes with his enchanting skills. Though cutting down an enemy was more of a human thing, it could be satisfying.

Unfortunately, he could not test out his Berserker Rage or use his superior ability in the air and snatch shards out of the hearts of the falling scourglings. Because when they exited the volcano, they were scorching hot. Most came out glowing orange and red with some kind of earth elemental touch to them. Even with his Toughened Skin, he could not get too close.

If they landed in vegetation, they started fires. However, a few minutes out of the volcano had them cooled down enough to approach. He often broke off from killing new ones to go harvest shards from the cooled, stiffened dead.

Unfortunately, those shards were only those odd blanks without a proper rank. He threw them in his Personal Space anyway. There had to be some use for them.

The best part of this eruption was that he gained levels in his movement skills. Experience appeared to be accelerated.

In fact, Brixaby was getting even more levels in movement skills than he had when he was fighting those scourglings in his forge challenge.

Flying Sprint, Pinpoint Turn, Trick Flying, Barrel Roll, and **Flying Accuracy** all received multiple levels.

But even with all this, he was only one dragon and could not kill them all. The scourglings that escaped his wrath usually recovered from being ejected out of the volcano and ran straight into the forest, where their hot hides inevitably started a forest fire.

That was not an issue. Plants grew back, and his retinue were all far too strong and clever to get caught in a forest fire. He caught glimpses of Joy's bright pink hide in the foliage as she hunted scourglings while being careful of the flames. With her abilities, a single scratch from her venomous claws meant certain death. He fully expected that she and her rider were getting their own shards as a bounty.

Meanwhile, Sams and Horatio were on the opposite slope of the volcano, which was much more rocky and provided little cover from aerial attacks. Brixaby wasn't quite certain how light could injure something that was already glowing hot from lava, but occasionally he would catch bright flashes out of the corner of his eye as Sams or his rider powered themselves up from the sun. Then, suddenly, a swath of scourglings on the far slope would die.

Arthur had tried to explain what Horatio had told him about invisible burning light, but Brixaby didn't have the patience to listen. He just trusted his retinue to do their job.

Finally, the other two dragonless humans were off a little ways in a freshwater lagoon. Occasionally, Brixaby would climb high enough to see over the top of the forest and check on them. He saw multiple versions of the boy, all confusing the scourglings. The girl seemed to be doing most of the fighting, using one of the swords that Brixaby had left her.

They were, in Brixaby's opinion, in very little danger. By the time the scourglings had reached that far, the molten hot hides had cooled down, making them stiff and awkward. Perfect practice for somebody who didn't even have a dragon to aid them.

Yes, he was feeling quite self-satisfied, right up until the point where the volcano sputtered out three final scourglings, and then no more.

"That cannot be it!" Brixaby used his **Flying Sprint** skill to quickly take himself over the mouth of the volcano. He had to do this quickly because those hot gasses were corrosive and could burn through his scales despite his protections.

The open throat of the volcano glowed ominously orange. And . . . was there something moving inside?

He grinned a feral dragon's grin, and flitted through the turbulent air to get clear of the volcano. Then he accessed his **Mental Thought** subskill, a reward for eating a mind card. With that, he spoke into the minds of his retinue. *We may have a demi-scourgling emerging.*

At least, he certainly hoped so. The emergence of a demi-scourgling meant that there was a Legendary card at play.

The creature that crawled out of the mouth of the volcano was huge and so hot that its hide glowed white with streaks of red and orange. It was shaped like an iguana with an extra-long, backward-facing shield over its head to protect its neck and spine. That told Brixaby that was its most vulnerable point.

It was as long as three horses put together, nose to tail. But to Brixaby's disappointment, the power he sensed coming out of it was Rare. This was a mega-scourgling, not a demi.

Still, it should provide him with some valuable cards to harvest.

After it crawled out, the volcano coughed as if it had been stuffed up behind the mega-scourgling and waiting to explode again.

This time, no more scourglings flew out, but dozens of glowing lava bombs did. Brixaby was hard-pressed to dodge out of the way. It wasn't just the balls of lava that exploded when they hit the ground, but the shards of molten rock that flew along with it and filled the sky like rain. He nearly lost the tip of his bottom-right wing trying to avoid one deadly shower. And for the first time, he was glad Arthur was not with him. If he'd been hit . . .

Then again, he would have told Brixaby to stay away from the edge of an erupting volcano, and he might have had a point.

Most unfortunately, Brixaby's distraction allowed the mega-scourgling to start heading down the lush, rainy slope of the volcano. Wherever it stepped, plants exploded into flame and rock melted.

The lava bombs were reaching the top of their arc and starting to fall down again. Looking at the distance, some might even hit the lagoon. Brixaby quickly sent a mental message to Marion and Soledad to take cover. He didn't know how they could, considering they were wingless, but Brixaby could not possibly think of every detail. He had bigger scourglings to fry.

More lava bombs were ejected and fell into the jungle, starting new fires. These joined others that had already been started by red-hot scourglings. He suspected that soon they would have a conflagration on their hands.

Joy and Cressida flew out of the jungle. Since Joy had kept well clear of the mouth of the volcano, she was able to keep an eye on falling lava bombs. She made an *ooh* sound as she spotted the mega-scourgling.

"Is that the boss?"

"It is no boss! If anything, I am the boss of it," Brixaby said, irritated.

And he proved that he was much better in every way by inhaling deep and directing the full force of his Stunning Shout directly at the mega-scourgling.

He had been practicing with his shout over the eruption, and like everything else in this challenge, it had leveled up. Now it had reached level 15.

Harnessing that power, he directed it in a tight, focused beam to the base of the creature's neck, in a gap between its back and the fleshy shield that extended backward from its head. He intended to carve through flesh and sever the spine . . . or whatever equivalent a scourgling had.

His stunning beam hit, but instead of cutting through like a scalpel, the hide rippled. No, it was not hide at all. The irritating creature was covered completely in molten lava.

There was more than one way to kill a scourgling. They could not live if their magic was ripped out of their hearts!

With a growl, Brixaby dived.

Joy yelled a warning, but Brixaby ignored her.

What did she know about snatching cards from enemies? Nothing!

By the time he got thirty feet above the creature, the sheer heat of that molten rock made him pull up sharply. It was like hitting a wall of fire, and if not for his Toughened Skin, he might have already been burned.

"Brixaby, look out!" Joy yelled, too close behind him. When had she dived? He glanced over and saw her coming in fast, close enough that they were in danger of crashing. What was she thinking?

Then in the next second, Cressida shouted something as a red-and-orange whip of lava came straight up from the mega-scourgling. It impacted a hastily thrown-up shield by Cressida. Some of that lava was reflected straight back to the scourgling, but as it was already coated, that was not a problem for it.

Brixaby's Counterfeit Siphon card activated.

New Counterfeit spell obtained: Mana Shield
Remaining Time: 59 Minutes 59 Seconds

New Counterfeit spell obtained: Right Back at Ya
Remaining Time: 59 Minutes 59 Seconds

Cressida dropped the shield a moment later, and Brixaby and Joy quickly put space between themselves and the scourgling.

Brixaby tried not to show that he was shaken. Even his Scales as Hard as Stone card wouldn't have helped if that lava whip had landed on him, and again, if he'd had Arthur riding along . . .

Arthur would have never allowed me to get that close to a lava scourgling. The thought came in a small voice, which he rejected immediately, even though he knew it was correct.

Well, no matter. They still had to kill the enemy and harvest its delicious cards.

"If it reaches the tree line, what's left of the island will burn," Joy said in a mournful tone.

Brixaby perked up. "Excellent. It will burn its own cover away, and that will make it all the easier for us to attack at range."

She gave him a shocked look. "Brixaby, don't you remember the challenge? We have to save the island, and right now, it's burning down. If we don't do something soon, there'll be nothing left to save."

He looked around and took in the multiple growing fires with a new light. She . . . might have a point.

Perhaps he should not have sent Sams and Horatio to protect the rockier downslope. That side of the volcano dumped straight into the water, and the scourglings taking that track would not have burned anything. But he had been thinking more about the harvest of shards and destroying the enemy as simply and efficiently as possible.

Saving stupid trees on top of that complicated the matter horribly.

Speaking of Sams, the large dragon had finally arrived. He took one sweeping look over the battlefield, snorted, and said, "Keep your eyes peeled for more of those lava bombs. Better yet, close your eyes in three . . . two . . . one . . ."

Brixaby did as he was told, and even through his closed lids he sensed a bright, piercing light. Opening them a moment later, he saw rock scorched in a dark ring around the scourgling . . . and it barely seemed to be affected at all.

New Counterfeit spell obtained: Sunlight Mirror
Remaining Time: 59 Minutes 59 Seconds

Annoyed, he accessed his copied Sunlight Mirror spell to cast his own beam. And even though Brixaby was a Legendary dragon—it stood to reason that anything he fired would be much brighter and more powerful—his beam was lesser and didn't even scorch the rock, much less do anything to the scourgling other than illuminating it a little.

Sams had his linked rider with him, and was likely using an entire deck's worth of internal cards to boost all their light-based attacks.

How annoying.

Ignoring them, the mega-scourgling continued doggedly to the tree line. It was close enough that the few remaining scraggly trees at the front of the line were aflame.

Cressida yelled, and a moment later her bear made of fire galloped through the air as if there was an invisible staircase that led down toward the scourgling. Brixaby didn't have much hope for it considering it was also a being made of fire, but he was proven wrong a moment later.

The heat from the lava did not affect the bear at all, and when it landed on the scourgling's back, it lifted a giant paw and slammed down into it, carving some of the lava away.

The scourgling finally reacted, throwing its tail in a whip to catch the bear, but Cressida's summon was made of flames, and there wasn't anything physical to strike at . . . though the wind of the tail did seem to dampen the flame a little.

Brixaby got an idea. He looked to Cressida and said, "Send your water cranes down and have them strike a specific point right behind the head. Pour all of your power into it. All of your mana."

She frowned. "Shouldn't we aim for the joints? Slow it down?"

"We do not need to slow it down. We need to kill it!"

She looked doubtful but nodded. Then three cranes made of water appeared and shot straight down. One was knocked away by the tail, but two others had a successful suicidal dive and struck one after the other at the point Brixaby had described.

The creature tossed its head back and bellowed, and though much of the water was instantly lost to steam, Brixaby saw a dark patch grow on the hide.

"Again! More cranes!"

"I can't do much more," Cressida said. "Two more waves like that will probably take the rest of my mana, then I won't be able to use a shield against the lava bombs."

"I'll keep an eye out," Joy said. "We'll dodge in time."

That was a good thing because more lava bombs had just erupted from the volcano with such vigorous frequency that Brixaby thought the scourgling might have some sort of control over it.

Cressida cast her cranes, and by the time the third group had appeared, she looked fatigued. But by then, she wasn't the only one suffering.

The mega-scourgling now had a patch of cool stone nearly three feet long and the same length wide. The scourgling thrashed around wildly, throwing out lava whips in different directions. It didn't seem to have the ability to look straight up to see and attack the dragons, but some of those whips were not so accidentally landing on the back of its neck and reheating the cooled rock.

It was time.

Brixaby folded his wings, tucked his legs, and tipped his head so that his nose acted like the point of an arrow. He dived down at maximum speed in the way that only a purple could.

One lava whip arced up at him, but he avoided it by mere feet and was moving so fast that the massive heat didn't sting him. And when he hit that wall of heat from the scourgling itself, he activated Cressida's mana shield.

It was a huge drain on his own mana pool, but he kept it up. He only needed it for seconds.

He dropped it just before reaching the scourgling. The heat hit him like a physical thing. Worst of all on his wing membranes, which stung like they were being hit by needles from the heat. His wings, the attached muscles on his chest, everything, screamed at the effort of pulling up at the last second.

He ignored that and reached down. The tips of his claws scraped the cooled stone at the back of the scourgling's neck, and with a mental wrench, he pulled out two full cards and a handful of shards.

The scourgling collapsed inches away from the trees.

Unfortunately, the first few dozen feet were already starting to catch on fire, but at least the thing would not make it farther into the jungle.

Brixaby arrowed upward, shaking out stinging claws and shaking his wings to rid himself of heat. He even double-checked just to make sure they weren't on fire. They weren't, but he'd definitely been singed.

It had been worth it.

Above, Joy and Sams roared, and he heard the triumphant yells of their humans.

Behind them, the volcano coughed and died.

Triumphant, Brixaby sailed over the tops of trees, a few of which were not burned, and landed with a sploosh in the lagoon. Though the crystal-clear water was now tainted by fire ash, the cool water stung in a good way. He dipped under for a second.

On the beach, several Marion clones who had been keeping watch puffed out of existence. Then the real Marion came out from the trees.

"You're burned," he called.

"It is but a surface burn," Brixaby growled. "I will heal."

He gave him a hard, assessing look, then nodded. "You will, but I assume you have some burn cream or something like in your Personal Space? I doubt Arthur would have let you leave his sight without it."

"I do," Brixaby grumbled, because it was the truth.

Remembering the supplies his rider had foisted on him, he grabbed a few squares of gelatin made from the healing chicken soup and popped them in his mouth. Then Brixaby waded out of the water and pulled out a jar of oil-based salve. He allowed the dragonless human to apply the salve to the burns on his wings and stomach.

Meanwhile, Brixaby admired the new pair of Rare cards. His reward for an excellent kill.

Joy and Sams landed nearby. All gathered round to see what Brixaby had gotten.

Lava Whip
Rare
Elemental Combat
Using a nearby source of heat that is at least as combustible as a flame,
the wielder will be able amplify that energy and kindle something greater.
Using mana, they will generate a whip made of pure molten rock. Length of
whip and effectiveness will depend on skill with the weapon.
Warning: This card does not protect against thermal damage. This card does
not unlock mana.
Seek additional cards in this set for more elemental whip skills.

For the Love of Lava
Rare
Elemental Combat
Using a nearby source of heat that is at least as combustible as a flame, like
a spark to tinder, the wielder of this card will have lava come out of their
pores to create a shield of incredibly hot liquid rock. While the outer shell is
too hot for most to touch (or get close to), the wielder's body will remain a
pleasant temperature. Lava shield effect ends when the lava cools down into
lava rock. It is highly recommended the wielder cancels that effect before
they are encased in stone. Card usage is limited to once every 24 hours on a
rolling basis. This card does not use mana.

Joy's head drooped. "Oh, nothing to put out the fires."

"Why do you care about stupid trees so much?" he asked, annoyed. This was supposed to be his moment of triumph. "The challenge is over, isn't it?"

"If it was over, wouldn't there be a way to leave?" Cressida asked, which was annoyingly logical.

"Besides," Joy added, "I got a side quest to save the forest."

That piqued his interest. "What is the reward?"

"An important life lesson."

He snorted in disgust. But . . . the two of them might have a point. A tiny one.

He had killed the mega-scourgling, and yet they were still here. Perhaps the challenge was to kill the mega-scourgling *and* all its lesser scourglings? Or do all that and save the stupid trees as well?

But no, Brixaby felt like it must be something else. The cards he had were a Rare ranked pair, but not overly powerful.

Both required an inconvenient source of heat nearby. The Lava shield did not seem useful while flying at all. Besides, Brixaby did not like the idea of cooled lava rock getting stuck between his scales.

And the shards he had picked up were completely blank, like the others.

"Did anybody harvest shards worth anything?" he asked.

"No, just more blanks," Horatio said with a thread of disappointment in his voice. "I figure they'll be worth something and that this isn't a big waste of time . . . Well, I hope."

Brixaby wasn't going to waste any more time guessing. He accessed his Call of the Heart card and focused his full attention on the grand prize of this challenge. Instantly, he knew where to find it. His true prize was so close, in fact, that it did not come with an accompanying map.

"That is it," he said, "the volcano."

Then he shook the annoying healer human off before flapping into the air.

"Brixaby!" Joy took off to follow him, leaving her rider behind.

Sams made moves to follow as well, but he was only a yellow and so much larger that he needed a much wider launch point to get into the air. He was in no way comparable to the speed of a purple.

Brixaby aimed straight for the volcano, which was now completely silent, without even a wisp of smoke coming out of the top.

"Brixaby, wait up!" Joy yelled. Puffing, she was able to catch up to him, which was irritating. Perhaps his wings were a bit more singed than he wanted to admit, otherwise she would have no chance of matching him in the air.

"Where are you going?" Joy asked.

"The true prize is within the volcano," Brixaby said. "I intend to secure it before this challenge ends."

"You can't go into a volcano! It's too hot in there . . . Oh, no. It isn't," she said as the two of them were easily able to fly over the mouth.

Looking down, the depth of the volcano was not glowing anymore, and there was none of those terrible corrosive gasses, either. It was as if it had been quiet for centuries.

"Brixaby, I don't have a good feeling about this."

She had feelings about *everything*. So, ignoring her, he tucked his sore wings in and dived right in. The throat of the volcano was dark and foreboding, but not nearly as bad as those terrible tunnels back in that free hive that the Mind Singer had taken over.

For a moment, it was as if he was there again. He could almost smell the overpowering stench of scourge-rot in his nostrils.

Why was he thinking about that right now? He dismissed the memory, and a moment later he was through and winging into a wide cavern. And there, sitting on a pedestal made of stone, was a card. Legendary power seemed to come off it in waves, and Brixaby practically salivated.

"It is mine," he hissed, landing so he could run straight toward it.

In the next second, Joy tackled him.

She was trying to take his card! Brixaby almost triggered his Berserker Rage, but then . . . a trickle of what Joy had been yelling finally caught his attention. He had been ignoring it for the last few moments.

"Activate your Mental Shield! Brixaby! Your Mental Shield! Do your shield thing!"

On reflex, Brixaby concentrated on the skill that he had honed while fighting in the doomed free hive. Why was he thinking about that terrible place again when there was a Legendary card in front of him?

The skill came up and something struck against it so hard that it shook his Mental Shield, but it held.

Blinking, Brixaby tried to look around. He was encased in Joy's wings, and through the sliver of an opening at the top, he saw her face. Her eyes were squeezed shut.

She seemed to be concerned he was no longer fighting. "Brixaby? Are you dead?"

"I'm not dead! Get off me."

"No, wait! Do you have your Mental Shield up?"

"Of course I do," he said, angry and embarrassed. Meanwhile, something was striking his shield from the outside. It was as if it was trying to batter its way in, but Brixaby had faced worse. It had no chance.

Well . . . no chance now that he was aware there was an enemy.

"Okay." She let out a breath of relief. "I'll let you go. Just . . . don't look at the cards."

"Cards?" he asked.

Ignoring him, she continued, "I have had a bad feeling all day. And then when you dived into the volcano, I got a quest."

"Why haven't I gotten a quest from you?" he demanded, but then realized with a shock that he had. He just hadn't paid attention to it.

New Quest: The Lie Behind the Illusion

You have been tricked! Bamboozled! Possibly scammed! Find out who, or what, is behind this lie for a reward.

Reward: Illusion card

Again, something battered at his shield, as if it were enraged.

Arthur had always been better at these mental skill things. He'd been better at planning and thinking for the both of them, too. He should be here with Brixaby. They were a team.

Now that his mental shields were up and he was able to think clearly again, he realized he dearly missed his rider.

Though . . . he supposed it wasn't *too* bad being encased in Joy's wings, though they could not stay here forever.

He wiggled. "Release me."

"Okay, but then we should get out of here—"

"No, my quest is to discover the lie of this place."

Joy hesitated, but then, carefully, she unfolded her wings, and Brixaby was able to stand on his own. Though his mental shields were up, he was very careful not to look at the podium. He had a feeling that if he did, he might very well be caught again.

However, it seemed that the chamber inside the volcano had changed . . . or perhaps now that he had his Mental Shield up, he saw it for what it really was: a large chamber made of glittering crystal, and the floor was absolutely covered in glowing runes.

This volcano was enchanted.

"Are you okay down there?" Sams called from above.

"Yes," Joy said, "but don't come down. There's a nasty illusion. Brixaby is using his Mental Shield, and I'm not looking. Join us and you'll get caught, too. So just stay up there."

With a bit of guilt, Brixaby accessed the area-of-effect portion of the skill and extended it over Joy. He should have done it from the beginning.

She shivered. "Oh, that's much better. But no offense, I'm still not opening my eyes."

He paused for a moment, thinking. "Perhaps put your wings over your eyes, too. This illusion is strong."

"I know," she said, doing as he suggested. "I keep hearing whispers, even with your shield over me. Whatever you're about to do, please hurry."

Brixaby let his mind sink into his Personal Space.

Once there, he spent a few moments growling and pacing. He pushed over a stack of metal ingots, and they crashed to the floor in a satisfying clatter. But that still did not bring him back into balance.

As much as it pained him to admit . . . he may have been too rash during this challenge. He often chafed against Arthur's restrictions and admonitions to be careful and to think about things. But perhaps, sometimes, that wasn't too bad of an idea.

If Joy was right, the forest that they had been charged with protecting was burning. And instead of killing the remaining scourglings, he had flown off to collect the grand prize, leaving the rest of his retinue behind.

That was not the mark of an effective leader.

And then he had almost been caught by some enchanter's trap.

With another growl, he went to his Mental Bookshelf, which he shared with Arthur, and pulled out volumes on runes. Even though he had access to Arthur's Eidetic Memory, perusing the books calmed him down. He compared the runes in the book to the ones that he had seen on the floor. Most were unfamiliar, but some were close enough to the examples on the pages that he was at least able to know how to destroy them safely.

He had flown straight into an array that was meant to focus the power of a card. He suspected it was one with illusion or mind powers.

Coming out of his Personal Space, he located the proper series of runes and ran a claw down the line, down the middle of them, destroying their cohesion. Slowly, the line of runes dimmed and lost power. And then, so did the rest of the floor.

The battering against his Mental Shield stopped.

Once the last of the light faded, he turned to the pedestal.

And there, he saw two cards, still Rare ranked, yet infinitely more valuable to him.

One was a trap card: Card of Covetousness.

The second was the promised illusion card: Mind Trap.

CHAPTER 44

Arthur blurted out his next words before he gave any thought to them. "Why hasn't anyone harvested this scourgling?"

The man with the curly hair gave him a baffled look. "Uh, harvest for what?" His gaze landed on the nearest scourgling in the water tanks. "You don't intend to . . . eat this, do you?"

In answer, Arthur strode to the scourgling laid out on the table. He reached for it.

"For God's sake, put on some gloves!" someone behind him yelped, but Arthur was already gesturing over the distinct glow in the chest.

The entire room fell silent as two shards drifted up. Arthur plucked them out of the air and then turned, palm out, to show them.

Immediately, the small group exploded into questions.

"What did you do?"

"What is that?"

"Hey, he stopped the glow!"

"What are those things?"

Deftly, Arthur held a shard up between his fingers. It was not a corner piece, but still oddly shaped. And like the shards Brixaby and the others in his retinue had received, it was blank without a feeling of rank to it.

That actually helped to settle him. It was a reminder that this place and these people weren't real, and this was not truly the past. This was a scenario—a challenge to solve by the Dark Heart.

Perhaps part of that challenge was to teach these people about cards? It was the only way he could think of that they could use to defend themselves against the scourgling horde outside.

This is a challenge, he thought. And, steeling himself, he accessed his Subtle Influence card to add weight to his words.

Subtle Influence
Common
Mind

The wielder of this card will be granted the power to subtly influence direct conversations in which they are participating. The wielder will be able to push a subtle weight to all of their words, which will have the effect of nudging a conversation in the direction they wish. This is a minor influence and may be counteracted by a strong will. Conversely, this card will have a greater effect on an unsteady, weak, or compromised mind. This is an active skill that uses mana.

These people were strong willed, so he knew he'd have a battle ahead to convince them. But this card would add extra weight to his words.

"This is a sliver of a card," Arthur began, and was almost immediately interrupted.

A young woman gasped. "You mean, a *magic* card?"

The people standing next to her looked uncomfortable, and the curly-haired man turned with a frown.

"There's no such thing."

"But what about all that stuff on social media before the networks went down?"

"They were a bunch of loons, Kelly," said another man. "People were seeing monsters attacking their cities, and they immediately looked toward conspiracy theories and end-of-the-world scenarios. And magic." He shook his head.

Others spoke up.

"Well, how do you explain what he just did?"

"Isn't there a point where high technology becomes indistinguishable from magic?"

"Causation doesn't equal correlation . . ."

The group started to argue among themselves, which wasn't productive or helpful. Arthur put a stop to it.

"You think this is a trick?"

He stepped a few paces to the right where another dead scourgling drifted in a water tank. This one had the general shape of a skunk—he didn't envy the people who'd brought it in.

As it was behind thick glass, he wouldn't be able to harvest it the normal way. So he simply reached for its chest and used Brixaby's Call of the Void.

They might be in different challenges, but they were still linked and had access to one another's cards.

This time he ended up with three shards. Turning, he held them out to the group and opened his other hand to show the original shards from the first scourgling.

"Okay, how the hell did you do that?"

The man who had spoken so repressively to Kelly came forward and practically pushed Arthur aside to clumsily wave his hand at the scourgling. Of course, there was no effect.

"This one has already been harvested. See? There's no glow. And doing it from something you can't touch takes experience," he added, on a lie. "You might want to try with one that's out in the open."

"So what do those card slivers do? Where are they coming from?" Kelly asked, frustrated. "We've done necropsies on those subjects, and there's nothing behind the glow. We certainly didn't pull slivers out—"

"Shards," Arthur said. "They're called card shards."

"Fine, we didn't see anything like that there." She crossed her arms over her chest and glared. Arthur sensed it wasn't that she didn't believe him, she just felt lost and frustrated by something she couldn't understand.

He'd been in that position enough times to sympathize.

Arthur started to reply but was cut off by a triumphant shout.

"Oh my God, you guys! Look! I did it! Holy crap!"

Another woman with tight curly hair stood near a far wall that was covered in drawers. She'd pulled one out to show another scourgling corpse and had easily harvested two more shards. "If that guy's a magician, I guess I am, too."

Some people went over to join her and poke at the shards. Others, however, turned to Arthur. There was much less hostility in their gazes.

"All right," the man who'd pushed him aside said. "What do those sliv— those shards do, exactly?"

Arthur picked his words carefully. "From what I know, if you put enough of them together, like a puzzle, then you get a magical card. Then you use these cards to fight scourglings."

"How?" someone asked. "Challenge them to a d-d-duel?" But he didn't seem serious, so Arthur ignored him.

Kelly said, "If that's true, we need to call the general down and read him in."

"Why? So he can condescend to the 'eggheads' some more?" But the person who said that was already pulling a slim, card-sized device out of their pocket and was putting it to their ear. They spoke briefly, and a moment later lowered the device. "He's coming down."

So, within a few minutes, Arthur found himself explaining all over again the very basics of the concepts of cards. This time to a stern-faced general.

At least he got a **General Teaching** skill out of it.

"Show me," the general said at the end of it.

So Arthur went to another scourgling that had been laid out on a table within the last few minutes. The general's focus went sharp when Arthur showed him the shards he'd pulled out.

"I've . . . heard of something like this, in whispers. Classified whispers." He reached up and rubbed at his forehead. "Some people called it magic, but there ain't no such thing. And you're telling me that these aren't aliens?" He looked back at Arthur, clearly hoping he would tell him that this was anything but magic.

Arthur didn't get it, but he carefully kept it off his face. "I don't know what the scourglings are, other than the antithesis of life. But if you want to fight back, these cards are how you do it." He let his Subtle Influence card put emphasis on his last words.

The general grunted. "Good old-fashioned guerrilla warfare. Take the enemy's weapon and use it against them."

Under his direction, everyone started harvesting scourglings. Though no one "got the trick" of getting shards from the ones in the tank without removing the body first. When asked, Arthur only shrugged.

By the time they were done, there were more than enough shards for at least an Uncommon card. The limiting factor was the corner pieces.

But there was another problem.

Soledad, Brixaby, and Cressida had all gotten enough shards in their pre-challenges to make at least a Common card. But when they'd put them together . . . nothing happened. They remained inert and rankless.

So Arthur helped the rest of the group—they kept referring to themselves as the science department—put the shards together, but cautioned them that he didn't know what would happen next.

However, when the last piece was pressed into place, the entire configuration flashed. The different pieces joined together, and a new card was born into the world, complete with images.

Basic Tricolored Fireball
Uncommon
Elemental Combat

Using mana, the wielder of this card will be able to summon a series of three fireballs at a time: red, blue, and white. Red burns at the lowest temperature and functions much like a regular fire. Blue burns at a higher temperature and for a longer time than red. White burns at the highest temperature with the ability to melt most metals. However, once released, the white fireball will burn itself out within ten seconds. This card does not unlock mana.

Hurriedly, Arthur explained all that he "understood from social media"—a phrase he'd picked up from the others—about mana.

"So this will allow any soldier to put down a gun and pick up a, what, wand?" The general didn't wait for a reply before he sighed, grabbed the card, and stuffed it in his pocket. "I suppose mad times come with mad solutions."

"One card isn't going to be enough," Arthur said.

"I ain't an idiot, son." But a moment later, he tempered his tone. "You say these shards come out of the, uh, scourglings." His lips twisted into something like a grin. "Well, we currently have thousands of them massed outside our blast doors. Lucky us."

He made to leave, but Arthur stopped him.

"General, there's one more thing. It's important."

He turned back. "Go on."

Arthur hesitated for a moment, then used a few words of vocabulary he'd picked up over the last few minutes. He only hoped he was saying it right. "Before we were evacuated, my, um, colleagues learned that these scourglings are toxic. If you have a card in your deck, it doesn't affect you." *Unless you're in the middle of a scourgling nest and breathe rot-saturated air for weeks on end*, he mentally added. "But I'm sure you've heard of scourge-rot. It can spread through the air, and we have dozens of scourgling bodies in here."

The general nodded. "We'll get some HEPA filters in here." He paused. "Maybe tape up those vents. You say that the cards help ward the sickness off? Well, in my view, that's all the more reason to get people some of this here magic."

Arthur nodded vigorously. "Remember, cards can't be given to children under twelve. Anyone younger needs to be kept away from this room." He wasn't sure what HEPA filters were, but he was becoming more and more impressed by these people's technology. Perhaps that would help the problem.

"Well, if we have children fighting for us, then we're further up a creek without a paddle than I thought." He clapped Arthur on the shoulder. "Good work. We'll get you and your group some fresh corpses soon. Learn what you can from these things, and let me know if you come up with anything else."

He left Arthur with the scientists and their endless curiosity.

From there, Arthur spent the next couple hours answering basic card questions, sometimes multiple times. He got the impression that a few of them were trying to trick him with similar questions just to see if he would provide different answers. Apparently, they were still having issues with believing in magic.

If not for his Subtle Influence mind card, they might have not believed him this much.

Judging by the general's attitude, he had previously had an explanation about cards, or something very close to it. He had been primed to believe. These scientists . . . they took more time.

Which meant they took out their frustration by being argumentative with one another. Arthur spent too much time breaking up little spats between them. Between all that, his **Leadership** skills shot up another five points. His **Acting** gained another three because people would occasionally ask questions about his background. And, of course, Arthur had no idea what they were talking about or what to say without seeming strange, so he had to dissemble.

However, the long day was catching up to him. Arthur's body was not nearly as athletic or trim as the one he was used to. He sat down at a desk, only meaning to rest his aching legs for a moment. Cradling his chin in a hand, he listened to the drone of scientists. And before he could stop himself, he had dozed off.

The next thing he knew, he was being shaken awake. "Billy! Rise and shine, man."

"What? Who?" Arthur asked. While his voice was still a man's, it was a little higher than usual.

The person shaking his shoulder snorted. "Cute. It's time for your shift, man. They said they'd wake you up early for the kitchen, and here it is."

He was in a bed, he realized. But wasn't he just in a lab?

He sat up and saw that he was in a very small room, and there were three other people sleeping in pallets next to him. It seemed that space was at a premium. The light was dim, but there was just enough light to see by. He looked down at his hands and saw that they had changed again. He had longer fingers, slightly darker skin, but that skin was younger. He was once again a different person, but it looked like he was still within the same facility. And curse his luck, once again, he was a cook.

He was given a quick change into a clean shirt and pants and then led down another hallway into a very large kitchen.

Well, here, at least, he felt at home.

He quickly found out that cooking here was different from any restaurant situation. For one thing, the facility, which everybody here called the bunker, had limited ingredients. Ingredients that he had to stretch to feed over nine hundred people.

The complex cooking equipment was completely unfamiliar to him, but as his new persona was one of the recent evacuees, he was only expected to do the basics.

"Give me a knife," Arthur said. "I can cut anything."

His tier-three Cooking Class said that he would be able to add magical attributes to skills over level 50. That meant his knife skills, but there was no magic here.

However, his high levels meant he had no trouble with whatever they put in front of him to prepare.

He quickly gained a reputation for competency, and that gave him more work, which he didn't mind. After he was done with the prep work, he helped with a vat of steamed vegetables that was bigger than the largest bathtub he had seen back at Wolf Moon Hive.

While doing that, he received a brand-new skill for his Cooking Class: **Bulk Cooking**.

It didn't matter the time or place, people liked to talk in the kitchen. Rumors of magical cards were starting to spread. Some people scoffed at the idea, but many more looked vaguely interested. Others talked about powers they'd seen. Arthur didn't say anything, but just let the conversation flow around him.

"I saw lights come out of his fingers, and then bam, a can of soda exploded across the room!"

"You should have slapped him upside the head for wastin' a good Coke. If they don't get a handle on this soon, no one's gonna have a Coke again."

"That's not the point, man. He did it with his mind!"

"Nah, you sound like what they are all saying on the internet about that mass ritual and—"

"Those are crazies."

"Yeah, maybe they were. But then monsters started popping up out of the ground, so maybe we got caught up in their craziness. You know what I mean?"

The next day, he woke up as another older man, one who volunteered in the medical unit as a nurse.

In between leveling up his **First Aid** and **Basic Nursing** skills, making people comfortable and treating basic injuries, he spotted something that was all too familiar.

"Heal—" He caught himself just before he called for a healer. "Doctor!" he said sharply instead, to get the nearby woman's attention.

She was the leader here but was more overworked than the rest of them, with deep bags under her eyes. She turned to Arthur with a look of exasperation. "Yes?"

He gestured to the bed. "This child is ill. Please take a look."

"The one with the mild fever?" she muttered, but came over to sit with the boy, who was shivering as if he were out in a snowstorm, even though it was a comfortable temperature in the room.

She frowned at the spots on the boy's arm that Arthur pointed out. "What is this? Dirt?"

She tried to rub the marks away, but of course, they didn't disappear. It never would, Arthur knew.

Those spots were the signs of impending scourge-rot.

Quietly, Arthur moved aside the blanket and lifted the boy's shirt. There were even more signs of rot, like pockmarks, on the child's chest.

The mother looked on in worry. "Chicken pox?"

"Maybe, though I've never seen it present quite like this." Then the doctor started talking to her about the child's history, including "shots" and things that went over Arthur's head without any context.

It didn't matter. He knew with grim certainty that the child was too far gone.

I told the general that scourge-rot traveled through the air, but maybe I wasn't forceful enough or . . . ?

"Have you been around scourglings?" he asked the child, and was surprised over how forceful his own voice was.

"Those monsters?" the mother asked.

"N-not the alive ones," the boy muttered through chattering teeth.

The doctor must have heard at least something about scourge-rot, because she leaned forward. "Dead ones?"

"No," the mother said firmly. A little too firmly for Arthur's tastes, and the way the boy looked up at her as if for confirmation was telling. He was checking to see what story the mother wanted him to tell.

Arthur wavered for a moment, but then firmed. "This is important. What your boy has, he can only get from being around scourglings. If it's in the air—"

She glared at him. "What are you trying to say? That we're, what, keeping one as a pet? That I let my child play with monsters?"

"Has he been in the labs?" Arthur pressed.

"No!" Her face twisted into a grimace of hate. "Everyone knows it's the scientists who are responsible for this mess! I wouldn't let him anywhere near them."

It suddenly became too much for the boy. "I'm sorry," he blurted, though saying it so forcefully made him stop to cough. A deep, wracking, wet cough that went on and on.

The doctor put a device in her ears that was attached to a rope with a disc at the end. She placed the disc against his chest and frowned. But when the boy caught his breath, he looked at Arthur. "Daddy took me to the military area to show me the monsters. It's because we can get weapons from them. Because . . ." He broke off for another round of coughing. "'Cause he said they can save the world. But it was supposed to be a secret."

"When was this?" his mother demanded. "How could he? Kyle, you should have told me."

By this time, the doctor had removed the device and looked at the mother. Her expression was carefully blank.

"I'll get an expectorant to help that cough." But when she stood, she gripped Arthur's arm and pulled him around the next corner, out of sight of mother and child. Her gaze was fierce on him. "I saw the look on your face. What do you know?"

Arthur didn't bother asking what she had heard in the boy's chest. He remembered his friend, Ernie, dying back at the border village . . . and he had only been one child of many through Arthur's early years.

"I know that you'll need a healing card to save him," he said frankly.

"One of those *magic* cards—" she started to say with derision thick in her voice.

He cut that off before she could gather momentum. "Yes, one of the magic cards. What's attacking him isn't something you can see with your instruments or fix with your medicine, is it? You've had others with the rot, too."

She wavered for a moment before she nodded. "Before I came here," she said shortly.

Arthur didn't bother to ask further questions. Every evacuee had terrible stories in their recent past. The fact that many people didn't want to talk about their awful experiences worked well for him, as he could cover his identity and gaps in knowledge.

"What do you know?" the doctor pressed.

"I keep my ears open," Arthur said. "You've heard of the card shards you get from the scourglings?" He waited for her nod to continue. "Well, if you put them together—and I mean *you*—then you're more likely to get a card that you need. It's not guaranteed, but if I were you, I would ask the general for some shards. You're needed to heal the sick, so he should approve you. And then think of that kid and what you can do for him as you put them together."

She gave him a long look. Doubt was heavy in her eyes. Eventually, though, she nodded. "Over the last few weeks, I've seen weirder stuff than all my years practicing, and I used to work in downtown Queens."

Arthur had no idea what that meant, but sensing that it was supposed to be a joke, he smiled.

"I'll get that cough expectorant. I'm not sure what it will do for him, other than keep him calm. Can you and the other nurses keep an eye on things here until I get back?"

Relief swept through him. She was going to take his advice. "I will."

The doctor arrived back a few hours later, and Arthur saw a new gleam in her eyes. She walked straight to the back beds where the boy and his mother were placed behind a privacy curtain.

Unfortunately, he didn't see her cast the healing as he was busy dealing with another intake—not a scourge infection, but a very badly sprained ankle. By the time he looked up from properly wrapping the injury and gaining another level in **First Aid**, the boy was not only looking much healthier, but he was walking out of the medical facility alongside his mom under his own power. There was no trace of the rot on him.

The doctor stopped to check Arthur's work. She nodded at his bandaging.

Once the patient with the sprained ankle was sent away, Arthur took the opportunity to ask, "Well?"

"It's a Common card, which they say is the lowest," she said shortly. "I can only use it once a day. But . . . he's all better. Just like that." She snapped her fingers, and for a moment, her face was alight in wonder. Her expression crashed a moment later. "It's a miracle, but only one every twenty-four hours." She shook her head and frowned. "There's only two MDs here, and I'm the only one on day shift. If this spreads . . ."

"That's the thing about cards," Arthur said, "if there are others who get medical types, they can help out, too."

She looked at him for a moment. "I didn't think about that. Instant doctoring." She shook her head, steeled herself, then went to check on other patients. But to Arthur's eye, it looked like there was a little more spring in her step. She had just gained a dollop of hope.

Arthur didn't gain a healing class that day, even though he felt close to it. But he couldn't feel bad about it. He'd done good work.

Arthur continued waking up as a new person every morning. Some were expected to be professionals in their field—like the times he was an electrical engineer or a biologist back in the labs. With those, he floundered and had to lean heavily on his **Acting** skills. Even if he got the basics skills of their profession, he was not truly the expert he pretended to be.

So, when something like that happened, he feigned sickness and exhaustion. Thankfully, no big emergency happened in the bunker that required his expertise.

Other times, he was expected to do more mundane jobs. One of his favorites was as an animal caretaker for the livestock that had been saved with the evacuees. This was extra important, as he was expected to make this small population last as long as possible. Hens could at least serve the rest of the facility by laying eggs, though the roosters were immediately sent up to the kitchens.

Slowly, slowly, as the days wore on, and he found himself in a different skin each time, he suspected that his real goal—aside from gaining different skills in multiple areas—was to educate and help people accept the idea of cards.

From what he heard, soldiers were often sent outside to "engage with scourglings" and either bring the corpses in for study or harvest the shards. Any combat cards were given back to the military, while utility-oriented ones were distributed to the rest of the base.

Arthur never woke in the body of a soldier or a guard. It made sense, as this was supposed to be a utility challenge.

But even the stretched food was starting to run low. Every noncombatant was on rations. At least there was enough water to drink, thanks to the formation of an Endless Well and Groundwater Purification card.

News was becoming grimmer. Word from the soldiers was the number of scourglings up above seemed endless, and almost all lines of contact to civilization had been cut.

Worse, sometimes small pockets of scourglings would manage to find a way in and try to overrun the facility. So far, it was only a few at a time, but it would send panic through the population. Arthur would evacuate with the rest of the civilian population from one section or floor to the other when there had been a breach. He hated those times—he felt useless.

There has to be a way to win this challenge, he thought over and over again.

He was doing what he could in little ways, one day and one life at a time. It helped to level his skills in many different areas. Still, what was the point of all this?

I must be here to help them survive . . . but how?

Maybe if he had arrived here with the rest of his retinue, if they were working together as a team . . .

He missed his friends and hoped that their challenge was going well. At least, he could still feel the link with Brixaby in his heart. That at least reassured him. They were alive, and Arthur would see this challenge through as well.

His first major breakthrough with his skills, oddly enough, came when he became a janitor. A female janitor.

It wasn't the first female body he had woken up in, but every time was an intensely uncomfortable experience. Breasts got in the way of *everything*, and the less said about relieving himself, the better.

Today, he woke up as a woman everyone called Gilda. She seemed to have a large circle of friends who were cleaners and enjoyed gossiping. One lady Melanie had a husband who was well-connected enough to get one of the few Rare-ranked cards. She apparently hadn't joined them for today's cleaning shift, and everybody else was aflutter over where she was.

Arthur just let them talk and kept his ears open. His **Tidying** skill was up to level 50, thanks to his third-tier Cooking Class, so he had to consciously slow down so he didn't leave the women in the dust . . . as it were.

Suddenly, one put down a mop that she'd been using to swab the tile floor. "Whoa, girl, took you long enough to get here. And what's that glow about?"

The missing Melanie had joined the group, and she was all smiles. "The general's office called me in, and I got a card!"

The other women squealed and dropped everything to gather around her. After a startled moment, Arthur did, too.

Melanie fumbled, but then clumsily projected an image of her card out. "It's only an Uncommon," she said while they read, "but . . . well, here it is!"

Spring Clean
Uncommon
Utility

The wielder of this card will be able to cast a spell to make themselves 25% more efficient in all cleaning tasks with a three-point increase in dexterity while the spell is active. Furthermore, anything that is cleaned while under the effect of this spell will automatically gain a sense of freshness for twenty-four hours. This spell uses stamina and not mana.

One of the women whistled. "Mana. Wow, my son used to play those video games and talked about all that—" She stopped suddenly, her face crumpling.

Everyone looked away uncomfortably. Arthur took it that the son had not made it to the evacuation point.

"Well, let's see you use it, Melanie," Arthur said.

"Yes!" Also clearly looking to change the subject, she grabbed a feather duster and started working on a shelf. Immediately, the area she dusted became suspiciously clean.

Arthur's Counterfeit Siphon kicked in.

New Counterfeit spell obtained: Spring Clean
Remaining Time: 11 Hours 59 Minutes 59 Seconds

Arthur was hit with an idea. His **Tidying** skill was up to 50. Did that mean that he could integrate a magical effect within it?

He immediately grabbed up his broom and started sweeping furiously, focusing on the **Tidying** skill. Then he, too, cast Spring Clean. He was lucky it was a skill mostly without visible effects. But he did not receive an alert that his **Tidying** skill was any different.

No, wait, that was supposed to be in conjunction with his Cooking Class. Wasn't it? But what if he . . .

"I gotta go," he said quickly. "I forgot . . . Uh, I'm needed in the kitchens. Bye!"

The other women gave him an odd look but didn't stop him as he hurried out.

Over the last few weeks, Arthur had become so familiar with the underground base that he felt like he could navigate it with his eyes closed. Thankfully, the large kitchens weren't very far away.

As soon as he opened the double doors, he saw that the staff was busy preparing lunch. He was able to sneak in without much notice. A couple of people glanced his way, but he just smiled at them and acted like he belonged there.

There was a sponge by a sink full of dishes. He got it and started scrubbing at some extra food that had been burnt to the bottom of a pan. As he did, he concentrated both on his **Tidying** skill and his Cooking Class as he cast Spring Clean.

Alert: Your **Tidying** skill has gained the attribute: Spring Clean.
Tidying will now be 25% more efficient when Spring Clean is in effect.
This attribute uses stamina.

"Yes!" he hissed, and resisted the urge to jig in place.

This was a huge moment. Ever since he had gotten Master of Skills, he had been stymied by the fact his skills were all mundane and not magical. Even his Counterfeit Siphon ran out after a certain period of time.

But this . . . he could feel that Spring Clean had integrated with his **Tidying** skill. It would be with him, even after the timer on Counterfeit Siphon expired. He hadn't received the freshness bonus, but this was an excellent start.

It was the happiest he'd ever been washing dishes. Feeling generous, Arthur decided to take care of the rest of the sink.

But there soon came a commotion by the side of the kitchen. It seemed that Melanie was not the only one who had gotten a new card today. Many of the cooks had left their stations and were gathered around, oohing and aahing over something that Arthur couldn't quite see.

He walked over and joined the group just in time for a young man, who was smiling, to say, "Yeah, it's a form of telekinesis—it would have been given to one of the soldiers, or maybe even one of the bosses, but it only works on kitchen equipment. So it came to me."

Then he demonstrated by holding his hand out to a few pans that were on the counter next to him. They lifted into the air, to the shock and delight of the rest of the staff.

New Counterfeit spell obtained: Kitchen Confidentially Telekinetic
Remaining Time: 59 Minutes 59 Seconds

Arthur stealthily moved over to one of the knife drawers, and with trembling fingers, he picked up a butcher's knife. Then he concentrated on his **Knife Work** skill and the new Telekinetic spell. The knife hovered over his palm.

Alert: Your **Knife Work** skill has gained the attribute: Kitchen
Confidentially Telekinetic. Using willpower, you now have basic
telekinetic control over knives.

He grinned.

"Gilda, what are you doing here?" someone asked from behind him.

Arthur let go of the skill and caught the handle of the knife as it fell back in his palm. Turning, he quickly made up the excuse of being sent to work prep in the kitchens.

The man, who obviously knew Gilda, narrowed his eyes. "We have more than enough help."

So Arthur was kicked out of the kitchen, but he still couldn't keep the grin off his face. His good mood lasted until the next life.

A few days later, he found himself again working with animals, not as a caretaker, but apparently as one of the animal doctors.

He was called to a storage room the facility used to house the hens. All of them were dead, and he found scourge-rot in the feed. That meant that the chickens couldn't be used to eat. This was a heavy blow to the base, and an unfortunate sign that despite all the protections, the rot was spreading. Some people blamed the labs or the soldiers who went out and fought scourglings. Those accusations caused infighting and resentment in the population.

Arthur suspected the rot was seeping in from the outside.

After that, each day brought more and more warning signs.

A small group had established some herb gardens and vegetable beds they called "victory gardens." Overnight, the plants wilted beyond saving. One of the researchers was brought down to take a look, and he said that there was no bacteria growth whatsoever in the soil. Arthur wasn't certain what that meant, but he recognized the gray look of the dirt.

"Add some cattle manure to it," the researcher said. "I'd say use the leavings from the chicken pens, but those are under quarantine."

Arthur nodded and went to do as he was told, though he was certain it wouldn't work. The soil had become like dead land. Without dragon soil, they'd never grow anything here again.

A few days later, Arthur found himself in the unique opportunity to be a civilian executive assistant to the general.

Thanks to other jobs before, he had a keyboard touch-typing skill, which would be useless outside the Dark Heart but allowed him, along with his **Acting** skill, to blend in.

The whole underground base now had a grim air around it. There were more and more emergency alarms as scourglings found a way to dig in through any soft spot in the base. Arthur felt on edge, and he couldn't shake the feeling of impending doom.

On his way to the general's office, which would be his workspace for the day, his **Tidying** skill twinged at him. He looked up and saw that someone had missed a bit of lichen growing on one of the granite rock walls that were here and there in the underground mountain. He rubbed his hand over it and saw it crumble away. The lichen had been killed, just like the garden beds had been killed . . . and just like how people were starting to sicken from the rot.

When he got into the office, he saw the general working at his own desk, a grim expression on his face as he looked at maps. Arthur couldn't take it anymore. He didn't care if this broke his character.

"General, how bad is it?" he demanded more than asked.

The general looked up, surprised, and pursed his lips. But instead of telling him off, he just sighed. "Arthur, we've worked together for how long? Twenty years? Trust me when I say, you don't want to know."

Arthur flinched in surprise. For the first time, the name of the person whose life he'd assumed shared his own. Though the general still said it in that twangy Texan way.

Arthur swallowed. "I heard rumors up above that all the trees are dying, and even the soil . . . We won't be able to grow anything down here."

The general looked at him for a moment, as if wondering if he should give him the bad news. "Yes," he said slowly. "Whatever these things, these *scourglings*, emit from their bodies, it's toxic to everything. It's not radiation, not poison . . . the damned eggheads in the labs can't figure out what it is. And slowly but surely, it's seeping down to us. I'm sure you've heard rumors of the last stand?"

He hadn't, but Arthur nodded anyway.

"It's coming soon," the general said, "so prepare yourself. But"—he smiled suddenly, and it was unexpectedly boyish—"don't worry, not all hope is lost. These things use card powers on us, and now we can use card powers on them. And I personally just got something fun up my sleeve. It's the highest rank of cards we've seen so far."

With a sense of dread, Arthur knew exactly what he was going to say.

Sure enough, thinking he was confiding in a longtime friend, the general said, "It's called Master of Cards, and I don't mind saying . . . it's got a hell of a kick to it."

This was it. *This* was why he had been brought here. Arthur had experienced things and situations he had never imagined existed, upgraded and fleshed out varieties of skills in almost all areas, and perhaps learned a bit about the first days of cards.

But this was the real prize, and it was in the heart of the man sitting behind a desk in front of him.

Arthur was linked to Brixaby's Call of the Void. He could rush over and snatch the card from the general's heart. With his strength attributes, Arthur was almost certainly stronger than him. And by wearing the body of his trusted assistant and friend, the general wouldn't see it coming.

There was even a sharp knife, called a letter opener, sitting on Arthur's own desk, waiting for him to grab it.

The general would maybe even be briefly incapacitated after Arthur took the card. It hadn't been in his heart for long, so he would recover quickly. Arthur would have to finish him off, add the card to his own set as a three of a kind, and run.

This is a challenge. It's a fake world. He's not real. It wouldn't be murder.

But Arthur had been a part of this community for weeks. And this man was everyone's leader. The one with the vision, who kept everybody—civilian and soldier alike—calm. He was the parental figure people railed at when things didn't go their way and the benevolent giver who awarded cards.

If he died, if he was *murdered*, what would happen to the rest of the people here?

Perhaps sensing that he'd given Arthur something to think about, the general turned his back to walk back around his desk.

The time to act was now. Arthur could use the letter opener with his Nice Shot card and his body enhancements. That card was calling to him.

The people here need their leader.

Arthur closed his eyes, sick that he had thought seriously of doing it, and equally sick that he wasn't going to do it.

I can't, he told himself and the Dark Heart. *Whether this challenge is full of real people or not . . . I can't do that to them.*

Skill level gained: Self-Insight (Insight Class)
Level 9

And suddenly, pressure that he had not been aware of before passed. Or maybe he was literally sensing his moment of opportunity fly by.

Suddenly, the door burst open as a guard, red-faced and sweaty, his eyes wild, burst in. "General! We have a scourgling breach on sub-level three. It's a bad one, sir."

Sub-level three. That was where most of the civilians were housed.

The general whipped back around. "Then why haven't the alarms—"

Immediately, the entire base was plunged into red emergency lights as the sirens began to wail. Overhead, the calm voice of another guard in charge rang out, "Breach: sub-level three. I repeat, there has been a breach on sub-level three. Civilians, please report to your assigned safe-stations. All combat teams to muster on sub-level two."

They would gather at sub-level two to engage the enemy on three.

A queasy feeling tightened Arthur's stomach. He knew, he *knew* that he had just failed this challenge, and this was the Dark Heart's way of shutting things down.

Last time, the world had gently come apart around him. This time . . . well, he'd thrown in his lot with the people here. Now he was to share their fate.

If that was the case, he didn't intend to go down without a fight.

Meanwhile, the guard continued talking. "The scourglings have taken on some sort of earthworm-type shape. The front line managed to burrow right in through the walls. The ones coming in behind are all sorts of beetles or bugs. It's a massacre out there."

All the faces that Arthur had come to know over the last few weeks in this challenge flashed to his mind. Arthur ignored the grief that threatened to swamp him. Standing from his desk, Arthur said, "How can I help?"

The general turned and looked at him, hard. "We don't need a noncombatant mucking things up for the rest of us. You're to evac to your safety station."

"General, I can do more," he said, and then grabbed for the letter opener, fully intending to use his Nice Shot to at least demonstrate—

Then the general's expression changed, perhaps seeing his certainty. "On second thought . . ." He strode to a wall, pushed aside a painting, and opened up a concealed area that Arthur had no idea had been there.

Behind sat what looked like a lock box, only without any runes. Like everything else in this world, the locking was done through electricity. The general tapped in a combination on a keypad and then opened up the box.

He grabbed a slim wooden box that sat within and held it out to Arthur. It was made in the exact dimensions of a card. "If you want to help, run these to the doctors on duty. You know where the medical bay is? Sub-level two?"

Of course he did. Arthur nodded.

Without waiting for a further answer, the general turned to the guard to start barking additional orders. Arthur was as good as excused.

Taking the box, Arthur ran out the door. Only when he turned the corner down the hall did he stop. Then, plastering himself against the wall so he wouldn't be in the way of people running back and forth, he opened the box.

There were three cards stacked on one another. All were Rare-ranked and medical.

Moderate Heal External Wound.

Moderate Strength Illness Diagnosis.

Moderate Body Polish.

Judging by the similar names and the looks of the cards, they were from the same set.

His first instinct, of course, was to hide the cards away in his Personal Space. But his soul flinched at that. He had done a good amount of healing from his fractured card anchor, but he wasn't sure he was up to adding that sort of magical weight. At least not without good reason.

After that, of course, he felt a moment of shame.

He had just told himself that he wasn't willing to kill the general to harvest his cards, real person or no. Now he was seriously thinking of stealing from healers who could help people recover from this breach.

Then again . . . had killing the general been part of the challenge after all?

After all, the guard who had burst into the room had been armed. All the guards were. If he had walked in to see Arthur hovering over the man's body . . . he would have shot Arthur or used a combat card on him. And that was that.

If I die here, is that real?

He didn't want to find out.

He couldn't let himself think of that too closely. Now he had a decision to make about three very valuable cards. Not personally to him, but to Marion.

One thing was for sure, he wasn't going to run through this base with an obvious card-shaped box.

So he slipped them into the wide leg pocket on his thigh, thanking whoever created pants for these people that they made the pockets so ridiculously oversized.

Then he ran to the medical bay.

It wasn't easy. People were in a full panic. This was a serious breach. The moment he got down to level two, he heard the whistling of scourglings from just below his feet as well as the shouting from guards, occasional firing of weapons, and the whoosh of fire and the gurgle of water as people used elemental weapons against the scourglings.

He hoped it would be enough.

The medical bay was even worse, as people were being dragged in, and anyone who could help was in a full rush. Arthur couldn't even spot the doctor in the crowd.

And worse, over it all, he could smell the scent of scourge-rot.

It was coming through the vents. Soon, anybody without a card in their heart would be infected.

Arthur was almost ready to grab one of the nurses—it was one that he might have shared the body of a few weeks ago—and just push the cards onto him, when a scream came from the back med-bay room.

Pushing through the crowd in the waiting room, Arthur went to go see.

The brickwork on the far wall was starting to bulge out. It was as if something from the other side was digging its way in.

Oh no.

Summoning his inner Brixaby, Arthur roared at the top of his voice, "Everyone! They're about to come through the walls. Evacuate the patients! Go back into the hallways."

"They're starting to come up from the third floor," someone else yelled. "They're going to be in the halls soon!"

Arthur yelled back, "They're going to be in this room in a minute."

A brick fell down off the wall as if to punctuate his statement. Behind it, the tip of a giant beetle leg poked out. That got everyone moving.

Everything was falling apart. There would be no grand last stand the general had envisioned. Just a desperate fight for survival.

But I'm not going down without trying, he thought, and stepped to the nearest counter where fresh trays of instruments were set out. That was one good thing about being in a medical room: There were lots of sharp objects.

On the tray lay scissors, needles for suturing, and several scalpels. These were the ones that were meant to be washed—or sanitized, as these people called it. Now, it and the contents of the rest of the trays were Arthur's weapons.

This was going to be difficult, but he had stretched the bounds of his **Knife Work** and **Butchering** skills before. Namely, in his Legendary recruit sparring. He told himself this would be no different.

With a light touch on his **Meditation** skill, Arthur blocked out the chaos around him—crying, screaming people, patients who were complaining about being moved again, and the horrified shouts as the wall bulged further. This medical facility was at the edge of the base, against what should have been only rock and earth. Now it bulged as if something alive pulsed from behind the wall. Dust drifted through cracks in the cinderblocks.

Arthur concentrated, combining his Nice Shot card with his **Butchering** and **Knife Work** skills that had been enhanced with telekinesis. He put his hand over the medical instruments. They rose into the air. Then, at a thought, they began to orbit him from shoulder to waist diagonally like he was wearing bandoliers.

"What the hell is he doing?" Someone gasped.

"Got a combat card," Arthur said through gritted teeth. Using separate skills for things they were not meant for wasn't as easy as he made it look. "Get out of here. I'll keep them back, give you time."

He heard "Bless you!" and thank-yous from the men and women as they rushed the last of the patients out.

Then the brickwork that made the back wall fell in, and an earthworm longer than Arthur's forearm—but with teeth sticking out of an unnatural jaw—crawled in.

Arthur shot the scalpels forward. The small blades cleaved the worm in two. It flopped around, still biting madly.

So Arthur pulled out metal shrapnel from his Personal Space. He had piles of it. All razor sharp. Like with the metal instruments, they circled in a tight whirlwind an inch away from his body. The shrapnel he shot out peppered the scourgling until it was cut into chunks.

But more earth was being pushed forward from behind it. A wave of soft soil buried the closest empty beds.

Arthur stepped back, and then a scourgling shaped like a beetle, brown and ugly and shielded from the front of its horned head to its sore-pitted back, scuttled in.

It didn't have armor on its legs, so Arthur aimed carefully for that. He lost contact with the knives and scalpels once they were a few feet away from his body, which was better than a few inches, like with the Nice Shot card. But using his **Throwing Accuracy**, all of his shots hit home.

He cut the legs out from under the beetle. It fell, clacking mandibles that could have snapped a man's leg in two. It was followed by more scourglings that looked like ants, termites, and other small burrowing creatures.

It was obvious how they had found their way down here. He suspected that the earthworms had chewed their way through rock somehow, maybe with some earth capabilities. The others had tunneled in afterward.

He was lucky in some ways. There were wolves or those terrible birds with teeth that got him before.

They pushed more and more of the brickwork out, but he was able to slaughter them as they emerged. He had more than enough shrapnel to protect the sick and injured who were evacuating behind him.

Meanwhile, there was chaos from that direction, too. He heard scourgling whistles from the direction of the hallway. A glance told him the last of the patients were being dragged by grim-faced volunteers out of the waiting room, which adjoined the med-bay.

He only needed to hold the line for a few more moments. Arthur started to back up, still firing.

Then he heard someone yell, "Is that it, is everybody out?"

"I'm still here," Arthur called, and kept backing up. The incoming scourglings used the opportunity to rush forward, but he cut them down with a wave of razor death.

A few rooms away, in the main hallway, he heard more screaming and then, "Shit! They're here! They're coming down the hall. Blast the charges!"

Arthur didn't know what that was, but he got the context.

"We can't!" he heard. "There are people—"

"That's an order!"

Arthur turned to run. He made it to the waiting room before a small explosion took out the ceiling of the hallway beyond. Arthur was thrown back a few feet and rolled. The only thing that kept him alive was the fact that the scourglings had been knocked back, too.

For a dazed second, Arthur couldn't hear anything but a high whine. He sat up to his knees, saw scourglings, and started firing shrapnel. There was no art to it, and many pieces flat-out missed. But it finished off the half-stunned scourglings and allowed Arthur to wobble back to his feet and take on ones that had started to charge from behind.

Only when he had created a little breathing room did he cast a glance back over his shoulder.

The waiting room was half filled with rock and soil, all brought in from the hallway. He guessed that the scourglings had made it to the second floor and someone had collapsed the hall to seal it shut.

He'd saved them, and in return, they had trapped him.

He had no time to be indignant. There were more scourglings coming. With gritted teeth, Arthur turned back to the rear wall and sent a flying wave of razor shrapnel outward.

The only thing that he had going for him was that the lights stayed steady. He could at least see.

He didn't know how long he kept killing for. He just shot shrapnel at anything that moved, and though some scourglings took longer to emerge from the rear wall than others—like the earthworms—he wasn't in any danger. Though he couldn't feel a rank from them, they fought like Commons.

There were so many that they had to crawl on top of one another to try to get to him. He caught glimpses of tunnels with even more scourglings behind. But when they crowded close, Arthur backed up a step and kept firing.

Finally, the flow of scourglings slowed until, eventually, they stopped.

His breath was heaving, and he pulled out a skin from his Personal Space and greedily drank water, wiping his forehead afterward.   .

Overhead, the lights flickered. Nothing more emerged from the tunnels.

"What do I do now?" Arthur asked aloud. But he already knew.

He stepped forward and slowly, methodically collected the pieces of shrapnel. That was easy, as it just took a wave, and his **Knife Work** telekinesis lifted them and brought them close so he could store the pieces back into his Personal Space. And, of course, he harvested the scourglings.

He had a vague hope that maybe he could find an earth-type card in the pile, but all he came up with were shards . . . A variable mountain of shards, and they were blank.

"I can put them together, hope for an earth card, or something to get me out of here. A portal would be great."

Where would he put the card? In his heart?

Arthur shook his head and reached to pat his leg pocket. He still had the medical cards.

"Marion will love these, if I can get out of here . . ." He turned again toward the sealed waiting room and hallway. It was entirely blocked from floor to ceiling with tons of debris. No way he could dig himself out.

Then his gaze turned back to the tunnels the scourglings had come out of. Arthur instinctively winced away from that thought. Surely this was just a pause between waves and more scourglings would be coming through . . .

But they had come from the surface, right? What if he could follow the tunnels and find his way up and out? Surely there'd be more scourglings on the way, but maybe survivors from the bunker had made their way to the surface, too. This may be their last stand, and Arthur could help.

Maybe *that* was the point of this challenge.

A moment later, he felt like a complete idiot. He could use his Call of the Heart. If there was any way out, the Legendary-ranked seeking card would find it.

Ah, but the Call of the Heart needed to know what to look for as specifically as possible. What did he want the most?

Perhaps it was that he'd used his **Meditation** skill so freely during the fight, but when Arthur searched his heart, he found he really didn't want to continue this fight with the survivors. He wanted the rewards of this challenge. Yes, he had gotten three medical cards, but he'd been here for weeks. Surely there were more, greater rewards.

Maybe he could get a second crack at the Master of Cards in a way that wouldn't make him lose sleep at night.

Arthur closed his eyes and concentrated on the card.

He didn't receive a map. To his shock, he felt like the reward was close. He *knew* he needed to go into the tunnels.

The surface was the answer, then. Maybe he'd be able to find the general's body and harvest Master of Cards.

With that thought in mind, he took a breath and moved forward.

He had to pull some of the scourglings out of the half-blocked tunnel—he'd done a thorough job and some of them were in parts. Nothing jumped out behind them, and the tunnel beyond was so small that he had to crawl. It was also pitch black.

"I really don't like this," he muttered, then pulled something else out of his Personal Space. He had been in this base for weeks, and these people had all sorts of interesting tools for him to store. One of the most impressive was called an "LED flashlight."

He grabbed one of the couple dozen he had stored in his Personal Space and shined it down the tunnel. No movement.

With the flashlight in one hand, he started to crawl forward. The stench in the tunnels reminded him viscerally of the Mind Singer's hive.

Arthur kept going. Every moment, he expected more scourglings to arrive and try to swamp him . . . but he couldn't even hear a whistle.

Perhaps the rest had taken other tunnels to flood the rest of the bunker? He certainly hadn't killed all of them.

The soil around him was cracked and gray, not with rock, but with desiccated earth.

Even if these survivors got out, they couldn't plant crops here. This whole area was turning into dead land. They'd have to find somewhere else, an oasis of life. Then hold on and try to survive.

Arthur had never really thought too much about the past, other than in general terms with the Rowantree family, but he suddenly felt more respect for his distant ancestors.

Some people had lived and went on to build kingdoms.

Arthur continued on.

The tunnel sometimes grew so wide that he could actually get up and walk for a few dozen feet. Then, it would narrow again, forcing him to crawl, then drag himself forward on his stomach with the earth pressing above and below.

He had never felt true claustrophobia until now, and he had to fight the urge to go back, or just scream. But he continued, an inch at a time.

After one terribly tight squeeze where it had gotten so narrow he half had to dig his way forward, he was finally able to rise fully to stand again. He stood there and breathed and realized he felt slightly different in an indefinable way.

On a hunch, he turned his flashlight on his own hands. They were *his* hands again, for the first time in weeks.

"I'm me again." It was his voice, too.

He checked Call of the Heart periodically. There was no map, just a vague feeling of forward. So that was where Arthur went, forward or left or right as the card told him.

And just when he felt like he would be crawling forever, Arthur fell.

He yelped, and the flashlight went tumbling out of his hands, casting light in wild directions as it tumbled along with him. He felt wide-open air for a few horrible seconds, then hit the ground hard. Thankfully, his Toughened Skin and Blunt Force Impact bodily enhancements meant he didn't damage himself.

The flashlight clattered near him, and he quickly scooped it up, swinging it this way and that.

He was in a natural cave complete with stalactites and stalagmites. It was small, and he heard dripping water, but there were no scourgling whistles.

And sitting there in the middle were two dragon eggs.

Arthur stared, thinking perhaps that he had mistaken them for scourgling ovoids, and that he was in a nest of some sort. That would at least make sense.

He edged forward.

They were up on a raised flat rock, as if someone had put them on display. He reached out and touched one. It was hard. Not like a soft, slick scourgling ovoid.

These really were dragon eggs. Two of them, actually. Each stood about the height of his knee.

Where was the mother dragon?

He knew how protective they could be of their eggs, unless she was killed by scourglings.

What dragon would lay her eggs here, in the deadlands, surrounded by scourglings? No, it didn't make sense. It must be a reward placed by the Dark

Heart. Or maybe there was a connection between scourglings and dragons that had run deep in those early days. Something he wasn't sure he wanted to think too closely about.

He swept the flashlight over the eggs again, checking them for cracks. The shells were intact. Both were . . . oddly blank. Not white like a dragon with mind powers. He didn't feel a sense of power from the eggs at all. Though when he rested his hand on them, they were both warm, as if alive. One twitched slightly.

They were as blank as the shards that he had collected from the scourglings.

Also, the fact that there were two eggs was a point for this being a Dark Heart reward. His team had two dragonless people.

That decided it. Placing his hands on the eggs, he stored them in his Personal Space.

Arthur winced at the feeling of being stretched. The eggs had no rank but were definitely heavy with magical weight. He was glad that he'd carried the medical cards in his pocket.

Then he continued down through the cave. There was a bend that came to a completely white space beyond. As if this was the place where the world—or this specific challenge—had ended.

Arthur stepped into it.

CHAPTER 45

When Arthur arrived back at the pavilion, he barely recognized it. Not because it had been weeks, possibly months, since he had last seen this room, but because it had changed drastically.

It was deeper, with the ceiling now at least two stories high. The kitchen had been expanded to include grilling stations and long countertops, while the area that had been filled with multiple bunk beds had been reduced to five. Most noticeably, the stairway that had led down from the trapdoor was now widened to a ludicrous degree and featured huge shallow steps that he imagined someone would place at the foot of a palace. That was matched by an equally giant door at the top—one big enough for a dragon Sams's size.

When the trapdoor had been the size to let in a person, it had taken him using all of his Strength attributes and Marion's help to open it. Now it would need a pulley system to slide the cover over.

Fresh from the challenge, he knew how to rig one up.

Arthur took in all the changes in a flash. Then he heard a booming voice, "Arthur! You made it!"

In the next moment, he was enveloped by black wings and the not-unpleasant scent of dragon. Brixaby did not hug him exactly, but he leaned his head, hard, on Arthur's shoulder.

"Of course I did," Arthur replied, leaning against his dragon. "Did I make you wait for long?"

In the next moment, Brixaby seemed to have recovered himself. He dropped his wings, backing away. "We just arrived." He looked Arthur up and down. "You are in one piece. Excellent. As you can see, I have brought my retinue back alive and victorious."

Arthur glanced around, swiftly counting heads. Everybody else was busy gazing around at the changed pavilion with wonder.

"How long have we been gone?" Soledad wondered. Her forehead and nose were sunburned. "They couldn't have done this in just a few days."

"A few days?" Arthur said, but then he spotted Cressida.

She, too, was sporting a sunburn, and it made the freckles on her face stand out. Her red hair was awry, escaping from its usual tight rider's bun in a halo, and she looked absolutely beautiful.

He stepped forward and caught her in a hug. "I missed you."

She squeezed him. "You're all right?"

He nodded, but inside, his mind flashed to all the people he had gotten to know—and who he had been—over the last few weeks in the bunker.

It was too easy to tell himself that those people had never been real . . . and on the off chance they had been, that they'd been dead for centuries. Maybe thousands of years. But they had been his reality, and he suspected it would be a while before he felt fully recentered in this world.

"I'll be all right," he said, squeezing her tight again.

"You should check on Brixaby," she murmured, too quietly for the proud dragon to hear.

Releasing her, he took a closer look at his dragon and startled. He hadn't caught it when he'd been enveloped in Brixaby's wings, but now he easily spotted raw patches along his belly and the underside of his wings.

"Brixaby, what happened to you?"

"I fought a lava-based mega-scourgling," Brixaby said proudly, though for some reason, he threw an annoyed glance at Soledad.

"The burns are minor," Marion put in. "I've treated them with a salve. He'll be uncomfortable for about a week, but it hasn't stopped him from flying."

Arthur went to check for that himself. He bent to examine the welts closer and noted the burn salve. Though he would have rather seen a bandage, they were not yet done with these challenges, and any visible bandage would be a target for any enemy to hit.

"You might lose a few scales," Arthur allowed. When dragon scales became too damaged, they dropped off and grew back. The important thing was, the hide underneath the scales still looked undamaged. "You'll look a little patch-worked for a while. It looks like your stomach got the worst of it—that's a good thing, as your wings don't have scales to protect them."

Brixaby puffed up proudly. "It was worth it. Come, you may now ooh and aah over my magnificent reward—"

Joy pointedly coughed.

To Arthur's utter shock, Brixaby caught himself and said quickly, "Of course, my retinue helped as well."

Arthur's eyebrows rose. What exactly had happened in the challenge? In the next second, his attention was diverted as Brixaby pulled out two

Rare cards from his Personal Space. They were impressive and scary in equal amounts.

Mind Trap

Rare

Illusion

The wielder of this card will be able to target an enemy and trap them in an illusion where they are about to gain the object of their desires. While in this state, the target will be immune to all additional magical attacks by the wielder but will be susceptible to suggestions. The target's ability to resist or even break free is dependent on the rank of the card within their own heart and any resistance skills. Mana is required for the creation and running of the mind trap. The trap has no time limit, only a limit of mana.

Card of Covetousness

Rare

Trap

The wielder of this card will be granted the remarkable ability to add additional cards of Rare rank and below into their heart deck, exceeding the wielder's natural heart deck limit. However, for every extra card, the wielder will lose a vital or important memory and all context of that memory. The memory lost is random and permanent. The wielder will not regain the memory upon removal of this card. Once this card is added to the heart deck, there is no limit on the amount of additional cards that may be added afterward.

"These are some dark cards," Arthur murmured. "I hope you don't expect me to use the Card of Covetousness."

Brixaby gave him a look like he was being ridiculous. "And risk you forgetting me?"

Arthur smiled, but it died a moment later. "Brix . . . I don't even think you should eat these cards. You could gain power from them, but the risk of keeping one of their bad effects . . ."

Cressida, who'd been listening, piped up. "The illusion card might not be so bad, but that other trap card . . ." She leaned in and tapped a nail over the description. "Did you see that it didn't say something like, 'for every additional card once the heart deck is full . . .'? That means, if someone were to add that card as their first or second, they'd lose a vital memory for every additional card. I think the trap is for the poor idiot who adds it to their deck. Who would do that?" she added in disgust.

"Someone who didn't care what card they had, as long as they had one," Arthur murmured. Such as someone who lived near the deadlands and needed to be protected from rot. But that was the very best situation he could think of. "Put those cards back in your Personal Space, Brix. And . . . be careful with them."

Despite the fact that they were powerful, he was a little surprised. Were those *all* the rewards they received? After all, he'd briefly had the chance to gain a Legendary card.

Speaking of . . .

"Well," he said, grinning at Soledad and Marion. He needed to find a way to take the sting out of the inevitable backlash when Brixaby heard he had not killed the general for the Legendary card, and he knew just how to do it. "Let me show you what I got from my challenge."

Then he pulled out two dragon eggs, letting out a mental sigh of relief as the weight left his Personal Space.

Soledad let out a shocked shriek of joy, clapping her hand over her mouth. "Is that—?"

Marion didn't say anything, but his eyes grew very wide.

"Dragon eggs?" Brixaby cocked his head to the side. "Did you go to a hive?"

"No," Arthur said. "I'm not quite sure how they appeared, really. I went to a place like the city-state here. There were no dragons."

Joy thrust her head forward, practically knocking Brixaby away to sniff over the eggs. "Are they supposed to be white like that? Well, they're not white, not really," she corrected. "They're just . . . kind of without color. It's really weird."

Marion squatted down and adjusted his glasses, looking closely. "I've seen dragon eggs before, but I've never seen anything like this. You're correct: They're not white, they're sort of devoid of color or the texture that dragon eggs have." He looked up at the other dragon riders. "Is this normal?"

Both Cressida and Horatio shook their heads. "It looks white to me, and usually a white one means you're dealing with a dragon with a mind card," Horatio said. "Which wouldn't be great because you two don't have those types of cards."

Arthur winced, flashing to the nasty Trap and Illusion "reward" cards he had just seen. Mind cards weren't dark just because a card delt with the mind, although he'd hardly seen good ones that weren't healing.

"I think they're a little like how the shards appear here: unranked," Arthur said. "Or unattributed, for lack of a better word. The trick will be to see if we can get the hatchlings to link with you two." He paused, realizing that he was assuming a lot. "You guys do want the eggs, right?"

"Yes," Soledad said immediately. Then she bit her lip. "But I don't . . . *like* the idea of linking with a mind dragon."

Joy jerked in surprise. "Oh! Quick! Who has one of those weird blank shards? Give one to me!"

Brixaby was the first to move, quickly summoning a shard from his Personal Space.

"Did you receive another quest?" he asked eagerly.

"Yeah, but it doesn't tell me anything useful. I'm supposed to help you two figure out how to hatch some dragons," she said, very carefully taking the shard, which looked incredibly tiny and delicate pinched between her nonvenomous claws.

"Joy, dear, you can't hatch these," Cressida said, and there was a distinct note of worry in her voice. Female dragons could get wildly possessive over eggs.

"No, no," Joy said impatiently. "These aren't *my* eggs. Of course I can't hatch them. I just have a strong feeling these weird shards and these weird eggs are connected. Sorry, eggs," she added, "but you *are* a little weird."

Still holding the shard carefully pinched between two claws, she very carefully pressed it to the shell of the closer of the two shells.

Instantly, the shard disappeared, and the egg took on the palest of pink hues.

There was a general gasp and sounds of amazement from the group.

"I knew it." Joy sat back on her haunches, looking smug.

"How did you know?" Horatio asked.

"Easy! They're cardless, so how could they have any specific magic to them? And the magic creates color. So, obviously, the solution is to give them card powers. And what makes cards? Shards! You two should do the rest," she added to Soledad and Marion. "Give them as many shards as they can hold."

Immediately, Soledad started emptying her pockets of all the shards she had picked up in both of her challenges.

Marion, however, frowned down at the second egg. And Arthur realized that he had never answered the question whether he wanted to be a dragon rider or not.

He stepped over to his friend. "The egg is yours if you want it," Arthur said, "but if you don't, I can put it back into my Personal Space, and it will be fine there." He paused for a moment and asked the real question. "Do you want to be a dragon rider?"

"I want to be a healer," Marion said. "Or at least . . . I know I'm smart enough to be one, and I thought it would give me purpose."

That wasn't an answer to his question, so Arthur waited.

Sure enough, Marion continued. "You know that I mostly came to Buck Moon Hive to protect my sister, but . . . yes, I admit I had dreams of possibly riding a dragon. What little boy wouldn't? I just didn't expect . . ." He trailed off. "I do still want to be a healer."

"Well," Arthur said, "why not both?" And then he pulled out the trio of healing cards from his jacket pocket.

During the transition from the challenge back to the pavilion, the cards had moved from the strange leg pants pocket to his normal jacket. Apparently, they were an official reward from the Dark Heart, as he hadn't lost them.

Marion stared, dumbfounded. "Where did you get these?"

"I got them during the challenge, of course."

"Wow," Horatio said. "What did you get for me?"

Arthur answered flatly. "New retinue hatchlings for your dragon to boss around."

"Thank you," Sams said.

Marion was still staring at the cards. "You're really giving these to me? These are a trio. Do you know how much they're worth?" He shook his head and answered his own question. "No, of course you know their worth, and you can't use them yourself."

"I would like you on my retinue, both of you," he said, including Soledad in the conversation, who nodded as if to say *of course*. "But whether you pick the egg or not, these cards are yours. They're three of a kind, so they only take up one space in your heart."

Marion took them with slightly unsteady hands, fanned them out to look at them again. Then he smiled and put them in his heart.

He shivered for a moment and closed his eyes, and when he opened them, Arthur thought he saw a flash of silver magic behind his eyes. He had never seen that before with anybody who had added a card. Then again, he'd never seen someone just add three of a kind at once.

"I guess I'm committed," Marion said lightly. Then he knelt and started pulling shards out of his own pockets.

But that still left the problem of Soledad. She was still pulling shards out of her pockets. How many did she have?

"Soledad, we need to talk about getting you some cards."

"Oh, don't worry about that," Cressida muttered.

Soledad smiled brightly. "Go teach your mother to suck eggs," she said fondly.

"Excuse me?" Arthur asked.

But at that moment, Soledad projected a pair of cards from her heart. Lava Whip and For the Love of Lava.

Arthur realized with a start that she did have Rare power emanating from her. He just hadn't bothered to look.

"Those were *my* winnings from the combat with the mega-scourgling," Brixaby grumbled. "Soledad insisted on claiming them, as she did not have any other cards, and they would not properly fit anybody's deck."

"Yeah." Horatio had a dopey smile on his face that Arthur did not understand at all. "That girl knows what she wants."

Brixaby continued, growing louder with indignation. "And when I suggested that I eat them, I was outvoted."

He sounded quite put out.

Arthur was just amazed that Brixaby had allowed a vote in the first place. It might have been because he was burned and not feeling quite himself. Then again, Soledad did have a forceful personality when she wanted.

Speaking of, she had finally finished emptying out her pockets, carrying bags, satchel, and what looked like a waterskin she'd dumped out and replaced with shards. She had quite the pile, whereas Marion only had a couple of handfuls.

"Wait," Arthur said, then steeled himself. This was not going to be popular. "Everybody, bring out your shards, and we will split them evenly between Soledad and Marion."

The reaction was instant.

"What?" Horatio said, aghast.

"What do you mean split them?" Soledad demanded. "I saved like a thousand turtles to get these shards, and killed some scourglings with a knife!"

"That was a sword," Brixaby said. She ignored him.

Arthur made a cutoff gesture. "These will need to be Rare-ranked dragons to link with you, which will take a lot of shards to rank them up high enough."

"Yeah!" Soledad gestured to her huge pile of shards. "Which is why I need to use every one."

"Soledad, don't be greedy," Cressida said. She started emptying her shards out of a glittery little bag she kept on her at all times that looked a lot like her card-anchor bag. "With all of us contributing, you'll end up with more shards. *Obviously.*"

That calmed her down a little.

Horatio quickly said, "Soledad can have my shards. I mean, both of you can," he added when Arthur and Sams gave him a look.

Brixaby, however, made no move to add to the pile.

"Brixaby," Arthur said patiently, "the more shards we put into the eggs, the stronger the dragons will be. And they're going to be part of *your* retinue."

Brixaby could be incredibly greedy and short-sighted, but he was not a fool. The strength of his retinue reflected back on him. He turned and growled at the eggs. "Do not disappoint me. I will be very *displeased* if you come out weak."

Then he started unloading shards from his own Personal Space. He had . . . a lot of shards. Arthur didn't, and he felt a little bad for telling everybody else to give away their shards when he didn't have much to contribute.

But there was no more grumbling. Even Soledad looked pleased when it was clear that, even splitting her shards with Marion, she came out way ahead with the addition of everybody else's.

They split the pile in half, and one by one, Soledad and Marion started pressing the shards to their respective eggs.

It was a long process, and Arthur and the others started comparing stories about their challenges as the two would-be riders worked. As they did, the shells lost that blank nothingness and grew more defined.

Soledad's, which was the one with the pale pink hue, grew redder and redder, and then started developing spots along the shell, dark and deep as Brixaby's hide. It gained features like crags and fissures. Very earthy, though anyone who touched the egg would see that this was an illusion.

"Oh, it's polka-dotted," Joy said.

Meanwhile, Marion's grew bright as a newly struck silver coin. There were no additional features. It was a single monochrome color, but glowed as if drawing from a deep well of power.

Good, Arthur thought. He'd always had a secret fondness for silvers, starting from the day he'd met Doshi, though he would never tell Brixaby.

Though the shells absorbed the shards almost instantly once they were pressed to them, with the size of the piles they had to work through, it took some time.

Joy sat by, advising them as if she were an expert. "Why don't you go ahead and talk to your dragon? Tell them that you can't wait to meet them, and that you're going to be their rider and take care of them forever and ever. It's scary when you first break out of the shell, and I think they'd like to see a face matching a voice that they recognize."

Soledad was enthusiastic about the idea. She started chatting about how she was very happy to meet the dragon whenever he or she came out. That by bonding with her, it would grow big and strong and that they would fight many scourglings.

Marion was much more reserved, almost unenthusiastic. Arthur briefly worried. Though he did sit with the egg and pat it as he fed it shards, murmuring very quietly so no one could hear him.

Arthur didn't quite get around to telling everybody about the general and the Master of Cards. He knew what everyone's reaction would be.

They had not been there. They would not understand.

But he also sensed that Brixaby was holding something back from his retelling of the combat challenge, too. If he had to guess, it had something to do with the volcano where he had found the two dark cards. This was reinforced by the way that Joy kept shooting him quick looks.

Finally, Marion and Soledad pressed the last of the shards to their eggs.

"What happens now? When's it going to hatch?" Soledad asked.

Everybody looked to Joy, who fluttered her wings anxiously.

"I don't know. Eggs hatch when they want to hatch. I didn't lay these. Maybe you should ask it to hatch?"

To Arthur's surprise, Marion was the first to act. He placed his hand on the top of his silver egg, which now gleamed so much it was another light source, and said, "Do you want to hatch now?"

Then he jerked in surprise, his eyes going wide as he looked at something that no one else could see.

Soledad hurried to follow his example but had a similar reaction. Then she frowned.

"What is it?" Arthur asked.

"I received a notice from the Dark Heart, I believe," Marion said darkly. "It says that the egg cannot hatch while the territory is in dispute."

"The territory is in dispute?" Horatio asked. "What does that mean?"

But Arthur suddenly knew, and Brixaby did, too. They both sprinted for the stairway leading to the door. But of course, Brixaby was faster and flew up the stairwell instead.

The moment he was out of the trapdoor and outside, he roared.

"Intruders!"

CHAPTER 46

Arthur got to the top of the stairwell and looked out. A handful of rough-looking men and women all surrounded the edges of the pavilion, staring back at him.

However, none had stepped on the slate rock platform that was under the roof. It likely had to do with the shield—almost completely translucent except for a bubble haze—that wavered right on the edges. Arthur hadn't noticed it before. Then again, he hadn't had strangers practically on the doorway to his territory before.

Arthur's hand slipped into his jacket pocket where he felt the territory card, which held everyone's names who was allowed in. Whoever these people were, they were too late to take over his territory.

"Well," said one man who had the air of the group leader. He wore a dark wide-brimmed hat in the style of the locals, and a long coat with a hem that brushed the top of his boots. He grinned at Arthur, unafraid. "You saved us the trouble of announcing ourselves. Thank you. With all the fun we've had today, my throat was starting to get a bit dry."

The rest of his group chortled.

"What do you want?" Arthur asked flatly.

"Simple: your cards and your shards, and then we'll agree to leave you in peace."

"You dare challenge us?" Brixaby boomed. "Go away before I teach you a lesson about respect."

Arthur frowned. "We have several dragons with us. This isn't a fight you want."

"That's what that thing is?" the man nodded to Brixaby who buzzed almost to the height of the roof with anger. Though he was smart enough to keep within the boundaries of the shield. "A dragon?"

Narrowing his eyes, Arthur moved away from the trapdoor, watching the man's face closely as Sams poked his head out. Not being intimidated by Brixaby was one thing, but Sams was a large dragon. Several of the would-be bandits stepped back, clearly intimidated as the giant dragon emerged. It was a lucky thing that the pavilion was so large because Sams still fit under it, but only with his tail tucked in. Joy came out next, causing additional murmurs. Obviously, some people had not known that he had three dragons with him.

Arthur let the moment play out. It was one thing to be brave in front of people you were trying to rob. It was another to do the same in front of giant beasts with teeth and claws. Joy looked around, saw the group, and grinned, showing off her intimidating green teeth.

Horatio, Cressida, Soledad, and Marion filed out next.

Including the dragons, the bandits were outnumbered.

"I don't know what you think your plan is," Arthur said. "You can't cross into my territory, and my retinue isn't stupid enough to go out and fight you," he said pointedly. Brixaby looked like he dearly wanted to. So did Joy.

"Well, I'll give you this . . . You have quite the colorful . . . What did you call them? Retinue?" the bandit leader said.

"And they have the cards to fight, too. Move along," Arthur said.

"No," he replied calmly. "I don't think I will, but I'll tell you what. I'll give you one more chance: your cards or your lives. And just because you didn't comply the first time, you get to forfeit your heart cards, too."

"Ruffians," Soledad said, and spat to the side.

His gaze landed on her, and his smile became downright sunny. "Soledad Boudreaux, right?" he said, and she froze. Everybody looked at Soledad. "Yep, I heard that you had been spotted with these dragon riders, too."

He looked at Arthur. "Add the girl in," he said, "and I'll let you keep your heart cards."

"You aren't in a position to negotiate," Arthur said.

He was about to tell Brixaby to give them a taste of his Stunning Shout when Joy warned, "Arthur, I just got a quest to rescue a princess!"

"I'm not a princess," Soledad snapped.

"I'll take that as a no," the leader drawled, and suddenly, the territory card in Arthur's jacket felt hot with power. And the invisible barrier that separated them all rippled like the rainbow edge of a soap bubble and fell down.

One of the bandits, the one with bright blond hair, flickered. Suddenly, he was right in the middle of their group, slashing with a dark blade at Horatio's neck.

Why him? Arthur thought in shock. *Why not me?* But the answer was obvious. As his rider, he stood next to Sams, and as the biggest, Sams looked to be the most threatening.

An instant before the knife hit, a mana-bubble shield appeared between Horatio and the blade, cast by Cressida. The dagger hit the shield and bounced back with equal kinetic force, nearly striking the blond man.

Sams roared and swiped a giant paw at the man who'd threatened his rider. But the man blinked away before the paw hit.

Then it was pure chaos as the rest of the bandits took the distraction as a chance to charge forward. Only the leader stayed in place, still grinning and occasionally making small movements with his hands.

"I have been waiting to use Berserker's Rage!" Brixaby cried.

Arthur yelled. "No, wait—"

But his dragon's eyes grew from his normal bloodred to a shining, unearthly glow. Brixaby launched himself head-on at a bandit with his claws out.

But just before he struck, the whole pavilion swung around them in a way that did not make sense. It was as if invisible angles had just come into being for an instant before everything popped back into place. But now there was a pillar between Brixaby and the man where there hadn't been one before. Brixaby hit it so hard that he left a dent. Thankfully, his Toughened Skin kept him from getting hurt. He swung about, roaring in rage to target another bandit instead of chasing the one he had been after.

He should have used his Stunning Shout on the leader, but he did not seem to be in his right mind.

Meanwhile, Horatio cast a burning light ray at another advancing bandit who slid out of the way with an almost bone-cracking grace. The bandit instantly popped back up, still advancing forward. Arthur didn't worry too much about him. Cressida was near him and would be able to provide another shield if needed.

Arthur turned away, and his eyes locked on the head bandit. He activated his Nice Shot card and **Knife Work** skills. The man was easily forty feet away. Arthur charged his shrapnel and fired them. What was good enough for a scourgling was good enough for a bandit. But every time he shot one out, something rose between them: a tree, a rock, another pillar.

Then the man made a sweeping gesture with his hand. Suddenly, all of them were down underneath the main pavilion.

Brixaby, who had been mid-dive on a bandit as they teleported, caught the man by the shoulders, lifting him up into the air. But he was so full of rage that he didn't even kill him properly or steal his cards.

He just shook him, and the man's head flopped back and forth. His upward arc was too steep, and he was too focused on the bandit he was punishing.

Brixaby hit the ceiling and staggered in the air, so surprised he let go of the bandit. The man fell and managed to land with natural grace.

"Brixaby," Arthur snapped, "turn off your Berserker Rage."

This was falling apart. Even taken by surprise, they should have had a handle on these bandits. But Brixaby was out of control, his group was scattered, and while they were coming together and starting to work as a team—Cressida was covering Horatio and Marion—Soledad was just standing there, glaring at the bandits as if they'd done her personal wrong.

It was up to Arthur and Horatio to try to kill them at range, but they kept missing because of the weird object-repositioning power the leader had. This was a mess.

And abruptly, the man who could teleport in a blink was next to Soledad, his dark blade against her throat.

"Stop," the leader said boredly, and his voice echoed out with the authority of another card skill. "I'd like to have her as ransom—her family is paying a good price, but I'll kill her if I need to."

Family?

"I'm not going back there," Soledad yelled, "that place is a charnel house."

"Now, that's not up to you, missy."

Arthur shot a look at Brixaby and saw that his eyes had dimmed to normal. Though, to Arthur's eye, his wing beats were more labored. The anger had overtaken him and left him exhausted.

"You're not taking her anywhere!" Cressida yelled and sent out Wicker. The fire bear charged forward with a crackling roar.

The bandit leader started to move his arm, probably to reposition them again with his weird teleport power, but abruptly . . . Wicker started to fall apart midcharge. Within a few steps, the flames disintegrated.

Arthur did not understand until the man who held Soledad screamed as his clothes caught on fire. He ripped the dagger across her throat, but that throat was now red hot and encased in liquid lava.

Oh, right. Her cards needed a source of heat.

Suddenly, the room was full of Marions, all screaming and running at each one of the bandits. The bandits attacked back, killing the illusions, but it was impossible to tell which was the real one.

Arthur ran behind one of the illusions, and when it was dispelled by the extra-flexible man, Arthur was revealed.

He didn't bother with his Nice Shot card, as everything he had fired so far had been unexpectedly blocked. Instead, he threw a wild punch that must have looked overt and ridiculous. The man barely had to flex to catch his wrist. He smiled.

Arthur grinned back and took the final step forward, reaching to rip out seven cards he felt in the man's heart.

The man staggered back with a gasp and fell down, shaking hard in the beginning of a seizure.

Suddenly, Cressida and Joy erupted out of the shadow of another bandit, who had been standing back, probably for mana support. Joy bit down on him, and it was impossible to say what killed him—the dragon's jaws or venomous teeth.

In an instant, Arthur's retinue had taken back control of the fight.

And just like that, they were teleported again. They all stood in the same relative positions that they were in before, but now they were outside at the edge of the pavilion.

A giant wall of earth roared up between the remaining bandits and Arthur's retinue.

They're running, Arthur thought.

"You're not getting away that easy!" Horatio stepped forward. He glowed with every flashing color. Sams had once made a comment about Horatio getting better at his light-based cards, and now Arthur saw the result. He was not just flashing in the basic rainbow spectrum. The lights were running up and down his body in a geometric pattern, which was a stark example of how much his level of control of the Rainbow Knight card had advanced.

Those lights streamed to Sams, who took it up within himself.

The sun, which was a reflection of the pit of the Dark Heart, suddenly flared yellow and real. The bandits began to scream.

"We surrender!" someone yelled from the other side of the wall.

Sams looked at Arthur, his top lip curled up in a snarl. After all, one of the bandits had tried to kill his rider.

Arthur sighed and made a cutoff motion. The sun dimmed to normal.

"The eggs," Soledad said. She had cooled down, and black bits of rock flaked off her body, leaving her skin whole. There were deep cut lines in the soil where she had flexed out with a lava whip and killed yet another bandit. "We need to check on the eggs. If they were cracked in that fight—"

"Yes, go check on them," Arthur said. "You too, Marion." But he barely needed to tell them twice. The two ran back down to the pavilion's stairwell.

Brixaby buzzed down next to Arthur. The moment Arthur was aboard, they flew up and over the top of the earthen wall. Brixaby was quiet, and Arthur could tell he was sulky and embarrassed.

Three men and their leader groaned, surrounded by black earth. A couple tried to pull shirts over their heads to keep away from the burning light.

Don't anger a yellow who has the full force of a light deck, Arthur thought.

The leader looked like he had a high-grade sunburn. As Arthur dismounted and walked over, the man held up his hands, which had welts on them.

He smiled at Arthur as if this had all been a joke taken too far.

"All right, all right, we'll leave."

"Tell me what you did," Arthur said. Off to the side, Cressida and Joy, and Sams with Horatio landed at different points around the bandits. They were surrounded. "How did you steal my territory?"

"Nothing was stolen," the bandit leader said in a placating tone. "Look at your card."

He did and saw a whole host of names that had been added that he didn't recognize. The first was named Storm Wind Rick, who he assumed was the leader. This was followed by other names he supposed were the other bandits, as several of them were crossed out.

"All is fair in the Dark Heart," Rick said.

"You threatened to kill those in my retinue," Brixaby said dangerously.

"That may be so, but only my men were killed."

"Fine," Arthur growled. "I want you out of my sight."

Brixaby looked outraged for a half second until Arthur added, "But as recompense for my time, you and your remaining men are going to give me all of the cards left in your card anchors. My dragon will know if you hold any back."

Joy growled and flexed her venom claws. Horatio activated his Rainbow Knight and lights spun all over his skin in ominous, dizzying patterns.

Rick hesitated, and to Arthur's surprise he looked around him at Brixaby. "I heard about you. You're the dragon that eats cards."

"I'll eat every one of *your* cards in front of you," Brixaby promised in a low hiss.

Rick smiled. "I also heard that dragon riders get their powers from their beasts. Is that right?" Rick made a sharp gesture, and a wicked dragger flew out from underneath the wide sleeves of his trench coat.

Arthur flinched, but the dagger curved around him and struck Brixaby right in the chest.

Arthur cried out in shock, and the man whipped around to send another dagger at Joy. It immediately struck one of Cressida's shields, but the tip of the dagger hit the shield and stayed there, making a scraping sound of metal as it dug in. It was poised to strike right at Joy's heart.

Turning, Arthur ran toward Brixaby. But Brixaby yelled, "Duck!"

Arthur fell forward and flattened himself on the ground.

His dragon let out a Stunning Shout. Leaving his mouth, it was shaped like a crescent blade and flew harmlessly over Arthur and hit Rick with enough force to knock him off his feet.

As Arthur looked up at his dragon's puffed-out chest, he saw that the dagger was stuck at the point of Brixaby's heart . . . but was stopped by his Toughened Skin.

Then Sams called the power of the sun down again.

The bandits died, but Sams, who had more fighting experience than them all, made sure to keep the bodies intact enough to harvest the cards.

CHAPTER 47

I'm sad that the bandits had to die," Joy said as Arthur and the others went around harvesting the remains. They had to wait a few minutes, as the ground around what was left of the corpses was too hot to step on even with shoes.

"I'm not," Brixaby muttered.

"Nor am I." Sams flexed his neck to nudge Horatio, who pretended to bat him away.

Cressida knew exactly what to say to soothe her dragon. "On the other hand, now that our territory is no longer in dispute, those eggs should be hatching soon."

"Oh! Right!" Joy perked up.

"You never said what the reward was for your egg hatching quest," Brixaby pointed out. "Was it these cards?"

"Of course not, silly. It was two new friends. And I want to see them be born! C'mon, let's go!"

Arthur held up a hand. "Wait a moment. I want to see how that bandit leader was able to break through the shield. If others can do it, we need to know."

With that, he harvested the lump of char that had been Rick. Wary of destroying the anchor deck, Sams had concentrated his power only on torsos and heads. Killing shots.

Arthur quickly skimmed through the cards he found for the most interesting. Not only did he want to know how Rick had broken into his territory, but he also wanted a portal-type card for Brixaby.

Despite his rush, he paused when he came to several familiar cards. His heart dropped. "Oh no."

"What is it? Another trap card?" Brixaby sounded a little too enthusiastic about that.

Arthur turned the cards for Brixaby to see: Maniac Kludger and Natural Mechanic.

Cressida, who was nearby, glanced at them, too. She shot Arthur a confused look. "I don't get it."

"These belong to a friend that we made hunting scourglings," Arthur admitted. "I'm surprised that they got to them."

"You guys, I don't want to miss the hatching," Joy whined.

There was nothing he could do for Claude at the moment. Arthur flipped through the rest of the cards. The last was the answer to what he needed to know.

Material Dungeoneer
Rare
Utility
Using mana, the wielder of this card will be able to furnish and manipulate materials inside a dungeon. It cannot create an initial access point for a dungeon, nor alter dungeon creatures without the aid of a dungeon blueprint. Seek cards within the same set to gain additional dungeoneering powers.

Arthur's eyebrows rose. "I guess the Dark Heart is a type of dungeon after all."

Horatio, who shamelessly read over Arthur's shoulder, scoffed. "Figures. He wasn't teleporting us. He was just"—he fluttered his fingers in the air—"moving the stuff around us."

"The eggs—" Joy began.

"Yes, yes, dear." With a smile, Cressida went to her dragon.

Arthur kept a hold on the cards as he mounted Brixaby and they flew back over the hill to the pavilion. Brixaby, showing off, buzzed directly down the stairwell in a way that Sams and Joy could not.

They found Marion and Soledad crouched anxiously by the eggs. One of them had gotten the idea of taking the bedding from the bunks and padding the shells in a pseudo-nest. The eggs looked entirely unharmed from the fight, and there were no cracks or even striations in the shells, but they were jerking back and forth rapidly as the little dragons inside fought to get out.

Joy galloped down the stairs. Sams took a more sedate way in, with Horatio having dismounted and running down on foot.

Marion glanced over to them. "Well, I guess you guys all survived."

"They're gone," Arthur said. "We got their cards."

Marion and Soledad could read between the lines and knew what that meant. Marion looked away, but Soledad kept her gaze on Arthur, her chin raised in defiance.

"Princess?" Arthur asked pointedly.

"He was exaggerating to puff himself up. I might have been someone like that if N'awlens wasn't dying." She stared hard at Arthur. "I ain't going back there."

"Oh, you'll fit right in here," Horatio drawled. He pointed to Cressida. "She's a fancy noble, Arthur was sort of a noble, too. That guy next to you used to be a prince. As for me? I'm practically royalty too, back in my old hive."

Sams snorted his disagreement at that.

"What if this doesn't work?" Marion blurted, cutting through Horatio's nonsense. "What if I don't have a card that matches this dragon?" As hesitant as he was before, he looked like he was going to be sick while waiting.

That was the big question. No one said anything for a moment, though glances were exchanged.

"You're the one who fed it shards," Joy said brightly. "Of course it will match to you."

But no one knew that for sure. And judging by Marion's expression, he was less than convinced. Soledad looked anxious as well.

"Well," Arthur said, "its shell is silver, so if the dragon is too, it will likely be attracted to something to do with strong magic."

"What color does a healing dragon have?" Marion asked.

"Green," Joy said unhelpfully, "but maybe silver, too. I think. But green is nature, and healing is naturey . . . right?"

They looked at one another, unsure.

Marion pressed his lips together. "I have an illusion and healing cards. Is that enough? Did you harvest anything from the bandits that could help?"

Brixaby bristled. Clearly, he wanted the first pick of the cards.

"I don't know if right when the thing is about to hatch is the time to add something new to your deck," Horatio said. "Hatchling dragons can be kind of sensitive."

"I added a card to link with Joy," Cressida countered.

"I don't think it will hurt," Arthur said, though he wasn't entirely certain. But he quickly pulled out the stack from his pocket and flipped through the cards. As was usual with the locals, there were quite a few body-modification cards, most of which he didn't think anybody here would want. What was Instant Dinosaur Foot, and why would somebody want that?

"I have ten points of strength . . . but that probably won't help with being a dragon rider." He flipped through some more. The combat cards were fairly mundane. He read them off as he flipped through them. "Ice Daggers, Water Whip, Sharpened Sword . . . a net made of mana that always binds up their enemies. I'm surprised they didn't use more of these, but I think they probably just added them and didn't have a lot of practice. A lot of these are Commons."

"He'll need a Rare," Cressida said, and everybody nodded.

"I get dibs on any fire-type cards," Soledad said.

Brixaby let out an aggrieved growl, but her request made sense.

Arthur came again to Claude's cards and set those aside, too.

"No fire cards, or portal," he grumbled. "Here's a couple interesting ones . . . Assassin Dagger. It's an Uncommon, but I'm sure that's the one he used to try to kill Brix and Joy. There's Teleport in a Blink. That's useful, but it only allows one person to teleport at a time. And this next one . . . it's Rare." He held up the dungeoneering card, thought for a moment, then held it out to Joy. "Do you have any feelings about this card?"

"What?" Distracted, she turned her head away from where she was watching the still-jerking eggs intently. "No, not really, but I would like that Teleport in a Blink one for myself."

"Then I want the ten points of strength," Horatio said.

"We are not giving out cards until I have had my own pick," Brixaby said. "And besides, the dungeoneering card should obviously go to Marion."

"What?" Arthur looked in surprise at his dragon.

"Of course." Brixaby was equally baffled at Arthur's reaction. "He wants pure magic, and there's nothing more magical than a dungeon."

"He is correct," Sams said. "I once knew a dragon rider in Horatio's father's day who had a dungeoneering card."

"What color was his dragon?" Horatio asked.

"Silver."

Arthur would have liked the dungeoneering card for himself, but he had little room in his heart deck for anything radically different from his existing cards. He consoled himself with the thought that if it was going to someone in his retinue, he would still have access to the card in a way. So he shrugged and held it out to Marion. "It's a Rare," he said again, meaningfully.

Marion took the card and gazed down at it. It said something about how nervous he must have felt about the hatching that he immediately put it into his heart without much fanfare.

He gave them a sickly grin. "If my career as a healer doesn't work out, maybe a dungeoneer would be a good second choice. I could build myself an endless library . . . Oh . . ."

"What is it?" Arthur asked. He glanced at the silver egg, but it was still shifting back and forth without a crack.

"Whoever had this had a lot of control over this area," Marion said idly. "And not a lot of imagination." Then, with a wave of his hands, the eggs were no longer sitting propped up on the floor, surrounded by hasty sheets and pillows they'd torn off nearby beds, but a soft padding of straw. "That's much better."

"Okay, but what do we do when they hatch?" Soledad bit out.

Cressida answered. "They will look into your heart deck and decide if what you have is a match to their core card. They'll offer their own, and then you link the two."

"And create a new card," Joy finished. She and Cressida shared a fond look, likely remembering their own moment of linking.

"Dragon-created cards are obviously the most powerful," Brixaby added.

Suddenly, there was a snapping sound. A jagged crack ran down Soledad's egg, from top to bottom.

The features of the egg had continued to develop over the course of the battle. This one definitely looked like an active volcano, complete with red-and-orange lava . . . But the black spots that had become fissures were deep, deep black, like looking at the darkest part of the night. Arthur wasn't exactly sure what that meant. The shell did not necessarily match the future dragon—Joy's had been like gemstones, which definitely reflected her glittering personality, if not her powers. But it certainly was a hint.

As if not wanting to be outdone by its sibling, Marion's egg started to hatch as well. The very tip popped off, and the white membrane inside was slashed open by a tiny tooth on top of a wet silver snout. The hatchling's nostrils breathed in its first gust of air.

But then, all at once, attention was back to the red-and-black egg as a vividly dark red wing popped out of the crack, followed by claws that scrabbled and pushed.

Soledad reached down to help, but before she could touch it, the shell fell apart to reveal a striking deep red dragon with a rather squarish head who sat awkwardly on the remains of his shell. Soledad raised her hand as if to pet the little hatchling, but then paused.

"Hello," she breathed.

The dragon blinked up at her with unsettling, dark, almost-black eyes with darker irises. Its eyes seemed to be too large for its head, giving it an odd appearance somewhere between cute and strange.

It stared at Soledad for a few long moments.

"Soledad, project your cards to it," Cressida insisted. In the excitement of the hatching, she seemed to have put any enmity for the other girl behind her.

"Of course. Oh, yeah, right." Soledad gestured, and her two cards appeared, projected between herself and the dragon.

The baby red peered at them for a moment, studying closely.

Arthur didn't think that the little dragon could read, but the magic of the cards meant that they could be understood. Besides, Rare cards had moving pictures.

"Yes . . ." the hatchling said in a surprisingly mellow tone. "Your deck is somewhat unbalanced, but this will do perfectly for now." Then he projected his own card to fit along with Soledad's.

The face of the card was visible just long enough for Arthur to take in the title. A Touch of Summer and Winter.

That was a little unusual. The natural magic of red dragons meant that they usually dealt with high energy, which classically meant fire. But some, such as Shadow, had access to more esoteric types.

Then again, this red was a Rare dragon, and judging by the way his scales glittered under the lights, a shimmer type as well.

But in the next moment, Soledad scooped up her little dragon as if she had longed to cuddle him for hours instead of moments.

Arthur looked away to give them a moment, and instead met Brixaby's bloodred gaze. The dragon was not often touchy-feely, but he ducked his head and bumped the top of his skull against Arthur's chest very gently.

At that moment, Marion's hatchling finally seemed to win its battle over the egg. The shell more or less crumbled around it, leaving a very delicate, very feminine-looking silver looking bemusedly up at the world.

Crouching to her level, Marion gestured to bring all of his cards out. The silver looked at them, smiled, and started to gesture to her own chest.

Then, she suddenly stopped and recoiled.

She backed away a couple steps, stumbling over the remains of her shell, shaking her head. "I can't," she said in a tiny, fluty little voice.

"Why not?" Marion hurriedly asked. "Is something wrong? Do you need another card?"

She backed up another step, shaking her head, though she stared at Marion with hunger and horror equal in her baby blue eyes. "I want to; you're perfect for me. But I *can't.*"

"Why not?" Brixaby demanded. "He is not, perhaps, as good as my rider, but he is perfectly acceptable. Besides, there are no other choices around here. You must pick him!"

Sams took on a slightly different tactic, bending his head to waft warm breath over the tiny hatchling. "What is wrong, little one?"

Arthur glanced at Joy to see what she had to say. She only watched on, slightly curious, but not too invested now that the eggs were hatched.

The little silver just shook her head again, staring at Marion as if begging him to fix what was wrong.

His shoulders slumped. "It's my heart," Marion said. "You feel the pain there."

"Yes, it hurts."

"It's because I had a Legendary card," Marion said, defeat thick in his voice. "And she's a Rare. My heart is too damaged for her."

CHAPTER 48

N o," Arthur said.

Everyone turned to stare at him, puzzled. Well, everyone but Marion who was gazing at his dragon with a look of utter defeat on his face.

"No," Arthur said again, stepping forward to place a hand on Marion's shoulder. "Remember, we're in the Dark Heart. Rules can be changed here."

"Arthur . . ." Cressida started, but then trailed off. She looked like she didn't know what else to say, as if she hardly dared to hope.

"Stand up, Marion," Arthur said. "This isn't over yet."

Marion looked up at him and must have seen the firm resolve in Arthur's expression. He sniffed once, nodded, and stood. When he spoke, his voice was wobbly.

"Y-you're right, of course. There are more challenges ahead." He gestured to the nearby wall.

Arthur followed his gaze and saw that the challenge doors had been reset again. Now they looked like they were made of steel, and again over them were the signs: UTILITY, PUZZLE, COMBAT.

He thought of his weeks in the last challenge. Of getting to know people he didn't even know were real or not. The gains . . . but also the emotional sacrifices.

And Marion would have to do it with his heart ripped in half.

"No," Arthur said for a third time. "I don't know about you guys, but I'm tired of waiting for my reward. I want it now."

"As do I," Brixaby piped up. "So we shall defeat the next challenge together and show this place what we are made of."

"Or," Arthur said, "we bypass it altogether. You have a dungeoneer card, Marion. Why don't you make another door straight to the core of the Dark Heart?"

Horatio whistled. "Is that possible?"

Everyone looked at Marion, who bit his lip and stared at the wall in thought. "I believe it should be."

"Wait, if this was possible, why didn't the bandits do it?" Cressida asked.

Sams's answer dripped with scorn. "Because they were thieves who were only interested in hunting down other people."

"He's right," Horatio said grimly. "We're putting our lives on the line with every challenge. So why do that when they can just hunt people they see as weak or exhausted after coming out of another challenge? Yeah, mana and stuff is renewed when we come out, but I don't know about you guys—I'm tired. It takes a bite out of you, every time."

"I said it before," Marion added. It looked like he was warming to the subject. "The last man who had this card wasn't exceptionally creative. He could have molded this world almost any way he wanted, and he used the card to simply move the land around us."

"He did almost get the drop on us," Horatio reminded him.

Cressida held out a hand to stop the conversation before it could go off the rails. "Wait, if we do this . . . won't it be cheating? Won't there be retaliation?"

Arthur shrugged and smiled at her. "I've learned more and more that some rules are meant to be broken."

"Yes," Brixaby agreed. "Especially when there are rewards on the other side."

Cressida turned to her dragon. "Joy?"

"I . . . don't know," Joy said cautiously. "It's not like I can tell the future. I just have a stronger sense of intuition, and it's not telling me one thing or another."

Brixaby opened his mouth, but she preempted him and said, "No quests, either."

Marion looked down at his little dragon, who stared up at him with pleading eyes. "You can fix it?"

"Yes," Marion said, and strode forward to the blank wall to the side of the doors. Placing his hand flat on the wall, he bowed his head as if he were concentrating fiercely.

"It isn't going to be easy, and there will be limits to what I can do. It feels like I can only get us to the outer edge of the center, and it will be up to us to do the rest," he said after a minute. "And I'm sorry, Joy and Sams, but I can't make the way big enough to fit you."

Sams shifted in place. "The Dark Heart took us to the challenge even though we were standing outside the trapdoor earlier."

"That was the Dark Heart's door. This is mine," he said, and spread his hands across the wall. A doorway grew in the middle—pitch black with a gold knob.

Arthur thought Brixaby would be able to just squeeze through if he sucked in his breath.

"You will go in," Sams said to Horatio, who was looking doubtful. "And get a reward that complements our decks."

He visibly shook himself and said, "Yeah, of course, buddy," casually, as if they weren't about to face the very core of the Dark Heart, which likely meant the hardest challenge of them all.

"You too, Cressida," Joy said. It was clear she was putting a positive face on, but she wasn't going to stop her rider. "I'll protect the pavilion."

Cressida went over to give her dragon a quick hug.

Arthur looked to Soledad. "I want you and . . ." He paused.

"His name is Equinox," Soledad said proudly.

"Yes," Equinox said. "The balance between day and night."

That didn't make any sense to Arthur—didn't his card have to do with the seasons, somehow?—but he nodded anyway. "I want you two to stay back and protect the territory until we go back."

"No problem." Soledad didn't seem bothered about sitting this one out. Possibly because her dragon was so small. "It will give us a chance to practice with our cards."

"Ohhh, lava," Joy said. "Probably take that outside when you practice, though."

Arthur thought for a moment before he pulled a big hunk of bison meat from his Personal Space to offer it to Equinox. The little red hatchling pounced on it right away, though when Arthur tried to offer the silver the same, she shied away.

Because Joy and Sams were giving him looks, not too unlike expectant dogs at the dinner table, he unstored an entire bison haunch along with a barrel of water.

Brixaby watched on with an odd look on his face.

"Oh, are you hungry, too?" Arthur asked, feeling inconsiderate.

"No, but it is possible for me to unstore the contents of my Personal Space. Then Sams, Joy, Equinox, and his linked rider can come with us."

Arthur felt like slapping his forehead. Except that brought up a new problem. "We're not exactly going to a regular Dark Heart challenge. If we all leave, will we lose the territory?"

It wasn't that he was overly attached to this pavilion, even with its convenient underground room. It was that by now, many territories had likely been taken over. He didn't want to fight or trick someone out of another.

Cressida looked torn, then sighed. "No, Soledad is the right one to stay behind with her hatchling dragon. But she shouldn't be expected to protect it alone. Joy and Sams should stay. Besides, I think they're busy having lunch."

Horatio nodded his agreement.

With everyone ready, Marion opened the door. Unlike with the Dark Heart challenges, they had to step through the door.

On the other side, they found an enclosed staircase that led down into a black tunnel.

Brixaby grunted when he saw the stairwell, which was much too small for him to fly down. Then he dug out a lit torch from his Personal Space.

With a grin, Arthur unstored his LED flashlight and turned it on. The beam illuminated all the way down the steep stairwell.

"What is that?" Brixaby all but ripped it out of his hands and looked at it closely, wincing away when he accidentally shined the flashlight in his own eye.

"It's a tool I picked up from my challenge. I told you, they had strange stuff there. Let's move fast—if this runs out of energy, I don't have a way to recharge it."

Yes, he had stored quite a few flashlights in his Personal Space, but waste not, want not.

The little silver hatchling had followed them through and to the landing. Marion extended a hand to her, but she shook her head again, looking miserable.

"That won't do," Cressida said briskly. Then she bent and scooped her up.

The little silver squawked. "You're not meant for me! You belong to someone else!"

"That's right, but today I'm only carrying you. It's a long way, and I don't want your legs to get tired."

The little silver didn't look happy, but she didn't protest anymore, though her gaze was fixed on Marion as they started down the stairwell.

Arthur sensed that with every step they took down, they were coming closer and closer to a source of power. It was a feeling of oppression, of being squeezed and yet still able to breathe. He didn't like it.

"What is this place, exactly?" he asked Marion.

He adjusted his glasses. "As far as I can tell, each step we take bypasses another challenge level."

Arthur was so surprised that he stopped in place, almost causing Horatio to crash into him. "What?"

"I'm sorry, was what I said unclear?" Marion asked blandly.

Horatio was flummoxed. "There have to be hundreds of stairs! You're telling me that if we wanted to get to the final level the normal way, we'd have to go through all of this? What happened to three or four levels?" He looked at Cressida accusingly.

She shrugged. "I told you that information on Dark Hearts is hard to come by."

"But . . . but that's not fair!"

"I'm starting to get the feeling that Dark Hearts aren't meant to be fair," Arthur muttered.

And with that dour comment, they continued downward.

Brixaby, of course, had a slightly different take on the situation. "If we received rewards such as dragon eggs and Rare cards from the first challenge, imagine the power and rarity of the hardest of challenges!"

"What's better than a Rare?" Horatio asked. "I mean, obviously Legendary, but how many Legendary cards can this thing have?"

"I don't know," Arthur said. "But what worries me is how much power is represented here. Remember, the Dark Heart ripened ahead of schedule. I think it can afford to give some cards away."

They were quiet as they continued to make their way down, and the oppressive sense grew. At the very bottom stood a landing with another door. This was not the smooth black as before, but gilded with gold and encrusted with gems.

"Do you think these are real diamonds?" Horatio asked. "Hey, Arthur, you have a chisel or something in that Personal Space, don't you?"

Arthur ignored him and stepped forward, resting his hand on the intricate door handle. He looked at the others. "You ready?"

Everyone nodded. Even Horatio, after a moment.

Arthur opened the door, and even though he did not step in, immediately they were all inside . . .

Where they were being oppressed, crushed by a weight that was physical, mental, and spiritual all at once.

Arthur fell to his knees and heard his friends all collapse as well. They were in a dark room without any boundaries or borders or up or down. And off in the distance—so far that it didn't seem possible, yet he could see it anyway—a pair of red scourgling eyes watched them and laughed.

He knew in his heart that these were the eyes of a Scourge God.

CHAPTER 49

Desperately, Arthur activated his Mental Shield along with his area-of-effect one to try to help his friends. To the side, he saw Cressida try to do the same with her mana shield, but the moment it went up, it was snuffed out like a candle flame. Her power was Rare.

Beside him, Brixaby roared in frustration and pain. The mental shields were barely holding up. They felt as thin as eggshells, and it would take only the lightest additional pressure to crush them.

We need to head back to the door. This is too much . . .

But Cressida, Horatio, Marion, and the hatchling dragon were all flat on the ground, either passed out or close to it.

The bare gaze of a distant Scourge God was too much for them. And it was close to breaking Arthur.

Then that red pair of eyes was joined by another and another and another. Until there were seven pairs looking at him.

He didn't know why the pressure hadn't increased—that should be more than enough to kill him. It didn't make sense.

Until a voice he had hoped to never hear again said, "I see rumors of your demise were exaggerated."

Lung Bai, King Elizar's Mythic dragon, stood near him. Or seemingly so. Her long body was as semitransparent as a ghost, and she carried a sense of distance around her, though she did seem closer than the Scourge Gods.

She stared down at Arthur and Brixaby with unblinking slit-pupiled eyes.

Arthur tried to reply, but it came out as a gurgle. He tasted iron in his mouth. Blood.

From beyond hissed seven unified voices that threatened to tear the skin from Arthur's bones.

"They are ours. Our feast. Our cards."

Lung Bai sent a derisive look over her shoulder and flicked her tail. "Silence, creatures."

And abruptly, through a working of her nullification magic, their voices were gone.

The pressure on Arthur lessened enough for him to inhale a shuddering breath. Brixaby did too, and leaped to his feet only to sweep his wings forward in a bow. "Mythic."

Behind, the rest of his retinue stirred, but they were still clearly suffering from the pressure—Lung Bai had only reduced it, not eliminated it. As Rares, they had less resistance.

Marion reached over and grabbed the little dragon from Cressida's slack arms, holding her close.

Lung Bai looked less than impressed. "You have run away from your responsibilities and right into the claws of the Scourge Gods."

"I didn't run away," Arthur gasped, which was a flat-out lie, so he padded it with the truth. "We were seeking something to destroy the scourglings—to help the hive."

"You foolish children went to a kingdom that has turned against dragons and then into the Dark Heart, the domain of the scourglings, thinking you could find weapons to use against them." Every word was angrier and angrier, and Arthur was certain he would soon feel his own cards being locked away again . . . but for now, he still had them.

That gave him courage. Getting his breath back, he said, "What the hives are doing is not working. There are more and more eruptions. Am I supposed to just sit back and let it happen?"

"Lung Bai," said another voice from just off to the side. "I thought your ridiculous kingdom forbade pairs of Legendary cards."

Arthur glanced and saw that past Lung Bai were four other pairs of eyes, and the size and shape told him they were other dragons.

The new speaker stepped closer and resolved into a semitransparent pale pink dragon. Her body shape was closer to Sams's or Joy's than Lung Bai's, though she was easily three times the size of Sams and had living crystals growing from out past her elbows and knees in spikes. Her back ridges were made of flashing crystal, and a circlet of gems surrounded her head.

Lung Bai was shaped unlike any dragon Arthur had seen. Her head was the same width as her long neck and pointed with two swept-back horns. The rest of her was snakelike with sharp narrow wings in the middle of her back.

"Yes," Lung Bai whisper-hissed. "These two have long been a pain in my tail."

"Mm." The pink swept a bored look over them. Then she paused and thrust her head forward to look closely at Marion's little silver, who had peeked her head out. "That is an Origin hatchling."

Suddenly, Arthur felt the pointed attention of all the Mythics on him. It was nearly as bad as the Scourge Gods, and he once again felt briefly at a loss for air until Lung Bai made a noise of disgust and the pressure eased.

But now another dragon had come closer. It was an elderly orange with a clearly broken back. He dragged himself close on two strong forelegs, while his back legs and tail trailed behind him. All of his attention was on the silver.

"An Origin hatchling? Impossible . . ." he breathed, then trailed off as he stared.

"Not all the Origin eggs have been found," said the pink. "But how did that Rare come across it?"

"I found the egg," Arthur gasped. No reason to tell them about Soledad's hatchling and possibly put him in danger.

"In *this* Dark Heart? Which level?" the orange barked. "Oh, Lung Bai, let up on him and allow him to speak. Crystal, help her."

Abruptly, the pressure lessened by a few more degrees. Arthur stood fully and noticed that Brixaby and the rest of his retinue were recovering.

"I found it in the first challenge," Arthur said.

One of the other, still-hidden dragons made an annoyed growl. "Another Dark Heart that's about to erupt, and if it's already spitting out rewards like that . . ."

"Did you go back in time?" the orange asked.

"Yes. Or I think so. Was that real?"

"It is the only way I can think of for you to return with an egg that was created of the first dragons, and some of the most powerful."

"It is only a Rare," Lung Bai snapped. "And a hatchling."

"I hatched as a Common," Crystal said to her. "Your starting power does not matter, only what you do with it."

Now that Arthur could properly breathe and had answered some questions, he felt like he deserved a couple answers of his own. "What is this place?"

"You have stepped through the doorway to the realm of the Mythics, foolish boy," Lung Bai told him. "Using a cursed Dark Heart of all things!" She looked angry enough to spit.

"To defeat a Dark Heart nowadays is an extraordinary feat," the orange murmured. "These are not simply foolish children, Lung Bai. To get this close to a core means they have defeated the traps and tricks of dozens, perhaps hundreds, of challenges."

Arthur was not going to tell them they had bypassed all of that using a dungeoneer card. But his attention was caught on one word. "Traps?"

"You don't think we made these things?" Another Mythic joined them. He was a younger blue and had a rather peaceful expression on his face. "The Scourge Gods have long learned to bait them with cards and rewards, with levels that become progressively harder and harder until by the end, they are virtually impossible." He gave Arthur a long look, one which told him he knew he'd cheated somehow. "When entire groups of hopefuls or strong solo delvers are wiped out, what do you think happens to their cards?"

Brixaby answered, "They are returned to the heart."

"Yes," Lung Bai said. "And thus, the Dark Heart grows stronger until it once more erupts and takes down the city that has grown around it. I like to think of it as the scourgling way of farming."

"Except scourglings know no bounds and are wiping away human habitations far more quickly than they can be built back up, and killing the land behind it," the orange added blandly.

That made a certain amount of sense. Arthur had suspected a certain level of chicanery when the general had flaunted the Master of Cards. If Arthur had taken it, the guard announcing the scourgling attack would have seen it. Then Arthur's life could have very well ended.

If he hadn't had access to Brixaby's Call of the Heart, he would have never found his way through those scourgling tunnels, much less found eggs that had been hidden.

Arthur had only gotten out of that challenge by cheating.

His attention was pulled back when the pink dragon spoke.

"That is all beside the point. If I am not mistaken, we have Mythic candidates in front of us, with an Origin hatchling in his retinue. And they have blundered onto the doorstep of a Scourge God."

The still-hidden dragon scoffed again. "A purple as a Mythic candidate. We truly are in dark times."

Arthur exchanged glances with Brixaby. *Mythic candidates?*

"They are hardly candidates," Lung Bai said. "With a pair of Legendaries between them."

"I'm about to add another to my deck," Arthur said. All the visible dragons swung their heads to him. "Uh, if I can get to the core."

"*If.*" Crystal snorted. "Young purple, you did not choose a confident one."

Brixaby had been somewhat subdued—at least for himself—in the presence of the Mythics. Now he bristled at her words. "Arthur is cunning and perfect in all the ways you will never know. He got himself and the rest of his retinue here on the strength of utility cards. Do not underestimate him. Or me," he growled, buzzing up to her eye level.

She snorted, sending him flipping back in the air.

"What say you?" the orange asked. "Do we risk this chance?"

"Aye," Crystal said.

"Yes," said the blue.

The orange nodded to indicate his vote.

After a pause, the hidden dragon sighed and said, "Whatever."

Only Lung Bai was quiet. She stared hard at Arthur. "I told you before that you would only have one chance, and now I am on the verge of giving you another. But I don't think you understand what a gift this is."

"Then tell me," Arthur said. "We only meant to challenge the Dark Heart and gain its rewards. Not . . . Scourge Gods."

"The Scourge Gods have poisoned this heart—all hearts—and made them nearly impossible to accomplish," Lung Bai said. "We can hold their influence off you, but for only this level. Complete it, and you will gain your reward. I assume that is the next Legendary card in your set?"

Arthur nodded.

"Good, I would do this for nothing less. Understand: this will cost us power, and thus, power for the world. Make your reward count and do great things with it."

Crystal lowered her head. "What she means is to complete your sets— together—and ascend to Mythic."

"You may have noticed, but we and our riders are outnumbered," the blue added.

Arthur hesitated. This challenge they'd just set before him was more than he had ever thought he could accomplish. Was it too much?

Brixaby, of course, said, "Yes, naturally. My card will make finding the other Legendaries quite easy."

"There are two more conditions," Lung Bai said.

The other Mythics groaned.

"What's that?" Arthur asked warily.

"The first is that you return to Wolf Moon Hive and take your place as leader. My kingdom cannot afford to have a hive falter in these times."

Which meant Whitaker was likely driving it to the ground. Not a surprise.

"What is the second condition?" Arthur asked.

"That you send one of your retinue to me—the Origin rider. I sense that the former prince Marion has three-of-a-kind healing set in his heart. He will do everything he can to heal his father's mind."

Arthur shot a glance at Marion, who had by now sat back up to his knees, cradling his silver dragon. Meeting his gaze, Marion nodded.

Arthur looked back at Lung Bai. "Surely, he already has the best healers in the land."

"You know of the specific overlapping powers of three of a kind," Lung Bai said dryly. "Yes or no?"

Arthur hesitated. Marion had already agreed, but he was the one responsible for his friend. "Whether he succeeds or not, he and his dragon will be returned whole and healthy to me. He won't be punished."

"Of course," she said impatiently. "And in return, I will extend you royal amnesty for your . . . many transgressions. But Arthur, you must succeed. You *must* find that card."

Her last words were unexpectedly anxious, and Arthur was reminded again that there were five Mythics and seven Scourge Gods.

"I agree," he said.

The world was washed in white. The last of the terrible pressure eased. And suddenly, Arthur and his retinue were again standing somewhere else entirely.

CHAPTER 50

Arthur found himself in a cozy living space, complete with a fireplace, cushioned seating, and even a writing desk in the corner. There were no windows, but a single oak door stood dominating the room with large writing over the top that read: ONE CHALLENGER MAY ENTER.

There were several lines of smaller writing underneath that he couldn't quite read from a distance.

Marion, Cressida, Horatio, and the little silver dragon, who'd had the pressure worse than Arthur and Brixaby, all gasped for free breath.

"What . . . was *that?*" Horatio said.

"That dragon with the long body is the Mythic bonded to our king," Arthur said. "And the rest . . . I don't know. Rulers of other kingdoms, I think."

"Mythics," Cressida said weakly. She seemed overwhelmed.

Arthur turned to Marion. "I'm sorry, but I had to agree to send you back to your father—"

Marion cut him off. "It's fine. I understand, and the important thing is we need to move on and finish this next challenge. I'm more worried about her." He looked down to the little silver in his arms. She was all but flopped over his forearm and looked quite out of energy.

It was no wonder: She had faced the might of Scourge Gods and Mythics on her first day of hatching. And without the strength and comfort of a linked rider.

Arthur nodded. While this place seemed to be a place of rest, he didn't think they would have the time.

He stepped closer to the door and read the smaller lines under the *One challenger may enter* statement.

Wonder upon wonders, it seemed to be a description of what they would face next.

Your team may send one champion. If they are successful, all will be rewarded. If not, all will be ejected down to the previous challenge, and, if successful, may try again.

That was both more explanatory and fairer than what they had experienced before.

"I like the extra instructions," Cressida said, "but I don't think we'll want to see what happens on the next-hardest level from here without the Mythics' help. We'll only get one try at this."

"That's why I'm going in," Arthur said.

"Not without me," Brixaby growled.

"Only one challenger, Brixaby," Arthur said. "You know it has to be me."

The dragon made a spitting sound that was not too far off from the disgusted noise Lung Bai had made. "You and I are a pair. It should treat us as one."

"If it doesn't," Arthur said, walking to the door, "then wish me luck."

He didn't let himself think about all he had learned from the Mythics. The fact that the challenge in the bunker had likely been real with people who had lived all that time ago. The hope, expectation, and pressure that he and Brixaby would be the next Mythic pair. And his pending return to Wolf Moon Hive. Not to mention Lung Bai's unrevealed anxiety. He must get this card. He put that all to the side and turned the doorknob.

Abruptly, he stood in a place that was familiar—back in that room that he had experienced under Ravi's guided meditation.

Five card slots stood blazing before him. Two were filled with Master of Skills and Master of Body Enhancement. On the other side stood two empty slots. And in the middle was the ghostly visage of Master of Cards.

And right in front, blocking his way, stood his cousin, Penn.

If I want that card, I'm going to have to fight him to the death, Arthur thought.

Sure enough, his cousin's face twisted in hate, and a dagger appeared in his hand.

"Betrayer," Penn sneered, and advanced on Arthur.

No, Arthur thought.

Penn rushed forward.

Do something, Arthur's instinct screamed.

"Fight me, you coward," Penn said. "Fight me like a true man."

Fear and adrenaline coursed through him. In the back of his mind, Arthur suspected this was a face-your-fear challenge. Penn's weapon even caught the light as he came close.

He didn't close his eyes, he didn't lift his arms to defend himself, and Penn . . . didn't slash down.

Arthur had been through this song and dance before. They had fought each other to a stalemate. Maybe it would be so in real life, too.

"We're family, Penn."

Though Penn did not take the fatal strike, he did press the edge of his dagger to Arthur's neck. He practically spat in his face. "Family? You've all but destroyed us."

"I can all but fix you," Arthur said.

"Liar!"

"Penn, if I was lying, I'd rip the card out of your heart right now."

Penn glanced down and paled when he saw Arthur's hand hovering a spare inch over his heart. He backed away.

"You can't fight me and win. All you have is tricks!"

It felt like something snapped in Arthur. "Yes, I can," he said, frustrated. "You have a Master of Combat. So what? I have a whole retinue of powerful dragons and their riders behind me. Through them, I have access to lava power, an assassin pair that can kill you with a scratch and teleport anywhere you have a shadow. I have a pair that can call down the heat of the sun on you, and now, if you can get a lucky shot in, I have a healer who will fix it. That's not even getting into my own Legendary dragon. You're nothing, Penn. I have all that, and I am *still* afraid of you," he roared.

Penn sneered. "As you should be. You're not going to take my card."

"Yes, I am," Arthur said, "and I'm going to be a Mythic."

"Mythic?" Penn barked out a scornful laugh. "You? How? By cheating?"

"Of course by cheating!" Arthur roared back. "I never take the direct route. I've already accepted I have to face you, and don't know how I'm going to take that card from you . . . but I promise, I swear, Penn, that somehow, I'm going to make it right between us. One way or another."

And with that, some lingering burden that he had not been aware of fell away. None of it erased what he had done to Penn. He had stolen the Master of Body Enhancement card that had been meant to save Penn's family from debt. Arthur had tricked and wronged Penn in several ways leading up to Brixaby's hatching.

And if he had to do it all over again, he would. But that didn't mean that he had to be the same man going forward.

Arthur stared at his cousin. "Penn, facing you means facing what I've done and then doing worse. It scares me even more than facing down those Scourge Gods . . . or even more than losing Brixaby. I don't know why or how it wormed so deep in my heart, but I'm not refusing to fight you because I'm scared. I'm refusing to fight you because when it really happens, I'm certain that we won't need to."

Skill level gained: Self-Insight (Insight Class)
Level 20

He had jumped up over ten levels in one go.

And of course, those levels were only a representation of his progress, because along with that self-realization and acknowledgment of his deepest, most shameful fear came acceptance.

With a feeling of loosening bands, Arthur's heart deck expanded. He felt he could easily fit five more cards in there. For a moment, he reveled in it, this feeling like all boundaries could be erased, if only he learned to get out of his own way.

His emotions came crashing down a moment later. After all, he was still facing a murderous cousin.

"You're wrong," Penn said, lifting his dagger again.

Arthur sighed. He needed to look past his own fear and self-doubt to see the reality: This wasn't his cousin. This was a challenge he needed to beat.

"I guess we'll find out," Arthur said.

Penn's face twisted and came at him again. Arthur didn't doubt he meant business this time.

Still, Arthur did nothing to protect himself. He stood there while Penn closed in and brought his dagger down.

New combat skill gained: Heart-Piercing Strike (Final Blow Class)
Remaining Time: 9 Minutes 59 Seconds

Arthur activated his Phase In, Phase Out, a card he and Brixaby had been careful not to show the Dark Heart yet.

One that Penn would know to watch out for. If he were real.

Penn stumbled through him, and Arthur phased back in, reached out, and ripped the card out of his back.

The fake Penn exploded into a million points of light, and the card dissolved in his hand as well.

Then, abruptly, he was standing in the cozy waiting room again. He backed away hurriedly.

"What's wrong?" Brixaby asked. "Are we going in?"

"I was just . . . I did it," Arthur said in surprise. "*I did it.*"

"What, in a second?"

"It wasn't a second to me," Arthur said, "but yeah, I won the fight."

Cressida clapped her hand over her mouth and pointed. "He did! Look!"

Where one door had been, now two stood. And above them was written: *Fear conquered! Congratulations! You and your team may step forward to claim a reward.*

The door on the right said: *One granted wish.*

The door on the left said: *One card from the heart library.*

The room shuddered around them suddenly, as if something large had bashed up against the wall.

A distant voice in Lung Bai's breathy whisper said, "*Hurry.*"

"Okay," Cressida said, "you're going to have to tell us the whole story later, but for now, let's get this done."

Marion said, "I'm going for the wish." He started for the right-hand door, then paused and transferred the silver dragon back to Cressida. The silver started to complain, but Marion touched under her chin and said, "I'm going to get my heart fixed. Pick a good card for the both of us, okay?"

The little dragon perked up a little. "Okay, be careful."

"I will." Marion smiled and turned to walk through the wish door.

"Well, what are we waiting for?" Horatio said, and headed straight for the card door.

Everybody else followed.

Around them, the room continued to shake.

Marion stepped through the wish door and felt the question more than heard it.

Lay your petition in front of the Dark Heart. What is your wish?

"I wish for my heart deck to be repaired," he said clearly, focusing hard on the words to prevent an intrusive thought from popping in like, *I want a million gold coins.*

There was a pause. Then suddenly, a plinth appeared in front of him, and on it a single card was propped up.

"I thought the other guys were getting cards," Marion muttered but went over to it.

Wish to Repair a Heart Deck
Rare
One-Time Use
Upon placing this card in a heart deck, all physical, mental, spiritual, and magical damage will be healed and the heart deck will be restored to pristine condition.
Warning: *As this is a Rare card, the wielder's heart deck will be restored to Rare rank and will no longer carry any lingering benefits of a once-Legendary wielder.*

Marion snorted. After giving up his Legendary card and the rest of his royal inheritance, he had stubbornly resisted adding cards to his deck. This would be the sixth one this week.

"Well, here goes," he said, and added it to his heart.

He disappeared in a flash of light, returning to the cozy waiting room.

Arthur, Brixaby, and Cressida stepped into a library. Instead of books or scrolls, it was filled with cards. Endless cards, stacked end to end, each in their own jeweled cases. The rows of shelves seemed to go on and on.

However, the outer walls shook as if caught in a permanent small earthquake. The jeweled cards rattled on their shelves, and Arthur got the unsettling impression that the whole place was ready to fly apart in a moment.

"*Hurry*," the ghostly voice said again. The Mythics who were keeping back the influence of the Scourge Gods were running out of time.

"You heard her," Arthur said. "Brixaby, get us a portal card."

Brixaby grinned evilly back at him. "I will get the best of the best."

Everyone split up, though Arthur ran straight down the front row of shelving.

Each section was labeled: Combat, Utility, Nature, Elemental, Healing, and so on, with different subsections for them all.

Arthur kept running. All of these cards were Common, Uncommon, and Rare. He was searching for a greater prize.

He poured all the experience of his **Running** and **Sprint** skills into his speed.

There, at the end of the shelving, was a short set of steps to a more elaborate second level. These, of course, were where the Legendary cards were. And past that, he sensed something even more powerful, something that he could only glance at, like the way he could only glance at the sun. There was a Mythic—maybe even several Mythic cards—in this library.

For the space of a thought, he wondered how he could possibly take one of those out of here . . . But even if he could, he would never use it. To do so would mean that he would have to unlink from Brixaby. That was not an option.

Arthur kept his gaze firmly on the Legendary cards. This section was obviously smaller, but there still had to be hundreds of Legendaries here. So much power, so much potential for good and evil.

And outside, distantly, he heard a whistle of a Scourge God that cut to the core.

He refocused and searched the sections: Combat, Spells, Nature, Mind, Elemental, Healing, Utility.

There.

Arthur ran down the row and concentrated on Brixaby's Call of the Heart to guide him.

Then he saw it. The card that had once lived in the heart of a general who had fallen to scourglings, been picked up, recycled through countless lives, and eventually found its way to the Dark Heart.

It sat in a jeweled case. Arthur picked it up with reverence. It opened as if waiting for him.

Master of Cards
Legendary
Meta

This card grants the wielder an extreme affinity with cards within their own heart deck and in others. The wielder will have an unusual level of control of their own heart deck and will be able to change parameters. In addition, the wielder will gain an extrasensory perception of others' cards. With practice, an advanced wielder may be able to interact with cards within another's heart deck without permission.

The wielder will be able to direct the formation of new cards using card shards toward a desired outcome.

Using an extreme amount of mana, the wielder will be able to make small, permanent changes to the properties and rules of cards, including linking cards within a different deck.

This is a meta-only card. Seek additional cards in this set to include combative, magical, body, and utilitarian abilities.

The general had been right. This card had quite a kick to it.

Arthur slid it into his heart. It didn't even twinge.

The moment he did, he was transported in a burst of light. But not before receiving a message.

Card synergy found. You have added a third card from the same set (Master of Skills + Master of Body Enhancement + Master of Cards) to create a three of a kind. Due to this pairing, you are able to create new classes which include utility-, body-, and card-based skills. These new classes may add to your attributes.

You have unlocked advanced controls within your heart deck.

Brixaby had become acutely, *uncomfortably* aware of his failings recently. He could act brashly, and some might even say just with a tiny, itty-bitty bit of callousness. Which was fine. He was a Legendary dragon. Arrogance was expected.

But over the last several days through the Dark Heart challenge, he had been faced with the extremely uncomfortable fact that he had come close to getting his own people killed through his arrogance. That was unacceptable.

Thus, he had been slightly tempted by the wish room. It could fix him. Probably.

Though he wasn't certain he needed to be fixed. Though perhaps he could be even better if he had a bit of empathy. Or was a touch more considerate.

But he didn't want the Dark Heart to change his personality. He liked who he was.

Bah. Self-reflection was tiresome.

In the end, he hadn't picked the wish room because he didn't know exactly what he wanted—he only knew he had a *teeny tiny* bit more growing to do than he originally thought.

But when Arthur mentioned the portal card, he knew that would be the perfect reward. They had long been stymied by not being able to travel the world at will.

He considered following Arthur to the Legendary section, but that would be a waste. The other cards in his set were not here. He felt it.

And unfortunately, his secondary core could not fit another Legendary not of his current Call set.

So Brixaby went to the Rares and started perusing, though quickly. The shaking was growing worse.

Ignoring the sounds of massively over-ranked beings fighting from outside—that was their problem, not his—he found the portal cards.

There were several. Some with severe mana drawbacks, others with time drawbacks, or distance drawbacks. Brixaby skimmed through them until he found the perfect card.

He even had a place in his secondary core for it. See, he was growing.

"What card do you want?" Cressida asked the little silver. She longed to go through the cards herself, but she was not entirely certain what she wanted.

"That way," the silver said. "I can feel a good card that would match Marion and I."

It was the Nature section.

"I don't want another animal card. This theme is getting ridiculous," Cressida grumbled.

But when the silver picked her card, Cressida saw the one next to it, and she had to admit it was perfect.

Cuddle Kittens

Rare

Summon

Using mana, the wielder of this card will be able to summon three incredibly fluffy big-eyed mewing kittens made of air and pure love. These precious bundles of cuddles want nothing but to tumble and play and utterly distract the wielder's enemies with their mind-altering cuteness. Allies are resistant to Cuddle Kittens but have a 10% chance of misfiring an attack out of an instinctive desire, should one of the little darlings get in the way. Enemies with strong mind shields may show resistance. Cuddle Kittens may be resummoned upon destruction. But who would dare harm one of them?

"Joy's going to love this," she said with a wince before putting it into her heart. Both she and the silver flashed away.

"Sams wanted a light card," Horatio muttered, snatching the card in front of him on the shelf. "But I don't think he'll get too mad at me for this."

Arthur arrived back in the cozy waiting room at the same moment as the others. Everybody was smiling.

The little silver let out a squeal upon seeing Marion. She literally flew out of Cressida's arms and into his. "You're fixed! I can feel it! You're whole again!"

Marion caught her, and without further ado, she projected her card.

Breath of Healing

Rare

Healing

The wielder of this card has the ability to breathe life to restore the sick, injured, and mentally unbalanced. Internal injuries and genetic issues cannot be cured by the Breath of Healing. This card unlocks mana, however, Breath of Healing does not require mana unless being used as a wide area-of-effect spell.

Reading that card, Arthur had an inkling of why the Mythics were so interested in an Origin dragon.

Marion projected his three-of-a-kind healing cards, and when they linked, he let out a joyous laugh, spinning her around. Fine stress lines that Arthur had hardly noticed before were now stark for being gone from his face. He looked healthier than Arthur had seen him since Buck Moon Hive.

Arthur opened his mouth to ask what everybody got, but then the room shook so violently that they all staggered.

And in the distance, he heard roaring and crashing. From the sounds of it, the Scourge Gods and the Mythics were having a battle.

"Let's get out of here."

Marion hurriedly led them back to the stairwell, which led back up to their territory.

EPILOGUE

They did not dally on the stairwell back to the pavilion. The shaking from outside—the incalculably distant sound of roars and whistles all the more terrifying because they could hear them—hurried them on.

The shaking and noise stopped the moment they reentered the door that led to the pavilion, but the waiting dragons were still visibly worried.

Joy let out a happy cry when they appeared, and practically seized Cressida to pull her in close and nuzzle her. "You're okay! I didn't get a quest or intuition or anything to tell me what was going on. It was so scary!"

"Where have you guys been?" Soledad said. "I thought that time didn't really pass when you were in challenges."

Arthur guessed that more had worried them than the wait. "What happened?"

Sam gestured with his snout. "We received that message a few minutes ago."

The three challenge doors were gone. In their place was a message:

The team that has claimed this territory has finished all applicable levels. Time remaining to exit the Dark Heart: 49 minutes, 17 seconds . . . 16 seconds . . . 15 seconds.

Failure to leave Dark Heart and relinquish your territory will result in escalating penalties.

"They only gave us an hour?" Arthur asked, then shot a look at Horatio. "Don't tell me that doesn't seem fair."

"It's not fair, but now we know why," Horatio muttered, shuddering dramatically.

"Why?" Soledad asked.

"I'll tell you later," Arthur said. "Let's move."

If they were forced to travel on foot and without any speed enhancements, the hour limit might be a problem. But flying on dragons, it wouldn't be an issue.

Still, after learning what he had about the Dark Heart, Arthur wanted to get out of there. Especially since there was a not-insignificant chance that whatever battle they'd caught a glimpse of might spill in.

As he ascended the stairs, he heard Joy say behind him, "Wait, so we can't do any more challenges? Boo. I was hoping for some more good cards."

"I got us a good card," Cressida told her.

Then a moment later, Joy exclaimed, "Those are the cutest kittens I've *ever* seen!"

Arthur fully expected to have to travel back to the spot between the hills where they had first arrived. Maybe an exit had opened there. Or maybe it would be another trap and they'd have to search for the real way out with a limited amount of time and risk those escalating penalties.

However, upon reaching the top of the staircase, he spotted a new entrance-way that stood in the middle of the pavilion. It was simply a frame floating in midair with a dark space behind it. Seeing it reminded Arthur of the place with the Scourge Gods and shuddered. But he felt no terrible pressure from beyond it. That was clearly the exit.

I guess we won't have to fly out of here, he thought. After all, they were still mounted on their dragons, with the hatchlings and their new riders seating themselves on Sams and Joy.

As they approached, the frame obediently expanded to include a dragon the size of Sams.

They went through it one by one and found themselves standing at the pit of the Dark Heart. Above them, streams of people were still descending into the pit.

Arthur touched Brixaby's neck. "Should we try to warn them?"

"It may not do any good," Horatio muttered. "I don't think they'll listen."

But Brixaby was already inhaling. Arthur knew he was more than willing to shout and be heard.

Several days later

Arthur stared hard at the card placed on the table in front of him. It was one that had been recovered from the bandits, which meant it was likely stolen from someone else.

People often put down Common-ranked cards, and the description for this one wasn't particularly impressive. But now he had a sense of how much energy was stored in the card.

Beautiful Bouquet
Common
Nature

Using mana, the wielder of this card will be able to generate pink flowers in the breed and variety that the wielder imagines.

It was a very simple card, and its simplicity was the reason why Arthur had chosen to work on it. Concentrating on the word *pink*, he focused hard and imagined the letters changing one by one. It was more than simply reworking what was on the surface. A matrix lay just underneath. A complex play of energy that existed within every card. He was only starting to learn how to decipher it.

Arthur concentrated so hard that beads of sweat popped out of his forehead, but he did not dare even to raise an arm to wipe it away.

Finally, with a sudden drop of mana, followed by a wave of exhaustion, the change clicked into place. The description now no longer read *pink flowers*. It read *purple flowers*.

That small change had cost him three quarters of his mana.

But this was an improvement. When he had started experimenting a few days ago, a little change like this would have nearly knocked him flat.

Skill level gained: Card Intuition (Card Smith Class)
Level 8

Skill level gained: Card Manipulation (Card Smith Class)
Level 7

This was good. This was *progress*.

Arthur leaned back in his chair and looked around. It certainly wasn't silent in the barn. Brixaby was working on something by his forge. Meanwhile, safely out of range of any sparks, Equinox and Marion's dragon, Asha, were wrestling together. They were already growing fast—faster than Arthur normally expected from other dragons, including Rares.

Their riders were currently out of the barn, and Arthur and Brixaby had chosen to keep an eye on them. Marion was back at the hospital. It was, unfortunately, doing very brisk business. When the survivors of the Dark Heart returned, they often were not unscathed.

Meanwhile, Soledad was out shopping for the group. They were running low on bison meat again. Of course, Arthur had his emergency stores . . . and some additional emergency stores in his Personal Space. But he didn't want to dip into that. Young dragons ate a lot, and Soledad had wanted some fresher, bloodier meat for them.

Sams and Horatio had made the excuse of going out to hunt any remaining scourglings beyond the walls with the guards. Arthur suspected that they were still integrating the new Rare card that Horatio had added. His friend was being cagey on the details, but Arthur hadn't pressed. He sensed that Horatio wanted to show it off to Soledad when he was ready.

Meanwhile, Cressida and Joy were at the library. After listening to the Mythics' conversation, Cressida had a renewed interest in history, and Joy wanted to sun herself on top of the library roof.

It was a nice afternoon, which was why Arthur wasn't too surprised when it was rudely interrupted.

A knock came at the barn door. Before he could rise, Asha broke off from playing with Equinox to yell, "I got it!"

She floundered over, mostly running, but aided by awkward beats of her wings. Unless they were purples or the rare blues with four wings, it took time for young dragons to learn how to fly.

Leaping, Asha pulled at the rope that connected to a pulley system Arthur had set up. The heavy barn door swung wide to reveal Oversheriff Walker standing on the other side.

Landing again, Asha looked up at her and said, "Hello, who are you?"

The sheriff looked mildly surprised, but only a little. She'd probably grown used to weirdness around Arthur.

"I'm Oversheriff Walker." She touched her hat.

Standing, Arthur slid the Common card back into his Personal Space. It twinged a little, but nothing he could not handle.

"Sheriff," he said, "why don't you come in?"

She did, and he gestured for her to have a seat across his desk.

"I'm glad to see you," he said, "but I half expected you to be delving the heart by now."

"I could say the same for you," she said.

With a polite smile, Arthur concentrated on his Charming Gentle-Person card. "How can I help you?"

She gave him a look as if he should already know, and the truth was, he had some guesses. But what she did next surprised him. From her belt, she pulled out a small leather bag and tossed it to the table between them.

"I intercepted this on the way here—saw it was for you and thought that I would save the deliverer a trip."

Arthur picked it up and looked inside. It was a bag of twenty card shards: the blank ones, straight from the Dark Heart. He had put out a bounty for those and paid in advance. Someone had taken him up on it.

"The question is," she said, "why didn't your team, which is one of the strongest left in the city, come back with any shards?"

That answer was easy, and for once, Arthur did not mind telling the truth. "All of our extra shards went to them." He gestured to Equinox and Asha, who had resumed their tumbling together. They looked like puppies.

She did a double take. "You need shards to breed dragons?"

"We only have one dragon of breeding age," Arthur said with a laugh. "No, we got these two from the Dark Heart."

"I see." She clearly didn't, but she leaned forward. "And your team is one of the few who have returned."

"Yes," Arthur said, his mood lowering. "At least, in one piece. I know people weren't happy about us broadcasting that the heart eats people."

She snorted. "To put it lightly."

What they were both not saying was that hardly anyone had been in the mood to listen while descending the pit, and once they reached the top, Arthur was officially told to knock it off. Of course, that didn't stop Brixaby from bellowing warnings in ears and in minds on the long, slow, extended journey back. People heard. He didn't think that many had listened, but they'd heard.

"Too many people have failed to return, and word is starting to spread that this heart is more than most can bite off and chew." Walker sighed. "I had hopes of going in myself, once the fervor died down a little."

"Don't," Arthur said. "It's not worth it."

"Why not?"

Ah, so now the city officials were starting to ask questions.

It made sense. The line waiting for the heart had finally dwindled to nothing, and yet not a lot of people had come back out. It could be that many were still doing challenges, but Arthur wasn't optimistic. He had even considered returning to the heart to grab people who were in trouble, or to just hunt bandits.

But when Arthur and Brixaby tried to go back in, they found that when they descended into the pit, the entrance did not open for them. Once they had defeated the final challenge of the Dark Heart, there would be no readmittance.

There was no reason to keep the truth away from Walker now. Especially now that her bosses were in the mood to listen. "We found out some truths," he said bluntly. "You think it's a gift, but we learned that the Dark Heart is a trap baited by high-ranking scourglings."

"You're talking about it erupting?" Walker asked, visibly alarmed. "Even after we opened it?"

"Sheriff, what do you think happens when somebody dies in there with a heart full of cards?"

"I don't know."

"It gets returned to the heart, and a lot more people are going in than coming out."

She sat on that for a moment, though she didn't look shocked. It wasn't too hard to figure that much out, if someone were already suspicious of the heart and thinking the right way.

"Do you think it will erupt?" she asked bluntly.

When. Not if.

That was the big question that kept him up at night.

Arthur hesitated. "That's why we're still here," he said. "My team ended up removing a few powerful cards on our way out, as well as those baby dragons you see. They represent a lot of power. And I suspect there might be other influences that have . . . put a cap on this cycle's eruption—for the time being." Though he worried how much it had cost the Mythic dragons to interfere.

The people who had managed to come back out after Arthur's retinue hadn't reported comparable rewards. There was a reason why less "bait" was being seeded around.

Too bad the Mythics wouldn't—or couldn't—do that for all Dark Hearts.

"But I'm almost certain that your Dark Heart will ripen faster than ever next time. And yes, it will likely erupt. We'll stay for another few weeks to be safe, but then we're going to be on our way."

She blinked. "But . . . with the cards you surely got out of it . . . you're not going for leadership?"

"I don't want to be a leader here," Arthur said. "This is not my city, or my kingdom."

"Poor Dannill," she said sarcastically.

He shrugged. "He's gotten his money. Have you seen the toys they're selling at the market? Stuffed dragons are all the rage."

"I suppose." She was quiet for a moment before she let out a sigh. "Well, if you're telling the truth about not seeking leadership, that will relieve a few people around here."

Arthur suspected that was the true reason she had come, which meant that she wasn't taking him as seriously as she ought. "Unless you can find a way to vent the Dark Heart before it ripens again, there's not going to be a city to lead."

She gave him a hard look. "I heard you, but I can't stop people from going in and taking a chance. They have a right."

"A right to die?"

"Not everybody dies, and that's the way we do things here. The best of the best pull out the strongest cards from the Dark Heart. That's why they're elected as leaders. It's how we reshuffle our government and keep it strong. Furthermore, we sell that opportunity for advancement to people. If we take that opportunity away, there will be riots."

"If you don't, there will be an eruption," Arthur said.

Though, to a degree, he understood her point. This place's whole social structure and economy, as well as everybody's hopes, were all pinned on the Dark Heart. People put their lives on the line, enduring the deadlands, just for the hope of retrieving powerful cards.

Arthur and Brixaby couldn't sit on the mouth of the Dark Heart and refuse to let more in. They were powerful, but the might of the entire city would be against them.

It left him with a sour taste in his mouth, but he had seen people turn back when Brixaby broadcasted his warning.

"If you have any sway here at all, spread the message to those going in not to go past the first couple of levels," Arthur said. "It gets progressively harder. If they listen, they can at least come out with some kind of reward. But if they get greedy and make one false move . . ."

She nodded. "That might be an acceptable middle ground. It's something we can do." She rose as if to go.

Arthur asked, "Has there been any word on Claude? I issued a missing person's report . . ."

She did not pretend like she didn't know what he was talking about. He knew she was keeping an eye out for him.

"No," she said. "But some reported missing persons are still being found. You never know. He might be in for a long challenge. I'm told that some of them last for years . . . objectively."

He nodded. "Thank you."

Arthur couldn't quite let himself grieve yet. Those two cards he'd found in the bandit's deck had been the *only* two Mechanical-type cards in there. And an adventurer like Claude would surely have more.

Maybe he had shed them or offered them as a bribe just for a chance to get away. Then he'd stayed in the heart to try to replace them.

Or maybe he was gone, and Arthur was fooling himself. Either way, he chose to have hope.

He walked the oversheriff out. When he closed the door, Brixaby came over. The tips of his claws were smoking from the heat of the forge, though it didn't seem to bother him. "What did she want?"

"Snooping around to see if we want to stay as leaders here."

"*Here?*" Brixaby asked. "In this little dragonless city?"

"We could find a way to safely vent the Dark Heart after it closes again," Arthur said, just for the sake of taking a different position. "That would really help these people."

"Or we could complete our sets like we originally set out to do, become Mythics, come back, and vent it then," Brixaby said. He had taken up the challenge of leaping to the next rank with gusto, especially since he already wanted to complete his set. Arthur couldn't say he minded it too much.

He turned to his desk. "She did bring a gift."

He walked back to his workstation, and Brixaby followed curiously. Upending the little leather bag, Arthur shook out the blank shards. Then, with a light touch on his Master of Cards, he sat down and started to look them over.

Some people had experimented with the blank shards once they were outside the heart, but they were just as useless as they were outside of challenges. But now Arthur had his Card Intuition and a plan. He spent a few minutes arranging the shards.

Each was a different shape, and there were no corner pieces. They still fit together if he put them together just so. Finally, when he was finished, he had a small solid square.

To his Master of Cards, they hummed with power.

"Brixaby, please hand me Repair Cards."

The moment it was out of Brixaby's Personal Space, it started shedding mana in the form of throwing sparkles. Arthur could feel the matrix underneath it unraveling like threads from a shirt that had been washed too many times. But when he gripped an edge, it stopped.

Carefully, he placed it on the table and held it. With his other hand, he slowly nudged the square of shards over the card.

Once it was centered, he relaxed his hold just a little. The square of shards melted over the card like wet candle wax and sank into the broken areas of the magical matrix underneath.

The matrix already knew what shape it should be. It had been that way for centuries. Using the extra power of the shards, it became whole again, brand new and perfect.

Repair Cards

Rare

Meta

The wielder of this card will be granted the ability and suite of basic skills in order to repair a damaged or malfunctioning magical card. When using any of these skills to repair a card, chances of spontaneous card fragmentation or scourge spawning are reduced by 25%. The skills which are granted are based on personality and ability in similar repair crafts. This card is skill based and uses mana. This card does not unlock mana.

"I did it," Arthur breathed.

And that wasn't all.

New skill gained: Card Smith (Card Smith Class)

Due to your card's bonus traits, you automatically start this skill at level 5.

"Hmm. Not quite as good as a blacksmith," Brixaby said when he told him, "but useful."

"I don't know, I like the title of Card Smith. Next stop is getting it as a class."

Grinning, Arthur slipped the new cards into his heart. With its recent expansion, there was no pain or added magical weight.

Then he spent a few minutes using his brand-new Repair Cards to fix the other two.

Card Sympathy

Rare

Meta

The wielder of this card will be granted the understanding of magical cards on a fundamental and instinctual level. Every card has its secrets that are not spelled out in the description. The wielder of this card will automatically be granted more insight into their own cards, and others that they see. The wielder will have unusual insight on how to best use compatible cards for the best effect.

Seek out other cards in this set to add to meta card knowledge.

Card Shard Insight

Rare

Meta

The wielder of this card will be granted unique insight on the nature of card shards on an instinctive level. The wielder will be able to position shards in the optimal position for the desired outcome when creating a card, as well as receive a 25% greater chance of harvesting a corner piece. In addition, the wielder will have a 5% chance of spontaneously harvesting a card shard of a higher rank than a scourgling's baseline rank.

Alert: Three of your cards share a set synergy.

Card Repair

Card Sympathy

Card Insight

These three cards have been combined into three of a kind.

Alert: Due to this Rare find, your basic Luck stat has been temporarily increased by +1.

Being three of a kind, they only took up one spot in his heart deck. They felt right there, and he could tell that they would match nicely with his new Master of Cards.

He looked at Brixaby. "What about your new Void Portal card?"

Brixaby, of course, had chosen probably the most ominous card that Arthur had ever heard of. But it was a portal strong enough to get him and his retinue to most places they pleased—at the cost of nightmares. They hadn't used it yet, but the description said power visions of death would open a temporary tear in the world and conduct those who the wielder thought was worthy through on a rowboat. It was an awful card, but the cost in mana was incredibly reasonable.

Brixaby grinned, showing teeth. "There was no problem adding it to my secondary core. Say the word, and we can portal anywhere."

"Soon. We're not quite ready to leave."

He didn't care what Lung Bai said, he and Brixaby would return to Wolf Moon Hive, but only when they were ready. Arthur still wanted to keep an eye on the Dark Heart to make sure it wouldn't erupt.

"Arthur," Brixaby said, "I do not *hate* the idea of returning to Wolf Moon, but I do dislike the thought of staying there forever."

"We promised that we would return and be leaders," Arthur said, "but we can always be leaders in our own way. Besides, they want us to ascend to Mythics, which means that we're going to be searching out other cards, right?"

Brixaby brightened.

Of course, the moment they arrived back at the barn after leaving the Dark Heart, they had used Brixaby's Call of the Heart to search for a card in his set. The answer was a surprise.

"Will we be going to Blood Moon before or after Wolf Moon?" Brixaby asked with an evil smile.

"Everything I've ever heard of Blood Moon says that they're elites and unfriendly."

Brixaby grinned. "Then stealing my next Legendary card from them will be fun."

ABOUT THE AUTHOR

Honour Rae is the author of the popular LitRPG series All the Skills, which has been praised by Matt Dinniman, Shirtaloon, and Aleron Kong. She lives in Northern California.

THANK YOU
FOR SUPPORTING HONOUR RAE

CONNECT WITH THE AUTHOR
BY VISITING THE FOLLOWING:

Continue building your deck with the *All the Skills* audiobook.

Experience Arthur's journey as performed by master of narration Luke Daniels.

AVAILABLE ON AUDIBLE!

RESPAWN YOUR CURIOSITY

follow us on our socials

podiumentertainment.com

@podiumentertainment

/podiumentertainment

@podium_ent

@podiumentertainment